One night, joking with an elderly male cardiac patient named Bruce Weiler, R.J. took both his hands in hers and squeezed them.

She couldn't let go.

It was as if they were linked by . . . what? She felt faint with certain knowledge she hadn't possessed a few minutes before. She wanted to scream out a warning to Mr Weiler. Instead, she muttered a dazed pleasantry and spent the next forty minutes poring over his records and taking his pulse and blood pressure again and again and listening to his heart. She told herself she was having a mental breakdown; nothing in Bruce Weiler's chart or vital signs indicated that his mending heart was anything but strong and getting healthier by the moment.

In spite of that, she was positive he was dying.

She said nothing to Fritzie Baldwin, the chief resident. She was able to tell him nothing that made any sense, and he would have ridiculed her savagely.

But in the small hours of the morning, Mr Weiler's heart blew out like a faulty inner tube, and he was gone.

CHOICES

NOAH GORDON

WARNER BOOKS

A *Warner* Book

First published in Great Britain in 1995 by Little, Brown and Company
This edition published by Warner Books in 1996

A CIP catalogue record for this book
is available from the British Library.

ISBN 0 7515 1474 8

Typeset by Palimpsest Book Production Limited, Polmont, Stirlingshire
Printed and bound in Great Britain by Clays Ltd, St Ives plc

Warner Books
A Division of
Little, Brown and Company (UK)
Brettenham House
Lancaster Place
London WC2E 7EN

This book is for Lorraine, my love.
And for our children –
Michael Gordon;
Lise Gordon and Roger Weiss;
and Jamie Beth Gordon, who had the warmth
and imagination to see the magic in heartrocks.

Notes and Acknowledgements

During the writing of this novel a number of physicians shared with me their very limited time, answered my questions, and loaned me books and materials. Among them were private practitioners – Richard Warner, M.D., of Buckland, MA; Barry Poret, M.D., and Nancy Bershof, M.D., both of Greenfield, MA; Christopher French, M.D., of Shelburne Falls, MA; and Wolfgang G. Gilliar, D.O., of San Francisco, Calif.

I received help also from academic and hospital physicians. Among these were Louis R. Caplan, M.D., chairman of the Department of Neurology at Tufts University and Neurologist-in-Chief at New England Medical Center, Boston, MA; Charles A. Vacanti, M.D., professor of anesthesiology and chairman of the Department of Anesthesiology at the University of Massachusetts Medical Center, Worcester, MA; and William F. Doyle, M.D., chairman of the Department of Pathology, Franklin Medical Center, Greenfield, MA.

I received help from Esther W. Purinton, R.N., Director of Quality Management at Franklin Medical Center, and from midwife Liza Ramlow, CMW. Susan Newsome of the Planned Parenthood League of Massachusetts talked with me about abortion; so did Virginia A. Talbot, R.N., of Hampden

Gynecological Associates and the Bay State Medical Center, Springfield, MA., and Kathleen A. Mellen, R.N. Polly Weiss of West Palm Beach, FL, provided reasoned insights about the anti-abortion movement.

As usual, I found help in my home town. Margaret Keith furnished anthropological information about bones, Don Buckloh of the U.S. Department of Agriculture and farmer Ted Bobetsky told me about husbandry; Suzanne Corbett talked with me about horses; EMTs Philip Lucier and Roberta Evans refreshed my memories of a hilltown ambulance service; and Denise Jane Buckloh, the former Sister Miriam of the Eucharist, OCD, provided insights into Catholicism and sociology. Attorney Stewart Eisenberg and former Ashfield Police Chief Gary Sibilia advised me about prison sentencing, and Russell Fessenden provided information about his late grandfather, Dr. George Russell Fessenden, an early country doctor.

Roger L. West, DVM, talked with me about bovine obstetrics, and dairy farmer David Thibault of Conway, MA, allowed me to witness his delivery of a calf.

Julie Reilly, objects conservator at the Winterthur Museum, Winterthur, Del., provided details about dating old ceramics, and I received help from Susan McGowan of the Pocumtuck Valley Memorial Assn., Old Deerfield, MA. I am grateful also to the Memorial Libraries at Historic Deerfield, and to the staffs at the Belding Memorial Library in Ashfield and at the libraries of the University of Massachusetts in Amherst.

I thank my literary agent, Eugene H. Winick of McIntosh & Otis, Inc., for his friendship and support.

Lastly, I thank my family. Lorraine Gordon is skilled at fulfilling multiple roles – wife, business manager, literary guide. Lise Gordon is my valued editor as well as my daughter. Roger Weiss, computer maven as well as son-in-law, kept my technology current and working. Daughter Jamie Beth Gordon generously allowed me to share with my characters and readers her creative passion for heartrocks (the term

Heartrocks ™ is legally protected by her and may be used only with her permission). Michael Gordon, my son, offered valued advice on several levels; and when emergency surgery kept me from accepting the James Fenimore Cooper Prize in person, he attended the awards ceremony in New York and delivered my remarks.

This book is theirs, with my love.

CHOICES is the third book of a trilogy about the Cole family of physicians. The first two novels in the series, THE PHYSICIAN and SHAMAN, have won literary prizes and are international best sellers. The trilogy has occupied my life for thirteen years, and it has taken me from the 11th century to the present day, a fascinating voyage. I am grateful that I was able to make it.

Ashfield, Massachusetts
February 1995

The difficulty in life is the choice.
—George Moore
The Bending of the Bough

I have never had a money practice; it would have been impossible for me. But the actual calling on people, at all times and under all conditions, the coming to grips with the intimate conditions of their lives, when they were being born, when they were dying, watching them die, watching them get well when they were ill, has always absorbed me.

—William Carlos Williams MD
Autobiography

The close-up, reassuring, warm touch of the physician, the comfort and concern, the long, leisurely discussions . . . are disappearing from the practice of medicine, and this may turn out to be too great a loss . . . If I were a medical student or an intern, just getting ready to begin, I would be more worried about this aspect of my future than anything else. I would be apprehensive that my real job, caring for sick people, might soon be taken away, leaving me with the quite different occupation of looking after machines. I would be trying to figure out ways to keep this from happening.

—Lewis Thomas MD
The Youngest Science: Notes of a Medicine Watcher

I
THE THROWBACK

1

An Appointment

R.J. woke.

As long as she lived, from time to time in the middle of the night she would open her eyes and search the darkness in the tense certainty that she was still an overworked resident physician at the Lemuel Grace Hospital in Boston, grasping at a nap in an empty patient room in the middle of a thirty-six-hour shift.

She yawned while the present flooded into her consciousness and she knew with great relief that the residency was years behind her. But she closed her mind to reality because the luminous hands of the clock told her she had two hours left and she had learned in that long ago residency to milk every moment of sleep.

She emerged again two hours later to greying light and no panic and reached over and killed the alarm. Invariably she awoke just before it rang, but she always set it the night before anyway, just in case. The special shower head thrummed the water into her scalp not quite bruisingly, as reviving as an extra hour of sleep. The soap slid over a body ampler than she thought desirable, and she wished there were time for a run, but there wasn't.

As she used the dryer on her short black hair, still thick and good, she appraised her face. Her skin was fair and clear, her nose narrow and somewhat long, her mouth wide and full. Sensual? Wide, full, and unkissed for a long time. There were bags under her eyes.

'So, what do you want, R.J.?' she demanded rudely to the woman in the mirror.

Not Tom Kendricks any longer, she told herself. Of that she was certain.

She had selected her clothing before she went to bed, and it waited at one side of the closet, a blouse and tailored slacks, attractive but comfortable shoes. In the hallway she saw through the open door to Tom's bedroom that the suit he had worn yesterday was still on the floor where he had dropped it the night before. He had been up earlier than she and was long gone from the house, needing to be scrubbed and in the operating room by 6:45.

Downstairs, she poured a glass of orange juice and forced herself to drink it slowly. Then she put on her coat, picked up her briefcase, and went through the unused kitchen and out to the garage. The little red BMW was her indulgence, as the grand antique house was Tom's. She enjoyed the purr of the engine, the responsiveness of the wheel.

It had snowed lightly during the night, but the Cambridge road crews did a good job removing snow, and she had no trouble once she was past Harvard Square and JFK Boulevard. She turned on the radio and listened to Mozart while drifting with the tide of traffic moving down Memorial Drive, then she took the Boston University Bridge across the Charles River to the Boston side.

Early as it was, at the hospital the staff parking lot was almost full. She slid the BMW into a space next to a wall, to minimize the chance of damage from a neighbor's carelessly opened door, and then walked briskly into the building.

The security guard nodded. 'Mornin, Dockuh Cole.'

'Hi, Louie.'

At the elevator she said hello to several people. She got out at the third floor and walked quickly into room 308. She always got to work very hungry in the morning. She and Tom rarely had lunch or dinner at home, and never breakfast; the refrigerator was empty except for juice, beer and soft drinks. For four years R.J. had stopped at the crowded cafeteria every morning, but then Tessa Martula had become her secretary and insisted on doing for her what she doubtless wouldn't have agreed to do for a man.

'I go there to get my own coffee, so it doesn't make sense not to get yours,' Tessa had insisted. So now R.J. put on a fresh white coat and began to review the case histories that had been left on her desk, and seven minutes later she was rewarded by the sight of Tessa bearing a tray containing a toasted bagel and cream cheese, and coffee black and strong.

While she made short work of the food, Tessa came in again with the appointment schedule, and they reviewed it.

'Dr Ringgold called. Wants to see you before you start your day.'

The chief of medicine had a corner office on the fourth floor. 'Go right in, Dr Cole. He's expecting you,' his secretary said.

In the inner office, Dr Ringgold nodded, pointed at a chair, and closed the door firmly.

'Max Roseman had a stroke yesterday while he was attending the communicable diseases meeting at Columbia. He's a patient at New York Hospital.'

'Oh, Sidney! Poor Max. How is he?'

He shrugged. 'Surviving, but he could be better. Profound paralysis and sensory impairment of the contralateral face, arm and leg, for starters. We'll see what the next few hours bring. I just got a courtesy call from Jim Jeffers in New York. He said he'll keep me informed, but it's going to be a long

3

time before Max returns to work. Matter of fact, given his age, I doubt he'll ever be back.'

R.J. nodded, suddenly watchful. Max Roseman was associate chief of medicine.

'Someone like you, a good female physician and with your background in law, would bring new dimensions to the department as Max's successor.'

She had no desire to be associate chief, a job of many responsibilities and limited power.

It was as if Sidney Ringgold could read her mind. 'In three years I reach sixty-five, the age of compulsory retirement. The associate chief of medicine will have a tremendous advantage over other candidates to succeed me.'

'Sidney, are you offering me the job?'

'No, I'm not, R.J. Matter of fact, I'm going to talk with several other people about the appointment. But you would be a strong candidate.'

R.J. nodded. 'Fair enough. Thanks for filling me in.'

But his glance held her in her chair. 'One other thing,' he said. 'I've been thinking for a long time that we should have a publications committee to encourage staff physicians to write and publish more. I'd like you to set it up and chair it.'

She shook her head. 'I simply can't,' she said flatly. 'I'm already stretching to handle my schedule.' It was true; he should know that, she thought with resentment. Mondays, Tuesdays, Wednesdays and Fridays, she dealt with patients at her hospital office. Tuesday mornings she went across the street to give a two-hour class at the Massachusetts College of Physicians and Surgeons on the prevention of iatrogenic illness, sickness or injury caused by a doctor or a hospital. Wednesday afternoons she lectured at the medical school on the avoidance and survival of malpractice suits. Thursdays she performed first-trimester abortions at the Family Planning clinic of Jamaica Plain. Friday afternoons she worked at a PMS clinic which, like the iatrogenic illness course, was begun because of her persistence and over the objections of some

4

of the hospital's more conservative doctors.

Both she and Sidney Ringgold were conscious of her debt to him. The chief of medicine had sponsored her projects and promotions despite political opposition. At first he had looked upon her warily – a lawyer turned physician, an expert on illnesses caused by the mistakes of physicians and hospitals, someone who did peer-review work and judged her fellow physicians, often costing them money. In the beginning, some of her colleagues had referred to her as 'Dr Snitch', an appellation she wore proudly. The chief of medicine had watched Dr Snitch survive and prosper and become Dr Cole, accepted because she was honest and tough. Now both her lectures and clinics had become politically correct, assets so prized that Sidney Ringgold often took credit for them.

'Perhaps you can trim some other activity?' Both of them knew he was talking about Thursdays at the Family Planning clinic.

He leaned forward. 'I'd like you to do this, R.J.'

'I'll give it serious thought, Sidney.'

This time she made it out of the chair. On the way out, she was annoyed with herself, realizing she was already trying to guess the other names on his list.

2

The House on Brattle Street

Even before they were married, Tom had tried to convince R.J. that she should exploit the combination of law and medicine to produce optimum annual income. When, despite his advice, she had effectively turned her back on the law and concentrated on medicine, he had urged her to develop a private practise in one of the affluent suburbs. While they were buying their house he had grumbled about her hospital salary, almost 25 percent lower than the income would have been from a private practise.

They had gone to the Virgin Islands for their honeymoon, a week on a small island near St Thomas. Two days after they returned they had started looking for property, and on the fifth day of their search a real estate woman had taken them to see the distinguished but run-down house on Brattle Street in Cambridge.

R.J. had viewed it without interest. It was too large, too expensive, too badly in need of repair, and there was too much traffic going by the front door. 'It would be crazy.'

'No, no, no,' he had murmured. She remembered he had been so attractive that day, his straw-colored hair in a designer trim, and wearing a beautifully cut new suit. 'It wouldn't be crazy at all.' Tom Kendricks saw a handsome Georgian house on a graceful heirloom street with red brick sidewalks that had been trod by poets and philosophers, men you read about in textbooks. Half a mile up the street was the stately house in which Henry Wadsworth Longfellow had lived. Just beyond that was the Divinity School. Tom already was more Boston than Boston, getting the accent just right, having his clothes tailored by Brooks Brothers. But in fact he was a midwestern farm boy who had gone to Bowling Green University and Ohio State, and the thought of being Harvard's neighbor – almost *part* of Harvard – fascinated him.

And he was seduced by the house – the exterior of red brick with Vermont marble ornamentation, the handsome thin columns alongside the doors, the small antique panes on each side and above the doorway, the matching brick wall around the property.

She thought he was joking. When it became apparent he was serious, she was dismayed and tried to talk him out of it. 'It would be *expensive*. Both the house and the wall need repointing, the roof and the foundation need repair. The real estate company's description says right up front that it needs a new furnace. It doesn't make sense, Tom.'

'Sense is what it does make. This is a house to be owned by a couple of successful doctors. A statement of confidence.'

Neither of them had saved much. Because R.J. had received a law degree before entering medical school she had managed to earn some money, enough to finish her medical education and training with only a reasonable debt. But Tom owed a frightening amount. Nevertheless, he argued stubbornly and at length that they should buy the house. He reminded her that already he had begun to make very good money as a general surgeon and insisted that when her smaller income was added to his, they could easily afford the house. He said it again and again.

It was early enough in the marriage so that she was still besotted. He was a better lover than he was a person, but she

7

didn't know that then, and she listened to him with gravity and respect. At last, bemused, she had given in.

They spent a good deal of money on furnishings, including antiques and near-antiques. At Tom's insistence, they bought a baby grand piano, more because it looked 'just right' in the music room than because R.J. was a pianist. About once a month her father took a taxi to Brattle Street and tipped the cabbie to carry in his cumbersome viola da gamba. Her father was happy to see her settled, and they played long and fulsome duets. The music covered a lot of scars that were there from the start and made the large house seem less empty.

She and Tom ate most of their meals out and didn't have live-in help. A taciturn black woman named Beatrix Johnson came every Monday and Thursday and kept the house clean, only now and again breaking something. The yardwork was done by a landscaping service. They rarely had guests. No hung shingle encouraged patients to enter the front gate of their home; the only clue as to the identity of the inhabitants came from a pair of small copper plates Tom had fastened to the wood on the right-hand side of the front door frame:

Thomas Allen Kendricks MD
and
Roberta J. Cole MD

In those days, she called him Tommy.

When she left Dr Ringgold she did morning rounds.

Unfortunately, she never had more than one or two patients in the wards. She was a general physician interested in family practise, in a hospital that didn't have a department of family practise. That made her a kind of jack-of-all-trades, a utility player without classification. Her work for the hospital and the medical school fell between departmental boundaries; she saw pregnant patients, but someone in Obstetrics delivered the babies; in the same way, almost always she referred her patients to a surgeon, a gastroenterologist, any one of more than a dozen specialists. Most of the time she never saw the patient again, because follow-up care was done by the specialist physician or the home-town family doctor; usually patients came to the hospital with only those problems that might require advanced technology.

At one time, political opposition and the sense that she was breaking new ground had lent spice to her activities at the Lemuel Grace, but for a long time now she had lost her sense of joy in medical practise. She spent too much of her time reviewing and signing insurance papers – a special form if someone needed oxygen, a special long form for this, a special short form for that, in duplicate, in triplicate, every insurance company with different forms.

Her office visits were apt to be impersonal and brief. Faceless efficiency experts at insurance companies had determined how much time and how many visits she could allow for each patient, who was quickly sent off for lab work, for X-rays, for ultrasound, for MRI – the procedures that did most of the real diagnostic work and protected her from malpractise suits.

Often she pondered, who were these patients who came to her for help? What elements in their lives, hidden from her almost cursory glance, contributed to their illness? What would become of them? There was neither time nor opportunity for her to relate to them as people, to really be a physician.

That evening she met Gwen Gabler at Alex's Gymnasium, an upscale health club in Kenmore Square. Gwen was R.J.'s medical school classmate and best friend, a gynecologist at Family Planning whose breeziness and salty tongue disguised the fact that she was hanging on by her fingernails. She had two children, a real estate broker husband who had run into hard times, an overcrowded schedule, bruised ideals, and depression. She and R.J. came to Alex's twice a week to punish themselves in a long aerobics class, sweat out foolish desires in the sauna, soak away fruitless regrets in the hot tub, have a glass of wine in the lounge and gossip and talk medicine throughout the evening.

Their favorite wickedness was to study the men in the club and judge their attraction solely by their appearance. R.J. found she required a hint of the cerebral in the face, a suggestion of introspection. Gwen liked more animal qualities. She was an admirer of the owner of the club, a golden Greek named Alexander Manakos. Easy for Gwen to dream of muscular but soulful romance and then go home to her Phil, myopic and stocky but deeply appreciated. R.J. went home and read herself to sleep with medical journals.

On the surface, she and Tom had the American dream, busy professional lives, the handsome house on Brattle Street, a farmhouse in the Berkshire Hills that they used for extremely rare weekends and vacations. But the marriage was ashes. She told herself it might have been different if they had had a child. Ironically, the physician who frequently dealt with infertility in others had been infertile for years. Tom had had semen analysis and she had had a battery of tests. But no cause of the infertility was uncovered, and she and Tom had been quickly caught up in the responsibilities of their medical personas. Those demands were so heavy for each of them that gradually they had drifted apart. If their marriage had been more substantial, doubtless in recent years she would have considered insemination or *in vitro* fertilization, or perhaps adoption. By now, neither she nor her husband was interested.

Long ago R.J. had become aware of two things: that she had married an insubstantial man and that he was seeing other women.

3
Betts

R.J. knew Tom had been as surprised as anyone when Elizabeth Sullivan had come back into his life. He and Betts had lived together for two years in Columbus, Ohio, when they were young. At that time she was Elizabeth Bosshard. From what R.J. heard and saw when Tom talked about her, he must have cared for her a great deal, but she had left him after she met Brian Sullivan.

She had married Sullivan and moved to the Netherlands, to The Hague, where he was a marketing manager for IBM. Several years later he was transferred to Paris, and less than nine years after their marriage he had suffered a stroke and died. By that time Elizabeth Sullivan had published two mystery novels and had a large readership. Her protagonist was a computer programmer who travelled for his company, and each book took place in a different country. She travelled wherever the books led her, generally living a year or two in the country she was writing about.

Tom had seen Brian Sullivan's obituary in the *New York Times* and had written a letter of condolence to Betts and received a letter in return. Other than that, he'd not even had a postcard from her, nor had he thought much about her for years until the day she telephoned him and told him she had cancer.

'I've seen doctors in Spain and in Germany, and I know the disease is advanced. I decided to come home to be sick. The physician in Berlin suggested someone at the Sloan-Kettering in New York, but I knew you were a doctor in Boston, so I came here.'

Tom knew what she was telling him. Elizabeth's marriage, too, had been childless. She had lost her father in an accident when she was eight, and her mother had died four years later of the same kind of cancer that Betts now had. She had been raised well by her father's only sister, who now was an invalid in a nursing home in Cleveland. There was no one but Tom Kendricks for her to turn to.

'I feel so bad,' he told R.J.

'Of course you do.'

The problem was well beyond the skills of a general surgeon. Tom and R.J. talked it over, considering whatever they knew about Betts's case; it was the first time in a long while that they had shared such a meeting of the minds. Then he had arranged for Elizabeth to be seen at the Dana-Farber Cancer Institute, and he had spoken to Howard Fisher about her after she was examined and tested.

'The carcinoma is widely traveled,' Fisher had said. 'I've seen patients go into remission who were worse off than your friend, but I'm sure you understand that I'm not hopeful.'

'I do understand that,' Tom had said, and the oncologist had blocked out a treatment regimen that combined radiation and chemotherapy.

R.J. had liked Elizabeth at sight, a full-bodied, round-faced woman who dressed as wisely as a European but who had allowed middle age to make her comfortably heavier than was fashionable. She wasn't prepared to give up; she was a fighter. R.J. had helped Betts find a one-bedroom condominium on Massachusetts Avenue, and she and Tom saw the ailing woman as often as possible, as friends and not as doctors.

R.J. took her to see the Boston Ballet do *Sleeping Beauty* and to the first autumn concert of Symphony, sitting high up in the balcony and giving Betts her own seventh-row center seat in the orchestra.

'You have only the one season ticket?'

'Tom doesn't go. We have different interests. He likes to go to hockey games and I don't,' R.J. said, and Elizabeth nodded thoughtfully and said she had enjoyed watching Seiji Ozawa conducting.

'You'll like the Boston Pops next summer. People sit at little tables and drink champagne and lemonade while they listen to lighter stuff. Very *gemütlich*.'

'Oh, we must go!' Betts said.

The Boston Pops wasn't in the cards for her. Winter was very young when her disease took hold; she had needed the apartment only seven weeks. At Middlesex Memorial Hospital they gave her a private room on the VIP floor and her radiation treatments were stepped up. Very quickly her hair fell out and she began to lose weight.

She was so sensible, so calm. 'It would make a really interesting book, you know?' she said to R.J. 'Only, I don't have the energy to write it.'

A genuine warmth had developed between the two women, but late one night when the three of them sat in her hospital room it was Tom she looked at. 'I want you to make me a promise. I want you to swear you won't allow me to suffer or linger.'

'I do,' he said, almost a nuptial vow.

Elizabeth wanted to review her will, and to draw up a

13

living will stipulating that she didn't want her life artificially prolonged by drugs or technology. She asked R.J. to get her a lawyer, and R.J. called Suzanna Lorentz at Wigoder, Grant, & Berlow, the firm where she had once worked briefly herself.

A couple of evenings later, Tom's car was already in the garage when R.J. got home from the hospital. She found him sitting at the kitchen table, having a beer while he watched television.

'Hi. That Lorentz woman call you?' He snapped off the TV.

'Hi. Suzanne? No, I haven't heard from her.'

'She called me. She wants me to be Betts's legal health care agent. But I can't. I'm her associate physician of record, and it would represent a conflict of interest, wouldn't it?'

'Yes, it would.'

'So will you? Be her legal health care agent, I mean?'

He was gaining weight and looked as if he hadn't been sleeping enough. There were cracker crumbs on his shirt front. She was saddened by the fact that an important part of his life was dying.

'Yes, that will be all right.'

'Thank you.'

'You're welcome,' she said, and went up to her room and went to bed.

Max Roseman faced a long convalescence and had decided to retire. R.J. didn't get the news from Sidney Ringgold; indeed, Dr Ringgold made no official announcement. But Tessa came in with the intelligence, beaming. She wouldn't reveal her source, but if R.J. had to bet, she'd have placed her money that Tessa had been told by Bess Harrison, Max Roseman's secretary.

'Word has it that you're among those being seriously considered as Dr Roseman's replacement,' Tessa said. 'Whoo-eee! I think you have a real good chance. I think that for you the job of associate chief would be the first rung of a tall, tall ladder. Would you rather aim at becoming dean of the medical school or director of the hospital? And whatever you end up doing, are you going to take me with you all the way?'

'Forget it, I'm not going to get that job. But I'm always going to take you with me. You hear so many rumors. And you get my coffee every morning, you damn fool.'

It was one of many rumors that floated all about the hospital. Now and again someone would say something sly and knowing, sending her a message that the world was aware of her name on a list. She wasn't holding her breath. She didn't know if she wanted the job enough to accept it if it were offered.

Soon Elizabeth had lost enough weight so that for a brief time R.J. was able to get a faint inkling of what she had looked like as the slim young girl Tom had loved. Her eyes seemed larger, her skin grew translucent. R.J. knew she teetered on the brink of gauntness.

There existed between them a curious intimacy, a world-weary knowledge that was closer than sisterhood. Partly, it was due to the fact that they shared memories of the same lover. R.J.'s mind wouldn't allow her to imagine Elizabeth and Tom having sex. Had his lovemaking habits been the same? Had he cradled Elizabeth's buttocks in his hands, had he kissed her navel after he was spent? Elizabeth must have some of the same thoughts when she looked at her, R.J. realized. Yet there was no jealousy in them; they were drawn close. Even burdensomely sick, Elizabeth was sensitive and astute. 'Are you and Tom going to split?' she asked one night when R.J. had stopped to see her on the way home.

'Yes. Very soon, I think.'

Elizabeth nodded. 'Sorry,' she whispered, finding the strength to console; but clearly, the confirmation came as no great surprise to her. R.J. wished they could have known each other for years.

They would have been wonderful friends.

4

Moment of Decision

Thursdays.

When R.J. was younger she had made a great many political statements. Now, it seemed to her that she had only Thursdays.

She placed special value on babies and disliked the notion of cancelling them. Abortion was ugly and messy. Sometimes it got in the way of her other professional activities because a few of her colleagues disapproved, and for public relations reasons her husband had always feared and hated her involvement.

But there was an abortion war waging in America. A lot of doctors were driven from the clinics, intimidated by the ugly and unsubtle threats of the anti-abortion movement. R.J. believed it was a woman's right to make decisions about her own body, so every Thursday morning she drove to Jamaica Plain and sneaked into the Family Planning clinic the back way, avoiding the demonstrators, the placards shaken at her head, the crucifixes jabbed at her, the thrown blood, the bottled fetuses stuck into her face, and the name-calling.

On the last Thursday in February she parked in the driveway of Ralph Aiello, a neighbor who was paid by the abortion clinic. The snow in the Aiello back yard was deep and new, but he had earned his money by shoveling a narrow path to the gate in the back fence. The back yard of the clinic property was on the other side of the gate, where another narrow shoveled path led to the rear door of the clinic building.

R.J. always made the walk from her car a quick one, afraid that demonstrators would burst around from the sidewalk in front of the clinic, and angry and illogically ashamed that she had to sneak to her work as a doctor.

On that Thursday there was no noise coming from the front of the building, no screams, no curses, but R.J. was particularly troubled, having stopped to see Elizabeth Sullivan on her way to work.

Elizabeth had traveled beyond the point of any hope and had entered the realm of intractable pain. The button she was allowed to press for self-medication had been inadequate almost from the start. Whenever she regained consciousness she suffered terribly, and now Howard Fisher had begun to give her very heavy doses of morphine.

She slept in her bed without moving.

'Hi, Betts,' R.J. had said loudly.

She had placed her fingers against Elizabeth's warm, faintly pulsing neck. In a moment, almost against her will, she had enclosed the other woman's hands in her own. From somewhere deep within Elizabeth Sullivan information had flowed into R.J. and found its way into her consciousness. She had sensed the smallness of the reservoir of life, depleting steadily in incremental amounts, with infinitesimal slowness. Oh, Elizabeth, I'm sorry, she told her silently. I'm so sorry, dear.

Elizabeth's mouth had moved. R.J. bent over her, straining to hear.

'. . . Green one. Take the green one.'

R.J. had mentioned the incident to one of the ward nurses, Beverly Martin.

'God love her,' the nurse said. 'Usually she never wakes up enough to say anything.'

That week it was as if the screws suddenly were tightened on all the torture vises that brought stress to R.J. An abortion clinic in New York State had been set afire in the night, and the same sick passion was alive in Boston. Large, turbulent protest demonstrations, manic at times, had hit two clinics in Brookline, run by Planned Parenthood and Preterm. They had led to disruption of services, a large police response, and mass arrests, and it was expected that the Family Planning center in Jamaica Plain was next.

In the staff room, Gwen Gabler was drinking coffee, uncharacteristically quiet.

'Something wrong?'

Gwen set down her cup and reached for her purse. The sheet of paper was folded twice. When R.J. opened it, she saw a wanted poster, the sort displayed in post offices. It bore Gwen's name, address, and photograph, her weekly schedule, the fact that she had left a lucrative ob-gyn practise in Framingham 'to get rich performing abortions', and the crime for which she was wanted: murder of babies.

'It doesn't *say* dead or alive,' Gwen said bitterly.

'Did they make up a poster of Les, too?' Leszek Ustinovich had practiced twenty-six years as a gynecologist in Newton before joining the clinic. He and Gwen were the only full-time physicians at Family Planning.

'No, I'm the chosen goat here, apparently, although I understand Walter Hearst at the Deaconess Hospital has been similarly honored.'

'What are you going to do about it?'

Gwen tore the poster in half, and then in half again, and dropped the pieces into the trash basket. Then she kissed her fingertips and gently slapped R.J.'s cheek. 'They can't drive us away if we won't let them.'

R.J. finished her coffee thoughtfully. She had been doing first-trimester abortions at the clinic for two years. She had had post-residency training in gynecology, and Les Ustinovich, a superb teacher with a lifetime of experience, had trained her in the first-trimester procedure. First-trimester procedures were absolutely safe when done carefully and correctly, and she was careful to be correct. Still, every Thursday morning she was as tense as though she had to spend the day doing brain surgery.

She sighed, threw her paper cup away, got up and went to work.

The next morning at the hospital Tessa gave her a very solemn stare along with her coffee and bagel. 'It's getting down to the crunch. Serious stuff. The word we have is that Dr Ringgold is discussing four names, and you're one of them.'

R.J. swallowed a bite of bagel. 'Who are the other three?' she said, unable to resist.

'Don't know yet. I heard only that every one is a heavy hitter.' Tessa gave her a sidelong glance. 'Do you know there has never been a woman in that position?'

R.J. smiled less than joyfully. Pressure was no more welcome because it came from her secretary. 'That isn't a surprise, is it?'

'No, it isn't,' Tessa said.

That afternoon R.J. was walking back from the PMS clinic when she met Sidney in front of the medical office building.

'Hiyuh,' he said.

'Hi there to you.'

'Have you decided anything concerning that request I made of you?'

She hesitated. The truth was, she had pushed it from her mind, not wanting to deal with it. But that was unfair to Sidney. 'No, I haven't. But I will in a very short time.'

He nodded. 'You know what every teaching hospital in this

city does? When they need somebody to fill a leadership job, they look for a candidate who's already created interest in himself because he's a hotshot bench scientist. They want someone who's published a number of papers.'

'Like the young Sidney Ringgold, with his papers on weight reduction and blood pressure and onset of disease.'

'Yes, like that long-ago young hotshot Sidney Ringgold. Research is what got me this job,' he agreed. 'It's no more logical than the fact that search committees looking for a college president always choose someone who has been a distinguished teacher. But there you are.

'You, on the other hand. You've published a few papers, and you've created a couple of stirs, but you're a doctor, not a bench-science investigator. Personally, I think this is a good moment in time to have a physician of people as the associate chief of medicine, but I need to make an appointment that will win a consensus of approval from the hospital staff and the medical community. So if a non-research type is going to be appointed associate chief of medicine, she has to have as much professional leadership in her résumé as is humanly possible.'

She smiled at him, aware he was her friend. 'I do understand, Sidney. And I'll get back to you very soon with my decision about chairing the publications committee.'

'Thank you, Dr Cole. Enjoy your weekend, R.J.'

'You too, Dr Ringgold.'

A weirdly warm storm blew in from the sea, pelting Boston and Cambridge with heavy rains and defrosting the late winter's snow. Outside, all was puddles and dripping, and the gutters were awash.

She lay in bed Saturday morning, listening to the downpour and thinking. She didn't like her mood; she was increasingly morose, and she knew that kind of thing could affect her decisions, if she allowed it.

20

She wasn't enthusiastic about being Max Roseman's successor. But she wasn't enthusiastic about her medical life as it existed at the moment, and she found herself responding to Sidney Ringgold's faith in her, and to the fact that again and again he had given her opportunities that other men would have denied her.

And she kept seeing the look on Tessa's face when she said that no woman had ever been associate chief of medicine.

Midmorning she got out of bed and put on her oldest sweatsuit, a windbreaker, her most disreputable running shoes, and a Red Sox cap that she pulled down hard over her ears. Outside, her feet squished through the water, soaked before she was twenty yards from the house. Despite the thaw it was winter in Massachusetts, and she was wet and shivering, but as she jogged her blood began to sing and she warmed quickly. She had intended to go only to Memorial Drive and back, but the running was too good to cut short and she loped alongside the frozen Charles River, watching the rain on the ice, until she began to tire. On the way back cars splashed her twice, but it hardly mattered; she was wet as a swimmer. She let herself into the house through the back door and left her drenched garments on the tile floor of the kitchen, wiping herself with a dish towel so she wouldn't drip on the rug on her way to the shower. She stayed under a very hot spray for a long time, until the mirror was so fogged she had no reflection when she got out and rubbed herself dry.

She had just begun to dress when she made up her mind to go for it, and to chair Sidney's committee. But not to replace anything in her schedule. Thursdays would stay Thursdays, Dr Ringgold.

She had gotten only as far as underpants and a Tufts University sweatshirt, but she picked up the portable phone and called his home number.

'It's R.J.,' she said when he answered. 'I didn't know if you guys would be home.' The Ringgolds owned a beach house on

21

Martha's Vineyard, and Gloria Ringgold insisted they spend as many weekends as possible on the island.

'Well, but the lousy weather,' Dr Ringgold said. 'We're stuck here for the weekend. You'd have to be a complete idiot to go out on a day like this.'

R.J. lowered the back of the seat and sat down on the toilet and laughed. 'You're absolutely right, Sidney,' she said.

5

An Invitation to the Ball

On Tuesday she taught an iatrogenic illnesses class at the medical school, pleasing to her because it was fiercely debated for almost the entire two hours. A few students still came to medical training in the smug expectation that they would be taught to be gods of healing, educated into infallibility. They resented discussion of the fact that in the course of trying to cure, doctors sometimes cause their patients injury and harm. But most of the students were aware of their place in time and society, sensitive to the fact that an exploding technology hadn't obliterated the human ability to make mistakes. It was important for them to be acutely aware of situations that could cause harm or death to their patients and waste their hard-earned incomes on malpractise settlements.

A good class. For the moment it made her more content with her lot as she made her way back to the hospital.

She had been in her office only a few minutes when Tessa told her Tom was on the line.

'R.J.? Elizabeth went early this morning.'

'Ah, Tom.'

'Yes. Well, she hurts no more.'

'I know. That's good, Tom.'

23

But *he* still hurt, she realized, and she was surprised how profoundly she hurt for him. What she felt for him was no longer a blaze, but undeniably a live spark of emotion remained. Perhaps he needed company. 'Listen. Do you want to meet me some place for dinner?' she said impulsively. 'Maybe go to the North End?'

'Oh. No, I— ' He sounded embarrassed. 'Actually, I have something I can't get out of this evening.'

Comfort from somebody else, she thought wryly and not without regret. She thanked him for letting her know about Elizabeth and went right back to work.

Late that afternoon, she received a call from one of the women in his office. 'Dr Cole? This is Cindy Wolper. Dr Kendricks asked me to tell you he won't be home at all tonight. He has to go on a consult, to Worcester.'

'Thank you for calling,' R.J. said.

But the following Saturday morning Tom asked her to brunch in Harvard Square. It surprised her. His usual Saturday routine was morning rounds at the Middlesex Memorial Hospital where he was a visiting surgeon, and then tennis, with lunch afterwards at the club.

He was buttering pumpernickel very precisely when he told her. 'An incident report has been filed against me at Middlesex.'

'By whom?'

'A nurse who was on Betts's ward. Beverly Martin.'

'Yes. I remember her. But, why on earth . . .?'

'She reported that I administered an "inappropriately large" injection of morphine to Elizabeth, causing her death.'

'. . . Oh, Tom.'

He nodded.

'What will happen now?'

'The report will be considered at a meeting of the hospital's medical incidents committee.'

24

The waitress came by and Tom stopped her and asked her to bring more coffee.

'It's no big deal, I'm certain. But I wanted to tell you about it before you heard it from somebody else,' he said.

On Monday, in accordance with the wishes she had expressed in her will, Elizabeth Sullivan was cremated. Tom, R.J. and Suzanna Lorentz went to the funeral home where Suzanna, as the attorney handling the estate, was handed a square box made of grey cardboard, containing the ashes.

They went to lunch at the Ritz, and Suzanna read parts of Betts's will to them over salads. Betts had left what Suzanna described as 'a considerable estate' to support and encourage the care of her aunt, Mrs Sally Frances Bosshard, patient at the Lutheran Home for the Aged and Infirm of Cleveland Heights, Ohio.

Following the death of Mrs Bosshard, the remaining money, if any, would go to the American Cancer Society. To her beloved friend Dr Thomas A. Kendricks, Elizabeth Sullivan had left what she hoped were good memories and an audio tape of Elizabeth Bosshard and Tom Kendricks singing 'Strawberry Fields'. To her new and valued friend Dr Roberta J. Cole, Elizabeth Sullivan had left a six-piece silver coffee service of French design and eighteenth-century manufacture, silversmith unknown. The silver service and the tape cassette were in storage in Antwerp, along with other items, mostly furniture and artwork that would be sold, the proceeds to be added to the monies going to Sally Frances Bosshard.

Of Dr Cole, Elizabeth Sullivan requested one last favor. She wished her ashes to be given to Dr Cole for placement in the earth, 'without ceremony or service, at a beautiful place of Dr Cole's choosing'.

R.J. was stunned, both by the bequest and by the unexpected responsibility. Tom's eyes glistened. He ordered a bottle of champagne, and they drank a toast to Betts.

In the parking lot, Suzanna took the small square cardboard box from her car and gave it to R.J. R.J. didn't know what to do with it. She put it on the passenger's side of the seat in the BMW and drove back to Lemuel Grace.

On the following Wednesday morning she was awakened at 5:20 a.m. by the loud and shockingly intrusive sound of bell chimes announcing that someone was at the front door.

She struggled out of bed and into her robe. Unable to locate her slippers, she padded into the cold hallway in her bare feet.

She went downstairs and peered through the glass at the side of the door. It was still dark outside, but she could make out two figures.

'What do you want?' she called, not about to open the door.

'State police.'

When she turned on the light and looked out again, she saw it was so, and she unsnapped the lock, suddenly terribly afraid.

'Did something happen to my father?'

'Oh, no, ma'am. No, ma'am. We would just like a word with Dr Kendricks.' She was a wiry corporal, in uniform, alongside a beefy male trooper in civilian clothes: black hat, black shoes, raincoat, grey slacks. They gave off an aura of unsmiling competence.

'What is it, R.J.?' Tom said. He stood at the top of the stairs wearing his blue suit trousers with the dusty rose pinstripe, in stocking feet and undershirt.

'Dr Kendricks?'

'Yes. What is it?'

'I'm Corporal Flora McKinnon, sir,' she said. 'And this is Trooper Robert Travers. We're members of C-PAC, the Crime Prevention and Control Unit attached to the office of Edward W. Wilhoit, the district attorney of Middlesex

County. Mr Wilhoit would like to have a few words with you, sir.'

'When?'

'Well, now, sir. He'd like you to come down to his office with us.'

'Jesus Christ, do you mean to tell me he's working at five thirty in the morning?'

'Yessir,' the woman said.

'Do you have a warrant for my arrest?'

'No, sir, we do not.'

'Well, you tell Mr Wilhoit that I refused his kind invitation. In one hour I'll be in the surgical theater at Middlesex Memorial, operating on someone's gallbladder, somebody who's depending on me. You tell Mr Wilhoit I can come to his office at one thirty. If that's all right, he can let my secretary know. If it's not all right, we can work out another time that is mutually satisfactory. Got that?'

'Yes, sir. We understand that,' the red-haired corporal said, and they nodded and went out into the dark.

Tom stayed on the stairs. R.J. remained fixed in the bottom hallway, looking up, afraid for him. 'God, Tom. What's going on?'

'Maybe you'd better go there with me, R.J.'

'I was never that kind of lawyer. I'll come. But you'd better have somebody else come, too,' she said.

She cancelled her Wednesday class and spent three hours on the telephone talking to lawyers, people she knew would respect her confidentiality and give honest advice. The same name kept being mentioned: Nat Rourke. He had been around a long time. He wasn't flashy, but he was very smart and highly respected. R.J. had never met him. He didn't take the call when she telephoned his office, but an hour later he called back.

He said almost nothing while she laid out the facts of the case.

'No, no, no,' Rourke said gently. 'You and your husband will not go to see Wilhoit at one thirty. You will come to *my* office at one thirty. I have to meet with somebody here, briefly, at three. We'll go to the DA's office at four forty-five. My secretary will call Wilhoit with the new time.'

Nat Rourke's office was in a solid old building behind the State House, comfortable but shabby. The lawyer himself reminded R.J. of pictures she had seen of Irving Berlin, a small man with sallow complexion and sharp features, nattily dressed in dark and subdued colors, very white shirt, a university tie whose symbol she didn't recognize. Penn, she found out later.

Rourke asked Tom to recount for him all the circumstances leading up to Elizabeth Sullivan's death. He watched Tom intently, a good listener, not interrupting, staying with the narrative until the end. Then he nodded, pursed his lips, leaned back in his chair with his hands folded on his vested belly, over the Phi Beta Kappa key.

'Did you kill her, Dr Kendricks?'

'I didn't have to kill her. The cancer took care of that. She would have stopped breathing on her own, a matter of hours, a matter of days. She could never again be conscious, never again be Betts, without agony. I'd promised her she wouldn't suffer. She was already receiving very heavy dosages of morphine. I increased the dosage to make certain she wouldn't have further pain. If it brought death sooner rather than later, that was perfectly all right with me.'

'The 30 milligrams that Mrs Sullivan received by mouth twice a day. I would suppose it was a slow-acting form of morphine?' Rourke said.

'Yes.'

'And the 40 milligrams you gave her by needle, that was fast-acting morphine, in sufficient amount perhaps to inhibit her respiration?'

'Yes.'

28

'And if it inhibited her respiration sufficiently, that would cause death.'

'Yes.'

'Were you having an affair with Mrs Sullivan?'

'No.' They discussed Tom's early relationship with Elizabeth, and the lawyer seemed satisfied.

'Have you in any way benefited financially from Elizabeth Sullivan's death?'

'No.' Tom told him the terms of Betts's will. 'Is Wilhoit going to make something dirty of this?'

'Very possibly. He's an ambitious pol, interested in moving up in the world, lieutenant governor. A sensational trial would be a springboard. If he could get you convicted of murder in the first degree, sentenced to life imprisonment without parole, with big, black headlines, pats on his back, lots of splash, he'd be made. But first-degree murder isn't going to happen in this case. And Mr Wilhoit is too shrewd a politician even to bring the case to the grand jury unless he has a good chance to convict. He'll wait for the hospital medical incidents committee to give him direction.'

'What's the worst thing that can happen to me in this case?'

'Bleakest scenario?'

'Yes. Worst.'

'No guarantees that I'm right, of course. But I would guess your worst scenario would be conviction for manslaughter. The sentence would be incarceration. This kind of case, it's likely the judge would be sympathetic and give you what we call a "Concord sentence". He would sentence you to the Massachusetts Correctional Institution at Concord for twenty years, thus preserving his reputation as a judge who was tough on crime. But he'd be giving you easy time, because at Concord you would be eligible for parole after serving only twenty-four months of the sentence. So you could use the time to write a book, get famous, earn a potful of money.'

'I would lose my license to practice medicine,' Tom said

levelly, and R.J. could almost forget that she had stopped loving him a long time ago.

'Keep in mind that we've been talking about the worst scenario. The best scenario would be that the case doesn't go to the grand jury. Accomplishing the best scenario is why I get paid the big money,' Rourke said.

It was easy to move into a discussion of his fee. 'Case like this, anything could happen, or nothing. Ordinarily, if the defendant were someone not terribly respectable, I would ask for an initial retainer, twenty thousand. But . . . you are a professional man of high reputation and good character. I think your best bet would be to hire me on a time-spent basis. Two-and-a-quarter an hour.'

Tom nodded. 'Sounds like a bargain to me,' he said, and Rourke smiled.

They reached the high-rise courthouse at five minutes to five, ten minutes after Rourke had said they would get there. It was the end of the workday and people were pouring out of the building with the pleased energy of children released from school. 'Take your time, we're in no hurry,' Rourke said. 'It'll do him good to meet us on our own schedule. That business of sending troopers to fetch you at crack of dawn is strictly cheap intimidation, Dr Kendricks. An invitation to the ball, you might say.'

It was meant to tell them, R.J. knew with a chill, that the district attorney had gone to the trouble of learning Tom's timetable, not something he would do for a routine matter.

They had to sign in with the guard at the desk of the lobby, and then the elevator whisked them to the fifteenth floor.

Wilhoit was lean and tanned, a big-nosed man who smiled at them as cordially as an old friend. R.J. had looked him up. Harvard College, '72; Boston College Law School, '75; assistant DA, '75–'78; state representative, '78 until elected district attorney in 1988.

'How are you, Mr Rourke? A pleasure to see you again. Nice to meet you, Dr Kendricks, Dr Cole. Yes, sit down; sit down.'

Then he was all business, cool eyes and quiet questions, most of which Tom had already answered for Rourke during the course of the afternoon.

They had obtained and studied Elizabeth Sullivan's medical file, Wilhoit told them. 'It says that by order of Dr Howard Fisher, the patient in room 208 of the Middlesex Memorial Hospital had been receiving an oral morphine medication known as Contin, 30 milligrams twice a day.

'. . . Let's see now . . . At 2:10 a.m., the night in question, Dr Thomas A. Kendricks entered into the patient's record a written order for 40 milligrams of morphine sulphate to be injected intravenously. According to the medications nurse, Miss Beverly Martin, the doctor told her he'd give the needle himself. Martin said that half an hour later, when she entered room 208 to check the patient's temperature and blood pressure, Mrs Sullivan was dead. Dr Kendrick was seated next to her bedside, holding her hand.' He looked at Tom. 'Are those facts essentially correct as I have presented them, Dr Kendrick?'

'Yes, I would say they are accurate, Mr Wilhoit.'

'Did you kill Elizabeth Sullivan, Dr Kendricks?'

Tom looked at Rourke. Rourke's eyes were guarded, but he nodded, signifying that Tom should answer.

'No, sir. Cancer killed Elizabeth Sullivan,' Tom said.

Wilhoit nodded, too. He thanked them politely for coming, and he indicated that the interview was at an end.

6

The Contender

There was no further word from the district attorney, no story in the newspapers. R.J. knew silence could be ominous. Wilhoit's people were at work, talking to nurses and doctors at Middlesex, assessing whether they had a case, whether it would help or hurt the district attorney's career if he tried to crush Dr Thomas A. Kendricks.

R.J. concentrated on her work. She posted notices in the hospital and at the medical school announcing the formation of the publications committee. When the first meeting was held on a snowy Tuesday evening, fourteen people showed up. She had expected the committee to attract residents and young doctors, the unpublished. But several senior physicians attended too. It shouldn't have surprised her. She knew at least one man who had become a medical school dean without having learned how to write acceptable English.

She set up a monthly schedule of lectures by medical journal editors, and several of the doctors volunteered to read their own papers-in-progress at the next meeting so they could be critiqued. She had to admit that Sidney Ringgold had anticipated a need.

Boris Lattimore, an elderly physician on the hospital's visiting staff, pulled R.J. aside in the cafeteria and whispered that he had news for her. Sidney had told him the next associate chief of medicine would be either R.J. or Allen Greenstein. Greenstein was a hotshot researcher who had developed a much-publicized program for the genetic screening of newborns. R.J. hoped the rumor was wrong; Greenstein was daunting competition.

The new committee responsibility wasn't difficult; it added to her schedule and nibbled away at her precious free time, but she was never tempted to sacrifice her Thursdays. She was aware that without sanitary, modern clinics to end pregnancy, many women would die trying to do it themselves. The poorest women, those without medical insurance, money, or enough sophistication to find out where help was available, still tried to end their own pregnancies. They drank turpentine, ammonia, and detergent, and poked things into their cervixes – coat hangers, knitting needles, kitchen tools, any instrument that promised to bring on a miscarriage. R.J. worked at Family Planning because she felt it was essential for a woman to have adequate services available if she needed them. But it was becoming harder and harder for the medical staff at Family Planning. Driving home after a busy Wednesday at the hospital, R.J. heard on the car radio that a bomb had exploded at an abortion clinic in Bridgeport, Connecticut, knocking out a portion of the building, blinding a guard, and injuring a staff secretary and two patients.

The next morning at the clinic, Gwen Gabler told R.J. she was resigning, moving away.

'You *can't*,' R.J. said.

She, Gwen and Samantha Potter had been close friends since medical school. Samantha was a fixture on the faculty of the

University of Massachusetts medical school in Worcester, her anatomy class already a legend, and R.J. didn't get to see her as frequently as they would like. But she and Gwen had spent time together regularly and often, for eighteen years.

It was Gwen who had made it possible for her to continue to work at Family Planning, bolstering her when things became difficult. R.J. was not brave. She thought of Gwen as her courage.

Gwen smiled at her miserably. 'I'm gonna miss the hell out of you.'

'So don't leave.'

'I have to go. Phil and the boys come first.' Mortgage rates had soared and the bottom had dropped out of the real estate market. Phil Gabler had had a disastrous business year, and the Gablers were moving west, to Moscow, Idaho. Phil was going to teach real estate courses at the university and Gwen was negotiating for a job as a gynecologist-obstetrician with a health maintenance organization. 'Phil loves to teach. And HMOs are where it's at. We've got to do something to change the system, R.J. Before long, we're all going to be working for HMOs.' She and the Idaho HMO already had completed initial arrangements by phone.

They held hands tightly, and R.J. wondered how she would get along without her.

After Grand Rounds on Friday morning, Sidney Ringgold broke away from the gaggle of white coats and crossed the hospital lobby to where R.J. waited at the elevator.

'I wanted to tell you, I'm getting lots of positive feedback about the publications committee,' he said.

R.J. was suspicious. Sidney Ringgold didn't usually go out of his way to deliver back pats.

'How's Tom doing these days?' he said casually. 'I heard something about a complaint to the medical incidents committee at Middlesex. Is it apt to give him any real trouble?'

Sidney had raised a lot of money for the hospital, and he

had an exaggerated fear of bad publicity, even the kind that rubbed off on a spouse.

All her life she had intensely disliked the role of job candidate. She didn't give in to temptation, didn't tell him: *You can take the appointment and stuff it.* 'No, no real trouble, Sidney. Tom says it's just a nuisance, nothing to worry about.'

He leaned toward her. 'I don't think you have anything to worry about, either. No promises, mind, but things look good. They look very good indeed.'

His encouragement filled her with inexplicable gloom. 'You know what I wish, Sidney?' she said impulsively. 'I wish you and I were working to set up a family practise residency and clinic for Lemuel Grace Hospital, so the uninsured of Boston would have a place to get really top-flight medical care.'

'The uninsured already have a place to go. We have a drop-in clinic that scores high numbers.' Sidney's annoyance showed. He didn't like conversations about the medical inadequacies of his service.

'People come to the drop-in clinic only when they absolutely have to. They get a different doctor every time they come, so there's no continuity of care. They're treated for the illness or injury of the moment, and no preventive medicine is practiced. Sidney, we could start something if we turned out family practitioners. They're the doctors who are really needed.'

His smile was forced now. 'None of the Boston hospitals has a family practise residency.'

'Isn't that a wonderful reason to start one?'

He shook his head. 'I'm tired. I think I've done well as chief of medicine, and I have less than three years before retirement. I'm not interested in leading the kind of battle that would be necessary to set up a program like that. You can't come to me with any more crusades, R.J. If you want to make changes in the system, the way to do it is to earn your own place in the power structure. Then you can fight your own battles.'

*   *.   *

That Thursday, her secret backyard route into the Family Planning building was uncovered. The police detail that kept demonstrators pushed away from the clinic was late that morning. R.J. had parked in Ralph Aiello's yard and was going through the gate in the fence when she became aware of people pouring around both sides of the clinic building.

Lots of people, carrying signs, shouting and pointing their fingers at her.

Ah, no. She didn't know what to do.

She knew there would be violence, what she had always been afraid of. She steeled herself to walk through them in silence, without visibly trembling. Passive resistance. *Think of Gandhi*, she told herself, but instead she thought of doctors who had been attacked, clinic staff who had been killed or maimed. Crazy people.

Some of them ran past her, went through the gate and into the Aiello yard.

An aloof dignity. *Think peace. Think of Martin Luther King. Walk through them. Walk through them.*

She looked back and saw that they were taking pictures of the red BMW, crowding around it. Oh, the paint job. She turned around and pushed back through the gate. Someone punched her in the back.

'Touch that car and I'll break your arm!' she yelled.

The man with the camera turned and shoved it toward her face. The strobe lamp flickered again and again and again, nails of light piercing her eyes, screams like spikes driven into her ears, a kind of crucifixion.

7
Voices

She called Nat Rourke right away and told him about the confrontation at the clinic.

'I thought you should know, so it wouldn't be a surprise in case they tried to use my activities against Tom.'

'Yes. Thank you so very much, Dr Cole,' he said. He had a very courtly manner. R.J. couldn't tell what he was really thinking.

That evening, Tom came back to the house on Brattle Street early. She was seated at the kitchen table doing paperwork, and he came in and took a beer from the refrigerator. 'Want one?'

'No thanks.'

He sat down opposite her. She had an urge to reach out and touch him. He looked tired, and in the old days she'd have gone around and massaged his neck. At one time they were very touchy. He had massaged her often. Lately they had tended to demonize one another, but she couldn't escape the fact that he had had many sweet traits.

'Rourke called me,' Tom said, 'and told me about what happened in Jamaica Plain.'

'Oh?'

'Yeah. He, uh . . . asked me about our marriage. And I was frank and truthful in my answer.'

She looked at him and smiled. Then was then, she thought; this was now. 'Always the best way.'

'Yes. Rourke said if we're going to be divorced, proceedings should be instituted at once, so that any controversy about your work at Family Planning won't prejudice my defense.'

R.J. nodded. 'It makes sense to me. Our marriage has been over for a long time, Tom.'

'Yes. Yes, it has, R.J.' He smiled at her. 'Now would you like that beer?'

'No, thanks,' she said, and went back to her paperwork.

Tom took some of his things and moved out at once, so easily she was convinced he had somebody's place to move right into.

At first she could detect no change in the house on Brattle Street, because she was accustomed to being alone there. She returned each night to the same empty house, but now there was a sense of peace, an absence of the signs of him that used to annoy and aggravate. A pleasing expansion of her personal space.

Eight nights after he left, however, she began to receive telephone calls.

There were different voices, and they phoned all night at different hours, probably on shifts.

'You kill babies, bitch,' a man's voice whispered.

'You cut up our children. You vacuum up human beings as if they were trash.'

One woman informed R.J. pityingly that she was under demonic control. 'You will burn in hellfire for eternity,' the caller said. She had a throaty whisper and a genteel voice.

R.J. had her telephone number changed to an unlisted one. A couple of evenings later, when she came home from work she saw that large nails had been hammered into the expensively restored door of her heirloom Georgian house. They held a poster.

WANTED
WE NEED YOUR HELP TO STOP
DR ROBERTA J. COLE

The picture showed her looking angrily into the camera, her mouth open unflatteringly. The text beneath the picture said:

Cambridge resident Dr Roberta J. Cole spends most of each week pretending to be a respectable doctor and teacher at the Lemuel Grace Hospital and at the Massachusetts College of Physicians and Surgeons.

But she is an abortionist. Every Thursday she kills from 10 to 13 babies.

Please join us by:

1. Prayer and fasting – God is not willing that any should perish. Pray for Dr Cole's salvation.

2. Write and call her and share the gospel and your willingness to help her leave her profession.

3. Ask her to STOP DOING ABORTIONS! *'Do not participate in the unfruitful deeds of darkness, but instead even expose them.'* Ephesians 5:11

The base cost of an abortion is $250.00. Most doctors in Dr Cole's position earn 50 percent of the cost of each abortion. That would make Dr Cole's income from killing almost 700 children last year to be approximately $87,500.

The poster listed ways in which R.J. could be reached, giving her daily schedule and the addresses and telephone numbers of the hospital, the medical school, the PMS clinic and the Family Planning clinic. At the bottom of the poster was a line that read: REWARD: LIVES WILL BE SAVED IF SHE IS STOPPED!!!!!

There was an ominous silence during the week that followed. One morning the *Boston Globe* carried a story quoting local political activists regarding the fact that District Attorney Edward W. Wilhoit was testing the wind for a run at the lieutenant governor's office. That Sunday, a letter from the cardinal condemning abortion as mortal sin was read in all churches of the Boston archdiocese. Two days later, national media carried the story that yet another assisted suicide had been performed in Michigan by Dr Jack Kevorkian. That evening, when R.J. turned on her television for the 11 p.m. news, there was a soundbite of Wilhoit addressing a convention of senior citizens. He pledged to 'bring swift justice to the antichrist among us, who through feticide, suicide, and homicide seek to usurp the powers of the Holy Trinity.'

'I would hope that we can be civilized, no rancor or quarreling, and just split everything, assets and debts. Right down the middle,' Tom said.

She agreed. She was sure he would be kicking and screaming if there were real money to kick and scream about, but most of what they had earned had gone into the house and to pay his medical school debts.

Tom became embarrassed when he told her he was living with Cindy Wolper, his office manager – blonde, bubbly, in her late twenties.

'We're going to be married,' he said, and looked enormously relieved to have finally made the grade from marital cheat to one of the newly engaged.

Poor baby, she thought angrily.

Despite the declarations of civility, Tom brought a lawyer, Jerry Saltus, when they met to discuss the division of property.

'Do you plan to keep the Brattle Street house?' he asked.

R.J. stared at him in amazement. They had bought the house at his insistence and over her objections. Because of his obsession, they had sunk all their money into it. 'Don't you want the house?'

'Cindy and I have decided to live in a condominium.'

'Well, I don't want your pretentious house either. I never wanted it.' She was aware that her voice was rising, and that she sounded waspish, but she didn't care.

'What about the farmhouse?'

'. . . I suppose it should be sold too,' she said.

'If you'll handle the sale of the country place, I'll arrange to sell the house here. Okay?'

'Okay.'

He said he especially wanted the cherry breakfront, the sofa, the two wingback chairs, and the large-screen television. She'd have wanted the breakfront, but he agreed she could have the piano and a Persian rug, a hundred-year-old Heriz that she treasured. The other furniture pieces they divided by taking turns in choosing items. The agreement was swiftly and bloodlessly made, and the lawyer fled before they changed their minds and became ugly.

Sunday evening R.J. went to Alex's Gymnasium with Gwen, who would be leaving for Idaho in a couple of weeks. Before their aerobics class, R.J. was telling her about Tom and his future bride when Alexander Manakos came in with a repairman and went to the other side of the gym, discussing a broken exercise machine.

'He's looking over here,' Gwen said.

'Who?'

'Manakos. At you. He's looked at you several times.'

41

'Gwen. Don't be a fool.'

But the club owner patted the repair man on the shoulder, and began to walk in their direction.

'I'll be right back. I have to call my office,' Gwen said, and fled.

His clothes were as well-tailored as Tom's, but not from Brooks Brothers. His suits were freer, *au courant*. He was an extremely beautiful man.

'Dr Cole.'

'Yes.'

'I'm Alex Manakos.' He shook her hand almost impersonally. 'Is everything satisfactory for you, here at my club?'

'Yes. I enjoy the club very much.'

'Well, I'm glad to hear that. Are there any complaints I can remedy?'

'No. How do you know my name?'

'I asked somebody. I pointed you out to her. I thought I'd say hello. You look like a very nice person.'

'Thank you.' She was no good at this sort of thing and was sorry he had decided to approach her. Up close, his hair reminded her of the young Redford. His nose was hooked, which made him look somewhat cruel.

'Would you have dinner with me some evening? Or drinks, whatever you prefer. A chance to sit and talk, get to know one another.'

'Mr Manakos, I don't—'

'Alex. My name is Alex. Would you feel better if we were introduced by somebody you know?'

She smiled. 'That isn't necessary.'

'Look, I've startled you, coming at you this way, like a pickup. I know you're here for an aerobics lesson. Think it over, and let me know before you leave.'

Before she could open her mouth to protest, and tell him it wouldn't matter, he went away.

*　　*　　*

42

'You're going out with him, aren't you?'

'No, I'm not.'

'Why? He looks very nice.'

'Gwen, he's gorgeous, but I'm not attracted to him at all. Honestly. I can't tell you why.'

'So? He's not proposing marriage, or suggesting you spend the rest of your life with him. He simply asked you out.'

Gwen didn't let up. During the lesson, between every set she returned to the same subject.

'He seems to be very nice. When was the last time you had a date with a man?'

As she danced, R.J. considered what she knew about him. A former All-American basketball player at Boston College, he came from an immigrant family. In the lobby was an early picture of him on Boston Common, an unsmiling kid with a shoeshine box. By the time he entered college he had rented a cubbyhole shoeshine stand in a building on Kenmore Square and hired several people to work there. As his athletic legend grew, Alex's became the 'in' spot to get your shoes shined, and soon he had a larger shine parlour with a refreshment stand. He wasn't good enough for professional basketball, but he had graduated with a business degree and enough publicity to get whatever capital he needed from Boston banks, and he opened the health club full of Nautilus equipment and trained instructors. For old times' sake, the club had a shoeshine parlour, but the refreshment stand had become a bar and café. Now Alex Manakos owned the health club, a Greek restaurant on the waterfront and another in Cambridge, and God only knew what else.

She knew he was unmarried.

'When was the last time you even had a conversation with a man who wasn't a patient or a doctor? He seems very nice. *Very nice.*

'*Go out with him,*' Gwen hissed.

*   *   *

After R.J. had showered and changed, she went into the bar. When she told Alex Manakos she would be happy to get together with him some evening, he smiled.

'That's good. You're a physician, am I correct?'

'Yes.'

'Well, I never went out with a woman doctor before.'

What have I gotten myself into? she asked herself. 'You go out only with men doctors?'

'Ho ho ho,' he said, but he was looking at her with interest. So they worked it out and they had a date for dinner. Saturday.

The next morning, both the *Herald* and the *Globe* published stories on abortion in Boston. Reporters had interviewed individuals on both sides of the controversy, and each paper ran several pictures of activists. In addition, the *Herald* reproduced two of the posters of 'wanted' abortionists. One was of Dr James Dickenson, a gynecologist who performed abortions at the Planned Parenthood clinic in Brookline. The other was the poster of Dr Roberta J. Cole.

On Wednesday it was announced that Allen Greenstein MD had been appointed associate chief of the department of medicine at the Lemuel Grace Hospital, to succeed Maxwell B. Roseman MD.

For the next several days there were newspaper and television interviews with Dr Greenstein about the fact that in a few years newborn infants would be genetically screened, making it possible for parents to know the health dangers their children would face in the course of their lives, and perhaps what they would die of.

R.J. and Sidney Ringgold found themselves thrown together on Grand Rounds and at a departmental meeting, and passing each other several times in the corridors. Each time, Sidney looked into her eyes and greeted her warmly and pleasantly.

R.J. would have liked him to stop and talk. She wanted to tell him she wasn't ashamed of performing abortions, that she was doing a difficult and important job, one she had taken on because she was a good doctor.

So why did she feel hangdog and furtive as she walked the corridors of her hospital?

Damn them!

On Saturday afternoon she made certain she came home early enough to shower at her leisure and dress slowly and carefully. At seven o'clock she entered Alex's Gymnasium and walked into the lounge. Alexander Manakos was standing at one end of the bar, talking to two men. She sat on a stool at the other end of the bar, and presently he came over to her. He was even better-looking than she remembered.

'Good evening.'

He nodded. He was carrying a newspaper. When he opened it, she saw it was Monday's edition of the *Globe*. 'Is it true, what this says? That you, you know, provide abortions?'

This wasn't to be an accolade, she knew. Her head went up, she drew herself erect so she could look him in the eye. 'Yes. It's a legal and ethical medical procedure that's vital to the health and lives of my patients,' she said levelly, 'and I do it well.'

'You disgust me. I wouldn't do you with somebody else's dick.'

Very nice.

'Well, you certainly won't with your own,' she told him calmly, and she got off the stool and walked out of Alex's Gymnasium, passing a booth in which a motherly person with white hair was applauding, tears in her eyes. It would have been more comforting to R.J. if the woman hadn't been drunk.

* * *

'I don't need anyone. I can live my life by myself. By myself. *I don't need anybody, get it?*

'And I want you to get off my back, friend,' she told Gwen fiercely.

'Okay, okay,' Gwen said, and sighed, and escaped.

8

A Jury of Peers

The scheduled April meeting of the medical incidents committee of the Middlesex Memorial Hospital was postponed because of a springtime blizzard that covered the grimy snow and old ice with a clean white layer that would have been cheering earlier in the season. As it was, R.J. grumbled about still more snow. Two days later the temperature rose to 74 degrees, and the new spring snow and the old winter snow disappeared together, the gutters flowing with the runoff.

The medical incidents committee met on the following week. It was not a lengthy session. In the face of clear evidence and testimony that Elizabeth Sullivan was dying and in terrible pain, they decided unanimously that Dr Thomas A. Kendricks had not acted unprofessionally in heavily sedating Mrs Sullivan.

A few days after the meeting Phil Roswell, one of the committee members, told R.J. there had been no debate. 'Damn it, let's be honest. We all do that to hasten a merciful end when death is close and inevitable,' Roswell said. 'Tom wasn't trying to hide a crime, he wrote the order honestly, right there in her chart. If we punished him, we'd have to punish ourselves and most of the doctors we know.'

Nat Rourke had a discreet chat with the district attorney and came away with the knowledge that Wilhoit did not intend to bring Elizabeth Sullivan's death to the grand jury.

Tom was exultant. He wanted to turn a page in his life, anxious to get on with the divorce and begin his new marriage.

R.J.'s mood was exacerbated by the beggars who were everywhere. She had been born and raised in Boston and she loved it, but now she couldn't bear to look at the street people. She saw them throughout the city, sifting through the trash cans and dumpsters, trundling their few possessions in shopping carts stolen from the supermarkets, sleeping in shipping crates on cold loading docks, lined up for free meals at the soup kitchen on Tremont Street, taking over the benches in Boston Common and other public places.

To her, homeless people were a medical problem. In the 1970s, psychiatrists had lobbied to phase out the massive stone public asylums where the insane had been stockpiled under shameful conditions. The idea was that patients would be returned to freedom to live in harmony alongside the sane, as was being done successfully in several European countries. But in America the community mental health centers set up to serve the freed patients were underfunded, and they failed. Patients scattered. It was impossible for psychiatric social workers to keep track of someone who slept in a cardboard carton one night and miles away over a steam grate the next night. All over the United States, alcoholics, drug addicts, schizophrenics, and every variety of the mentally ill made up an army of the homeless. Many of them turned to begging, some soliciting on subways and buses with loud speeches and pitiful stories, others sitting against a building with a cup or overturned cap next to crude signs making their pleas: *Will work for food. Four children at home.* R.J. had read a study estimating that 95 percent of America's beggars were addicted to drugs or alcohol, and that some begged up to three hundred dollars a day, money they promptly spent on substance abuse. R.J. thought with great guilt of the 5 percent who weren't addicted, merely homeless and jobless. Still, she steeled herself against giving and was furious when she saw someone dropping a dime or a quarter into a cup instead of pressuring politically to get homeless people off the streets and into adequate care.

It wasn't only the homeless; all the ingredients of her existence in the city got on her nerves – the ending of her marriage, the depersonalization of her profession, the daily paperwork grind, the traffic, the fact that she hated to go to work now in a place where Allen Greenstein had beaten her out of a job.

Everything merged into a bitter cocktail. Realization slowly dawned that it was time for her to change her life drastically, to leave Boston.

The two medical communities where there were programs into which someone with her hybrid interests might fit were Baltimore and Philadelphia. She sat down and wrote letters to Roger Carleton at Johns Hopkins and Irving Simpson at Penn, asking if they were interested in her services.

Long ago she had arranged for her spring calendar to be clear for a week, dreaming about St Thomas. Instead, on a warm Friday afternoon she got away from the hospital early and went home to pack a few things she could wear in the country. She had to dispose of the Berkshires property.

She had left the house and was getting into the car when she remembered Elizabeth's ashes, and she went back inside and took the cardboard box from the top of the bureau in the guest room, where she had put it when she had brought it home.

She couldn't bring herself to put the ashes into the trunk with her suitcase. Instead, she placed the small box on the seat next to her and put her folded raincoat in front of it so it wouldn't roll off if she had to stop short.

Then she drove to the Mass. Pike and pointed the red BMW west.

9

Woodfield

Even before the Georgian house on Brattle Street had been restored and furnished to their satisfaction, her marriage to Tom had begun to unravel. When they had found a charming property on a Berkshires mountainside in the township of Woodfield, in western Massachusetts near the Vermont line, they bought it and used the project of a vacation home to try to reinvent their 'togetherness'. The small yellow frame house was about eighty-five years old, surviving sturdily next to an old tobacco barn that had begun to sag badly, like their relationship. There were seven acres of fields and thirty-nine acres of tangled old New England woods, and the Catamount, one of Woodfield's three small mountain rivers, ran through both the forest and the meadow.

Tom had hired a contractor to dig a swim pond out of a wet place in the pasture, and the bulldozer unearthed the small, stubborn remains of an infant child. The connective tissue had long since disappeared. What was left could have been mistaken for chicken bones save for the unmistakably human skull like a delicate hardened mushroom, in three sections. There was no grave marker and the land was too marshy to be a cemetery. The find had caused a local stir; nobody in the town knew how the fetus had gotten there.

Maybe the buried child had been Indian. The medical examiner said the little bones were old. Not eons, but certainly they had been buried long ago.

Found in the earth above the bones had been a small earthenware plate. When it was washed, a series of rust-colored letters came into view, now terribly faded. What had been written on the plate couldn't be read. Most of the letters were gone, but a few remained: *ah*, and *od*. And *o* and again, *od*. Despite the sifting, a few of the small bones never were recovered. The county medical examiner had pieced together enough of the tiny skeleton to determine that it had been almost but not quite full term, but the sex was unknown. The coroner took the bones away, but when R.J. asked if she could have the plate, he shrugged and gave it to her. She had kept it ever since in the breakfront in the parlor.

The Massachusetts Turnpike is unexciting over most of its length. It was only when she had left the Turnpike near Springfield and driven north on I-91 that she first saw the low, worn-down mountains and began to feel happy. I will lift up mine eyes unto the hills, from whence cometh mine help. In another half hour she was in the hills, climbing roads that twisted and undulated, passing farms and forest, until she turned onto Laurel Hill Road and then drove down the long and winding driveway to the wood-frame farmhouse, the color of butter, that hugged the fringe of woods at the far end of the meadow.

She and Tom hadn't used the country house since the previous fall. When she opened the door the air was heavy and slightly bitter. There were droppings on a windowsill in the parlor, like mouse feces only larger, and with a quick return of the bad feeling that had plagued her for days, she told herself there was a rat in the house. But in a corner of the kitchen she found the desiccated remains of a bat. The first job she gave herself was to fetch the dustpan and broom and dispose of bat and droppings. She turned on the refrigerator, threw up the windows to let in fresh air, and carried in her supplies, two cartons of groceries and a cooler with perishables. Hungry but unambitious, she made a supper of a hard and tasteless supermarket tomato, a kaiser roll, two cups of tea and a package of chocolate cookies.

Brushing the crumbs off the table, she realized with a pang that she had forgotten about Elizabeth.

She went outside and brought in the box of ashes from the car, setting it on the fireplace mantel. She would have to discover the beautiful place Elizabeth had trusted her to find, and bury the ashes. She was drawn outside again and took a few steps into the woods, but they were dark and tangled. There was no way to explore them except by climbing over or under downed trees and bulling through brush and brambles, and something in her wasn't ready for them, so she beat a hasty retreat and walked down the gravel driveway to Laurel Hill Road. It was an oiled gravel road, nearly three miles long, rising and falling in several hills. She was glad to walk. A mile and a quarter down the road, she approached the small white farmhouse and enormous red barn of Hank and Freda Krantz, the farmers who had sold Tom and her their place. She turned around before she reached their door, for the moment not wanting to answer questions about Tom and explain the end of her marriage.

The sun was down when she got back to the house, and the clear air was sharply cold. She closed all the windows but one. There was dry wood in the shed, and she built a small blaze in the fireplace and took away the chill. As dusk fell, the shrill of peepers in the pond spillway came through the open window, and she sat on the couch and drank hot, black coffee that was sweet enough to guarantee weight gain, and watched the fire.

*   *   *

The next morning she slept late, had eggs for brunch, and then indulged in a frenzy of housecleaning. Because she so seldom was required to do housework she enjoyed it, and now she gained satisfaction out of vacuuming, sweeping, dusting. She washed all the pots and pans but only a few dishes and utensils, just the things she would need.

She knew the Krantzes ate midday farm dinners promptly at noon, so she waited until 1:15 and then walked up the road and knocked on their door.

'Well, look who's here,' Hank Krantz boomed. 'Come in, come in.'

They welcomed her into their kitchen, and Freda Krantz poured her a cup of coffee without asking and cut a wedge from half a white cake that was on the counter.

R.J. didn't know them that well, really, seeing them only on her infrequent visits, but she saw honest regret in their eyes as she told them about the divorce and asked their advice about the best way to sell the house and land.

Hank Krantz scratched his face. 'You could go to a real estate agent in Greenfield or Amherst, of course, but nowadays most folks sell through a fella named Dave Markus, right here in town. He advertises and gets good prices. And he's a straight shooter. Not a bad sort at all for a fella from New York.'

They told her how to get to Markus's house. She drove first to the state highway and then off it and down a series of very bumpy gravel roads that didn't do her car any good. In a clover field a lovely Morgan horse, brown with a white face-blaze, ran alongside her car on the inside of the fence and then passed her, tail and mane streaming. There was a real estate sign outside a handsome log house looking out on a splendid view. A second sign made her smile:

I'm-In-Love-With-You
HONEY

Jars of amber honey were stacked in two old bookcases on the porch. Inside, radio rock music blared: The Who. A teenaged girl with long black hair came to the door. Freckled, heavy-breasted, angel-faced behind thick glasses, she was dabbing a cotton ball against a bloody pimple on her pointed chin.

'Hi, I'm Sarah, my father's away. He'll be back tonight.' She scribbled R.J.'s name and telephone number and promised her father would call. While R.J. bought a jar of honey, the horse whinnied behind the fence.

'He's such a damned busybody,' the girl said. 'Want to give him his sugar?'

'Sure.'

Sarah Markus got two cubes of sugar and gave them to her, and they walked to the fence together. R.J. presented the cubes timidly, but the big square horse teeth missed the flesh of her palm, and the lapping rough tongue made her smile. 'What's his name?'

'Chaim. He's Jewish. My father named him for a writer.'

R.J. was beginning to relax as she waved goodbye to the girl and the horse and drove back down the road lined with tall trees and old stone walls.

Main Street in Woodfield contained the post office and four businesses – Hazel's, an establishment that couldn't make up its mind if it was a hardware store or a gift shop; Buell's Expert Auto Repair; Sotheby's General Market (Est. 1842); and Terry's, a modern convenience store with a couple of gas pumps out front. R.J. was partial to the funky general store. Frank Sotheby always had a wheel of sharp, aged cheddar that made her mouth water. He sold maple syrup, cut his own meat, and made his own sausage, sweet and hot.

There was no lunch counter. 'Would you make me a sandwich, cheddar on a roll?'

'Why not?' the storekeeper said. He charged her a dollar, and fifty cents for an Orange Crush. She had her lunch sitting on the bench on the store porch, watching the village go by. Then

54

she went back into the store and recklessly cast aside her usual low-cholesterol approach to food, buying a sirloin steak, sweet sausage, and a wedge of the good cheese.

That afternoon she put on her oldest clothes and some boots and braved the woods. Just a few feet in, it was another world, cooler, dark, quiet with only the wind through billions of leaves, a gentle accumulated rustle that sometimes became as loud as surf and made her feel holy, and also a little scared. She was counting on the supposition that large animals and monsters would be frightened off by the disturbance she was making without trying, stepping on branches that snapped and generally moving clumsily through the close-grown forest. Now and again she came to a tiny clearing that gave respite, but there was no inviting place to rest.

She followed a brook to the Catamount River. She estimated she was close to the midpoint of her property, and she traced the river downstream. The bank was as overgrown as the woods and the going was hard; despite the spring coolness she found that she was sweating and exhausted, and when she came to a large granite rock that projected from the bank into the water, she sat on it. She studied the pool and could see small trout hovering at mid-depth in the shelter of the rock, sometimes moving in unison like a squadron of fighter planes. The water at the tail of the pool was rushing and high with snow-melt, and she lay full-length on the warm rock in the hot sun and watched the fish. Once in a while she felt a spray like a whisper of ice on her cheek.

She stayed out late until she was exhausted, then she struggled back through the woods, flopped on the couch and napped for two hours. When she woke up she fried potatoes and onions and peppers, and pan-fried the steak medium rare, and gobbled everything in sight, finishing with honey-sweetened tea. Just as the last light was squeezed out of the sky outside she was settling down for coffee before the fire and listening to another peepers concert, when the telephone rang.

'Dr Cole, God, it's Hank. Freda's shot, my rifle went off—'

'Where was she hit?'

'The upper leg, under the hip. She's bleeding something fierce, it's just pumping out.'

'Get a clean towel and press it against the wound, hard. I'm coming.'

10
Neighbors

She was on vacation, she had no medical bag. Her car wheels scattered gravel, the high beams battling crazy shadows as the BMW sped up the road and turned into the drive, the left tires wounding the lawn Hank Krantz maintained so neatly. She drove up to the front door and went into the house without knocking. The errant rifle was on the newspaper-covered kitchen table, along with rag patches, a ramrod, and a small can of gun oil.

Freda, white-faced, lay on her left side in blood. Her eyes were closed, but she opened them and looked at R.J. Hank had half-removed her jeans. He was kneeling, holding a saturated towel against her lower thigh. His hands and sleeves were smeared. 'My God. God in heaven, look what I did to her.'

He was in misery, but he was keeping a tight rein on himself. 'I called the town ambulance,' he said.

'Good. Take a fresh towel. Just put it on top of the soaked one and continue to bear down.' She knelt and with her fingers palpated the flesh where the thigh met the torso, next to the black pubic hair that showed through Freda's cotton underpants. When she felt the pulsations of the femoral artery she placed the heel of her palm over the spot and pressed.

57

Freda was a large and heavy woman, and years of farm work had made her muscular. R.J. had to bear down hard to try to compress the artery, and Freda opened her mouth to scream, but only a low moan came out.

'Sorry . . .' While the fingers of R.J.'s left hand maintained pressure, her right hand searched lightly and carefully under Freda's thigh. When she found the exit wound, Freda shuddered.

R.J. was taking the pulse in Freda's throat when the first animal wail of the siren reached them. Very soon, two vehicles stopped outside and doors slammed. Three people came in, a burly, middle-aged police officer and a man and a woman wearing red polyester jackets. The woman carried a portable oxygen tank.

'I'm a doctor. She's been shot, she has a broken femur and there's trauma to the artery, maybe it's severed. There's an entry wound and an exit. Her pulse is 119 and thready.'

The male EMT nodded. 'Shocky, all right. Lost a shitload of blood, hasn't she,' he said, taking in the mess on the floor. 'Can you keep holding the pressure point, doc?'

'Yes, I can,'

'Good, you do that.' He knelt on the other side of Freda. Without wasting time, he began doing a swift physical assessment. He was broad and overweight and young, scarcely more than a boy but with quick, capable hands.

'Was it just the one shot fired, Hank?' he called.

'Yes,' Hank Krantz called back angrily, upset by the implications of the question.

'Yeah, one entry wound, one exit,' the EMT said when he finished his assessment.

The small, blonde woman had already taken a blood pressure. 'Eighty-one over fifty-seven,' she said, and the other technician nodded. She set up the portable oxygen unit and fixed a non-rebreathing mask over Freda's mouth and nose. Then she cut away Freda's jeans and underpants, covering her

58

groin with a towel, and removed the sock and tennis shoe from her foot. Grasping the bare foot in both hands, the woman EMT began a steady, concentrated pulling.

The male technician wrapped an ankle hitch around his patient's foot. 'This is going to be clumsy, doc,' he said. 'We've got to get in there, past your hand, with the splint. You'll have to let up on the pressure for a few seconds.'

When she did, Freda's blood began to pump out again. Working quickly, the technicians proceeded to immobilize the leg in a Hare traction splint, a metal frame that fit snugly into the groin area at one end and extended all the way beyond the foot. As soon as she could, R.J. resumed the pressure on the femoral artery, and the bleeding eased. The splint was strapped to the thigh and, on the other end, was secured to the ankle hitch. A little windlass allowed the technicians to tighten it so manual traction no longer was needed.

Freda sighed, and the male EMT nodded. 'Yes, I imagine that feels some better, doesn't it?' She nodded back, but she cried out when they lifted her and was weeping as they set her down on the gurney. They moved out in a small mob, Hank and the policeman at the front corners of the gurney, the male EMT behind Freda's head, the blonde tech carrying the portable oxygen tank, and R.J. trying to maintain her weight on the pressure point as she walked along.

They lifted the gurney into the ambulance and locked it into place. The blonde switched Freda's mask from the portable tank to the on-board oxygen supply, and they elevated her legs and covered her with warm blankets against the shock. 'We're a crew member short. You want to come along?' the senior technician asked R.J.

'Sure,' she said, and he nodded.

The blonde woman drove, Hank beside her in the front seat. As they pulled away from the farmhouse, the driver spoke into her radio, telling the dispatcher they had picked up their patient and were on their way to the hospital. The police car led the way, roof light turning and its siren laying a ribbon of sound. The ambulance's external flashers had been on while parked, and now the blonde woman turned on a two-toned wail, alternatively *whup-whup-whup* and *ee-awe, ee-awe, ee-awe*.

It was difficult for R.J. to bear down on the pressure point while standing in the ambulance that jounced over bumps and lurched and swayed alarmingly around curves.

'She's bleeding again,' she said.

'I know.' The EMT was already laying out what looked like the bottom half of a space suit, a bulky garment that sprouted cables and tubes. He took a quick blood-pressure reading and pulse and respiration rates, and then lifted a radio-telephone speaker off the wall and called the hospital, requesting permission to use MAST trousers. After a brief discussion, permission was given, and R.J. helped him to move the trousers into place over the splint. There was a hiss as air was pumped into the garment over the injured leg and it ballooned and became rigid.

'I love this thing. Have you ever used one, doc?'

'I haven't done much emergency medicine.'

'Well, it does everything for you, all at once,' the man said. 'Stops the bleeding, reinforces the Hare splint to stabilize the leg, and pushes blood up to the heart and brain. But they make us get permission from medical control before we use it, because if there was internal bleeding it would cause a blow-out, push all the blood into the abdominal cavity.' He checked Freda to make sure she was okay, then he grinned and stuck out his hand. 'Steve Ripley.'

'I'm Roberta Cole.'

'Our demon driver is Toby Smith.'

'Hey, doc!' The driver didn't take her eyes off the road, but in the mirror R.J. saw a winsome grin.

'Hey, Toby,' she said.

Nurses were waiting at the ambulance entrance and Freda

was taken away. The two EMTs stripped the bloody sheets from the gurney and exchanged them for fresh sheets from the hospital supply room; they disinfected the gurney and made it up again before returning it to the ambulance. Then they sat in the waiting room with R.J. and Hank and the policeman. He said he was Maurice A. McCourtney, the Woodfield police chief. 'They call me Mack,' he told R.J. gravely.

The four of them drooped visibly; their job was done and reaction had set in.

Hank Krantz was making all of them party to his remorse. It was coyotes, he said, they had been around his farm for the better part of a week. He had decided to clean his deer gun and shoot a couple of them, to drive the pack away.

'Winchester, ain't it?' Mack McCourtney asked.

'Yeah, old lever-action Winchester 94, takes a .30–.30. I've owned it, must be eighteen years now, never had an accident with it. I set it down on the table a little hard, and it just banged off.'

'Safety wasn't on?' Steve Ripley said.

'Well, Jesus, I never keep a round in the chamber. I always empty the damn thing when I finish with it. I must of just forgot this time, the way I forget everything nowadays.' He glared. 'And you got some nerve, Ripley, asking me did she have more than one bullet in her. You think I shot my wife?'

'Listen. There she was on the floor, bleeding hard. I just had to know in a hurry if there was more than one wound to worry about.'

Hank's eyes softened. 'Yeah, and I shouldn't be giving you a bad time. You saved her life, I hope.'

Ripley shook his head. 'The real one saved her life is the doctor here. If she hadn't found the pressure point when she did, we'd be real sad right about now.'

Krantz looked at R.J. 'I'm never going to forget it.' He shook his head. 'Look what I did to my Freda!'

Toby Smith leaned over and patted his hand, leaving her hand on his. 'Listen, Hank, we all screw up. We all make

61

every kind of stupid mistake. All that guilt you're piling on yourself isn't going to help Freda one bit.'

The police chief frowned. 'You haven't got a milk herd any more. You've just got some beef steers, right? I wouldn't think coyotes would go after anything large as a beefer.'

'No, they won't go for a steer. But I bought four calves last week from Bernstein, that cattle dealer from out Pittsfield way.'

Mack McCourtney nodded. 'That explains it, then. They'll do a hell of a job on a calf, but not on a heifer.'

'Yeah, mostly they'll leave a heifer alone,' Hank agreed.

McCourtney left, needing to have the police car on patrol in Woodfield. 'You'll need to get back too,' Hank said to Ripley.

'Well, the neighboring towns can cover for us for a little while. We'll wait. You'll want to speak to the doctor.'

It was another hour and a half before the surgeon came out of the operating theater. He told Hank he had repaired the artery and placed a metal pin to rejoin the sections of Freda's broken femur. 'She's going to be just fine. She'll be here about five days. Five days to a week.'

'Can I see her?'

'She's in recovery. She'll be sedated all night. Best for you to go home, get some sleep. You can see her in the morning. You want me to send a report to your family doctor?'

Hank made a face. 'Well, at the moment, we don't have one. Our doctor's just retired.'

'Who was that, Hugh Marchant, over on High Street?'

'Yes, Dr Marchant.'

'Well, you get a new doctor, let me know who it is and I'll send him a report.'

* * *

'How come you travel all the way to Greenfield to see a doctor?' R.J. asked Hank on the way home.

'Well, because there isn't one who is closer. We haven't had a doctor in Woodfield for twenty years, since the old doctor died.'

'What was his name?'

'Thorndike.'

'Yes. Several people mentioned him when I first started coming here.'

'Craig Thorndike. People loved that man. But after he died, no other doctor came to Woodfield.'

It was close to midnight when the ambulance dropped Hank and R.J. at the Krantzes' driveway.

'You all right?' she asked Hank.

'Yeah. I won't be able to sleep, I know that. I guess I'll just clean up that mess in the kitchen.'

'Let me help you.'

'No, I wouldn't hear of it,' he said firmly, and suddenly she was glad of that, because she was very tired.

He hesitated. 'I thank you. Lord only knows what would have happened if you hadn't been here.'

'I'm glad I was here. You get some rest, now.'

There were large, white stars. The night held the memory of ice, a spring chill, but she was warmed as she drove back down the road.

11

The Calling

The next morning she awoke early and lay in bed reviewing the events of the previous evening. She guessed that the coyote pack Hank had wanted to drive away had moved off on its own to hunt elsewhere, because through the bedroom window she could see three whitetailed deer feeding in the meadow, their tails waggling as they cropped the clover. A car came down the road and the tails went up, showing their white flags of alarm. When the car passed, the tails dropped and waggled again, and the deer went back to feeding.

Ten minutes later a boy roared by on a motorcycle, and the deer broke for the woods with long, fearful bounds that were at the same time powerful and delicate.

When she got out of bed and called the hospital, she learned that Freda's condition was stable.

It was Sunday. After breakfast R.J. drove slowly to Sotheby's, where she bought the *New York Times* and the *Boston Globe*. As she was leaving the general store she met Toby Smith and exchanged good mornings.

'Well, you're looking rested after working late last night,' Toby said.

'I'm afraid I'm accustomed to late nights. Do you have a minute or two to talk, Toby?'

'I surely do.'

The other woman led the way to the bench on the store porch, and they sat. 'Tell me about the ambulance service.'

'Well . . . history. It was started just after World War II. A couple of people who had served in the armed forces as medics came home, and they bought a surplus army ambulance and began to serve the town. After a while the state began to test and certify emergency medical technicians, and a whole system of continuing education evolved. EMTs have to keep up with developments in emergency medicine and recertify every year. Here in town, we have fourteen registered emergency technicians, all volunteers. It's a free service to everyone who lives in Woodfield. We wear pagers and cover the town for medical emergencies around the clock. Ideally we like to have three people in the crew on every run, one behind the wheel, two riding in back with the patient. But much of the time we have only two, like last night.'

'Why is it a free service?' R.J. said. 'Why don't you bill insurance companies for transporting their clients to the hospital?'

Toby stared at her quizzically. 'We don't have big employers here in the hilltowns. Lots of our people are self-employed and just scraping by – loggers, carpenters, farmers, folks who do crafts. A big hunk of our population hasn't got health insurance. I wouldn't have it myself if my husband didn't have a federal job as a fish and game officer. I do bookkeeping on a freelance basis, and I simply couldn't afford to pay the premiums.'

R.J. nodded and sighed. 'I guess things aren't very different here than they are in the city, as far as medical coverage is concerned.'

'A whole lot of people gamble they won't get sick or be hurt. It scares the dickens out of a person to do that, but a lot of them have to do it anyway.' The ambulance service played an important role in the town, Toby said. 'Folks really appreciate that we're around. Closest doctor to the east is all the way into Greenfield. To the west, there's a general practitioner named Newly thirty miles away, just outside of Dalton on Route 9.' Toby looked at her and smiled. 'Why don't you come here to live year-round and be our doc?'

R.J. smiled back. 'Not likely,' she said.

Still, when she got back home she took out a map of the region and studied it. There were eleven small towns and villages in the area that Toby Smith said didn't have a resident doctor.

That afternoon she bought a houseplant – an African violet in plump blue blossom – and brought it to Freda in the hospital. Freda was still post-op and not talking much, but Hank Krantz was warmed by R.J.'s presence.

'I've been wanting to ask you. What do I owe you for last night?'

R.J. shook her head. 'I was there as a neighbor more than as a physician,' she said, and Freda looked at her and smiled.

R.J. drove back to Woodfield slowly, relishing the sights of farms and wooded hills.

Just as the sun was setting, her telephone rang.

'Dr Cole? This is David Markus. My daughter tells me you came to our place yesterday. Sorry I wasn't home.'

'Yes, Mr Markus . . . I wanted to talk with you about selling my house and land.'

'We can surely talk. When would be a good time for me to come by?'

'Well, the thing is . . . I still might want to sell, but suddenly I'm not all that certain. I have to do some deciding.'

'Well, you take your time. Think it all out.'

He had a nice, warm voice, she thought. 'But I'd like to talk to you about something else.'

'I see,' he said, although clearly he didn't.

'By the way, you make wonderful honey.'

She could feel his smile over the phone. 'Thank you, I'll tell the bees. They love to hear things like that, although it drives them crazy when I get all the credit.'

Monday morning was overcast, but she had a responsibility that was very much on her mind. She bulled her way back into the woods, getting a thorn scratch on the neck and several small gouges on the backs of her hands. When she reached the river, she traced it downstream as close as she could get to the banks, which sometimes were blocked to her by wild roses and raspberries and brambles. She followed the river the length of her land and considered several sites carefully, finally choosing a sunny, grassy place where a thick white birch arched over a small waterfall that made a lively plashing. She made another tortuous trip through the woods and came back carrying the spade that had hung from a nail in the barn, and the box containing Elizabeth Sullivan's ashes.

She dug a deep hole between two thick roots of the tree, and poured the ashes from the box. They were just fragments of bone, really. In the hungry blast of the crematorium, Betts Sullivan's fleshly self had vaporized and disappeared, flying off somewhere just as R.J. had always imagined the departing soul flew free of the world, when she had been a child.

She covered the ashes with earth, trod it down tenderly. Then, worried lest some animal dig them up, she found a round, current-washed rock in the river, almost but not quite too large for her to move, and in a series of lifts and drops, moved it onto the dug earth. Now Betts was part of this land. The strange thing was, increasingly R.J. had the feeling that in many ways, she was part of it too.

She spent the next couple of days investigating, gathering information, making lots of notes, scribbling figures and estimates. David Markus turned out to be a large, quiet man in his late forties, with rugged, somewhat battered features that were interesting in a Lincolnesque way (how could they have called Lincoln homely? she asked herself). He had a large face, a prominent, slightly crooked nose, a scar in the left corner of his upper lip, and gentle, easily amused brown eyes. His business suit was faded Levi's and a New England Patriots jacket, and he wore his thick, greying brown hair in an improbable ponytail.

She went to the town hall and talked to a selectwoman named Janet Cantwell, a bony, aging woman with tired eyes who wore ragged jeans, shabbier than Markus's, and a man's white shirt with the sleeves rolled up to her elbows. R.J. walked Main Street from one end to the other, and studied the houses and the people she met along the way, and the flow of traffic. She went to the medical center in Greenfield and talked with the hospital director, and sat in the cafeteria and spoke with several doctors as they ate their lunch.

Then she packed her bag and got into the car and drove toward Boston. The farther she got from Woodfield, the more she felt she had to return there. Whenever she had heard of someone who had received a 'calling', she had assumed the expression was a romantic euphemism. But now she saw that it was possible to be captivated by a compulsion so powerful that it couldn't be denied.

Better than that – this thing she was obsessing about made excellent, practical sense to her in terms of the rest of her life.

She still had several days of her vacation left, and she used them to make lists of things she must do. And to formulate plans.

Finally, she telephoned her father and asked him to meet her for dinner.

12

A Brush with the Law

She had contended with her father from the time of her earliest memory until she became an adult. Then something sweet and good had happened, a simultaneous mellowing and blossoming of feeling. On his part there was a different kind of pride in her, a re-evaluation of why he loved her. For her there was a realization that, even in the years when she had fumed at him, he had always been steadfast in his support of her.

Dr Robert Jameson Cole was the Regensberg Professor of Immunology at the Boston University School of Medicine. The chair he occupied was endowed by his own distant relatives. R.J. never had seen him embarrassed when that fact was mentioned by anyone. The original endowment had been made when he was a boy, and Professor Cole was so celebrated in his field that it would never occur to anyone that his appointment had come because of anything but his own accomplishments. He was a strong-willed achiever.

R.J. remembered her mother remarking to a friend that the first time her daughter had defied Professor Cole was when she had been born a female. He had counted on a boy. For centuries, Cole first-born sons had been named Robert, with middle names that began with the letter J. Dr Cole had given the matter serious thought and had picked out a name for his son – Robert Jenner Cole, the middle name to honor Edward Jenner, the discoverer of vaccination. When the baby turned out to be a girl, and when it became clear that his wife, Bernadette Valerie Cole, never could bear another child, Dr Cole insisted their daughter would be named Roberta Jenner Cole and would be called Rob J. for short. It was another Cole family tradition; somehow, to claim the child as a new Rob J. was to declare that yet another future Cole physician had been born.

Bernadette Cole had submitted to his plan except for the middle name. Not for her daughter a male name! So she had reached into her origins in northern France and the girl was christened Roberta Jeanne d'Arc Cole. Eventually Dr Cole's attempt to call his daughter Rob J. also failed. Soon to her mother and then to everyone who came to know her, she was R.J., although her father stubbornly clung to calling her Rob J. in tender moments.

R.J. grew up in a comfortable second-floor apartment in a converted brownstone house on Beacon Street, with giant antique magnolia bushes in the front yard. Dr Cole liked it because it was a few doors down from the brownstone where the physician Oliver Wendell Holmes had lived. His wife liked it because it was rent-controlled and therefore manageable on a faculty salary. But after her death from pneumonia, three days after her daughter's eleventh birthday, the apartment began to feel too large.

R.J. had attended public schools, but with her mother gone, her father felt she needed more control and structure in her life than he was able to provide, and he enrolled her in a day school in Cambridge, to which she traveled by bus. She had studied piano from the time she was seven, but when she was twelve she began taking lessons in classical guitar at school, and within a couple of years she was hanging around Harvard Square, playing and singing with other street musicians. She

70

played very well; she didn't have a great voice, but it was good enough. When she was fifteen, she lied about her age and became a singing waitress at the same second-story club where Joan Baez, who also was the daughter of a Boston University professor, had gotten her start. That September R.J. had sex for the first time, in the loft of the MIT boathouse, with the stroke of the MIT crew. It was messy and painful, and the experience turned her off from sex, but not permanently.

And not for long.

R.J. always thought the middle name her mother had chosen had done a great deal to shape her life. From childhood she was ever ready to do battle for a cause. And although she loved her father desperately, often it was Dr Cole with whom she contended. His yearning for a Rob J. who would follow in his medical footsteps was a constant pressure to his only child. Perhaps if it hadn't been there, her path would have been different. In the afternoons when she returned alone to the quiet apartment on Beacon Street, sometimes she went into his study and took down his books. In them she memorized the sexual parts of men and women, often looking up the acts about which her contemporaries whispered and sniggered. But she moved on to a non-prurient contemplation of anatomy and physiology; the way some of her contemporaries became interested in the names of dinosaurs, R.J. memorized the bones of the human body. On the desk in her father's study, in a small glass-and-oak box, was an old surgical scalpel of beaten blue steel. Family legend said that many hundreds of years ago the scalpel had belonged to one of R.J.'s ancestors, a great surgeon. Sometimes it seemed to her that helping people as a doctor would be a good way to spend her life, but her father was too insistent, and when the time came he drove her to a declaration that she would take a pre-law course in college. As the daughter of a professor, she could have attended Boston University with a tuition waiver. Instead, she escaped the long centuries of medical Coles by winning a three-quarters scholarship to Tufts University, bussing tables in a student dining room and working two evenings a week at the club in Harvard Square. She did go to law school at Boston University. By that time she had her own apartment on Beacon Hill, behind the State House. She saw her father regularly, but already she was living her own life.

She was a third-year law student when she met Charlie Harris – Charles H. Harris MD, a tall, skinny young man whose horn-rimmed glasses habitually slid down his long, freckled nose and gave his sweet amber eyes a quizzical look. He was just beginning a surgical residency.

She had never met anyone so serious and so funny at the same time. They laughed a lot, but he was humorlessly dedicated to his work. He envied her graceful scholarship and the fact that she actually enjoyed taking examinations, in which invariably she did very well. He was intelligent and had a good temperament for a surgeon but studying wasn't easy for him, and he had achieved because he labored at it doggedly: 'Gotta take care of business, R.J.' She was Law Review, he was on call. They were always tired and in need of sleep, and their schedules made it hard for them to see enough of each other. After a couple of months she moved from Joy Street into his converted stable off Charles Street, the cheaper of their two apartments.

Three months before she finished law school, R.J. discovered she was pregnant. At first she and Charlie were terrified but then they were filled with radiance at the thought of being parents and agreed they would be married at once. Several mornings later, however, while Charlie was scrubbing for the OR, he was suddenly doubled over by a piercing pain in the lower left quadrant of his abdomen. An examination revealed the presence of kidney stones that were too large for him to pass naturally, and within twenty-four hours he was admitted

72

to his own hospital as a patient. Ted Forester, the best surgeon in the department, performed the operation. Charlie appeared to sail through the initial post-op period, except that he was unable to void urine. When he hadn't urinated in forty-eight hours, Dr Forester ordered that he be catheterized, and an intern inserted the catheter and gave him relief. Within two days, Charlie's kidney was infected. Despite antibiotics, the staph infection spread through his bloodstream and localized in a heart valve.

Four days after the operation, R.J. sat by his bed in the hospital. It was obvious to her that he was very sick. She had left word that she wanted to see Dr Forester when he came on rounds, and she thought she should telephone Charlie's family in Pennsylvania, so his parents could talk to the doctor if they wished.

Charlie moaned, and she got up and washed his face with a wet cloth. 'Charlie?'

She took his hands in hers and leaned over and studied his face.

Something happened. A current of information passed from his body into hers, into her mind. She didn't know how, or why. It wasn't imagined, she knew it was real. In a way she couldn't understand, she was suddenly aware that they wouldn't be growing old together. She couldn't drop his hands, or run away, or even cry out. She just stayed where she was, bending over him, gripping his hands tightly as if she could hold him back, memorizing his features while she still had a chance.

He was placed in the ground in a large, ugly cemetery in Wilkes-Barre. After the funeral R.J. sat on the cut-velvet chairs in his parents' living room and suffered the stares and questions of strangers until she was able to flee. In the tiny toilet of the plane taking her back to Boston, she was racked by nausea and vomiting. For several days she thought constantly about how Charlie's baby would look. Perhaps grief did her in, or maybe what occurred would have happened even if Charlie were alive. Fifteen days after his death, R.J. miscarried his baby.

On the morning of the bar examination she sat in a room full of tense men and women. She knew Charlie would have told her to take care of business, and she formed a woman-size ice cube in her mind and placed herself in its very center, cold-bloodedly putting grief and discomfort and everything else beyond her consciousness and turning her attention to the many and difficult questions of the bar examiners.

R.J. retained the icy shield when she went to work for Wigoder, Grant & Berlow, an old firm that practiced general law, with three floors of offices in a good building on State Street. There no longer was a Wigoder. Harold Grant, the managing partner, was crochety, dried-up, and bald. George Berlow, who headed Wills & Trusts, had a paunch and a veined, whiskey-reddened face. His son, Andrew Berlow, fortyish and bland, was manager of major real estate clients. He put R.J. to work researching briefs and preparing leases, routine tasks that involved using lots of computer boilerplate. She found it tedious and uninteresting, and when she had been there two months she admitted this to Andy Berlow. He nodded and told her drily that it was foundation work, good experience. The following week he let her accompany him to court, but she remained unenthused. She told herself it was depression, and she tried to bear down hard during her workdays.

When she had been with Wigoder, Grant & Berlow not quite five months, she broke. It was not an emotional train wreck – more, a temporary derailment. One night when she and Andy Berlow had been working late, she joined him for a glass of wine that turned out to be a bottle-and-a-half, and they ended up in her bed. Two days later he took her to lunch and nervously explained that although he was divorced, he was 'involved with a woman, living with her, in fact'. He thought R.J. was gracious in her reaction; actually, the only man who interested her was dead. The thought caused the ice cube to crack and fall away. When she began to weep she went home from the office, and she stayed home. Andy Berlow covered for her, believing she was prostrate with love for him.

She needed to have a long talk with Charlie Harris. She ached to be his lover again, and she yearned for his phantom child, his might-have-been baby. She knew none of these desires could be fulfilled, but mourning had reduced her to basics, and there was one area of her life that she had the power to change.

13

The Different Path

Her decision to study medicine was what her father had always wanted, but Professor Cole loved her and approached it with caution.

'Is it because you feel that somehow you have to take Charlie's place?' he asked her gently. 'Is it that you want to feel and experience the things he did?'

'That's part of it, I admit,' she said, 'but only a small part.' She had given this a great deal of thought and had reached a mature decision, realizing for the first time that she had stifled any early desire to be a doctor because of her need to stand up to her father. Their relationship still had problems. She found it impossible to apply to the Boston University School of Medicine, where he was faculty. She was accepted at the Massachusetts College of Physicians and Surgeons with a deficiency in organic chemistry that she made up in summer school.

Student aid was inadequate for medical students. R.J. was awarded a one-quarter scholarship, and she expected to fall deeply into debt. Her father had helped her through law school, supplementing her scholarship money and earnings, and he was prepared to help her through medical school, although that would have been a hardship. But the people at Wigoder, Grant, & Berlow were intrigued by what she was undertaking.

Sol Foreman, the partner who managed medical litigation, asked her to lunch, although they hadn't met before.

'Andy Berlow told me about you. The truth is, Miss Cole, you're worth much more to our firm as a lawyer studying medicine than you have been as a law clerk in the real estate department. You'll be in a position to research the facts of important cases from a medical viewpoint, yet you'll be able to write briefs as a person educated in the law. We pay well for that kind of expertise.'

It was a welcome gift to her. 'When do you want me to begin?'

'Why not try your hand at it straight off?'

So while she studied chemistry in summer school, she had also researched the case of a twenty-nine-year-old woman dying from aplastic anemia as a result of being given penicillamine, which had suppressed the blood-forming function of her bone marrow. R.J. became familiar with every medical library in Boston, and she delved into card catalogs, books, medical journals, and research papers, learning a great deal about antibiotics.

Foreman seemed satisfied with the result, and at once he gave her another assignment. She prepared the brief for the case of a fifty-nine-year-old male teacher who had had a hip replacement in which deep infection, from inadequate filtering of contaminated air in the operating room, had smouldered for three years before bursting forth, leaving him with an unstable hip and a shortened limb.

Following that, her research led the law firm to refuse the case of a man who wished to sue his surgeon after a vasectomy had failed. R.J. noted that the patient had been warned by his surgeon of the possibility of failure and advised to use a contraceptive device for six months, which he had neglected to do.

The people at Wigoder, Grant, & Berlow were very pleased with her work. Foreman put her on a monthly minimum retainer with an override that she earned more months than not, and he was willing to assign as many cases to her as she would accept. That September, in order to make things still easier, she took another medical student as a housemate, a beautiful, serious black woman from Fulton, Missouri, named Samantha Potter. With only minimal help from her father, R.J. was able to pay her tuition and living expenses and run her car. The legal profession she had rejected now made it possible for her to study medicine without financial hardship.

She was one of eleven women in her class of ninety-nine students. It was as though she had been lost and stumbling and had finally found a clear and certain path. Every lecture was a source of enormous interest. She discovered she was fortunate in her choice of housemate. Samantha Potter was the eldest of eight children, brought up on a share-cropping farm that barely achieved subsistence in any given year. All the Potter children picked cotton and fruit and vegetables for other people, turning their hand to anything that brought in a little money. At sixteen, already a tall woman with broad shoulders, Samantha had been hired by a local meat-packing company to work after school and summers. The supervisors liked her because she was strong enough to lift the heavy frozen meat and was well-mannered and dependable. After a year of pushing an offal wagon, she had been taught to become a meat cutter. The cutters worked with power saws and knives sharp enough to slip through meat and connective tissue, and it wasn't uncommon for a plant employee to be seriously hurt. Samantha sustained a number of minor cuts and grew accustomed to bandaged fingers, but she avoided a major accident. Working every day after school, she became the first member of her family to gain a high school diploma. She worked as a meat cutter for five summer vacations after that, while she earned bachelor's and master's degrees in comparative anatomy at the University of Missouri, and she came to the medical school's first-year human anatomy class with impressive knowledge about animal bone, internal organs, and circulatory systems.

R.J. and Samantha developed a close friendship with one of the other women in the class. Gwendolyn Bennett was a feisty redhead from Manchester, New Hampshire. Medicine was changing quickly, but it was still pretty much a men's club. There were five female members of the faculty, but all the department chairs and the school administrative posts were filled by males. Male students were called on frequently in class while women tended to be overlooked. The three friends, however, were determined not to be ignored. Gwen had had experience as a women's rights activist at Mount Holyoke College, and she mapped their strategy.

'We have to volunteer answers in class. Faculty asks questions, we stick up our hands, right in their sexist faces, and give 'em correct answers. We get noticed because we work our asses off, right? It means we have to study harder than the men, be better prepared than they are, act generally sharper.'

It meant a crushing work load on top of the medico-legal research R.J. was doing in order to stay in school, but it was the kind of challenge she needed. The three of them studied together, drilled and grilled one another before examinations, and bolstered each other when they detected academic weaknesses.

The strategy largely worked, despite the fact that they quickly developed a reputation as aggressive women. A couple of times they believed their grades suffered because of an instructor's resentment, but most of the time they received the high marks they earned. They ignored the occasional sexual remarks made by male students and even, on rare occasions, by a faculty member. They dated only once in a while, not out of disinclination but because time

79

and energy had become vital commodities that had to be doled out stingily. Whenever they had a free evening, they went together to the anatomy lab, which Samantha had made her real home. From the beginning, everyone in the anatomy department knew that Samantha Potter was hot, a future professor in their specialty. While other students fought for an arm or a leg to dissect, there was somehow always a cadaver reserved for Samantha, and Sam shared with her two friends. Over four years they dissected four dead human beings – an elderly bald Chinese man with the overdeveloped chest that spelled chronic emphysema, an old black woman with grey hair, and two whites, one of them an athletic middle-aged male, the other a pregnant woman about their own age. Samantha guided R.J. and Gwen into the study of anatomy as if it were an exotic and wonderful country. They spent hour after hour dissecting, stripping the bodies down layer by layer, exposing and sketching muscles and organs, joints and blood vessels and nerves in exquisite detail, learning the wonderful intricacies and mysteries of the human anatomical machine.

Just before the beginning of the second year of medical school, R.J. and Samantha moved from the apartment in the mews off Charles Street. R.J. was glad to leave the converted stable; it was too full of memories of Charlie. Gwen joined them, the three of them renting a shabby railroad flat only a block from the medical school. It was on the fringe of a rough neighborhood, but they wouldn't waste precious time getting to labs or the hospital, and the evening before classes began, they threw an open-house bash. Characteristically, it was the hostesses who shooed the guests out the door at an early hour so they could be up to form in school the next day.

When their clinical work in the wards started, R.J. met it as though she had been preparing for it all her life. She saw medicine differently from most of her classmates, very much through her own eyes. Because she had lost Charlie Harris due to an unclean catheter, and because she still was an attorney working constantly on malpractise briefs, she tended to search for dangers to which most of her fellow-students were oblivious.

Researching a law case, she found a report by Dr Knight Steel of the Boston University Medical Center, who had studied 815 consecutive medical cases (excluding cancer, which carries a large risk of adverse results from chemotherapy). Of the 815 patients, 290 – *more than one out of every three* – developed an iatrogenic illness.

Seventy-three people, 9 percent, had complications that threatened their lives or left them permanently disabled – catastrophes that wouldn't have happened to them if they had stayed away from their doctors or their hospitals.

The mishaps involved drugs, diagnostic tests and treatment, diet, nursing, transportation, heart catheterization, intravenous treatment, arteriography and dialysis, urinary catheterization, and a myriad of other procedures that compose a patient's experience.

Soon it was clear to R.J. that in every aspect of medical care, patients were at risk from their benefactors. As increasing numbers of new drugs were put on the market, and as increasing numbers of tests and lab studies were ordered by doctors to protect themselves against malpractise suits, the possibilities of iatrogenic damage increased. Dr Franz Ingelfinger, the very respected professor of medicine at Harvard and editor of the *New England Journal of Medicine*, wrote:

> Let us assume that 80 percent of patients have either self-limited disorders or conditions not improvable, even by modern medicine. In slightly over 10 percent of the cases, however, medical intervention is dramatically successful . . . But alas, in the final 9 percent, give or take a point or two, the doctor may diagnose or treat inadequately, or he may just have bad luck. Whatever the reason, the patient ends up with iatrogenic problems.

81

R.J. saw that despite the high costs in human suffering and in money, medical schools weren't making students aware of the dangers of human mistakes in treating patients, nor were they teaching them how to react to malpractise suits, despite the proliferation of legal action against doctors. In the course of her own ongoing work for Wigoder, Grant, & Berlow, R.J. began to accumulate an extensive file of cases and data in both these areas.

The trio was broken up after graduation. Samantha had always known that she wanted to spend her life teaching anatomy, and she accepted a residency in pathology at Yale-New Haven Medical Center. Gwen hadn't had the slightest idea about a specialty through most of the four years of medical school, but ultimately her politics influenced her to choose gynecology, and she took a residency at the Mary Hitchcock Hospital in Hanover, New Hampshire. R.J. wanted it all, everything being a physician had to offer. She stayed in Boston, taking a three-year residency in medicine at the Lemuel Grace Hospital. Even during the worst of times – when dirty jobs were piled on her, and during the terrible grind, the sleeplessness and the marathon hours – she didn't doubt what she was doing. She was the only woman among the thirty internal medicine residents of her program. As in law school and medical school, she had to speak a little louder than the males, work a little harder. The doctors' lounge was male country, where her fellow residents hung out, spoke obscenely about women (gynecological residents were known as 'connoisseurs of the cunt'), and mostly ignored her. But from the start she kept her eyes on her goal, which was to become the best doctor she was able to be, and she was good enough to rise above sexism when she met it, as she had watched Samantha rise above racism.

*   *   *

Early in her training she had revealed evident talent as a diagnostician, and she enjoyed looking at each patient as a puzzle to be worked out by using her brain and her training. One night, joking with an elderly male cardiac patient named Bruce Weiler, R.J. took both his hands in hers and squeezed them.

She couldn't let go.

It was as if they were linked by . . . what? She felt faint with certain knowledge she hadn't possessed a few moments before. She wanted to scream out a warning to Mr Weiler. Instead, she muttered a dazed pleasantry and spent the next forty minutes poring over his records and taking his pulse and blood pressure again and again and listening to his heart. She told herself she was having a mental breakdown; nothing in Bruce Weiler's chart or vital signs indicated that his mending heart was anything but strong and getting healthier by the moment.

In spite of that, she was positive he was dying.

She said nothing to Fritzie Baldwin, the chief resident. She was able to tell him nothing that made any sense, and he would have ridiculed her savagely.

But in the small hours of the morning, Mr Weiler's heart blew out like a faulty inner tube, and he was gone.

A few weeks later, she had a similar experience. Troubled and intrigued, she spoke about the incidents to her father. Professor Cole nodded, a gleam of interest in his eyes.

'Sometimes doctors seem to have a sixth sense about the way a patient will respond.'

'I experienced this thing long before I became a doctor. I knew that Charlie Harris was going to die. I knew it with absolute certainty.'

'There's a legend in our family,' he said tentatively, and R.J. groaned to herself, not being in the mood to hear family legends.

'It was said that some of the Cole physicians down through the ages have been able to foretell death by holding the hands of their patients.'

The back of R.J.'s neck prickled, but she snorted.

'No, I'm serious. They called it the Gift.'

'Come on, Dad. Talk about superstition! That's straight from the days when they prescribed eye of newt and toe of frog. I don't believe in magic.'

'Nobody said it was magic,' he said mildly. 'I think some of our family were born with extra sensors that allowed them to collect information not available to most of us. Supposedly my grandfather, Dr Robert Jefferson Cole, and my great-grandfather, Dr Robert Judson Cole, both had the Gift when they were country doctors in Illinois. It can skip generations. Reportedly, several of my cousins had it. I was left the family's prize antiques, Rob J.'s scalpel that I keep on my desk, and my great-grandfather's viola da gamba, but I would have preferred the Gift.'

'Then . . . you've never experienced anything like that?'

'Certainly I've known whether particular patients were going to live or die. But, no, I've never had the sure knowledge of approaching death without signs or symptoms. Of course,' he said blandly, 'the family legend also says the Gift is dulled or ruined by the use of stimulants.'

'That leaves you out, then,' R.J. said. For years, until his generation of doctors had learned better, Professor Cole had enjoyed the frequent comfort of good cigars, and he continued to relish his regular evening reward of a good single-malt liquor.

R.J. had tried marijuana briefly in high school but never had taken to either kind of smoking. Like her father, she enjoyed alcohol. She hadn't allowed it to interfere with her work, but during times of stress she found a drink a distinct comfort, of which sometimes she availed herself greedily.

* * *

By the time she finished the third year of her medical residency, R.J. knew she wanted to treat entire families, people of all ages and of both sexes. But to do so adequately, she wanted to know more about the medical problems of women. She sought and received permission to take three rotation periods in obstetrics and gynecology instead of one. When she completed her medical residency she took a one-year externship in ob-gyn at Lemuel Grace, at the same time taking advantage of an opportunity to do the medical examinations for a large research program dealing with the hormonal problems of women. That year she took and passed the examination to become a fellow of the American Academy of Internal Medicine.

By that time, she was an old hand at the hospital. It was generally known that she had done a great deal of legal work for malpractise suits that often won large sums from insurance companies. Malpractise insurance rates were soaring. Some doctors said in open anger that there was no excuse for a physician to do work that would harm a fellow doctor, and throughout her years of training there were unpleasant moments when someone didn't bother to hide the animosity they felt toward her. But she worked on a number of court cases in which her legal briefs for the defendant had saved the doctor who was being sued, and that became widely known as well.

R.J. had a quiet reply for anyone who attacked her. 'The answer isn't to eliminate malpractise suits. The answer is to eliminate habitual malpractise, to teach the public to do away with frivolous claims and awards, and to teach doctors how to protect themselves during those times when they make the mistakes that happen to every human being.

'We feel free to criticize otherwise-honest police officers who protect crooked cops because of their Blue Code. But we have our White Code. It allows some doctors to get away with clinical shoddiness and bad medicine, and I say to hell with it.'

Someone was listening. Toward the end of her ob-gyn externship, Dr Sidney Ringgold, the chairman of the department of medicine, asked if she would be interested in teaching two courses, *The Prevention of and Defense against Malpractise Suits* for fourth-year students, and *The Elimination of Iatrogenic Incidents* for students in their third year. Along with the instructorship in the medical school came an appointment to the medical staff of the hospital. R.J. accepted at once. The appointment created grumbling and several complaints in the department, but Dr Ringgold weathered them calmly, and it had all worked out well.

After residency, Samantha Potter had gone straight into the teaching of anatomy at the state university's medical school in Worcester. Gwen Bennett had joined the established practise of a gynecologist in Framingham and already had begun working part-time in the Family Planning abortion clinic. The three of them remained close friends and political allies. Gwen and Samantha, as well as a number of other women and several foward-thinking male doctors, had backed R.J. resolutely when she proposed the establishment of the Pre-Menstrual Syndrome clinic at the hospital, and after a period of in-fighting with a few physicians who thought it a waste of budgetary funds, the PMS clinic had become an established service and a part of the teaching curriculum.

All the controversy had been particularly hard on Professor Cole. He was very much a member of the medical establishment, and the harsh criticism of his daughter, particularly the implication that she was sometimes a traitor to her fellow physicians, had been hard for him to bear. But R.J. knew he was proud of her. He had stood by her repeatedly despite their earlier difficulties. Their relationship was strong, and now she didn't hesitate to turn to her father again.

14

The Last Cowgirl

They met for dinner at Pinerola's, a restaurant in the North End. When she had first gone there with Charlie Harris she had to walk down a narrow alley between tenement buildings, then up a tall flight of stairs into what was essentially a kitchen with three small tables. Carla Pinerola was the cook, assisted by her elderly mother, who shouted and grumbled at her a lot. Carla was middle-aged, sexy, a character. She had had a husband who beat her; sometimes when R.J. and Charlie came into the restaurant there was a bruise on Carla's arm or she had a black eye. Now the old mother was dead, and Carla was never visible; she had bought one of the tenement buildings and gutted the first and second floors, turning it into a large and comfortable eating place. Now there was always a long line of patrons waiting for tables – business people, college kids. R.J. still liked it; the food was almost as good as in the old days, and she had learned never to go there without a reservation.

She sat and watched her father hurrying toward her, slightly late. His hair had become almost completely grey. Seeing him reminded her that she was getting older, too.

They ordered antipasto, veal marsala, and the house wine,

and talked of the Red Sox and what was happening to theater in Boston and the fact that the arthritis in his hands was becoming quite painful.

Sipping her wine, she told him she was preparing to go into private practise in Woodfield.

'Why private practise?' He was clearly astonished, clearly troubled. 'And why in such a place?'

'It's time for me to get away from Boston. Not as a doctor, as a person.'

Professor Cole nodded. 'I accept that. But why not go to another medical center? Or work for . . . I don't know, a medical-legal institute?'

She had received a letter from Roger Carleton at Hopkins saying that at present no money was budgeted for a position that would suit her, but he could arrange to have her working in Baltimore in six months. She had received a fax from Irving Simpson saying they would like to put her to work at Penn, and would she come to Philadelphia to talk about money?

'I don't want to do those things. I want to become a real doctor.'

'For God's sake, R.J.! What are you now?'

'I want to be a private practitioner in a small town.' She smiled. 'I think I'm a throwback to your grandfather.'

Professor Cole struggled for control, studying his poor child who had chosen to swim against the current all her life. 'There's a reason why 72 percent of American doctors are specialists, R.J. Specialists make big money, two or three times more than primary care physicians, and they get to sleep through the night. If you become a country doctor, you'll make a harder, tougher living. You know what I would do if I were your age, in your position, no dependents? I'd go back for all the training I could force myself to accept. I'd become a super-specialist.'

R.J. groaned. 'No more externships, my Poppy, and certainly no more residencies. I want to look beyond the technology, beyond all those machines, and see the human beings.

I'm going to become a rural physician. I'm prepared to earn less . . . I want the life.'

'The life?' He shook his head. 'R.J., you're like that last cowboy fella they keep writing books and songs about, who saddles up his bronc and goes riding through endless traffic jams and housing tracts, searching for the vanished prairie.'

She smiled and took his hand. 'The prairie may be gone, Pop, but the hills are right out there on the other side of the state, full of people who need a doctor. Family practise is the purest kind of medicine. I'm going to give it to myself as a gift.'

They took a long time over the meal, talking. She listened carefully, aware that her father knew a great deal about medicine.

'A few years from now, you won't be able to recognize the American health care system. It's going to change drastically,' he said. 'The presidential race is waxing hotter and hotter, and Bill Clinton has been promising the American people that everybody is going to have health insurance if he is elected.'

'Do you think he can deliver?'

'I really think he's going to try. He seems to be the first politician to give a damn that there are poor people without care, to confess he's ashamed of what we have now. Universal medical insurance would make things better for you primary care physicians, while lowering the incomes of specialists. We'll have to wait and see what happens.'

They discussed the financial requirements of what she proposed to do. The house on Brattle Street wouldn't bring much money after all the debts were paid; real estate prices were very depressed. She had made careful assessments of the money she needed to set up and equip a private practise and get through the first year, and she was almost $53,000 short. 'I've talked with several banks, and I can borrow the money. I have enough equity to cover the loan, but they insist on a co-signer.' It was a humiliation; she doubted they would make the same stipulation to Tom Kendricks.

'You're absolutely certain this is what you want?'

'Absolutely certain.'

'Then I'll sign the note, if you'll permit me.'

'Thank you, Pop.'

'In a way it drives me crazy to think of what you're doing. But at the same time, I have to tell you how much I envy you.'

R.J. raised his hand to her lips. Over cappuccino they reviewed her lists. He said he thought she had been too conservative, and that the figure she was borrowing should be ten thousand dollars higher. She was terrified of the financial depths and argued forcefully, but in the end she saw that he was right, and she agreed to dive even deeper into debt.

'You're a pistol, my daughter.'

'You're a pistol too, my old man.'

'Are you going to be all right, living up there in the hills all by yourself?'

'You know me, Dad. I don't need anybody. Except you,' she said, and leaned forward and kissed him on the cheek.

II
THE HOUSE
ON THE VERGE

15

Metamorphosis

She took Tessa Martula to lunch. Tessa wept into her lobster stew and was by turns sullen and heartbroken. 'I don't know why you have to cut and run,' she said. 'You were going to be my elevator, up and up.'

'You're a hell of a worker, you are going to do just fine. And I'm not running away from this place,' R.J. said patiently. 'I'm running toward a place I think will be better for me.'

She tried to feel as confident as she sounded, but it was like graduating from school all over again; she had so many fears and uncertainties. She hadn't delivered many babies in recent years, and she felt inadequate. Lew Stanetsky, the chief of obstetrics, gave her some advice, his manner a cross between concern and amusement. 'You're going to be a country doc, eh? Well, you'll have to hook up with an obstetrician-gynecologist if you're going to deliver babies out there in the hinterlands. The law says you have to call in an ob-gyn if you run into the need for things like caesareans, forceps births, and vacuum extractions.'

He arranged for her to spend long hours alongside the interns and residents in the hospital maternity clinic, a large room filled with birthing stools occupied by straining, sweating, and often cursing inner-city women, most of them Afro-American, allowing R.J. to oversee two lines of brown and purple pudendas stretching in the natural violence of the act of birth.

She wrote a solid and laudatory letter of recommendation for Tessa, but it wasn't needed. A few days later Tessa came to her, all smiles.

'You're never going to guess whom I am going to work for. Dr Allen Greenstein!'

When the gods are cruel, R.J. thought, they are bastardly cruel. 'Is he going to move into this office, too?'

'No, we're getting Dr Roseman's office, that beautiful, big corner office, opposite end of the building from Dr Ringgold's.'

R.J. hugged her. 'Well, he's a lucky man to get you,' she said.

It was surprisingly hard to leave the hospital, much easier to leave the Family Planning clinic. She gave Mona Wilson, the clinic director, six weeks' notice. Luckily Mona had been beating the bushes for a replacement for Gwen. She hadn't found a full-time person, but she had hired three part-timers and had no trouble staffing Thursdays without R.J.

'You gave us two years,' Mona said. She looked at R.J. and smiled. 'And you hated every second of it, didn't you?'

R.J. nodded. 'I guess I did. How did you know?'

'Oh, it wasn't hard to see. Why did you do it if it was so difficult for you?'

'I knew I was really needed. I knew women had to have this option,' R.J. said.

But as she left the clinic, she felt light as thistledown.

I don't have to come back! she thought exultantly.

She faced the fact that while it gave her enormous pleasure to drive the BMW, the car didn't make sense in terms of the spring mud and unpaved mountain roads she would come

94

up against in Woodfield. She carefully inspected a number of four-wheel-drive vehicles, deciding finally on the Ford Explorer, ordered with air-conditioning, a good radio and CD player, heavy-duty battery, and wide tires with a tread designed for muddy roads. 'Want my advice?' the salesman said. 'Order a come-along.'

'A what?'

'A come-along. It's an electric power winch that's attached to the front bumper. Runs off the car battery. It's got a steel cable and a snap hook.'

She was dubious.

'If you get stuck in the mud, you just wrap the cable around a big tree, and winch yourself out. Five tons of pulling power. It'll cost you another thousand, but worth every penny if you're going to be driving bad roads.'

She ordered the come-along. The dealer turned a cagey gaze on her little red car.

'A-l condition. All-leather interior,' she pointed out.

'I'll allow you twenty-three thousand, trade-in.'

'Hey. This is an expensive sports car. I paid more than double that.'

'Couple of years ago, right?' He shrugged. 'Check the Blue Book.'

She did, and then she put an advertisement in the Sunday *Globe*. An engineer from Lexington bought the BMW for $28,900, paying for the Explorer and giving her a small profit.

She drove back and forth between Boston and Woodfield. David Markus suggested she would be best off with an office on Main Street, in the center of the village. The street was built around the white, wood-frame town hall that had been converted from a church more than a century ago. It was adorned with a spire in the Christopher Wren tradition.

Markus showed her four places on Main Street that were empty or soon would be. The prevailing wisdom was that a doctor required from 1,000 to 1,500 square feet of space for an office suite. Of the four prospective properties, R.J. ruled out two at once as eminently unsuitable. One of the others appealed to her but would be cramped, having only 795 square feet. The fourth property, which the canny real estate man had saved until last, looked promising. It was across the street from the town library and a few houses away from the town hall. The outside of the house was well preserved and the grounds carefully tended. The interior space, 1,120 square feet, was shabby, but the rent was slightly less than R.J.'s estimate in the budget she had agonized over with her father and other advisors. The house was owned by an elderly woman named Sally Howland. She had plump red cheeks and a nervous but benevolent glare, and she said it would be an honor to have a doctor in town again, and on her property.

'But I depend on my rents to live, you understand, so I cannot come down on the price.' Nor could she afford to do the renovations R.J. would need, she said; but she would give permission for them, as well as whatever painting the doctor might like to have done at her own expense.

'It'll cost you to renovate and paint,' Markus told R.J. 'If you go for it, you ought to protect yourself with a lease.'

In the end, that's what she did. The painting was done by Bob and Tillie Matthewson, a husband and wife team who doubled as dairy farmers. The place was full of antique woodwork that they brought back to a soft lustre, and worn and scarred random-width pine floors that she had them paint teal blue. They covered the dead or dying wallpaper in every room with two coats of washable off-white. A local carpenter put up lots of shelves and cut a large square hole – behind which the receptionist would sit – through the interior wall of what used to be the parlor. A plumber put in two additional toilets, placed sinks in both the former bedrooms that would now be examining rooms, and added a tankless boiler to the furnace in the basement so R.J. would have hot water on demand.

Buying furniture and equipment should have been fun

but was a source of anxiety because she had to keep one eye on her bank balance. Her problem was that she had been accustomed to ordering the best of everything when it was needed at the hospital. Now she settled for second-hand desks and chairs, a gem of a Salvation Army rug for the waiting room, a good used microscope, a rebuilt autoclave. But she bought new instruments. She had been advised she needed two computers, the first for patient records, the second for billing, but grimly decided to make do with one.

'You met Mary Stern yet?' Sally Howland asked her.

'I don't believe I have.'

'Well, she's postmistress. She owns the heavy old upright scale that used to be in Dr Thorndike's office. Bought it at the auction after the doctor died twenty-two years ago. She's willing to sell the scale to you for thirty dollars.'

R.J. bought the scale, scrubbed it, had it checked and rebalanced. It became part of the office, a link between the town's old doctor and the new one.

She had intended to advertise for help, but there was no need. Woodfield had an underground communications system that worked efficiently and with the speed of light. Very quickly she had four applications from women who wanted to be her receptionist, and three applications from registered nurses. She was careful and took her time choosing, but Toby Smith, the personable blonde woman who had driven the ambulance the night Freda Krantz had been shot, was one of the applicants for the receptionist job. She had impressed R.J. from the moment they had met, and she had the added attraction of heavy bookkeeping and accounting experience, so she could keep the financial records. For her nurse R.J. hired solid, grey-haired, fifty-six-year-old Margaret Weiler, who was called Peggy.

She felt guilty when it came to discussing money with each

of them. 'What I can pay you at the start is less than you would be paid in Boston,' she told Toby.

'Listen, don't you sweat about that,' the new receptionist said forthrightly. 'Both Peg and I are tickled to be able to work right here in town. This isn't Boston. Jobs are hard to find in the country.'

David Markus came around to the emerging office now and then. He cast an experienced eye on the renovation work and sometimes offered her a quiet word of advice. A couple of times they had lunch at the River Bank, a pizza joint on the outskirts of the village; twice, he paid, once she did. She found herself liking him, telling him her friends called her R.J.

'Everybody calls me Dave,' he said. Then he smiled. 'My friends call me David.' His blue jeans were faded but always looked freshly washed. His ponytailed hair was always very clean. When they shook hands she could feel that his palm was muscular and work-hardened, but his nails were cut short and looked cared-for.

She couldn't make up her mind whether he was sexy or just interesting.

The Saturday before she moved from Boston, he took her on a real date, to dinner in Northampton. As they were leaving the restaurant, he took a handful of candy from the bowl by the front door, bits of coated chocolate. 'Mmmm, upscale M&Ms,' he said, offering her some.

'No, thank you.'

In the car she watched him chewing and lost a struggle to keep quiet. 'You shouldn't eat those.'

'Hey, I love 'em. I don't gain weight.'

'I love them too. I'll buy you some in a nice clean package.'

'You a cleanliness freak? I got these at a nice clean restaurant.'

'I just read about tests that were done on candy from

restaurant candy bowls. They found that in most cases the candy contained traces of urine.'

He looked at her in silence. He had stopped chewing.

'Male diners go to the men's room. They don't wash their hands. On their way out of the restaurant, they reach into the candy bowl . . .'

She knew he was trying to decide whether to spit or to swallow. There goes this relationship, she thought as he swallowed, lowered the car window, dumped the rest of the candies.

'That's a terrible thing to tell somebody. I've been enjoying restaurant candy for years. You've absolutely ruined that pleasure for me for all time.'

'I know. But if I had been eating them and you knew, wouldn't you have told me?'

'Maybe not,' he said, and when he started to laugh, so did she. They chuckled halfway up Route 91.

On the drive back up into the hills, and then sitting in his parked pickup truck in front of her house, they told each other about their lives. He was a jock as a youth, 'just good enough to get a lot of injuries in a lot of sports'. By the time he reached college, he had been hurt enough that he didn't play varsity anything. He majored in English at Hamilton College, did graduate work about which he was vague. Before coming to the hills of Massachusetts he had been a corporate real estate executive at Lever Brothers in New York, the final two years as vice president. 'The full catastrophe – the 7:05 train to Manhattan, the big house, the pool, the tennis court.' His wife, Natalie, had developed amyotrophic lateral sclerosis, Lou Gehrig's disease. They both knew what was involved, they had watched a friend die of ALS. A month after her diagnosis was confirmed, David came home to find that Sarah, then nine years old, had been left with a neighbor, and Natalie had placed wet towels around the garage doors, started her car, and died listening to her favorite classical music station.

He had hired a cook and a housekeeper so Sarah would be

cared for, and he had gotten drunk regularly for eight months. On a sober day he had realized that his bright, coltish daughter was failing in school and developing psychological problems and a chronic, nervous little cough, and he had gone to his first meeting of Alcoholics Anonymous. Two months later David and Sarah had come to Woodfield.

He nodded when he heard R.J.'s story a little later, over three cups of strong coffee in her kitchen.

'These hills are full of survivors,' he said.

16
Office Hours

She moved from Cambridge on a hot morning in late June, under high, dark rainclouds that promised thunder and lightning. She had thought she would be happy to leave the house on Brattle Street; but in the last days, as some of the furnishings were sold and some went to storage and some went to Tom – as piece by piece was carried out until her high heels made echoes in the empty rooms – she looked at the house with the forgiving eyes of a former owner and saw that Tom had been right about its dignity and splendor. She was reluctant to leave it; despite her failed marriage, it had been her nest. Then she remembered that it was like a large hole in the ground into which they had poured their money, and she was content to lock the door and drive out of the driveway, past the brick wall with sections that still needed work, her responsibility no longer.

She was aware that she was driving into the unknown. All the way to Woodfield, her mind grappled with medical economics, fearful lest she was making a disastrous mistake.

For several days she had toyed with a fantasy. Suppose she were to operate a practise on a cash basis only – able completely to ignore the insurance companies whence came most of the bad stuff that on occasion made doctoring unpleasant? If she were to drop her fee for an office visit steeply – say, down to twenty dollars – would enough patients come to keep her afloat financially? Some would come, she knew, sick people who weren't covered by medical insurance. But would anybody covered by Blue Cross-Blue Shield forget about the fact that he or she owned a paid-up insurance policy and volunteer to pay cash at Dr Cole's office?

She realized regretfully that most people wouldn't.

She decided to try to establish an unofficial fee of twenty dollars for those who were uninsured. Insurance companies would pay their usual forty to sixty-five dollars for an office visit by one of their clients, depending on the complexity of the problem, with an additional charge for house calls. Full physical examinations would be billed at ninety-five dollars, and all lab work would be done at the medical center in Greenfield.

She put Toby to work two weeks before the office officially opened, programming all the insurance company documents into the computer. She would do most of her business with the five largest insurance companies, but there were fifteen other companies from which many patients bought insurance, and about thirty-five smaller, marginal companies. All of them had to be in the computer, multiple forms from each firm. The exhausting programming was a one-time job, but R.J. knew from experience that it would have to be updated constantly as companies discontinued some forms, revised others, and added new ones.

It was a major expense, one with which her great-grandfather had not had to contend.

A Monday morning.

She arrived at the office early, her hurried breakfast of toast and tea turned into a cold ball of nervousness in her stomach. The place smelled of paint and varnish. Toby was already at work, and Peg arrived two minutes later. The three of them grinned at one another foolishly.

The waiting room was small, but suddenly it looked enormous to R.J., deserted and empty.

Only thirteen people had made appointments. People who had been twenty-two years without a local doctor must have grown accustomed to the fact that they had to go out of town, she told herself. And once people had forged a relationship with a physician, why should they go to somebody new?

Suppose no one showed up? she asked herself in what she recognized as unreasonable panic.

Her first patient was there fifteen minutes before his appointment, George Palmer, seventy-two years old, a retired lumber miller with a painful hip and three stubs where fingers should have been.

'Morning, Mr Palmer,' Toby Smith said calmly, as though she had been greeting patients for years as they came through the door.

'Mornin, Toby.'

'Morning, George.'

'Mornin, Peg.'

Peg Weiler knew just what to do, ushered him into an examining room, filled in the top of his chart, took a set of vitals and recorded his data.

R.J. enjoyed taking a very relaxed history of George Palmer. In the beginning, each of the office visits would require a lot of time because every patient was new to her and would require a full work-up.

In Boston she would have sent Mr Palmer and his bursitis to an orthopod for a shot of cortisone. Here she gave the injection herself and asked him to make another appointment to see her.

When she stuck her head into the waiting room, Toby showed her a bouquet of summer flowers, sent by her father, and a huge ficus plant sent by David Markus. There were six people in the waiting room, and three of them didn't have appointments. She told Toby to practice triage; anyone in pain or severely ill should be worked in quickly. Others should be given the first available appointment. She realized suddenly, with a strange mixture of relief and regret, that she didn't have time to spare, after all. She asked Toby to bring her a cheese sandwich on a kaiser roll from the general store, and a large decaf. 'I'll work through my lunch hour.'

Sally Howland was coming through the front door. 'I have an appointment,' she said, as if she expected to be challenged, and R.J. had to restrain herself from kissing her crabby landlady.

Both Peg and Toby said they would work through the lunch hour too, and that they had better order sandwiches of their own. 'I'll pay,' R.J. told Toby happily.

17

David Markus

He invited her to supper at his house.

'Will Sarah be there too?'

'Sarah is having a big, formal dinner with the cooking club at the regional high school,' he said. He regarded her contemplatively. 'You can't come to my house unless a third person is around?'

'No, of course I'll come. I was just hoping Sarah would be there.'

She liked their house, the warmth and friendliness of the thick log walls and comfortable old furniture. There were lots of paintings on the walls, the work of local artists whose names didn't mean anything to her. He gave her the tour. Eat-in kitchen. His office, full of real estate paraphernalia, a computer, a big gray cat sleeping on his desk chair.

'Is the cat Jewish too, like the horse?'

'Matter of fact, she is.' He grinned. 'We got her with a beat-up, horny old tomcat Sarah said was her husband. But the male hung around only two days and then ran off, so I named this one Agunah. That's Yiddish for deserted wife.'

His monastic bedroom. There was just a bit of sexual tension as she took in the king-size mattress and box-spring on legs.

There was another computer on the desk, a bookcase full of volumes about history and agriculture, and a pile of manuscript. Under probing, he admitted he was writing a novel about the death of small farms in America, and about the early farmers who settled the Berkshire hills.

'I always wanted to tell stories. After Natalie was gone, I decided to give it a try. I had Sarah to clothe and feed, so I stayed with real estate when we moved, but real estate is not exactly a pressured business out here. I have plenty of time to write.'

'How's it going?'

'Oh . . .' He smiled, shrugged.

Sarah's room. Terrible multicolored drapes on the windows; he said Sarah had tie-dyed them herself. Two Barbra Streisand posters. All over the room, trays of rocks. Big rocks, little pebbles, medium-sized stones, each of them roughly in the shape of a heart. Geological valentines.

'What are they?'

'She calls them heartrocks. She's been collecting them since she was a little girl. It's something Natalie started her on.'

R.J. had taken a year of geology at Tufts. As she looked at the trays she thought she could identify quartz, shale, marble, sandstone, basalt, schist, feldspar, gneiss, slate, a red garnet, all heart-shaped. There were crystals she couldn't even guess at. 'This one I moved in the bucket of the tractor,' David said, pointing to a heart-shaped granite boulder more than two feet tall, propped in the corner of the room. 'Six miles, from Frank Parsons' woods. It took three of us to carry it into the house.'

'She just finds them on the ground?'

'She finds them everywhere. She has a knack. I almost never find one. Sarah is tough, she rejects a lot of stones. She doesn't call it a heartrock unless it has a true heart shape.'

'Perhaps you should look more carefully. There are billions and billions of rocks out there. I'll bet I can find Sarah some heartrocks.

106

'You think so, eh? You have twenty-five minutes before I serve the food. What will you bet?'

'A pizza with everything. Twenty-five minutes should be enough time.'

'You win, you get a pizza. I win, I get a kiss.'

'Hey.'

'What's the matter, you afraid? Put your money where my mouth is.' He grinned, daring her.

'You're on.'

She didn't waste much time in their barnyard or drive, figuring they would keep the area around the house well patrolled. Their road was unpaved, full of stones. She walked down it slowly, head bent, studying the ground. She had never been aware how varied stones were, how many shapes they came in, long, round, angular, thin, flat.

Now and then she would stoop and pick up a stone, but it was never right.

After ten minutes had gone by, she was a quarter of a mile from the log house and had found only one stone that looked even remotely like a heart, but it was misshapen, too low on one side.

A bad bet, she decided. She wanted to find a heartrock. She didn't want him to think she had failed on purpose.

At the end of the allotted time, she was back at his house. 'I found one,' she said, holding it out.

He looked at it and grinned. 'This heart is missing . . . what's the name of the upper chamber?'

'Atrium.'

'Yeah. This heart is missing the atrium on the right side.' He carried it to the door, flipped it outside.

What happened next would be important, she told herself. If he used the bet to demonstrate his machismo, either with a clinch or an exchange of saliva, she would have no interest in him at all.

But he bent and barely touched her mouth with his lips, a kiss that was tender and incredibly sweet.

Ooh.

He gave her a simple but wonderful supper: a large, crisp salad made entirely from his own garden stuff, except for the tomatoes which were store-bought because his weren't ripe yet. It was served with the house specialty, a honey-miso dressing, and garnished with asparagus they picked and steamed just before they sat down to eat. He had made his own sprouts from a combination of seeds and legumes he assured her was a secret, and he had baked crispy rolls filled with tiny pieces of garlic that exploded flavor as she chewed.

'Hey. You're *some* cook.'

'I like to potchky around.'

Dessert was homemade vanilla ice cream, with a blueberry torte he'd baked that morning. She found herself telling him about the religious mixture of her clan. 'There are Protestant Coles and Quaker Regensbergs. And Jewish Coles and Jewish Regensbergs. And atheists. And my cousin Marcella Regensberg, who is a Franciscan nun at a convent in Virginia. We have something of everything.'

Over the second cup of coffee she learned something about him that was astounding. The 'graduate study' about which he had been vague was completed at the Jewish Theological Seminary of America, in New York.

'You're a *what*?'

'A rabbi. At least, I was ordained, a long time ago. I worked at it only a while.'

'Why did you quit? Did you have a congregation?'

'I just . . .' He shrugged again. 'I was too full of questions and insecurities to take a congregation. I had begun to doubt, I couldn't make up my mind about the existence of God. And I felt a congregation at least deserved a rabbi who had made up his mind about that.'

'And how do you feel now? Have you made up your mind since then?'

Abraham Lincoln looked at her for a long moment. How could blue eyes become so sad, hold such fleeting pain? He slowly shook his head. 'Jury's still out.'

He didn't blurt things. It was only after weeks of seeing him often that she learned details. When he had finished at the seminary he had gone directly into the army, ninety days at officers' school and then right to Vietnam as a second lieutenant chaplain. It was comparatively cushy work, safely behind the lines at a large hospital in Saigon. He had spent his days with the maimed and dying, his evenings writing letters to their families, and he had absorbed their fears and anger long before his own body was injured.

One day he was riding in the back of a troop carrier with two Catholic chaplains, Major Joseph Fallon and Lieutenant Bernard Towers, and they were caught in the street during a rocket attack. There was a direct hit on the front of the vehicle; in the rear seat the blast was narrow and selective. Bernie Towers, seated on the left, was destroyed. Joe Fallon, seated in the middle, lost his right leg at the knee. David suffered a serious wound in his left leg, into the bone. It required three operations, long recovery. Now his left leg was shorter than the right, but the limp was negligible, she hadn't even noticed it.

He had returned to New York when discharged and delivered one guest sermon in application for a job. It was in Bay Path, Long Island, at Temple Beth Shalom, the House of Peace. He spoke of keeping peace in a complex world. Halfway through the sermon, he looked up to where the temple decorating committee had placed a large plaque emblazoned with the first of Maimonides' Thirteen Articles of Faith: *I have perfect faith that the Creator, blessed be His name, is the author and guide of everything that has been created;*

and that He alone has made, does make, and will make all things.

It came to him in a moment of frozen terror that he could not with certainty agree, and he had somehow stumbled to the end of the sermon.

He had applied to Lever Brothers as a real estate trainee, an agnostic rabbi too full of doubt to be anybody's clergyman.

'. . . Could you still marry people?'

He had an attractive, slightly twisted smile. 'I suppose I could. Once a rabbi . . .'

'It would make a great combination of signs. *Marryin' Markus.* Right under, *I'm-In-Love-With-You Honey.*'

18

A Feline Intimacy

R.J. hadn't fallen in love with David Markus all at once. It had started as a small seed, an admiration of his face and strong, long fingers, a response to the timbre of his voice, to the softness in his eyes. But to her surprise – even to her fear – the seed had flowered, feeling had grown. They hadn't fallen into each other's arms – as if with their very patience, their mature caution, they were telling one another something. But on a rainy Saturday afternoon in his house, his daughter safely at the one-dollar movie in Northampton with friends, they kissed with a familiarity that also had grown.

He complained to her that he was having trouble describing a woman's body in his novel. 'Artists and photographers simply use models, a sensible solution.'

Very sensible, she agreed.

'So will you pose for me?'

She shook her head. 'No. You'll have to write from memory.'

Already they were unbuttoning buttons.

'You're a virgin,' he said.

She didn't remind him that she was a divorced woman, and forty-two years old.

'And I've never seen a woman before, we're both brand new, blank pages.'

Suddenly, they were. They inspected one another at length. R.J. found she had a hard time breathing. He was slow and very gentle, at first controlling the urgency and making it better, treating her as if she were made of very fine breakable stuff, without words letting her know things that were important. Both of them quickly became almost crazy.

Afterwards they lay as though comatose, still joined. When finally she turned her head, she looked into the unblinking green eyes of the cat. Agunah was seated on her haunches on a bedside chair, watching intently. R.J. had the certain knowledge that the cat understood exactly what had just been done.

'David, if this is a test, I have failed. Get her out of here.'

He laughed. 'It isn't a test.'

He disengaged, took out the cat and closed the door, came back. The second time was slower, calmer, and filled R.J. with happiness. He was considerate and generous. She explained that her orgasms were apt to be long and full, but once she had had one, the next one usually was somewhere a few days down the road. She was embarrassed in the telling, certain that his last lover had had climaxes like firecrackers, but he proved easy to talk to.

Eventually, he left her in the bed and made their supper. The door was left open again, and the cat returned to the room and the chair, but R.J. didn't mind, and she lay there and listened to David singing Puccini off-key and sounding very happy. The scent of their joining mingled with the perfume of his omelets, onions and peppers and tiny zucchinis frying until they were sweet as his kisses, rich as the promise of life. Later, when she and David lay next to one another, dozing, Agunah settled herself at the foot of the bed between their feet. When R.J. became accustomed, she liked it.

'Thank you for giving me a wonderful experience, all those important little details to write about.'

She glowered. 'I'll cut your heart out.'

'You already have,' he told her gallantly.

One out of every six patients who came to her didn't have medical insurance of any kind. A number of them didn't have the twenty dollars she had set as her fee for treating the uninsured. From some, she accepted payment in kind. She accumulated six cords of hardwood, split and stacked behind her house. She acquired a once-a-week cleaning woman for the house and another for the office. She got a regular supply of dressed chickens and turkeys and several sources of fresh vegetables, berries and flowers.

She was amused by the barter but worried about cash and about her debts.

She developed a clinical technique for working with patients who lacked insurance, aware that she would have to try to reverse ailments long neglected. But it wasn't people with complicated problems who bothered her most, it was those who didn't come at all because they couldn't pay and were too proud to accept charity. People like that sought out a doctor only in extremity, when it was too late to help them: the diabetes had resulted in blindness, the tumors had metastasized. R.J. saw several of these cases right from the start. She could do nothing but rage silently at the system and treat them.

She depended on word of mouth to get her message out into the hills: *When you're sick, when you hurt, come to the new woman doctor. If you don't have insurance, she makes arrangements about the money.*

As a result, some of the disenfranchised did come to her. Even when she didn't want their barter, some of them insisted. A man with Parkinson's disease fought his tremors to weave her an ash splint basket. A woman with ovarian cancer was making her a patchwork quilt. But many more people were scattered throughout the hills without insurance and without any kind of medical care at all. She knew it, and it ate at her.

She continued to see a great deal of David. To her surprise and regret, the warmth Sarah had shown toward her at their first meeting was soon noticeably lacking. R.J. understood that the girl was jealous of her, and she talked it over with David.

'It's natural that she should feel threatened by a woman who suddenly is occupying a good deal of her father's life,' she said.

He nodded. 'We'll just have to give her time to get used to it.'

That presupposed that the two of them were on a course she wasn't certain she wanted to follow. David was being honest about the way they had come to feel about one another. She was just as honest, with herself as well as with David.

'I just want to continue things the way they are, without making heavy plans for the future. It's too early for me to think about a lasting relationship. I have goals to accomplish here. I want to become established in the town as its doctor, and I'm not looking to make a permanent personal commitment right now.'

David seemed to latch on to the words *right now* and to take encouragement from them. 'Fine. We have to give ourselves time,' he said.

She was full of uncertainties, unable to know her own mind, but she found it possible to tell him about her hopes, and of her worries about money.

'I don't know medical economics, but there should be enough of a practise here to give you a damn fine income, mucho dough.'

'It doesn't have to be damn fine. I just need to get by. I don't have anybody to support but myself.'

'Still . . . why merely to get by?' He looked at her the way her father had.

114

'I don't care about money. What I care about is practicing world-class medicine in this small town.'

'That makes you some kind of saint,' he said almost fearfully.

'Get real. No saint would do what I just did to you,' she said practically, and grinned at him.

19

The House on the Verge

Slowly she and Peg and Toby worked the kinks out of the office routine. Slowly, too, R.J. learned the rhythms of the town and grew familiar with its pace. She sensed that people she met liked to nod and say, 'Hello, doctor!', felt their pride in the fact that the town had a physician again. She began making house calls, seeking out the homes of the bedridden, traveling to patients who found it difficult or impossible to get to medical care. When she had the time and they offered a piece of pie and a cup of coffee she sat with them at their kitchen tables and talked about town politics and the weather, and copied recipes into her prescription pad.

Woodfield sprawled over forty-two square miles of rugged country, and sometimes she was called into neighboring townships as well. Summoned by a boy who hiked three-and-a-half miles to get to a phone, she went to a cabin on top of Houghton's Mountain and strapped a sprained ankle for Lewis Magoun, a sheep farmer. When she came down the mountain and drove back to the office, she found Toby harried and anxious. 'Seth Rushton has had a heart attack. They called you first thing, but when I couldn't reach you, I telephoned the ambulance.'

R.J. drove to the Rushton farm to find that the ambulance had already left for Greenfield. Rushton was treated and was resting comfortably, but it was a valuable lesson. The following morning R.J. drove to Greenfield and bought a cellular bag phone. She kept it in the car, and she was never out of touch with her office again.

Now and then, as she made her way about the town, she passed Sarah Markus. She always sounded the horn and waved. Sometimes Sarah waved back.

Whenever David brought R.J. to the log house while Sarah was home, she could feel Sarah's watchful eyes as the girl analyzed everything that was said.

Driving home from the office one afternoon, R.J. passed Sarah galloping Chaim the other way. She admired how well the girl sat the horse, how effortlessly she posted, her dark hair streaming behind her. R.J. didn't toot a greeting, for fear of spooking the animal.

A few days later, sitting in her living room, R.J. glanced out of the window and saw, through the gaps between the apple trees, that Sarah Markus was walking her horse along Laurel Hill Road very slowly while she studied R.J.'s house.

R.J. was interested in Sarah in part because of the girl's father, but also because of Sarah herself, and perhaps for another reason. Somewhere in the back of her mind was an amorphous picture, a possibility she didn't dare to consider yet – the concept of the three of them together, she, David, and this girl as her daughter.

A few minutes later, horse and rider came back down Laurel Hill Road the other way, the girl still taking in the house and the land with her eyes. Then, when they had reached the end of the property, Sarah kicked her heels and Chaim began to trot.

For the first time in a long while, R.J. allowed herself to think of the pregnancy that had miscarried after Charlie Harris had died. If that baby had been born, she would be thirteen years old, three years younger than Sarah.

She waited by the window, hoping Sarah would turn the horse and ride past again.

One day when she came home from the office at dusk, R.J. found that a heart-shaped rock, as large as her hand, had been left on her porch by the front door.

It was a beautiful heartrock composed of two outer layers of dark gray stone and an inner layer of lighter rock that sparkled with mica.

She knew who had left it. But was it a gift of approval? A signal of truce? It was too pretty to be a declaration of war, R.J. felt certain.

She was happy to get it, and she took it inside and set it on the living-room mantel next to her mother's brass candlesticks, a place of honor.

Frank Sotheby stood on the porch of his general store and cleared his throat. 'I think they should both of them see a nurse, mebbe, Dr Cole? The two of them live all by themselves with a bunch of cats in that apartment above the hardware store. The smell. Whew.'

'You mean right down the street? How come I've never seen them?'

'Well, because they don't ever come out, hardly. One of 'em, Miss Eva Goodhue, is old as sin, and the other one, Miz Helen Phillips, that's Eva's niece, is lots younger but more'n a little dotty. They take care of each other after a fashion.' He hesitated. 'Eva calls me Fridays with her grocery list. I carry 'em an order every week. Well . . . her last check was refused by the bank. Insufficient funds.'

The dark, narrow stairway had no lightbulb. At the top of the stairs R.J. knocked, and after she had stood there for a long time, she knocked harder. Again and again.

She heard no footsteps, but she sensed slight movement behind the door. 'Hello?'

'. . . Who is it?'

'It's Roberta Cole. I'm the doctor.'

'From Dr Thorndike?'

Oh, baby. 'Dr Thorndike has been . . . gone . . . a good while. I'm the doctor now. Please . . . Am I speaking to Miss Goodhue or Mrs Phillips?'

'Eva Goodhue. What do you want?'

'Well, I'd like to meet you, Miss Goodhue, to say hello. Will you kindly open the door and invite me in?'

There was silence behind the door. The moment stretched and stretched. The silence thickened.

'Miss Goodhue?'

At last R.J. sighed. 'I've got a new office right down the street from you. Just down Main Street, first floor at Sally Howland's house. If you should ever need a doctor, either one of you, just telephone or send somebody to fetch me, okay?' She took one of her cards and slipped it under the door. 'Okay, Miss Goodhue?'

But there was no answer, and she went back down the stairs.

When she and Tom had made their infrequent trips to the country, sometimes they had seen an occasional glimpse of wildlife, rabbits and squirrels, chipmunks who nested in the overhang woodshed. But now that she lived in the house every day, she witnessed through the windows a variety of wild neighbors she hadn't met before. She learned to keep her binoculars at close hand.

From the kitchen window, one gray dawn, she saw a bobcat amble insolently across the meadow. From her home office overlooking the wet pasture, she saw four otter, up from the river to hunt in the marsh, running in a single undulating file so close to one another they appeared to be the curves of a serpent, a Loch Ness monster in her wet pasture. She saw turtles and snakes, a fat old woodchuck who ate the clover in the meadow every day, and a porcupine that waddled out of the woods to munch the early drop of tiny pale-green apples under the trees. The thickets and trees were full of songbirds and raptors. Without trying she saw a great blue heron and several varieties of hawk. From her front porch she witnessed a horned owl come down, fast as doom and soft as a whisper, and take a running vole from the meadow. Up, out, and away.

She described what she had seen to Janet Cantwell. The town selectwoman taught biology at the university in Amherst. 'It's because your house is on a verge, a meeting of several different environments. Wet pasture, dry meadow, deep woods containing ponds, the good river running through the whole thing. Creatures find wonderful hunting.'

As R.J. traveled the countryside she saw properties with names. Some signs were self-acknowledgements, Schroeder's Ten Acres, Ransome's Tree Farm, Peterson's Reward. Others were droll with Dunrovin and It's Our Place; or descriptive, Ten Oaks, Windcrest, Walnut Hill. Some of the names were too precious. She'd have enjoyed calling her place Catamount River Farm, but for many years that name had been on a house a mile upstream; besides, it would have been presumptuous to call her property a farm nowadays.

David, that man of many facets, had a basement full of power tools and had offered to make it possible for the new doctor to hang out a shingle.

She mentioned it to Hank Krantz, who came roaring and clattering up her driveway one morning on his big John Deere tractor, pulling his manure spreader. 'Get in,' he said, 'and we'll get you a log for your signpost.' So she clambered into the big metal spreader, providentially empty but redolent of cow shit, and held on in disbelief while he jarred and bumped her – a country woman at last – all the way to the river.

Hank chose a healthy, mature black locust tree in a stand on the riverbank and felled it with his chainsaw, trimming the log and putting it in the manure spreader to keep her company on the way back.

David fashioned a stout, square-cut signpost from the log, approving Hank's choice. 'Black locust is just about rot-proof,' he said, and set it three feet into the earth. An arm extended from it, with two eyebolts on the bottom surface from which the sign would be suspended. 'You want something besides your name? You want to call the place anything special?'

'No,' she said. Then she made up her mind, and she smiled. 'Yes, I do.'

She thought it was beautiful when it was done, painted the same beige-gray as the house, with the lettering in black.

The House
on the Verge
R.J. Cole MD

The sign puzzled people. On the verge of what, they asked her.

Depending on her mood she pleased herself by telling them the house was on the verge of solvency, on the verge of despair, on the verge of collapse, on the verge of answering the cosmic riddle of life. Pretty soon either they grew bored by her oddness or accustomed to the sign, and they stopped asking.

20
Snapshots

'Who's next?' R.J. asked Toby Smith late one afternoon.

'I am,' Toby said nervously.

'You? Oh . . . of course, Toby. Do you need a physical exam, or do you have a problem?'

'Problem.'

Toby sat by the desk and outlined the facts sparingly and clearly.

She and her husband, Jan, had been married for two-and-a-half years. For the past two years they had been trying to conceive a child.

'No luck at all. We make love all the time, desperately and much too often, really. It's ruined our sex life.'

R.J. nodded in sympathy. 'Well, give it a rest. It ain't what you do, it's the way that you do it. And *when*. Does Jan know you're talking with me about this? Is he willing to see me, too?'

'Oh, yes.'

'Well, we'll do a semen analysis and run some tests on you, for starters. After we gather some information, we'll be able to set up a regular drill for you.'

Toby regarded her seriously. 'I would appreciate it if you

would use another word, Dr Cole.'

'Of course. Schedule? We'll set up a regular schedule?'

'Schedule is fine,' Toby said, and they smiled at one another.

She and David had reached the stage where they asked each other a lot of questions, wanting to know one another in every way. He was curious about how she regarded her work, and it was interesting to him that she had been educated both as an attorney and as a physician.

'Maimonides was a lawyer as well as a doctor.'

'A rabbi too, no?'

'A rabbi too, and a diamond merchant, to bring bread into the house.'

She smiled. 'Maybe I should become a diamond merchant.'

She found it possible to talk about anything with him, an unbelievable luxury. He felt the same way about abortion that he felt about God: he was undecided. 'I think a woman should have the right to save her own life, to safeguard her health or her future, but . . . to me, a baby is a very serious thing.'

'Well, of course. To me, too. Conserving life, making it better – that's my job.'

She told him how it felt when she was able to help someone, really score points to drive away pain, to extend life. 'Like a cosmic orgasm. Like the world's biggest hug.'

He listened when she remembered agony too, times when she had made a mistake, when she realized that someone who had come to her for help had been harmed by her efforts.

'Have you ever ended somebody's life?'

'Hurried death in through the door? Yes.'

She liked the fact that he didn't say the obvious things. He only looked into her eyes as he nodded, and took her hand.

He could be moody. Real estate sales seldom influenced his

spirits, but she was able to guess whether or not his writing was going well. When it was going badly he took refuge in physical work. Sometimes on weekends he allowed her to share his garden chores, and she pulled weeds and dug her hands into the soil, loving the gritty contact of earth with skin. Despite her supply of fresh vegetables from the gardens of others, she wanted her own. He convinced her of the wisdom of a couple of raised beds, and he knew where she could buy some used barn beams with which to make the frames.

They removed the grassy topsoil from two rectangles on a gradual, south-facing slope in the meadow, block by block like Inuits building an igloo, and piled the sod upside down in the composter. They set flat stones in the ground in the shape of the beds, four feet by eight feet, using a bubble level to make certain the stones were even. On the stone base David built the bed frames, using two layers of the oak beams on each. The beams were difficult to handle and work. 'Hard as death and heavy as sin,' David grunted, but soon he had shiplapped the corners and had driven long galvanized spikes to form the frames.

He set down his sledge and took her hand. 'You know what I love?'

'What?' she asked, her heart pounding.

'Horse shit and cow shit.'

The manure available to them was from the Krantzes' cow barn. They mixed it with peat moss and soil and over-filled the beds, and then piled a foot of loose hay on top.

'It will settle some. Next spring, all you'll have to do is pull the hay aside and plant your seeds, and then add more mulch as things grow,' David said, and she looked forward to all of that with the anticipation of a child.

By the end of July she was able to see some financial trends in her practise. It became troublingly clear to her that certain patients ran up doctor's bills without any serious commitment to paying. Payment for treating insured patients, although slow, was guaranteed. Of the uninsured, some were destitute, and without hesitation or regret she wrote off their treatment – *pro bono*. But a few patients were reluctant to pay even though it was obvious they were able to do so. She had treated Gregory Hinton, a prosperous dairy farmer, for a series of ulcerated boils on his back. He had been to her office three times, each time telling Toby he would 'send a check', but no check had arrived.

While driving past his farm, she saw him enter the barn, and she turned the Explorer into his driveway. He greeted her pleasantly, if with curiosity. 'Don't need your services, glad to say. Boils are all gone.'

'That's good, Mr Hinton. Glad to hear it. I was wondering . . . well, if you could pay your bill for the three visits?'

'You were *what*?' He glared. 'Good Lord. Is it necessary to dun patients? What kind of a doctor are you, woman?'

'A doctor who has just begun a new practise.'

'You should be advised that Doc Thorndike always gave a person plenty of space about paying.'

'Dr Thorndike has been gone a long, long time, and I don't have that luxury. I'd appreciate it if you could pay what you owe,' she said, and bade him good day as pleasantly as she was able.

That evening David nodded slowly when she told him about the encounter.

'Hinton is a stubborn old skinflint. He keeps everyone waiting to be paid, so he can milk the last bit of bank interest out of every dollar. What you have to realize – what your patients must realize, too – is that you're running a business at the same time that you're doctoring them.'

She needed to work out a system for collections, David said. Any dunning should be done by someone other than the doctor, so R.J. could keep her 'image as a saint'. Collecting debts was pretty much the same no matter what the business, he told her, and together they mapped out a program that she explained the next morning to Toby, the delegated collector, who would send out bills once a month.

Toby knew the local population well and would make the difficult decision about whether a patient truly was indigent. Anyone who couldn't pay but who wished to barter work or goods would be allowed to do so. Anyone who couldn't give money or barter wouldn't be billed.

For those whom Toby believed capable of paying, separate computer categories were programmed for accounts that were up to 30 days overdue, 60–90 days overdue, and more than 90 days overdue. Forty-five days after the first bill was mailed, Letter No. 1 was sent, asking the patient to contact the doctor with any questions about the account. After 60 days, Toby would make a telephone call reminding the patient of the outstanding balance and recording his or her response. After 90 days, Letter No. 2 was sent, a firmer request for payment by a specific date.

David suggested that after four months the account should be turned over to a collection agency. R.J. wrinkled her nose in distaste; that didn't fit her vision of the relationships she wanted to build in a small town. She realized she had to teach herself to be a businesswoman as well as a healer; still, for the time being she and Toby agreed to hold off on dealing with a collection agency.

Toby came to work one morning with a piece of paper that she handed to R.J. with a smile. It was yellowed and crumbling and had been placed for protection in a clear plastic holder.

'Mary Stern found it in the files of the Historic Society,' Toby said. 'Since it was addressed to an ancestor of my husband's – the brother of his great-great-grandmother – she brought it over to our house to show it to us.'

It was a physician's bill, made out to Alonzo S. Sheffield, for 'Office visit, grippe – 50 cents'. The name printed at the top was Doctor Peter Elias Hathaway, and the date on the bill was May 16, 1889. 'There have been several dozen physicians

126

in Woodfield between Dr Hathaway and you,' Toby told R.J.
'Turn the bill over,' she said.

A verse was printed on the back:

> *Just on the brink of danger, not before,*
> *God and the Doctor we alike adore;*
> *The danger passed, both are alike requited;*
> *God forgot and the Doctor slighted.*

Toby returned the bill to the historical society, but not
before copying the verse and placing it into the computer
with Accounts Receivable.

David talked all the time about Sarah, and R.J. encouraged
him to do it. One evening he brought out pictures, four fat
albums that recorded the life of one child. Here was Sarah as a
newborn, held in the arms of her maternal grandmother, the
late Trudi Kaufman, a plump woman with a wide smile. Here
was serious little Sarah in her Teeterbabe, gravely watching
her young father while he shaved. Many of the pictures
engendered an anecdote. 'See this snowsuit? Navy blue,
her first snowsuit. She was just a year old, and Natalie and I
were making a big deal over the fact that we had been able to
switch her from diapers to training pants. One Saturday we
took her to A&S – Abraham & Strauss, the nice department
store in downtown Brooklyn. It was January, right after the
holidays, and cold. You know what it is to dress a little kid
for the cold? All the layers you have to put on them?'

R.J. nodded, smiling.

'She had so many layers of clothing she was shaped like a
little ball, a little Vienna roll. Well, we're in the elevator at
A&S, the elevator man is announcing the merchandize, floor
by floor. I had been carrying her, but now she's standing
between us, Natalie and I each have a hand. And I notice
the elevator man's face as he's reciting the merchandize, and

I follow his eyes. And I see that all around those two little white baby shoes there is a big wet circle in the carpet on the elevator floor. And Sarah's legs are a darker, wetter blue than the rest of her snowsuit.

'We had changes for her in the car and I ran to the garage and got them. So we had to take all those wet layers off and put all those dry layers on. But the snowsuit was soaked, so we had to go to Infants' Wear and buy another snowsuit.'

Sarah on her first day of school. Sarah as a skinny eight-year-old, digging in the sand on vacation at Old Lyme Beach in Connecticut. Sarah with braces on her teeth and a big, exaggerated grin to show them off.

David appeared in some of the pictures with her, but R.J. assumed that mostly he had been behind the camera, because Natalie was in many of the snapshots. R.J. studied her covertly, a pretty, self-assured young woman with long black hair, shockingly familiar because her sixteen-year-old daughter looked so much like her.

There was something wrong – sick – about envying a dead woman, but R.J. envied the woman who had been alive when all the pictures had been taken, the woman who had conceived and borne a daughter, taught and guided Sarah, given the girl her love. She recognized uncomfortably that some of her interest in David Markus stemmed from the fact that she yearned for a daughter herself, coveting the girl he and Natalie Kaufman Markus had brought into the world.

From time to time as she traveled the town she remembered Sarah and her collection, and she tried to keep her eyes out for heartrocks but never had any success. Mostly she was too busy to remember, and too short on time to spend pleasant minutes studying stones on the ground.

It happened by accident, a moment of serendipity. On a hot midsummer day she stole into the woods and took off her shoes and socks at the riverbank. She rolled up the legs of her slacks above the knee and waded blissfully in the cold water of the Catamount. In a moment she came to a pool and saw that it was full of fingerlings. She couldn't tell if they were brook trout or brown trout as they hovered in the clear water. Then, just beyond and below the trout, she saw a small whitish stone. Although she was conditioned by previous disappointments not to have expectations, she waded a few feet into deeper water, scattering fish in every direction, and reached down until her fingers closed on the stone.

A heartrock.

A crystal, probably quartz, about two inches in diameter, with a smooth surface made opaque by untold years of running water and grinding sands until the stone was just the proper shape.

She carried it home in triumph. In her bureau drawer was a small jeweler's box, and she emptied it of the pearl earrings it had contained and nestled the crystal into the velvet lining. Then she took the box and drove across town.

Fortunately, the log house looked deserted. Leaving the Explorer's motor running, she left the car and placed the little box in the middle of the top step, in front of Sarah Markus's door. Then she jumped into her car and made her getaway as gratefully as if she had just robbed a bank.

21
Finding Her Way

R.J. had said nothing to Sarah about the heartrock that had been left for her, and nothing was said by Sarah to indicate that she had found the crystal in the jewelry box.

But the following Wednesday afternoon when R.J. came home from the office, she found a small cardboard box by her front door. It contained a dark green, shiny stone with a ragged crack that started from the dip at the top and ran halfway through to the point at the base.

The next morning, on her precious day off, R.J. drove to a gravel pit in the hills that was used by the town highway department. Millions of years ago, a great torrent of ice had moved over the land, picking up and carrying soil, stones, and rocks, and great frozen chunks had broken off and fallen here to melt and become a river of water, washing up alluvial material into a moraine that now furnished material for the gravel roads of Woodfield.

R.J. spent all morning moving over the piles of stones, burrowing into them with her hands. There was stones of infinite hue and combination – brown, beige, white, blue, green, black, and gray. There were stones of diverse shape, and R.J. inspected and discarded thousands, one by one, without finding what she sought. Toward noon, sunburned and grumpy, she drove home. Passing the Krantz place, she saw Freda in the garden, waving the car to a halt with her cane.

'Picking beets,' Freda called when R.J. rolled down the window. 'Want some?'

'Sure. I'll come out and help.'

In the large garden on the south side of the big red Krantz barn, they had pulled the eighth big round beet when R.J. saw in the upturned dirt a piece of black basalt the size of the nail on her little finger and perfectly shaped. She began to laugh even as she pounced on it.

'May I have this?'

'Well, is it a diamond?' Freda said in astonishment.

'No, it's just a pebble,' R.J. said, and bore away the beets and the heartrock in triumph.

In the house she washed the stone and wrapped it in a paper tissue. Then she placed it in a plastic box that had housed a VCR tape. She found a cardboard box, fourteen inches square, and made popcorn, eating some for her lunch, and placed the VCR box in the small carton and filled it with popcorn. Then she got a larger carton, three feet by two feet, and placed the smaller carton inside, surrounded by balls of crumpled newspaper, and taped it closed securely.

She had to set the alarm in order to get up early enough the next morning so that David and Sarah would still be asleep when she went to their house. The sun was still low enough to glitter on the wet grass as she pulled up on their road, not daring to drive to the door. She carried the box down their driveway and set it on the front steps, just as Chaim nickered in the field.

'Aha! So it *was* you,' Sarah said from her open window.

In a moment she had come downstairs. 'Wow. This must

be a big one,' she said, and R.J. laughed at her expression as she lifted the box, with its lack of weight.

'Come in. I'll give you coffee,' Sarah said.

Seated at the kitchen table, they grinned at one another. 'I love the two heartrocks you gave me. I'll keep them always,' R.J. said.

'The crystal one is my favorite, at least at the moment. I change favorites a lot,' Sarah said, careful to be honest. 'They say crystal has the power to cure illness. Do you think it does?'

R.J. was just as careful. 'I doubt it, but then, I've never had any experience with crystals, so I'm not in a position to say.'

'Well, I think heartrocks are magical. I know they can be very lucky, and I carry one wherever I go. Do you believe in luck?'

'Oh, yes. I definitely believe in luck. I do.'

While the coffee was brewing Sarah put the package on the table and cut the tape. Getting through the various layers and obstacles, she laughed a lot. When she saw the tiny black heartrock she gasped. 'It's the best one yet,' she said.

There were paper balls and boxes and popcorn all over the table and the floor; R.J. felt as though they had been opening presents on Christmas morning. That was how David found them when he came downstairs in his pajamas, looking for coffee.

R.J. began to spend time on her house, enjoying the experience of making her own nest without having to consider the likes and dislikes of anyone else. She had received the books that had filled the library in the house on Brattle Street. Now she bartered pediatric care for four children, in exchange for carpentry work by George Garroway, their father. She bought seasoned lumber from a little one-man mill deep in the hills. In Boston the black cherry boards would have been kiln-dried and prohibitively expensive. Elliot Purdy did all the labor himself, logging trees on his own land, milling and carefully stacking and air-drying the lumber, so the price was reasonable, and R.J. and David carried the boards to her house in his pickup. Garroway filled the living-room walls with bookshelves. R.J. spent evening after evening sanding them and hand-rubbing them with Danish oil, often helped by David and sometimes joined by Toby and Jan, whom she rewarded with spaghetti dinners and opera on the CD player. When they were finished, the room took on the warmth that only glowing wood and the spines of many books could give.

Along with the cartons of books that she had trucked from the storage warehouse in Boston came the piano, which she placed in front of the living-room window, on the Persian rug that had been her favorite possession in the Cambridge house. The antique Heriz had started out brightly coloured 125 years ago, but through the long years the red had mellowed to rust, the blues and greens had softened into fine, subtle shades, and the white was now a delicate cream.

A few days later, a Federal Express van turned into R.J.'s driveway, and the driver delivered a bulky package with lading marks from The Netherlands. It turned out to be her legacy from Betts Sullivan, a beautifully worked silver tray, coffee pot, teapot, sugar bowl, and creamer. She spent an entire evening polishing the heavy pieces and then placed them on the lowboy where she could see them and the Heriz rug as she sat and played the piano in her home. She discovered deep contentment. It was an unfamiliar sensation, but one to which she could easily become addicted.

David exclaimed over the silver service. He was interested when she told him about Elizabeth Sullivan and moved when she took him to the small riverside clearing where she had buried Betts's ashes.

'Do you come here often, to speak to her?'

'I come here because I like this spot. But, no . . . I don't speak to Elizabeth.'

'Don't you want to tell her that her gift has arrived?'

'*She* isn't here, David.'

'How do you know that?'

'I just know. I buried just some bits of burnt bone under that rock. Elizabeth merely wanted her remains to be added to the earth in a pretty, wild place. This town, this place by the Catamount River, they meant nothing to her during her lifetime. She didn't know them. If souls can return after death – and I don't believe that happens, I think that probably dead is dead – but if it *could* happen, surely Betts Sullivan would go to some place that was significant to her?'

He was shocked, she could tell. And disappointed in her, in some important way.

They were completely different kinds of people. Perhaps it was true that opposites attracted one another, she thought.

Although their relationship was full of questions and uncertainties, they shared wonderful hours. They explored her property together and found treasures. In the middle of her woods was a series of water containments like the beads in an enormous necklace. It began with a tiny dam that enclosed a trickle too small to qualify as a real brook, producing a collection of water scarcely larger than a puddle. Working with unerring engineering instinct, beavers had built a series of dams and ponds beyond the first one, each somewhat larger than the last, ending in a pond that covered more than an acre. Wading birds and other wildlife came to the largest pond for nesting and to hunt trout, and it was a place of stillness and peace.

'I wish I could walk out here without crashing through trees and undergrowth.'

David agreed. 'You need a trail,' he said.

That weekend he brought cans of spray paint with which to mark a trail's course. They walked the route many times to make certain of it before they marked the trees, and then David came with his chainsaw and went to work.

They deliberately kept the way narrow and avoided dealing with dead falls or cutting large trees except to prune away lower branches that would impede a walker's progress. R.J. dragged away the limbs and small trees that David cut, reserving those thick enough to be firewood and making piles of the rest of the slash to provide shelters for small animals.

David pointed out animal signs, a buck tree where a deer had rubbed the velvet from his antlers, a dead trunk torn asunder by a black bear seeking grubs and insects, and now and again a pile of bear droppings, sometimes formless with berry diarrhea, sometimes exactly like human ordure except that it was of comically enormous caliber.

'Are there many bears around here?'

'Quite a few. Sooner or later you'll see one, probably from a distance. They don't let us get close. They hear us coming, smell us. They stay out of the way of human beings, for the most part.'

Some of the scenery was particularly beautiful, and as they worked she made mental note of several places where she wanted to build benches. For the time being, she bought two plastic chairs from the supermarket in Greenfield, and she placed them in a clump of brush on the shore of the large beaver pond. She learned to sit there for long stretches of time without moving, and sometimes she was rewarded. She watched the beavers, and a gorgeous pair of wood ducks, and a blue heron wading in the shallows, and a deer come to the pond for a drink, and two snapping turtles the size of Betts's silver tray. Sometimes she felt as if she had never been in a traffic jam.

Little by little, whenever they could find the time, she

and David cleared her narrow path through the whispering woods, all the way to the beaver ponds, and beyond, in the direction of the river.

22
The Singers

Despite all kinds of misgivings, she slid into the relationship.

It frightened her that a woman of her age and experience could become so completely unglued inside, as vulnerable as a teenager. Her work kept her apart from David most of the time, but she was capable of thinking of him at random and inopportune moments – of his mouth, his voice, his eyes, the shape of his head, the way he held his body. She tried to examine her reactions scientifically, to tell herself it was all biological chemistry: when she saw him, heard his voice, sensed his presence, her brain released phenylethylamine to drive her body crazy. When he stroked her, kissed her, when they had sex, the release of the hormone oxytocin made their lovemaking sweeter.

She drove him out of her mind ruthlessly during the day so she could function as a physician.

When they did get to spend time together, they couldn't keep their hands from one another.

It was a difficult time for David, a pivotal time. He had sent half his book and an outline to a leading publishing house, and in late July he was summoned to New York, to which he traveled by train on the hottest day of the summer.

He came back with a contract. The advance money wouldn't change his life – twenty thousand dollars, average support for a literary first novel that wasn't about a murder and a sexy detective. But it was a victory, with the added triumph that he had allowed his editor to dine him but not to wine him.

R.J. took him for a swank celebratory dinner at the Deerfield Inn and then accompanied him to an AA meeting in Greenfield. He had confessed to her at dinner that he was terrified about his ability to finish the book. She took note at the AA meeting that he didn't have the confidence to identify himself as a writer.

'I'm David Markus,' he said. 'I'm an alcoholic, and I sell real estate in Woodfield.'

When they returned to his house at the end of the evening they sat in the dark on the battered couch on the front porch, next to the jars of honey. They talked quietly and enjoyed the breeze that every now and again teased out of the woods and across his pasture.

While they were sitting there, a car came down the road and turned into the driveway, its yellow beams casting vine-shadows on David's face from the old wisteria that shaded the porch.

'It's Sarah,' he said. 'She went to the movies with Bobby Henderson.'

As the car approached the house, they heard the sound of singing. Sarah and the Henderson boy were harmonizing to 'Clementine', their voices thin and untrue. Obviously they were having a very good time.

David gave a snort of laughter.

'Shhh,' R.J. said quietly. The car came to a halt in front of the house, separated from the porch by only a dozen feet of air and the thick growth of wisteria.

Sarah started the next song, 'The Deacon Went Down to the Cellar to Pray', and the boy joined in. At the end of the song there was silence. Bobby Henderson must be kissing Sarah, R.J. thought. We should have let them know we're here, she realized, but already it was too late. She and David sat in the dark and held hands like an old married couple and grinned at one another in the dark.

Then Bobby began a song.

'The Ring-dang-doo, it's short and fat— '

'Oh, Bobby, you're such a pig,' Sarah said, but she giggled, and when he continued the song, she sang harmony.

'It's covered with hair . . .'
  (*'Lots of hair . . .'*)
'Like a pussy cat . . .'
  (*'A puss-y cat . . .'*)

David let go of R.J.'s hand.

'Yes, covered with hair . . .'
  (*'Curly black hair . . .'*)
'And split in two . . .'
  (*'Split right in two . . .'*)
'That's what they call . . .'
  (*''At's whatta-they-call . . .'*)
'Sarah's Ring-dang-doo!'
  (*'My Ring-dang-doo-oo-oo-oo-oo-oo!'*)

'Sarah,' David said loudly.

'Oh, God,' Sarah said.

'Get into the house.'

There was a spate of intense whispering, then a giggle. The car door opened and closed. Sarah ran up the front steps and past them without speaking, as Bobby Henderson's car shot away, made a tight turn in the barnyard, and went past the house again and down the road.

'Come on, I'll take you home. Then I'll deal with her.'

139

'David. Calm down. She hasn't committed a murder.'

'Where is her self-respect?'

'So . . . it's a mistake in judgement. A bit of teenage foolishness.'

'Foolishness? I should say so!'

'Listen here, David. Didn't you sing dirty songs when you were her age?'

'Yeah. I used to sing them with the guys. I never sang them with a respectable girl, I'll tell you that.'

'How sad for you,' R.J. said, and went down the steps and out to his car.

He called her the next day to invite her to dinner, but she was very busy; it was the start of a five-day marathon for her, nights as well as days. Her father had been right, her sleep was too often interrupted. The problem was that the medical center in Greenfield to which she sent her patients, half an hour away by fast ambulance during emergencies, wasn't a teaching hospital. In Boston, on the less frequent occasions when she was awakened at night, she had almost always been given a house physician's assessment of the problem and could return to bed after telling the resident what to do with the patient. Here, there were no house physicians. When she received a call, it was from a nurse, often in the middle of the night. The nursing staff was very good, but R.J. came to know the twisting Mohawk Trail too well as it appeared by day, at night, and in the dying dark of early morning.

She envied doctors in the European countries where patients were sent to the hospital along with their charts, and a staff of hospital doctors assumed full responsibility for their care. But she was practicing in Woodfield and not in Europe, so she made frequent trips to the hospital.

She had terrible premonitions about driving the Mohawk Trail when winter came and the road was slick, and that week during the most wearying of those exhausting trips she reminded herself that she had wanted to practice in the country.

It was the end of the week before she had time to accept David's invitation to dinner, but when she got to his house, he wasn't there.

'He had to take clients up to Potter's Hill to show them the Weiland place. A couple from New Jersey,' Sarah said. She was wearing a tee-shirt and shorts that lengthened her long, tanned legs. 'I'm cooking tonight, veal stew. Want some lemonade?'

'Sure.'

Sarah poured. 'You can have it on the porch, or you can keep me company in the kitchen.'

'Oh, the kitchen, by all means.' R.J. sat at the table and sipped while Sarah took veal chunks from the refrigerator, washed them under the tap, patted them dry with paper towels, and dropped them into a plastic bag with flour and seasonings. After she had shaken the bag and coated the veal, she poured a small amount of canola oil into a pan and put in the meat. 'Now, into the oven for half an hour at 400 degrees.'

'You look and sound like a great cook.'

The girl shrugged and smiled. 'Well. My father's daughter.'

'Yes. He's a terrific cook, isn't he?' R.J. paused. 'Is he still angry?'

'No. Dad gets mad, but he gets over it fast.' She took down a trug basket from a hook over the kitchen counter. 'Now, while the veal browns, we have to go outside and get the vegetables for the stew.'

In the garden, they knelt on opposite sides of the row of Blue Lake bush beans and picked together.

'My father is very funny about me. He would like to wrap me in cellophane and not unwrap me until I'm an old married lady.'

R.J. smiled. 'My father was the same way. I think most

parents would like to do that. They want so desperately to protect their kids from pain.'

'Well, they can't.'

'No, that's right, Sarah. They can't.'

'That's enough green beans. I'll get a parsnip. You pull about ten carrots, okay?'

The earth around the carrots had been hoed a lot and they came up easily, deep orange, short and broad-shouldered. 'Have you been going out with Bobby a long time?'

'About a year. My father would like me to meet Jewish kids, that's why we belong to the temple in Greenfield. But Greenfield is too far away for me to have really close friends there. Besides, he's spent my whole life telling me that people shouldn't be judged by their race or religion. Does all that change when you start dating?' She glowered. 'I noticed *your* religion didn't come into the picture when he started going with you.'

R.J. nodded, bemused.

'Bobby Henderson is really nice, and he's been very good for me. I didn't have many friends at school until I started going with him. He's a football player, and he'll be co-captain next fall. He's very popular so that's made *me* very popular, you know?'

R.J. nodded, troubled. She knew. 'One thing, though, Sarah. The other night, your father was right. You committed no crime, but your singing that song didn't show a lot of self-respect. Songs like that . . . they're like pornography. If you encourage men to thnk of women as sex objects, that's how they'll think about you, as meat.'

Sarah looked at R.J., no doubt reassessing her. Her face was very serious. 'Bobby doesn't think of me that way. I'm lucky he's my boyfriend. It isn't as if I'm this raving beauty.'

Now it was R.J.'s turn to frown. 'You're kidding, right?'

'About what?'

'You're kidding me or you're kidding yourself. You are a knockout.'

Sarah brushed the dirt from a turnip, added it to the basket and stood. 'Don't I wish.'

'Your father showed me a bunch of pictures, in those albums he keeps in the parlor. A number of them were of your mother. She was very beautiful and you look exactly like her.'

Deep within Sarah's eyes there was a subtle warming. 'People have told me I look like her.'

'Yes, you look very much like her. Two beautiful women.'

Sarah took a step toward her. 'Do me a favor, R.J.?'

'Of course, anything I can.'

'Tell me what I can do about these,' she said, covering her chin, on which there were two pimples. 'I don't understand why I have them. I scrub my face, and I eat the right things. I'm perfectly healthy. I never need a doctor. I've never even gone to the dentist for a filling. And I use face cream until my fingers fall off, but . . .'

'Stop using face cream. Go back to soap and water, and use a facecloth *gently*, because it's easy to irritate your skin. I'll give you a salve.'

'Will it work?'

'I think it will. Give it a try.' She hesitated. 'Sarah, sometimes there are things it's easier to talk to a woman about than a man, even your father. If you ever have any questions, or just want to gab about something . . .'

'Thank you. I heard what you said to my father the other night, sticking up for me. I appreciate it.' She came to R.J. and gave her a hug.

R.J.'s knees felt weak; she wanted to hug Sarah back, to stroke the girl's shining black hair. But she contented herself with patting her clumsily on the shoulder with the hand that wasn't holding the carrots.

23

A Gift to be Used

As a rule the hills were about ten degrees cooler than the valley, summer and winter, but that year the third week of August was sodden with heat, and R.J. and David sought the shade of the woods together. At the end of the trail they toughed it through the forest to the river, hard going, and made sweaty love in the pine needles on the riverbank, R.J. worrying about hunters. Then they found a sand-bottom pool and sat naked in the water, washing each other with their hands.

'Heaven,' she said.

'At least, the opposite of hell,' David said thoughtfully.

He told her a story, a legend. 'In Sheol, the fiery underground world to which all sinners go, souls are freed every Friday at sundown by the *malakh ha-mavet*, the Angel of Death. The freed souls spend the entire Sabbath soothing themselves by sitting in a cool stream, just as we're doing now. That's why in the old days some of the ultra-pious Jews wouldn't drink water all during the Sabbath. They didn't want to lower the healing waters occupied by the souls furloughed from Sheol.'

She was intrigued by the legend but was having troubling

thoughts about him. 'I can't figure you out. How much are you poking fun at piety, and how much is piety part of the real David Markus? Who are you to talk about angels, anyway? You don't even believe in God.'

He appeared to be mildly shocked. 'Who says? It's just . . . I'm not *certain* God exists, and if so, what he is – or she, or it.' He grinned at her. 'I believe in a whole order of higher power. Angels. Djinn. Kitchen ghosts. I believe in sacred spirits that serve prayer wheels, and in leprechauns and elves.' He held up his hand. 'Listen.'

What she heard was the complaint of the water, confident birdsong, the wind through megamultitudes of leaves, the velvet bee-drone of a truck on a far-off road.

'I feel the spirits every time I come into the woods.'

'I'm being serious, David.'

'So am I, damn it.'

She saw he was capable of spontaneous euphoria, of attaining a kind of high without swallowing alcohol. Or *was* it without swallowing alcohol? Was he safe from alcohol nowadays?

How healed was the weakness that lurked within his strengths? The errant breeze continued to move the leaves above them, and his forest imps nagged at her, pinched at the most sensitive parts of her psyche, whispered that although she was becoming more and more involved with this man, there was much she didn't know about David Markus.

R.J. had called a county social worker and reported that Eva Goodhue and Helen Phillips needed help. But the county authorities moved slowly, and before the call brought results, a boy came to her office one afternoon and reported that the doctor was needed at once in the apartment over the hardware store.

This time the door to Eva Goodhue's apartment opened for her and she absorbed the full blast of air so foul she had to fight against gagging. Cats were underfoot, rubbing against her legs as she avoided their excrement. Garbage overflowed a plastic container, and dishes bearing rot were piled in the sink. R.J. had supposed the summons was because Miss Goodhue was in trouble, but the ninety-two-year-old woman, dressed and spry, was waiting for her.

'It's Helen, feeling very poorly.'

Helen Phillips was in bed. Her heart didn't sound alarming when R.J. listened with the stethoscope. She needed a good scrubbing, and there were bed sores on her back and buttocks. She had indigestion, belched, broke wind, and was unresponsive to questions. Eva Goodhue answered every question for her.

'Why are you in bed, Helen?'

'She enjoys it, it's cozy. She likes to lie there and watch the television.'

From the condition of the sheets, it was obvious Helen took all her meals in bed. R.J. was prepared to prescribe a new and stern regimen: out of bed early in the morning, regular baths, meals eaten at the table, and pharmaceutical samples for the indigestion. But when she took Helen's hands in her own, she was afflicted with a flow of intelligence that filled her with sadness and terror. She was shaken. It had been some time since she had experienced the strange and terrible understanding, the certain knowledge for which there was no explanation.

She reached for the telephone and dialed the town ambulance, willing the dispatcher to pick up the receiver. 'Joe, it's Roberta Cole. I have an emergency and I need an ambulance fast. Eva Goodhue's, just down the street, over the hardware store.'

They were there in under four minutes, a remarkable response time. Nevertheless, Helen Phillips's heart stopped when the ambulance was halfway to the hospital. Despite frantic resuscitation efforts by the ambulance crew, she was dead on arrival.

*   *   *

R.J. hadn't received the message of impending death for several years. Now, for the first time, she acknowledged to herself that she possessed the Gift. She remembered what her father had told her about it.

She discovered she was ready to believe.

Perhaps, she told herself, she could learn to use it to fight the dark angel whom David called the *malakh ha-mavet*.

She made certain she carried a hypodermic needle and a supply of streptokinase in her medical bag, and she contrived opportunities to hold her patients' hands every time she saw them.

Only three weeks later, making a house call to Frank Olchowski, a math teacher at the high school who was in bed with the flu, she took the hands of Stella, his wife, and felt the signals she dreaded to detect.

She took a deep breath and forced herself to think calmly.

She had no idea what form the impending disaster would take, but the chances were highest that it would come either as a heart attack or a cerebrovascular accident.

The woman was fifty-three years old, about thirty pounds overweight, and distraught and puzzled. 'It's *Frank* who is sick, Dr Cole! Why have you called the ambulance, and why must *I* go to the hospital?'

'You must trust me, Mrs Olchowski.'

Stella Olchowski went into the ambulance, staring at her doctor strangely.

R.J. rode in the ambulance with her. She fixed the mask over Stella's face and adjusted the flowmeter on the tank to deliver 100 percent oxygen. The driver was Timothy Dalton, a farm worker. 'Make tracks. No noise,' she told him. He used the ambulance's flashers as the ambulance careened away, but he didn't sound the siren; R.J. didn't want Mrs Olchowski any more perturbed than she already was.

Steve Ripley was troubled, too, after he took a set of the patient's vital signs. The medical technician shot a puzzled glance at R.J. 'What's wrong with her, Dr Cole?' he said, reaching for the radiophone.

'Don't call the hospital yet.'

'If I bring somebody in with no symptoms and without submitting to the emergency room's medical control, I'm going to be in deep trouble.'

She looked at him. 'Go with me on this one, Steve.'

Reluctantly, he put the phone back on the hook. He watched Stella Olchowski and R.J. with increasing unhappiness as the ambulance made its way down Route 2.

They were two-thirds of the way to the medical center when Mrs Olchowski winced and clapped her hand to her chest. She groaned and looked wide-eyed at R.J.

'Take another set of vitals, fast.'

'Jesus, she's in severe arrhythmia.'

'Now you can call medical control. Tell them she's having a heart attack, that Dr Cole is with you. Request permission for me to administer streptokinase.' Even as she spoke, the hypodermic needle was entering flesh, her fingers depressing the plunger.

The cells of the heart muscle were perfused with oxygen, and by the time permission was given by medical control, the drug was beginning its work. When Mrs Olchowski was offloaded at the hospital by the emergency room staff, damage to her heart had been minimized.

For the first time, R.J. had learned that the strange message she sometimes received from patients could save their lives.

The Olchowskis told all their friends about their internist with the wonderful medical wisdom. 'She just looked at me, and that woman knew what was going to happen. She is some doctor!' Stella said. The ambulance crew agreed, and added their own embellishments to the story. R.J. began to enjoy the smiles that were directed at her as she went on her house calls.

'This town likes having a doctor again,' Peg told her. 'And they're proud to think they have a damn good one.'

It embarrassed R.J., but the message went out through the hills and valleys. Toby Smith came back from the state Democratic convention in Springfield and told her that a delegate from Charlemont had remarked that he had heard the lady doctor Toby worked for in Woodfield was a really warm, friendly sort of person. Always holding peoples' hands.

October brought an end to pesky insects and triggered incredible bursts of colors in the trees, a joyous streaking of the hills. The natives told her it was just a run-of-the-mill autumn, but she didn't believe it. On an Indian summer day she and David went fishing on the Catamount, and he caught three decent trout and she caught two, gills brightly colored for mating. When they cleaned the trout they saw that two of them were females full of eggs. David reserved the trout eggs to fry with hen's eggs, but R.J. avoided them, disliking all roes.

Sitting with him on the riverbank, she found herself telling him details about the experiences she would never dare tell a medical colleague.

David didn't smile. He listened with great interest – even, she realized, with envy.

'It's written in the *Mishnah* . . . Do you know what the *Mishnah* is?'

'Some kind of Hebrew holy book?'

'It's the basic book of Jewish law and thought, compiled 1,800 years ago. It records that there lived a rabbi named Hanina ben Dosa, who could work miracles. He prayed over the sick, and he used to say, "This one will live," or "This one will die," and it always turned out as he said. And they asked him, "How knowest thou?" And he said to them. "If my prayer is fluent in my mouth, I know he is accepted. And if not, I know he is rejected."'

She was annoyed. 'I don't pray over them.'

'I know. Your ancestors named it well. It's a gift.'

'But . . . *what is it?*'

He shrugged. 'A religious savant would say of both you and Rabbi Hanina that it's a message you alone are privileged to hear.'

'Why me? Why my family? And a message from whom? Certainly not from your angel of death.'

'I think your father probably was right when he guessed that it's a genetic gift, a combination of mental and biological sensors that allows you additional information. A kind of sixth sense.'

He held out both his hands to her.

'No. Go away,' she said when she understood.

But he waited with an awful patience until she took his hands in hers.

She felt only the warmth and strength of his grip, and a weakness of relief, and anger at him.

'You're going to live forever.'

'I will if you will,' he said.

He talked as if they were soul mates. She considered the fact that he already had had a strong love, a wife he had cherished and now mourned. She had had Charlie Harris, an early lover who had died while their union was still perfect and untested, and then a bad marriage to a selfish and immature man. She continued to grip David's hands, unwilling to let go.

24
New Friends

On a busy afternoon during office hours R.J. received a call from a woman named Penny Coleridge. 'I told her you were with a patient and would return the call,' Toby said. 'She's a midwife. She said she would like to get to know you.'

R.J. returned the call as soon as she was able. Penny Coleridge had a pleasant telephone voice, but it was impossible to guess her age over the phone. She said she had been practicing midwifery in the hills for four years. There were two other midwives – Susan Millet and June Todman – practicing with her. R.J. invited them to her house for supper on Thursday, her free afternoon, and after consulting with her colleagues, Penny Coleridge said all three would come.

She proved to be an affable, stocky brunette, perhaps in her late thirties. Susan Millet and June Todman were about ten years older. Susan was greying, but she and June were blondes who looked enough alike to be mistaken for sisters, although they had met only a few years earlier. June had received her training in the midwifery program at Yale-New Haven. Penny and Susan were nurse-midwives; Penny had trained at the University of Minnesota, and Susan had trained in Urbana, Illinois.

The three made it clear that they were happy to have a doctor in Woodfield. They told R.J. that some pregnant women in the hilltowns preferred an obstetrician or a family practitioner to deliver their babies and had to travel a good distance away to find one. Other patients preferred the less invasive techniques practiced by midwives. 'In places where all the docs are men, some patients have come to us because they wanted a woman to deliver their baby,' Susan said. She smiled at R.J. 'Now that you're here, they have a wider choice.'

Some years before, obstetricians in urban locations had worked to hobble midwives politically because they saw them as economic competitors. 'But out here in the hill country, doctors don't give us trouble,' Penny said. 'There's more than enough work to go around, and they're happy we're here, sharing the burden. By law, we have to be salaried workers, employed by a clinic or a physician. And although midwives would be perfectly capable of doing things like vacuum extractions and forceps births, we have to have a boarded obstetrician on call to do those things, just as you do.'

'Have you made connection with an ob-gyn to act as your backup?' June asked R.J.

'No. I would value your advice in that regard.'

'We've been working under a good young obstetrician, Grant Hardy,' Susan said. 'He's smart, he has an open mind, and he's idealistic.' She made a face. 'He's too idealistic, I guess. He's taken a job with the surgeon general in Washington.'

'Have you made a new arrangement with another ob-gyn, then?'

'Daniel Noyes has agreed to take us on. The trouble is, he's retiring in a year, and we'll have to start again with somebody new. Still,' Penny said thoughtfully, 'he might be just the ob-gyn to be *your* backup as well as ours. He's grouchy and crusty on the outside, but he's really an old dear. He's far and away the best obstetrician in the area, and an arrangement with him would let you take your time looking for another ob-gyn before he retires.'

R.J. nodded. 'That sounds sensible to me. I'll try to persuade him to work with me.'

The midwives were discernibly pleased when they learned that R.J. had had advanced training in obstetrics and gynecology and had worked in a clinic dealing with female hormonal problems. It was a relief to them that she was available in the event that a medical problem arose with one of their patients, and they had several women they wanted her to examine.

R.J. liked them as people and as professionals, and their presence made her feel more secure.

She dropped in often to see Eva Goodhue, sometimes bringing a package of ice cream or some fruit. Eva was quiet and introspective; for a few days R.J. suspected that was her way of grieving for her niece, but she had come to conclude that those qualities were aspects of Eva's personality.

The apartment had been thoroughly cleaned by the pastoral committee of the First Congregational Church, and Meals on Wheels, a non-profit agency that served the elderly, delivered a hot dinner every day. R.J. met with the Franklin County social worker, Marjorie Lassiter, and with John Richardson, minister of the church in Woodfield, to talk about Miss Goodhue's other needs. The social worker began with a blunt report of her financial status.

'She's broke.'

Twenty-nine years before, Eva Goodhue's only living sibling, an unmarried brother named Norm, had died of pneumonia. His death had left Eva sole owner of the family farm on which she had always lived. She had promptly sold it for just under $41,000 and rented the apartment on Main Street, in the village. A few years later her niece, Helen Goodhue Phillips, daughter of Harold Goodhue, Eva's other dead brother, had divorced her abusive husband and had come to live with her aunt.

'They were supported by Eva's money in the bank and by a small monthly welfare check,' Marjorie Lassiter said. 'They thought they were on easy street, even sometimes indulging in a weakness for mail order purchases. They always spent more than the capital earned annually, and the dwindling bank account has finally run out.' She sighed. 'It's not uncommon, believe me, for someone to outlive her money.'

'Thank God she still has the welfare check,' John Richardson said.

'That won't support her,' the social worker said. 'Eva's monthly rent alone is four hundred and ten dollars. She has to buy groceries. She's on Medicare, but she has to buy drugs. She has no supplemental medical insurance.'

'I'll look out for her medical care as long as she remains here in town,' R.J. said quietly.

Ms Lassiter gave her a rueful smile. 'But that still leaves fuel oil. The electric bill. The occasional purchase of a necessary article of clothing.'

'The Sumner Fund,' Richardson said. 'The town of Woodfield has a sum of money left it in trust, the interest to be utilized to help needy citizens. The expenditures are made quietly at the discretion of the three selectpersons, and are kept private by them. I'll talk to Janet Cantwell,' the minister added.

A few days later R.J. met Richardson in front of the library and he told her it was all set with the Board of Selectmen. Miss Goodhue would receive a monthly stipend from the Sumner Fund, enough to cover her deficit.

It was later that day, as R.J. finished updating the patient charts, that she realized a bright truth: as long as she lived in the kind of town that was willing to help an indigent old woman, she was content not to have shiny new plumbing in the town hall toilets.

* * *

'I want to stay in my own home,' Eva Goodhue said.

'And you will,' R.J. told her.

At Eva's suggestion, R.J. brewed a pot of blackcurrant tea, Eva's favorite. They sat at the kitchen table and talked about the physical examination R.J. had just completed. 'You're in remarkably good condition for somebody who is marching toward her ninety-third birthday. Obviously you have very good genes. Do you come from long-lived parents?'

'No, my parents died fairly young. My mother had a ruptured appendix when I was only five. My father might have lived to be old, but he was killed in a farm accident. A load of logs let go and he was crushed. That was when I was nine years old.'

'So who raised you?'

'My brother Norm. I had two brothers. Norm was thirteen years older than I, and Harold was four years younger than Norm. They didn't get along at all. Not at all. Fought and fought, and Harold up and ran away from the farm – just left it for Norman to worry about. He joined the Coast Guard and never did get home again, never communicated with Norm, although now and again I would get a postcard, and sometimes there was a letter for me and a small amount of money at Christmas.' She sipped her tea. 'Harold died of tuberculosis in the Naval Hospital in Maryland, about ten years before Norm passed away.'

'You know what boggles my mind?'

Eva smiled at the expression. 'What?'

'When you were born, Victoria was England's queen. Wilhelm II was the last emperor of Germany. Teddy Roosevelt was about to become president of the United States. And Woodfield – what changes you must have seen as they took place in Woodfield.'

'Not so many changes as you might expect,' Eva said. 'The automobile, certainly. Now all the main roads are tarred. And electricity is everywhere. I remember when street lamps came to Main Street. I was fourteen years old. I walked six miles

155

from the farm and back, after chores, so I could see the lights turned on. It was another ten or twenty years before the electric wires reached all the houses of the town. We didn't even have milking machines until I was forty-seven. *There* was a blessed change!'

She said little about Helen's dying. R.J. raised the subject, thinking it would be healthy for her to talk about it, but Eva only stared out of tired eyes as deep and fathomless as lakes.

'She was a dear soul, my brother Harold's only child. Of course I shall miss her. I miss them all, or at least most.

'I've lived longer than everybody I once knew,' she said.

25
Settling In

On a mild day in mid-October, R.J. was leaving the hospital in Greenfield when she passed Susan Millet standing in the parking lot talking with a ruddy-faced, balding man. He was large and tall but slightly crooked, as if his spine were made of bent tin, and his left shoulder was lower than his right. Chronic scoliosis, her mind registered.

'R.J., hi! Say, here's somebody I want you to meet. Dr Daniel Noyes, this is Dr Roberta Cole.'

They shook hands. 'So you're Dr Cole. Seems to me, all I've heard lately from the three midwives is your name. You're some kind of expert on hormones, I'm told.'

'Hardly an expert.' She told him about having worked in the clinic at Lemuel Grace Hospital, and he nodded.

'Don't contradict. That makes you more of an expert on hormones than we've had around here up to now.'

'I'm going to deliver babies, part of a full family practise. I need the cooperation of an ob-gyn who is on staff here.'

'You do, eh?' he said coolly.

'Yes.' They regarded one another.

'Well, are you asking me to work with you?'

He was crusty and cranky, she thought, just as the midwives

had described him. 'Yes, that's the idea. I realize you don't know much about me. Do you happen to be free for lunch?'

'No need to waste money buying me lunch. They've told me all about you. Did they tell you I was calling it a career in twelve and a half months?'

'Yes, they did.'

'Well, if you still want me to consult with you for that brief a time, it's fine with me.'

'That's great. I mean, I do.'

Now he was smiling. 'That's settled, then. So, how's about I take you to lunch at the world's best old-fashioned diner, and tell you some war stories about practicing medicine in western Massachusetts?'

He *was* an old dear, she could see that. 'I'd like that very much.'

'I suppose you want to come too,' he said dourly to Susan, who was wearing a satisfied expression.

'No, I have an appointment, but you two go ahead,' Susan said. She was laughing to herself as she walked to her car.

R.J. was busy, working long hours, and apt to be tired and unambitious when she had a little time off. The trail through the woods didn't progress far beyond the beaver ponds. When she wanted to go to the river, she still had to contend with a lot of rough hiking through heavy growth.

Late in the fall she and David had to stay out of the woods, which were full of hunters carrying loaded weapons, their trigger fingers itchy. She winced to see, again and again, whitetailed deer dead and broken, slung over the bumpers of cars and trucks.

A lot of people in the hills hunted. Toby and Jan Smith invited R.J. and David to dinner and served an impressive royal crown roast of venison.

'Got a young buck, a four-pointer, right up on the ridge above the house,' Jan said. 'I always go out on opening day with my Uncle Carter Smith, been hunting with him ever since I was a boy.'

Whenever he and his uncle got a deer they followed a Smith family tradition, he told them. They cut out the deer's heart while they were still in the woods, sliced it, and ate it raw. He was pleased to share that detail with them and he told the story well, giving them a sense of the love and kinship between the old man and the young man.

R.J. suppressed her distaste. She couldn't help imagining that parasitic diseases may have been invited into their bodies with the deer's heart, but she cast all such thoughts from her mind. She had to admit the venison made a splendid roast, and she ate her fill and sang its praises.

She had inserted herself into a culture that was remarkably unfamiliar to her. At times she had to swallow hard as she adjusted to traditions that were foreign to her experience.

A number of families had been in the town for many generations – Jan Smith's ancestors had walked all the way to Woodfield from Cape Cod in the final months of the seventeenth century, driving their cows in front of them – and they had intermarried, so everyone seemed to be everyone else's cousin. Some of those who came from old families in Woodfield were welcoming to newcomers, while others were not. R.J. observed that individuals who were more or less happy with themselves, secure in their own souls, usually opened themselves to new friendships. It was those whose ancestry and native status were their only hopes for distinction who tended to be critical and cold toward 'new people'.

Most of the town's residents were happy about the presence of the doctor. Still, the environment was largely unfamiliar to R.J., and often she got the feeling that she was a pioneer on a new frontier. A country practise was like doing high acrobatic work without a net. At the Lemuel Grace Hospital in Boston, labs and diagnostic technology had been at her fingertips.

Here, she was alone. High tech science was available, but she and her patients had to make an effort to reach it.

She didn't send patients away from Woodfield unless she had to, preferring to depend on her own skills and capability. But there were times when she contemplated a patient and a silent warning bell rang starkly in her head, and she realized that she needed help; then she referred the patient to Greenfield or Northampton or Pittsfield, or even to the greater specialization and technology in Boston or New Haven or Hanover, New Hampshire.

She was still feeling her way but she had come to know many of her patients intimately, to see into the corners of their lives that affected their health, in a way that was possible to a small-town doctor.

One night at 2 a.m. she was awakened by a call from Stacia Hinton, Greg Hinton's wife.

'Dr Cole, our daughter Mary and our two grandchildren are visiting us from New York. The littlest one, Kathy, she's two years old. She's an asthmatic, and now she's come down with a bad, bad cold. She's having a terrible time trying to breathe. She's all red in the face, and we're frightened. We don't know what to do.'

'Hold her over a steaming kettle and make a little tent around her with a towel. Just keep her there, and I'll come right over, Mrs Hinton.'

R.J. made certain a tracheotomy kit was in her bag, but when she got to the Hinton farm she saw it wouldn't be necessary for her to do a trache. The steam had already done some good. The child had a barking cough, but she was getting air into her lungs, and the redness was gone from her face. R.J. would have liked an X-ray to tell her whether it was epiglottitis, but a careful examination indicated to her that the epiglottis wasn't involved. There was a mucosal inflammation of the lower larynx and trachea. Kathy cried all through the examination, and when it was over R.J. remembered something she had seen her father do with pediatric patients.

'Would you like me to give you a tricycle?'

Kathy nodded, sniffling. R.J. wiped the tears from her cheeks, then she took a clean wooden tongue depresser and drew a tricycle on it with her ball-point pen. The little girl took it and looked at her with interest.

'Want one with a clown on it?'

Kathy nodded again, and soon she had a clown. 'Big Bird.'

'Oh-oh,' R.J. said. Her television memory was weak, but she managed to draw an ostrich with a hat, and the child smiled.

'Will she have to go to the hospital?' Stacia Hinton asked.

'I don't think so,' R.J. said. She left some pharmaceutical samples and two prescriptions to be filled in the morning, when the drug store opened in Shelburne Falls.

'You keep her breathing that steam. If she has any more trouble, call me right away,' she said. Then she walked woodenly to her car, drove sleepily home, and fell into her bed.

The next afternoon Greg Hinton came to the office and told Toby he had to speak to the doctor personally. He sat and read a magazine until R.J. was able to see him.

'What do I owe you for last night?'

When she told him, he nodded and wrote out a check. She saw that it covered everything he owed her for his past visits.

'I didn't see you last night,' she said.

He nodded again. 'I thought I'd better stay out of the way. I've been a stubborn fool. I guess I didn't feel comfortable, getting you to my house in the middle of the night after the way I've talked to you.'

She smiled. 'Don't worry about that, Mr Hinton. How's Kathy doing today?'

'Much better. And we thank you for that. No hard feelings?'

'No hard feelings,' she said and shook the hand he held out to her.

With his 175-cow herd, Greg Hinton could more than afford to pay for a doctor's services, but R.J. also took care of Bonnie and Paul Roche, a young couple with two small children, who were struggling to survive with an 18-cow dairy farm.

'Every month,' Bonnie Roche told her, 'I have a veterinarian come in to give our cows their tests and shots, but we can't afford medical insurance for ourselves. Until you came, my cows got better medical care than my kids.'

The Roches weren't an isolated case in America. In November, R.J. went to the old wooden town hall and cast a ballot for Bill Clinton as president of the United States. Clinton had promised her patients that he would provide medical insurance to everyone who didn't have it. Dr Roberta Cole intended to hold him to that promise, and she cast her vote as if it were a lance she was leveling at the health care system.

26

Above the Snow Line

'Sarah has had sex.'

R.J. waited a beat, and then she said carefully, 'How do you know that?'

'She told me.'

'David, it's absolutely wonderful that she could talk to you about something so intimate. You must have a remarkably good relationship with her.'

'I am devastated,' he said quietly, and she saw it was so. 'I wanted her to wait until she was ready. It was easier years ago, when women were supposed to be virgins until their wedding night.'

'She's seventeen years old, David. Some would say she's well behind the curve. I've treated eleven-year-old children who have had sex. Sarah has a woman's body, a woman's hormones. It's true some women wait for sex until they marry, but they've become a rare species. Even in the years when unmarried women were supposed to be virginal, a whole lot of them weren't.'

He nodded. He had been quiet and morose all evening, but now he began to speak tenderly of his daughter. He said he and Natalie had talked to Sarah about sex before and after she entered puberty, and that he realised he was fortunate she was still willing to talk to him openly.

'Sarah didn't say who her partner was, but since she's dating only Bob Henderson, it's safe to make a supposition. She said it was in the nature of an experiment, that she and the boy are very good friends, and they thought it was time they both got it over with.'

'Would you like me to have a talk with her about birth control, things like that?' R.J. hoped very much he would say yes, but he looked alarmed.

'No, I don't think it's necessary. I don't want her to know I've been talking with you about her.'

'Then I think you should talk with her about those things.'

'Yes, I will.' He looked more cheerful. 'Anyway, she told me the experiment is over. They value their friendship too much to spoil it, and they've decided to go back to just being best buddies.'

R.J. nodded doubtfully. She didn't tell him she had observed that once young people had sex, they almost invariably repeated the experience again and again.

She had Thanksgiving dinner at the Markus cabin. David had roasted the turkey and made re-stuffed baked potatoes, and Sarah had candied a panful of yams with maple syrup and made three-berry apple sauce from their own berries and fruit. R.J. brought pumpkin pies and apple pies with crusts she bought frozen at the supermarket and fillings she had prepared from scratch at three o'clock in the morning.

It was a quiet, very satisfying Thanksgiving dinner. R.J. was glad that neither David nor Sarah had invited anyone else. They ate the good dinner, drank mulled cider, and popped corn over the open fire. To complete her picture of what Thanksgiving would be if it were perfect, the overcast sky turned almost black at dusk and produced fat white flakes.

'Surely it's too early for snow!'

'Not up here,' David said.

By the time she went home, several inches of snow had accumulated on the road. The windshield wipers kept the glass free, and the defroster worked, but she drove slowly and carefully because she hadn't had the snow tires put on the car.

During all her winters in Boston, R.J. had loved the brief, mystical time when things were quiet and white during and immediately after a snowfall, but almost at once plows and trucks and cars and buses would begin to roar and snort, and the white world quickly became a dirty, dreary mess.

Here it was different. When she got to the house on Laurel Hill Road she built a fire and then turned off the lights and sat close to the flames in the darkened living room. Through the windows she saw that all around her house an accumulating blue-whiteness had taken over the woods and the fields.

She thought of wild animals hunkered down in their holes in the blanketed ground, in the small marble caves on the ridges, in the hollow trees, and she wished them survival.

She wished the same thing for herself. She had survived the easy first months as physician to Woodfield, the springtime and summer. Now nature in the mountains was showing teeth, and R.J. hoped she would be equal to the challenge.

Once the snow came to the high land it didn't go away. The snow line ended about two-thirds of the way down the long descent local residents called Woodfield Mountain, so that when R.J. drove down into the Pioneer Valley to go to the hospital or to a movie or a restaurant, she found a snowless landscape that for a few moments seemed as foreign as the far side of the moon. It would be the week following New Year's Day before the valley received a snowfall heavy enough to remain on the ground.

She enjoyed leaving the snowlessness and re-entering the white world of the hills. Although dairy farms were dwindling

165

in number, the town was accustomed to an old tradition that said all roads must be kept open so tank trucks could collect the milk, and she had little trouble reaching her patients for house calls.

One night in early December, she had gone to bed early but was awakened at 11:20 by the telephone's ring.

'Dr Cole? This is Letty Gates, over on Pony Road, and I'm hurt.' The woman was crying, breathing raggedly as she spoke.

'Hurt how, Mrs Gates?'

'My arm may be broken. I don't know, my ribs . . . It gives me pain to breathe. He did me bad.'

'He? Your husband?'

'Yes, him. Phil Gates.'

'Is he there?'

'No, he's gone off for more drinking.'

'Pony Road is up on the side of Henry's Mountain, isn't it?'

'Yes.'

'Well, okay. I'll be right along.'

First she telephoned the police chief. Giselle McCourtney, the chief's wife, answered the telephone. 'Why, I'm sorry, Dr Cole, but Mack isn't here. A big twelve-wheeler went off the highway on that icy stretch just past the town dump, and he's been down there since nine o'clock, directing traffic. He should be back any time, I expect.'

R.J. told her why her husband was needed. 'So will you send him up to the Gateses' farm as soon as he's free?'

'I surely will, Dr Cole. I'll try to raise him on the radio.'

She didn't have to place the car in four-wheel drive until she started up Pony Road. After that the rise was steep, but the hard-packed snow made a smoother ride than the dirt road would have offered in the summertime.

Letty Gates had turned on the strong light above their barn

166

door, and R.J. began seeing it through the trees while she was a good distance away. She drove into the barnyard and stopped the Explorer near the back steps. She had just gotten out of the car and was taking her bag from the back seat when the first sharp, loud report made her start, and something kicked up the snow near her booted foot.

At once she made out the figure of a man just inside the barn door, in the darkened interior. The outside light reflected off the snow to gleam dully on the barrel of what she guessed was a deer rifle.

'Get the fuck out of here.' He swayed as he called to her, lifting the rifle.

'Your wife is hurt, Mr Gates. I'm a doctor, Dr Cole, and I'm going into your house to take care of her.' Oh God, she thought, not smart at all. She didn't want to give him ideas, send him back into the house after the woman.

He fired again, and the glass in the right headlamp of her car exploded in a shower of shards.

There was no place where she could hide from him. He had a powerful weapon, and she had none. Whether she tried to duck behind the car or within it, all he had to do was take a few steps, and he could kill her if that was what he wanted to do.

'Be reasonable, Mr Gates. I offer no threat to you. I just want to help your wife.'

There was a third shot, and the glass in the left headlamp of the car disappeared. Then another shot blew away a chunk of the front left tire.

He was making junk of her car.

She was exhausted, sleep-deprived, and so terrified that she was past caution. The accumulated tensions of ripping apart her life and putting it together again in this new place – everything suddenly welled up within her and spilled over.

'Stop it. Stop it. Stop it. Stop it.'

She had lost control, abandoned reason, and she took a step in his direction.

He came to meet her, holding the rifle low but keeping

his finger on the trigger. He was unshaven, dressed in dirty overalls and a manure-stained brown barn jacket and a plaid woolen cap embroidered with *Plaut's Animal Feeds* on the front.

'I didn't have to come here.' She listened to her voice in astonishment. It was modulated and reasonable.

He looked puzzled as he lifted the rifle. At that moment they both heard the car.

For just long enough, he hesitated, and Mack McCourtney sounded the siren loud and low, like the growl of a giant animal. In a moment the car lumbered into the driveway, and McCourtney was there.

'Now don't you be a horse's prick, Philip. Put that gun down, or it will be real bad for you. Either you'll be dead, or you'll be in jail forever with no chance to get drunk at all.' The police chief was quiet and steady, and Gates set the rifle against the wall of the house. McCourtney handcuffed him and put him in the back of the jeep, which was as secure as a cell, reinforced by heavy wire gridwork.

Very carefully, as if she were walking over thin ice, R.J. went inside the house.

Letty Gates had multiple bruises from her husband's fists and what proved to be hairline fractures of the left ulna and of the ninth and tenth ribs on her left side. R.J. called the ambulance just as it returned from transporting the truck driver to the hospital.

Mrs Gates's arm was splinted and placed in a sling and bound to her chest with a wide cravat to support the ribs. By the time she was taken away by the ambulance, Mack McCourtney had gotten the spare tire onto R.J.'s car. The lampless Explorer was blind as a mole, but she followed behind the police jeep as McCourtney slowly drove down the mountain.

When she got home, she managed to get only partially undressed before she sat on the edge of her bed and cried and cried.

*   *   *

The next day she was busy during office hours, but Dennis Stanley, one of McCourtney's part-time special officers, drove the Explorer into Greenfield for her. He got a new spare tire and the Ford dealer replaced the headlights and the wiring for the left lamp. Then Dennis went to the county jail and gave the bills to Phil Gates, explaining that the judge might take it kindly when he considered the possibility of bail if Gates could say he was sorry and had already made restitution. Dennis brought Gates's check back to R.J. with the repaired car and advised her to cash it immediately, which she did.

Things slackened in December, and she welcomed the breathing room. Her father had decided to visit friends in Florida for Christmas, and he asked if he could spend four days beginning December 19 with R.J., to celebrate the holiday early.

The early celebration put Christmas on schedule with Chanukah, and David and Sarah said they would be glad to come to a holiday dinner.

R.J. cut a small tree from her own woods, which pleased her, and made a nice dinner for the four of them.

They exchanged gifts after the meal. She gave David a small painting she had bought of a cabin doorway that reminded her of his house, and a family-size package of M&Ms. For her father she had bought a jug of the Roches' maple syrup and a jar of I'm-In-Love-With-You Honey. For Sarah, she had a collection of Jane Austen's novels. Her father gave her a bottle of French brandy, and David gave her a book of poems by Emily Dickinson. Sarah had wrapped a pair of mittens she had knitted of undyed yarn and a third heartrock for R.J.'s collection. She told R.J. that in a way, her gifts were from Bobby Henderson too. 'The wool came from sheep raised by his mother, and I found the heartrock in their barnyard.'

R.J.'s father was growing older. He was more hesitant than she remembered, a little quieter and somewhat wistful. He had brought his viola da gamba. His hands were so arthritic that it hurt him to play, but he insisted that he wanted to make music. After the presents were exchanged, she sat at the piano, and they played a series of duets that went on and on. It was even better than the perfect Thanksgiving had been; it was the best Christmas R.J. had ever had.

After David and Sarah had gone home, R.J.'s father opened the front door and walked out onto the porch. It was crispy cold, so there was a sheen of ice on the surface of the snow, and the full moon cast a path of light across the meadow as if it were a lake.

'Listen,' her father said.

'To what?'

'To all the calm and bright.'

They did, standing there together, breathing in the cold air for a long minute. The wind was still, and there was a complete absence of sound.

'Is it always this peaceful here?' he asked.

R.J. smiled. 'Most of the time,' she said.

27

The Season of Cold

David came to her place one afternoon when she was away and snowshoed over the cleared path through the woods three times, packing down the deep snow so the two of them could travel the trail on cross-country skis. The trail was too short, too quickly covered by a skier; they agreed they would have to finish it in time to have better skiing the following winter.

The woods became a very different place in the cold season. They saw tracks that told of animals that in the summer would have passed through the woods unnoticed, spoor of deer, mink, coon, wild turkey, bobcat. One set of rabbit tracks ended in a broken place off the trail. When David stirred the snow with a ski pole he uncovered frozen blood and bits of white rabbit fur, where an owl had fed.

Snow was a serious reality of everyday life in the hills. At David's suggestion, R.J. bought a pair of snowshoes and practiced using them until she could make reasonable progress. She kept the snowshoes in the car, 'just in case'. In fact, she didn't have to use them that winter. But early in January there was a storm that even the town's old-timers called a serious blizzard. After a day and a night of steady, heavy snowfall, her telephone intruded just as she was sitting down to breakfast.

It was Bonnie Roche. 'Dr Cole, I have a terrible pain in my side, and I'm so nauseated I had to quit in the middle of milking.'

'Do you have a fever?'

'My temperature's a little over one hundred. But my side. It hurts like hell.'

'Which side?'

'On the right.'

'Low or high?'

'High . . . Oh, I don't know. In the middle, I guess.'

'Have you ever had your appendix removed?'

'No. Oh, God, Dr Cole, I can't go to the hospital, that's out of the question! We couldn't afford it.'

'Let's not assume anything. I'll come out to your place right away.'

'You can only get as far as the highway. Our private road isn't plowed.'

'Sit tight,' R.J. said grimly. 'I'll get there.'

Their private road was a mile and a half long. R.J. called the town ambulance squad, which had a rescue unit that used snowmobiles. They met her at the entrance to the Roche's road with two of the machines, and soon she was seated behind Jan Smith and hugging him, her forehead tucked into his back as they skimmed over the snow-buried dirt track.

When they arrived, it was clear at once that Bonnie's problem was appendicitis. A snowmobile wouldn't ordinarily have been R.J.'s transportation of choice for a patient with a hot appendix, but under the circumstances, it had to serve.

'I can't go to the hospital, Paulie,' Bonnie told her husband. 'I can't. Dammit, you know that.'

'Never you mind about that. You leave that to me,' Paul Roche said. He was tall and rawboned, in his twenties and still looking too young to drink alcohol legally. Every time R.J. had come to their farm, he had been working, and she hadn't ever seen him, out here or in town, when his worried boy's face wasn't creased with an old man's frown.

172

Despite Bonnie's protestations she was helped onto Dennis Stanley's machine, which moved off as slowly as Dennis could manage. Bonnie rode hunched over, guarding the appendix. At the plowed public road the ambulance and the crew were waiting, and they whisked her away, the siren splitting the silence of the town.

'About the money, Dr Cole. There's no insurance,' Paul said.

'Did you clear thirty-six thousand last year from the farm?'

'Clear?' He smiled bitterly. 'You're joking, right?'

'Then you won't be charged by the hospital, under the rules of the Hill-Burton Act. I'll see that the hospital sends you the papers to sign.'

'You mean it?'

'Yes. Only . . . I'm afraid the Hill-Burton Act doesn't cover doctor bills. Don't worry about my bill,' she forced herself to say. 'But doubtless you'll still have to pay a surgeon, an anesthesiologist, a radiologist, and a pathologist.'

It hurt her to see the worry flood back into his eyes.

That evening she told David about the Roches' predicament. 'Hill-Burton was meant to protect indigent and uninsured people from disaster, but it doesn't work because it pays only the hospital bill. The Roches are riding a fragile economic ship. The expenses that aren't covered may be heavy enough to sink them.'

'The hospital raises its charges to the insurance companies to cover what they can't collect from patients like Bonnie,' David said slowly. 'And the insurance companies raise the rates they charge for their insurance to cover their increased cost. So everybody who buys health insurance ends up paying Bonnie's hospital bill.'

R.J. nodded. 'It's a lousy, inadequate system. There are thirty-seven million people in the United States without any

173

form of medical insurance. Every other leading industrial nation in the world – Germany, Italy, France, Japan, Britain, Canada, and all the others – supplies health care to all its citizens, at a fraction of what the world's richest country spends for inadequate health care. It's our national shame.'

David sighed. 'I don't think Paul will make it as a farmer even if they survive this problem. The soil in the hills is thin and rocky. We have some potato fields and a few orchards, and some farmers used to grow tobacco. But the crop that grows best up here is grass. That's why we had a lot of dairy farms once upon a time. But the government doesn't support milk prices any more, and the only milk producers who can make money are the big-business outfits, enormous farms with giant herds, in states like Wisconsin and Iowa.'

It was the subject of his novel. 'Small farms around here have popped like balloons. With fewer farms, the agricultural support system has disappeared. There are only one or two veterinarians left to treat the herds, and agricultural equipment dealers have gone out of business, so if a farmer like Paul needs a part for a tractor or a baler, he has to drive clear into New York State or Vermont to find it. The small farmer is doomed. The only ones left are those with personal wealth or a few like Bonnie and Paul. Hopeless romantics.'

She remembered how her father had characterized her desire to practice rural medicine. 'The last cowboys, searching for the vanished prairie?'

David grinned. 'Something like that.'

'Nothing wrong with romantics.' She determined to do everything in her power to help Bonnie and Paul stay on their farm.

Sarah was off on an overnight field trip to New Haven with the school drama club, seeing a revival of *Death of a Salesman*, and almost shyly, David asked if he could spend the night.

It was a new wrinkle in their relationship; he wasn't

unwelcome, but suddenly he was in her living space in a more serious way, something that took getting accustomed to. They made love, and then he was there in her room, sprawled over more than half of her bed, sleeping as soundly as if he had spent the last thousand nights there.

At 11 o'clock, sleepless, she slipped from the bed and went into the living room and turned on the television for the evening news, keeping the volume low. In a moment she was listening to a United States senator castigating Hillary Clinton as a 'dreamy do-gooder' for vowing to gain passage of a universal health care act. The senator was a millionaire whose every medical problem was taken care of, free of charge, at the Bethesda Naval Hospital. R.J. sat alone before the flickering screen and cursed him in furious whispers until she began to laugh at her own foolishness. Then she clicked him off and returned to bed.

Outside, the wind screamed and moaned, and it was as cold as the senator's heart. It was good to snuggle up to David's warmth, one spoon fitting into another, and presently she slept as soundly as he.

28
Rising Sap

The advent of spring took her by surprise. The fourth week of a dun and cheerless February, while R.J. was still in the dead of winter psychologically, she began to notice people working in the woods by the roadsides as she drove past. They were tapping wooden or metal spikes into maple trees and hanging buckets on them, or running plastic lines like a giant network of intravenous tubing from the treetrunks into large collecting tanks. Early March brought the requisite weather for sugaring – frosty nights, warmer days.

The unpaved roads thawed each morning and were transmuted into canals of glue. R.J. found trouble as soon as she turned the car into the private road on the Roche place, and very soon the Explorer had churned into the gumbo up to its wheel hubs.

When she got out of the car, her booted feet sank as if something were pulling her into the earth. R.J. dragged the wire cable out of the winch in front of the Explorer and slogged down the road with it until more than a hundred feet of line lay in the mud behind her. She chose a huge oak tree that looked as though it were anchored in the earth for all time, encircling it with the cable and then snapping the hook over the line so the tree was captive.

The winch came with a remote control. She stood off to one side and pressed the button, then watched in fascinated delight as, gradually and inexorably, the cable was drawn into the winch and became taut. There was a loud sucking noise as the four tires were pulled from the thick ooze, and the car began to inch forward slowly, slowly. When it had moved about twenty yards toward the oak tree, she stopped the winch and got back in and started the engine. The wheels had purchase in four-wheel drive, and within minutes she had reclaimed the cable and was rolling toward the Roche barnyard.

Bonnie, minus her appendix, was home alone. She still couldn't do heavy labor, and Sam Roche, Paul's fifteen-year-old brother, came each morning before school and every evening after supper and milked the cows. Paul had taken a job as a shipper in the knife factory in Buckland, in order to try to pay the bills. He came home every day after three o'clock and spent what was left of daylight collecting maple sap and boiling it in the sugar house until the wee hours of morning. It was brutal work, collecting and boiling forty gallons of sap to get one gallon of syrup, but people paid well for the syrup, and they needed every dollar.

'I'm scared, Dr Cole,' Bonnie told R.J. 'I'm afraid he'll crack under the strain. Afraid one of us will get sick again. If that happens, goodbye farm.'

R.J. had fears about the same things, but she shook her head. 'We just won't let it happen,' she said.

Certain moments never would leave her.

November 22, 1963. She had been going into Latin class in junior high school when she heard two teachers talking about the fact that John F. Kennedy had been gunned down in Texas.

177

April 4, 1968. She had been bringing books back to the Boston public library when she saw a librarian crying and learned that an assassin's bullet had found Martin Luther King Jr.

June 5, that same year. She had been kissing her date outside the apartment where she lived with her father – she remembered the boy was chubby and played jazz clarinet, but she no longer could recall his name. He had just touched the fabric armor, made up of her thick sweater and her bra, that enclosed her breast. She was trying to figure out how to react to that when his father's car radio reported that Robert Kennedy had been shot and was believed to be dying.

She would add to those moments hearing that John Lennon had been assassinated and that the *Challenger* had exploded.

Now, in Barbara Kingsmith's house, on a rainy morning in mid-March, she had another terrible moment.

Mrs Kingsmith had a serious kidney infection; her fever hadn't impaired her garrulousness, and she was complaining about the colors used by painters on the inside of the town hall when R.J. heard a few words of a bulletin from the television in the den, where Mrs Kingsmith's daughter was watching.

'Excuse me,' she said to Mrs Kingsmith, and went to the den. The television was reporting that in Florida a Right-to-Life activist named Michael F. Griffin had shot and killed Dr David Gunn, a physician who worked at an abortion clinic.

Anti-abortion activists were raising money to buy Griffin the best defense lawyer available.

It made R.J. weak with fear.

When she left the Kingsmiths she went straight to David's house and found him in the office.

He held her, comforted her, listened as she talked about the distorted faces she had passed on so many Thursday mornings in Jamaica Plain. She told him of the eyes filled with hate, and revealed that now she knew what she had always expected on Thursdays: a gun pointed at her, a finger pulling the trigger.

*　　*　　*

She visited Eva more often than was necessary from a physician's perspective. Eva's apartment was just down the street from R.J.'s office, and she had come to admire the old woman and to use her as a means of knowing what the town was like when it was younger.

Usually she brought ice cream, and they sat and ate it and talked. Eva had a clear mind and a good memory. She told R.J. of the Saturday night dances that used to be held on the second floor of the town hall; everybody in town came, bringing their children. And of the days when there was an ice house at Big Pond, and a hundred men at a time swarmed out on the ice and cut it up into blocks. And of the spring morning when a loaded ice wagon and a team of four horses went through the ice and down, down in the black water, and all the horses and a man named Chink Roth were drowned.

Eva became excited when she learned where R.J. lived. 'Why, I lived only a mile or so from there most of my life. That was our farm, that place on the upper road.'

'Where Freda and Hank Krantz live now?'

'Yes! They bought from *us*.' In those days R.J.'s land was owned by a man named Harry Crawford, Eva said. 'He had a wife named Rosalie. He bought your land from us, too, and built your house on it. He had a small mill on the banks of the Catamount, with a millrace to supply power. He took logs from your forest and made and sold all kinds of wooden things: buckets, butter molds, paddles and oars, ox yokes, napkin rings, sometimes furniture. The mill burned down years ago. You should be able to see the foundation on the riverbank, if you look carefully.

'I remember, I was . . . oh, perhaps seven or eight years old, and I used to walk down there all the time and watch them sawing and hammering, building your house. Harry Crawford and two other men. I don't remember who the other two were, but I recollect Mr Crawford made me a little ring out of a two-penny nail.' She took R.J.'s hand and smiled at

179

her warmly. 'This makes me feel you and I are neighbors, don't you know.'

R.J. questioned Eva closely, thinking that the history of the Crawfords might shed some light on the tiny bones found when her pond was dug. But she learned nothing that was any help at all.

A couple of days later she stopped in at the old frame house on Main Street that was the Woodfield Historical Museum, and sifted through the historical society's records, some of them yellowed and musty. The Crawfords had had four children. A son and a daughter, Tyrone Joseph and Linda Rae, had died young and were buried in the main town cemetery. Another daughter, Barbara, had died in adulthood in Ithaca, New York; her married name had been Sewall. A son, Harry Hamilton Crawford Jr, had moved to California many years ago, and his whereabouts were unknown.

Harry and Rosalie Crawford had been members of the First Congregational Church of Woodfield. They had buried two children in the town cemetery; was it likely, R.J. asked herself, that they would have placed another infant into mucky, unconsecrated ground, without a headstone?

It wasn't. Unless, of course, there was something connected to that birth that the Crawfords were overwhelmingly ashamed of.

It remained a puzzlement.

R.J. and Toby Smith had developed into more than employee and employer. They were becoming close friends who could talk in confidence about the things that counted. It made R.J. more vulnerable in her failure to help Toby and Jan achieve a pregnancy.

'You say my endometrial biopsy was fine, and that Jan's sperm is okay. And we've been very good about doing exactly what you've advised us to do.'

'Sometimes we just don't know why there's no pregnancy,'

R.J. told her, feeling somehow guilty that she hadn't been able to help them. 'I think you should go to Boston to see a fertility specialist. Or up to Dartmouth.'

'I don't think I could get Jan to go. He's tired of the whole thing. We both are, damn tired,' Toby said peevishly. 'Let's talk about something else.'

So R.J. spoke frankly to her about David.

But Toby said little in reaction.

'I don't think you like David all that much.'

'That isn't true,' Toby said. 'I think David's just fine. Most people I know like him, but nobody I know has become close to him. He kind of . . . lives within himself, if you know what I mean.'

R.J. did.

'The important question is, do *you* like him?'

'I do, but that's not the important question. The important question is, do I love him?'

Toby lifted her eyebrows. 'So, what's the important answer?'

'I don't know. We're so completely different. He says he's a religious doubter, but he lives in a very spiritual place, a more spiritual place than I'm ever going to be able to share with him. I used to have faith only in antibiotics.' She smiled ruefully. 'Now I don't even have faith in them.'

'So . . . where are you two heading?'

R.J. shrugged. 'I'll have to make up my mind soon, otherwise it won't be fair to him.'

'I can't imagine you ever being unfair to anyone.'

'You'd be surprised,' R.J. said.

David was working toward the finishing chapters of his book. They were forced to see each other less often, but he was coming to the end of a long, hard effort, and she was happy for him.

She spent what little spare time she had by herself. Walking along the river, she found the foundation of Harry Crawford's mill, great blocks of hewn stone. Brush and trees had grown up, hugging and hiding the foundation, and several of the stone blocks had slipped into the river bed. She couldn't wait until David was free so she could show him the mill site.

Next to one of the big stone blocks she found a small heartrock, of a blue stone she couldn't identify. It didn't seem likely to her that it contained magic.

On impulse, she gave Sarah a call. 'Want to go see a movie with me?'

'Uh . . . sure.'

Dumb idea, she told herself severely. But to her pleasure, it worked out well. They drove to Pittsfield, where they had supper in a Thai restaurant and saw a movie.

'We'll do it again,' she said, meaning it. 'Okay?'

'Sure.'

But she became busy, and three or four weeks went by. Several times she saw Sarah on Main Street, and Sarah smiled to see her. It was becoming easier and more pleasant to run into her.

One Saturday afternoon Sarah surprised her by riding Chaim down her driveway and tying his reins to a rail of the porch.

'Hey. How nice. You want tea?'

'Hi. Yeah, please.'

R.J. had just finished baking scones from a recipe given to her by Eva Goodhue, and she served them.

'Maybe it's missing an ingredient. What do you think?' she said doubtfully.

Sarah hefted one. 'Could be lighter . . . Can lots of things cause you to miss a period?' she said, and R.J. forgot her baking problems.

'Well, yes. Lots of things. Is it the first time a period hasn't appeared on schedule? And is it only one period that's been missed?'

'. . . Several periods.'

'I see,' R.J. said cheerfully, in her most controlled friendly-doctor voice. 'Are there any other symptoms?'

Nausea and vomiting, Sarah told her. 'What you might call morning sickness, I suppose.'

'Are you asking about these things for a friend? And would she like to come and see me at the office?'

Sarah picked up a scone and appeared to consider whether or not to bite, and then returned it to the dish. She looked at R.J. in much the same way as she had looked at the scone. When she spoke, her voice held only the smallest amount of discernible bitterness, and just the slightest tremble.

'I'm not asking for a friend.'

III
HEARTROCKS

29
Sarah's Request

Sarah wore her hair that year in the fashion of dozens of smart young models and film actresses, in long, tangled ringlets. Her tender, troubled eyes were made larger and more luminous by the thick glasses. Her full-lipped mouth trembled slightly, and her hunched, tense shoulders seemed to expect the vengeful blows of a punishing God. The pimples on her chin were back, and there was another in the crease at the side of her nose. Even now, while carefully damming up her despair, she looked like the dead mother whose pictures R.J. had studied so covertly, but Sarah was taller and had inherited some of David's stronger facial features; she held the promise of a beauty more interesting than had been evident in the snapshots of Natalie.

Under R.J.'s careful questioning, what Sarah had described as 'several' missed periods turned out to be three.

'Why didn't you come to see me sooner?' R.J. asked.

'My period is so irregular anyway, I kept thinking it would come.'

And then too, Sarah said, she hadn't been able to make up her mind about what to do. Babies were so wonderful. She had spent lots of time lying on her bed, imagining the sweet softness, the warm helplessness.

How could this be happening to *her*?

'You used no contraception?'

'No.'

'Sarah. All those programs in your school about AIDS,' R.J. couldn't keep from saying with ill-disguised bitterness.

'We knew we wouldn't get AIDS.'

'How could you possibly know a thing like that?'

'We hadn't ever gone all the way before with anybody, either of us. Bobby used a condom the first time, but we didn't have one the next time.'

They didn't know zilch. R.J. fought for calm wisdom. 'So . . . have you talked about this with Bobby?'

'He's scared stupid,' Sarah said flatly.

R.J. nodded.

'He says we can get married, if I want to.'

'Is that what you want?'

'R.J. . . . I like him a lot. I even love him a lot. But I don't love him . . . you know, for always. I know he's way too young to be a good father, and I know I'm too young to be a good mother. He has plans to go to college and law school and be a bigshot lawyer in Springfield like his father, and I want to go to school.' She brushed a lock of hair from her eyes. 'I want to become a meteorologist.'

'You do?' Somehow, because of her rock collection, R.J. would have guessed at geology.

'I study the television reports all the time. Some of those weather assholes are just comedians who don't know a thing. Scientists keep learning new stuff about the weather, and I think a smart woman who works hard can go places.'

Despite what she was feeling, R.J. found herself smiling, but only briefly. She could see clearly where the conversation was heading, but she was waiting for Sarah to take them there. 'What are your plans, then?'

'I can't raise a baby.'

'Are you considering adoption?'

'I thought about it a lot. I'll be a senior in the fall. It's an important year. I need a scholarship to go to college, and I won't earn one if I have to deal with a pregnancy. I want to have an abortion.'

'You're sure?'

'Yes. It doesn't take long, does it?'

R.J. sighed. 'No, it doesn't take a lot of time, I guess. So long as there aren't complications.'

'Are there often complications?'

'Not very often at all. But there can be complications with anything. It's an invasive procedure.'

'But you can bring me someplace good, *really* good, can't you?'

The freckles stood out in the pale face and made Sarah appear very young and so vulnerable that R.J. found it hard to speak normally. 'Yes, I could bring you someplace really good, if that's what you end up wanting to do. Why don't we talk it over with your father?'

'No, he's not to know a damned thing! Not a single word, do you understand?'

'That's such a mistake, Sarah.'

'You can't tell me it's a mistake. You think you know my father better than I do? When my mother died, he became a falling-down drunk. This could make him drink again, and I won't risk it. Look, R.J., you're good for my father, and I can tell he thinks a lot of you. But he loves me too, and he has . . . an unrealistic picture of me in his mind. I'm afraid this would really do it for him.'

'But this is a terribly important decision, Sarah, and you shouldn't have to make it alone.'

'I'm not alone. I have you.'

It forced R.J. to say four very hard words. 'I'm not your mother.'

'I don't need a mother. I need a friend.' Sarah looked at her. 'I'm going to do this with or without your help, R.J. But I really need you.'

189

R.J. looked back. Then she nodded. 'Very well, Sarah. I'll be your friend.' Either her face or the words revealed her pain, and the girl took her hand.

'Thank you, R.J. Will I have to go away overnight?'

'From what you've told me, I believe you've entered the second trimester. An abortion in the second trimester is a two-day procedure. Afterwards, there will be bleeding. Perhaps no more than a heavy menstrual flow, but possibly more. You'll have to plan on being away from home at least one night. But, Sarah . . . in Massachusetts a female under eighteen needs the written consent of her parents to have an abortion.'

Sarah stared. 'You can give me the abortion, here.'

'No.' No way, friend. R.J. took her other hand too, feeling the reassuring youthful vigor. 'I'm not set up to do an abortion here. And we want you to be as safe as possible. If you're absolutely certain you want an abortion, you have only two choices. You can go to a clinic in another state, or you can request a hearing before a judge who can grant you permission to have an abortion in this state without parental consent.'

'Oh, God. I have to go public?'

'No, not at all. You would see the judge in the privacy of his chambers, just the two of you.'

'What would you do, R.J.? If you were in my place?'

She was cornered by this direct question. No evasion was possible, and she owed the girl an answer. 'I'd see the judge,' she said briskly. 'I could set up the interview for you. They almost never refuse permission. And then you could go to a clinic in Boston. I used to work there, and I know that it's very good.'

Sarah smiled and wiped her eyes with her fingertips. 'That's what we'll do then. But, R.J. What will it cost?'

'A first-trimester abortion costs three hundred and twenty dollars. A second-trimester abortion, the kind you need, is more complicated and more expensive, five hundred and fifty dollars. You don't have that kind of money, do you?'

'No.'

'I'll pay half. And you must tell Robert Henderson that he has to pay half. All right?'

Sarah nodded. For the first time, her shoulders began to shake.

'But right now, I have to arrange for you to have an examination.'

Despite what she had told Sarah, she already half-thought of her as . . . not her daughter, exactly, but at least someone with whom she had a strong personal connection. She could no more do an internal examination of Sarah Markus than if she herself had suffered the labor pains of Sarah's birth, or been there in the department store elevator when Sarah had made water on the carpet, or brought her to the first day of school.

She picked up the telephone and called Daniel Noyes's office in Greenfield and made arrangements to bring Sarah in for an office visit.

Dr Noyes said that as near as he could tell, Sarah had been pregnant for fourteen weeks.

Too long. The girl's firm young stomach was barely convex, but it wouldn't stay that way much longer. R.J. knew that with each passing day cells would multiply, the fetus would grow, and abortion would become that much more complicated.

She arranged a judicial hearing before the Honorable Geoffrey J. Moynihan. She drove Sarah to the courthouse, kissed her before leaving her in the judge's chambers, and sat on the hard bench of polished wood in the marble corridor, waiting.

The purpose of the hearing was to convince Judge Moynihan that Sarah was mature enough to have an abortion. To R.J., the hearing itself was a conundrum: if Sarah wasn't mature enough to have an abortion, how could she be mature enough to bear and raise a child?

The interview with the judge took twelve minutes. When Sarah emerged she nodded somberly.

R.J. put her arm around the girl's shoulders, and they walked that way to the car.

30

A Small Trip

'After all, what is a lie? 'Tis but the truth in masquerade,'
Byron wrote. R.J. hated the masquerade.

'I'm taking your daughter to Boston for a couple of days,
my treat, if it's okay with you, David. Girls only.'

'Wow. What's in Boston?'

'There's a revival road company production of *Les Mis-
érables*, for one. We'll pig out and do some very serious
window-shopping. I want us to get to know one another
better.' She felt demeaned by the deception, yet she knew
no other way.

He was delighted, kissed her, and sent them off with his
blessings, in high good humor.

R.J. telephoned Mona Wilson at the Jamaica Plains clinic and
told her she would be bringing in Sarah Markus, a seventeen-
year-old patient who had entered the second trimester of
pregnancy.

'This kid means a lot to me, Mona. A whole lot.'

'Well, R.J., we'll offer her every amenity,' Mona said, a little
less warm than she had been.

R.J. got the message that to Mona every patient was special, but she persisted doggedly. 'Is Les Ustinovich still working there?'

'Yes, he is.'

'Could she have Les, please?'

'Dr Ustinovich for Sarah Markus. She's got him.'

When R.J. picked her up at the log house, Sarah was too bright, too cheerful. She was wearing a loose two-piece outfit on the advice of R.J., who had explained that she would only have to disrobe the lower part of her body.

It was a mild summer day, the air clear as glass, and R.J. drove slowly and carefully down the Mohawk Trail and Route 2, making Boston in less than three hours.

Outside the clinic in Jamaica Plain there were two bored-looking policemen R.J. didn't recognize, and no demonstrators. Inside, the receptionist, Charlotte Mannion, took one look at her and let out a whoop. 'Well, hello, stranger!' she said, and hurried from behind her desk to kiss R.J.'s cheek.

The turnover had been high; half the staff people R.J. saw that morning were unknown to her. The other half made a fuss over seeing her again, which she found especially gratifying because it visibly gave Sarah confidence. Even Mona had gotten over her snit and hugged her long and hard. Les Ustinovich, rumpled and grumpy as always, gave her the briefest of smiles, but it was warm. 'How's life on the frontier?'

'Very good, Les.' She introduced Sarah to him and then took him aside and told him quietly how important his patient was to her. 'I'm glad you were free to take care of her.'

'Yeah?' He was studying Sarah's forms, noting that Daniel Noyes had done the pre-clinic physical instead of R.J. He looked at her curiously. 'She something to you? Your niece? Or a cousin?'

'Her father is something to me.'

'Oh-ho! Lucky father.' He started to turn away but came back. 'You want to assist?'

'No, thank you.' She knew Les was being gracious – a stretch for him.

She stayed with Sarah through several hours of first-day preliminaries, taking her through admitting and medical screening. She waited outside, reading a two-month-old *Time* during the counseling session, most of which would be a repeat for Sarah because R.J. had gone over every detail with her as carefully as possible.

The last stop of the day was in a procedure room for laminaria insertion.

R.J. stared sightlessly at *Vanity Fair*, knowing that in the room next door Sarah would be on the examining table, her feet in the stirrups, while BethAnn DeMarco, a nurse, inserted a two-inch twist of seaweed, like a tiny stick, into her cervix. In first-trimester abortions, R.J. had dilated the cervix with stainless steel rods, each one larger than the last. A second-trimester procedure required a larger opening to enable the use of a larger cannula. The seaweed expanded as it absorbed moisture overnight, and by the next day the patient didn't need further dilation.

BethAnn DeMarco accompanied them to the front door, telling R.J. the whereabouts of several people with whom they had worked. 'You might just feel a little pressure,' the nurse told Sarah casually, 'or the laminaria might give you some cramps tonight.'

From the clinic they went to a suite hotel overlooking the Charles River. After they registered and went up to the room, R.J. whisked Sarah off to Chef Chang's for dinner, thinking to razzle-dazzle her with sizzling soup and Peking duck. But razzle-dazzle was difficult because of discomfort; halfway through dessert they abandoned the ginger ice-cream because the 'little pressure' DeMarco had mentioned was rapidly becoming cramps.

By the time they got back to the hotel, Sarah was pale

and racked. She took the crystal heartrock from her purse and placed it on the night table where she could see it, and then she curled up like a ball on one of the beds, trying not to weep.

R.J. gave her codeine, and finally she kicked off her shoes and lay down next to the girl. She was painfully certain she would be rebuffed, but Sarah snuffled into her shoulder when R.J. put her arms around her.

R.J. stroked her cheek, smoothed her hair. 'You know, honey, in a way I wish you hadn't been so healthy up to now. I wish you'd needed a few fillings at the dentist's, maybe even had your tonsils and your appendix out, so you'd understand that Dr Ustinovich is going to take care of you and that this will pass.

'Just tomorrow, and then it will be over,' R.J. said, patting her back gently and even rocking her a bit. It felt right, and they lay like that for a long time.

Next morning they arrived at the clinic early. Les Ustinovich hadn't had his morning coffee yet and gave them a nod and a grunt. By the time he'd had his caffeine fix, DeMarco had ushered them into the treatment room, and Sarah was positioned on the table.

She was pale, rigid with tension. R.J. held her hand as DeMarco administered the paracervical block, an injection of 20cc of Lidocaine, and then started the IV. As luck would have it, DeMarco made a couple of false tries with the IV needle before she found the vein, and Sarah was gripping R.J.'s hand so tight it hurt. 'This will make you feel better,' R.J. said as DeMarco started conscious IV sedation, 100 mcg of Fentanyl.

Les Ustinovich came in and looked at their welded hands. 'I think you'd better go to the waiting room now, Dr Cole.'

R.J. knew he was right. She reclaimed her hand and kissed Sarah on the cheek. 'I'll see you in just a little while.'

In the waiting room she settled onto a hard chair between a skinny young man who was concentrating on biting off a cuticle, and a middle-aged woman who was pretending to read a tattered issue of *Redbook*. R.J. had brought the *New England Journal of Medicine* but she had a hard time concentrating. She was thoroughly familiar with the timetable and knew what was happening to Sarah. The curettage was done in two stages of suctioning. The first was called 'the long session' and took about a minute and a half. Then, after a pause, the second, touch-up suctioning was briefer. She hadn't had time to make her way through an entire article before Les Ustinovich came to the door and beckoned to her.

He had only one clinical manner, bluntness.

'She's aborted, but I perforated her.'

'Jesus Christ, Les!'

He froze her with a glance that brought her to her senses. He undoubtedly felt bad enough without salt in the wound.

'She jerked her body at just the wrong moment. God knows she wasn't feeling any pain, but she was a nervous wreck. The perforation of the uterus took place where she has a fibroid tumor, so there's some ripping and tearing. She's bleeding a lot, but she'll be all right. We've got her packed, and the ambulance is on its way.'

From then on, everything went into very slow motion for R.J., as if suddenly she existed under deep water.

She never had perforated a uterus during her time at the clinic, but she had always worked on women in the first trimester. Perforations happened very rarely, and they required surgical repair. Luckily, Lemuel Grace Hospital was only minutes away, and the ambulance was there almost before she had finished reassuring Sarah.

She made the short ride with Sarah, who was taken to the operating room on arrival.

She didn't have to request a surgeon. Sarah was assigned a gynecologist whom R.J. knew by reputation, Sumner Harrison. He was supposed to be very good, the luck of the draw.

The place that once had been so familiar to her was slightly out of focus. A lot of strange faces. Two familiar people smiled and said hello as they passed her in the corridor, hurrying from someplace to someplace.

But she remembered where the telephones were located. She picked up a phone, ran her credit card through the slot, and dialed the number.

He picked it up after two rings.

'Hello, David? This is R.J.'

31

A Ride Down the Mountain

By the time David got to Boston, Sarah was out of surgery and doing nicely. He sat by her bed and held her hand as she emerged from the anesthesia. At first Sarah wept to see him and watched him warily, but R.J. thought he handled her in exactly the right way; he was tender and supportive and gave no indication he wasn't completely in control of his thirst.

R.J. thought it best to give them some time alone. She wanted to know details of what had happened, and she telephoned BethAnn DeMarco and asked her if they might meet for dinner.

BethAnn was free, and they met in a small Mexican restaurant in Brookline, near where BethAnn lived.

'This morning was something, wasn't it?' DeMarco said.

'Some morning.'

'I can recommend the arroz con pollo, very good,' BethAnn said. 'Les feels bad. He doesn't talk about it, but I know him. I've worked at the clinic four years, R.J., and this is only the second perforation I've seen.'

'Who did the other one?'

BethAnn looked uncomfortable. 'It happened to be Les. But it was so innocuous it didn't require surgery. All we

199

had to do was pack her and send her home for bed rest. That wasn't Les's fault this morning. The girl just gave an involuntary lurch, like a big twist, and the curette penetrated. That doctor who examined her out where you live . . .'

'Daniel Noyes.'

'Well, Dr Noyes can't be faulted either. For missing the fibroid, I mean. It wasn't large, and it was in a little fold of tissue, impossible to see. If it had been just the perforation, or just dealing with the fibroid, it would have been easier to handle. How's she doing?'

'She seems to be fine.'

'Well, all's well that ends well. Me for the arroz con pollo. How about you?'

R.J. didn't care; she had the arroz con pollo too.

It wasn't until later that evening, when she and David were alone, that he began to formulate the hard questions that she found difficult to answer.

'What in hell were you thinking of, R.J.? Don't you know you should have consulted me?'

'I wanted to, but Sarah wouldn't hear of it. It was her decision, David.'

'She's a child!'

'Sometimes pregnancy makes women out of children. She's a seventeen-year-old woman, and she insisted on dealing with her own pregnancy. She went before a judge, who decided she was mature enough to end the pregnancy without bringing you into it.'

'I suppose you arranged for her to see the judge?'

'At her request. Yes.'

'God damn you, R.J. You acted as if her father were a stranger to you.'

'That isn't fair.'

When he didn't answer, she asked if he intended to

stay in Boston until Sarah was released from the hospital.

'Of course.'

'I have patients waiting to see me. So I'll go back.'

'Yes, you do that,' he said.

It rained hard for three days in the hills, but the day Sarah came home the sun was warm, and the spicy smell of the summer woods was in the soft breeze. 'What a day for riding Chaim!' Sarah said. It was good for R.J. to see her smile, but she was pale and tired-looking.

'Don't you dare. You stay in and rest for a few days. That's important. Do you understand?'

Sarah smiled. 'Yes.'

'This is a chance for you to listen to some ba-ad music.' She had bought the newest Pearl Jam CD, and Sarah's eyes filled when R.J. gave it to her.

'R.J., I'll never forget . . .'

'Never mind that. Now, you take care of yourself, sweetheart, and get on with your life. Is he still angry?'

'He'll get over it. He will. We'll honey-hug and sweet-talk him.'

'You're a great girl.' R.J. kissed her on the cheek. She decided she had to talk to David without delay. She walked out to the barnyard where he was unloading bales of hay from his pickup truck. 'Will you please come to dinner tomorrow night? Alone?'

He looked at her and then nodded his head. 'All right.'

The next morning shortly after eleven she was preparing to drive down into Greenfield to visit two hospitalized patients when her telephone rang.

'R.J., it's Sarah. I'm bleeding.'

'A lot or a little?'

'A lot. A whole lot.'

'I'll be right there.' She called the ambulance first.

Sarah had been content to sit for hours like an invalid on the old stuffed rocking chair next to the jars of honey and watch what she could see, squirrels chasing pigeons on the barn roof, two rabbits chasing one another, their neighbor Mr Riley driving by in his rusted blue pickup truck, a large and obscenely fat woodchuck browsing on the clover in the northwestern corner of the pasture.

Presently she watched the woodchuck scamper clumsily to pop into its burrow under the stone wall, and a few seconds later she saw why, because a black bear ambled out of the woods.

It was a small bear, probably born only last season, but its scent carried to the horse. Chaim's tail came up, and he began to prance in terror and to whinny loudly. At the sound the bear hightailed it back into the woods, and Sarah laughed.

But then Chaim's shoulder hit the one bad post in the barbed wire fence. Most of the posts were newly split black locust and would fight moisture for years. This one was pine, and it had rotted nearly in two at the place where earth met air, so that when the horse went into it with his shoulder it had fallen with only the slightest sound, allowing him to leap at once over the suddenly lowered strands.

On the porch, Sarah had set down her cup of hot coffee and risen. 'Damn. You! You bad Chaim, you!' she had called. 'You wait right there, you bad thing.'

On her way across the porch to the stairs she picked up a piece of old rope and a feed bucket that still contained a little grain. It was a good distance to go, and she forced herself to walk slowly.

'C'mere, Chaim,' she called. 'Come and get it, boy.'

She struck the feed pail with her fingers. Ordinarily that was enough to bring him to her, but he was still spooked by the bear scent, and he moved a little way up the road.

'Damn.'

This time he waited for her, turned so he could watch the edge of the woods. He never had kicked her, but she gave him no chance, approaching him carefully from the side and holding out the bucket.

'Eat, you dumb old thing.'

When he buried his nose in the pail, she let him get a mouthful and then slipped the rope around his neck. She didn't tie it, afraid he would spook again and get it caught on something that could choke him. She wished she could have swung up onto him and ridden him bareback. Instead she slipped the rope over his ears and past his eyes and held the two ends together with her hands, talking to him softly and tenderly.

She had to lead him past the break in the fence, all the way to the rude gate, and then lift the heavy poles out of their slots until the way was open for him to reenter the field. She was putting the poles back and worrying about how she could close up the fence until her father came home, when she became conscious of the wetness, of the shining-leather redness of her legs, of the shocking trail she had been leaving behind her, and the strength went out of all of her and she began to cry.

By the time R.J. reached the log house, the towels Sarah had fashioned into packs had proven woefully inadequate. There was more blood on the floor than R.J. would have imagined possible. She guessed that Sarah had stood there and bled, not wanting to ruin the bedclothes, but then had flopped back onto the bed, perhaps in a faint. Now her legs dangled beyond the crimsoned bed, her feet on the floor.

R.J. lifted her legs to the bed, removed the soaked towels and put in fresh pressure packs. 'Sarah, you have to keep your legs together hard.'

'R.J.,' Sarah said faintly. From very far away.

She was already semi-comatose, and R.J. saw that she wouldn't be able to control her muscles. R.J. took strips of cling bandage and tied the girl's legs together at the ankle and the knee, and then made a little pile of blankets and lifted Sarah's feet onto it.

The ambulance was there very soon. The EMTs wasted no time loading Sarah, and R.J. got into the back with Steve Ripley and Will Pauli and started oxygen therapy at once. Ripley did the workup and assessment en route, while the wailing ambulance rocked and swayed.

He grunted when the vital signs matched the numbers R.J. had recorded in the house before the ambulance came.

R.J. nodded. 'She's in shock.'

They covered Sarah with several blankets, kept her feet raised. Behind the grey oxygen mask covering her mouth and nose, Sarah's face was the color of parchment.

For the first time in a very long time, R.J. tried to will every cell of her being into direct contact with God.

Please, she said. Please, I want this kid.

Please. Please, please, please. I need this clean, long-legged girl, this funny, beautiful girl, this possible daughter. I need her.

She forced herself to take the girl's hands in her own, and then she couldn't let them go, feeling the trickling of the sand out of the hourglass.

There was nothing she could do to stop it, to reverse what was happening. She could only fuss with the oxygen to make certain it was pouring out its richest mixture and ask Will to radio the hospital so that a supply of matched blood would be available and ready.

When the Woodfield ambulance reached the emergency room, the waiting nurses opened the door of the rig and stood abashed and uncertain at the sight of R.J. unable to stop clutching Sarah's hands. They had never before seen an ambulance arrive containing a broken doctor.

32
The Ice Cube

Steve Ripley telephoned Mack McCourtney and asked him to get David Markus and bring him to the hospital.

Paula Simms, the emergency room doctor, insisted on giving R.J. a tranquilizer. It made her very quiet and withdrawn but otherwise had no discernible effect on her horror. She was sitting frozen next to Sarah, holding her hand, when David arrived, his eyes wild.

He didn't look at R.J. 'Leave us alone.'

R.J. went out into the waiting room. After a long while, Paula Simms came to her.

'He insists that you go home. I think you'd best do it, R.J. He's very . . . you know. Upset.'

Consciousness hurt unbearably. Sarah couldn't be gone forever like that, just . . . *gone*. It was hard for her to face. It hurt to think, even to breathe.

Suddenly the ice cube in which she had lived after Charlie Harris's death was back.

She made the first call to David that afternoon. After that, she telephoned every fifteen or twenty minutes. Each time she got his recorded business voice, so professional, so relaxed, thanking her for calling the Woodfield Realty Company and inviting her to leave a message.

Next morning she drove to his house, thinking perhaps he was sitting there alone, not picking up the phone. Will Riley, David's far neighbor from down the road, was putting a new fence post into the ground.

'He home, Mr Riley?'

'No. Found a note from him taped to my door early this morning, asking me to feed the animals for a couple of days. I thought the least I could do is fix the fence. Hell of a thing, isn't it, Dr Cole?'

'Yes. Hell of a thing.'

'That wonderful little girl.'

Sarah!

What was going on with David? Where was he?

When she went into the house it was just as it had been when she and the ambulance crew had left it, except now the blood had dried to a paste a quarter of an inch thick. She stripped the sheets and the blankets from the bed and placed them in a garbage bag. She used David's garden spade to scrape up the terrible pudding from the floor, then she carried it into the woods in a plastic bucket and buried it. She searched out David's stiff brush and soap and scrubbed the floor until the successive rinse waters turned from red to pink to clear. Under the bed, she found the cat.

'Oh, Agunah.'

She would have liked to pet the cat, hug her, but Agunah stared at her like a cornered lion.

She had to drive home fast in order to shower and get to the office in time to see patients. It was mid-afternoon when she met Toby in the hallway and learned what half the town already knew, that David Markus had taken his daughter back to Long Island for burial.

For a little while she sat at her desk and tried to make sense of the next patient's case history, but words and letters wriggled on the other side of a deep liquid glitter. Finally, she did something she had never done before. She told Toby to apologize and reschedule patient appointments. Sorry, terrible headache.

When she got home she sat in a chair at the kitchen table. The house was very quiet. She just sat.

She cancelled all appointments for four days. She walked a lot. Got out of the house and just walked, over the trail, over the fields, along the road, without knowing where, to start and look about her in surprise: how on earth did I get here?

She telephoned Daniel Noyes, and they met for an uncomfortable, sorrowful lunch.

'I gave her a good examination,' he said quietly. 'I couldn't see anything wrong with her at all.'

'It wasn't your fault, Dr Noyes. I know that.'

He gave her a long, searching look. 'It wasn't your fault either. Do you know that, also?'

She nodded.

Outside the restaurant, he kissed her on the cheek before he turned away and walked toward his car.

R.J. had no trouble sleeping. On the contrary, at night she sank into a deep and dreamless place of refuge. Mornings she lay under the covers in the fetal position, unable to move for long periods.

Sarah.

Her mind told her to reject guilt but she understood that guilt was hopelessly intertwined with her sorrow and from now on would be part of her.

She decided it would be better to write to David before she tried to talk with him. It was important to her that he understand that Sarah's death might just as easily have occurred following an appendectomy or a bowel resection.

That infallible surgery didn't exist. That it was Sarah's own decision to have had the abortion and that she would have had it even if R.J. hadn't agreed to help her.

R.J. knew it would be little comfort for David to be told that some losses are incurred even in the safest invasive procedures. That in electing abortion over pregnancy, Sarah had been increasing her chances for survival, because in the United States, one out of every 14,300 women who continue pregnancy will die, while of women who are aborted – even after fourteen weeks of pregnancy – one in 23,000 can be expected to die. And that since everyone's chances of dying every time he or she enters an automobile are one in 6,000, both pregnancy and abortion are extremely safe risks.

So Sarah's death as a result of a legal abortion was a rarity. A *rarity*.

She wrote letter after letter, until finally she finished one that satisfied her, and then she drove to the post office.

But instead of mailing it, she tore it up and threw the pieces in the dumpster. She realized she had written it as much for herself as for David. Anyway, how could it make a difference. What did he care about statistics.

Sarah was gone.

And so was David.

33
Inheritances

Day after day passed, and R.J. didn't hear a thing. She called Will Riley and asked him if he knew when his neighbor was coming home.

'No, I don't have any idea. He sold the Morgan, you know. Did it by phone. I got a letter from him, overnight mail, asked me to be there yesterday at four o'clock so the new owner could pick up the horse.'

'I'll take their cat,' R.J. said.

'That'll be good. She's out in my barn. I've already got four cats.'

So R.J. picked up Agunah and brought her home. Agunah minced through the entire house, every inch a visiting queen, inspecting with disdainful suspicion. R.J. hoped David would come home and claim her soon. She and the cat never had established a meaningful relationship.

She was chatting with Frank Sotheby at the general store a few mornings later when he wondered whether some other real estate person would move into town to take Dave Markus's place.

'I was surprised to hear he put his house on the market,' he said, regarding her closely. 'I understand Mitch Bowditch is handling it, over in Shelburne Falls.'

She drove down the Mohawk Trail to Shelburne Falls to have lunch and dropped in at the real estate office. Bowditch was a pleasant man, relaxed with people. He sounded truly regretful when he told her he had neither an address nor a telephone number for David Markus. 'I just have a letter authorizing me to sell the place fully furnished, as is. And a New York bank account to send the check to. David said he wants to unload it quick. He's a very good real estate man, and he set the price on the low side of fair. I should sell it pretty soon, I expect.'

'If he should call, would you kindly ask him to contact me?' R.J. said and handed over her card.

'I will be happy to do that, doctor,' Bowditch said.

In three days the cat ran away.

R.J. roamed up and down Laurel Hill Road and walked the trail through the woods, calling.

'AAGUUUUNAAAAAH!'

She thought of all the critters that would consider a housecat a meal: bobcats, coyotes, mountain lions, large winged raptors. But when she got back to the house, there was a message on the answering machine from Will Riley's wife, Muriel, saying the cat had made her way through the hills back to their barn.

R.J. picked her up again, and two days later Agunah left again and returned to the Rileys.

Three more times the cat ran away.

By that time it was late in September. Will grinned at her when she showed up to claim her unwilling guest. 'It's okay with us if you just leave her here,' he said, and R.J. agreed at once.

Still, she felt a reluctance. 'Shalom, Agunah,' she said, and the damned cat yawned at her.

On her way back down the road, as she passed the log house she saw that a new blue jeep with New York registration plates was parked in the drive.

David?

She pulled in behind it, but when she knocked on the front door, Mitch Bowditch opened it. Beyond him was a man with a tanned face, thin greying hair and a brushy mustache.

'Hi, there. Come on in and meet another physician.' He introduced them. 'Dr Roberta Cole. Dr Kenneth Dettinger.' Dettinger's handshake was friendly but brisk.

'Dr Dettinger's just bought the place.'

She controlled her reaction. 'Congratulations. Will you practice here?'

'Oh, God no! I'll just use it for weekends and vacations. You know.'

She knew. He had a practise in White Plains, child and adolescent psychiatry. 'Very busy, long hours. This place, it'll be like heaven to me.'

They all three moved out into the back yard toward the barn, past the half dozen hives.

'You going to keep bees?'

'No.'

'Want to sell the hives?'

'Well. You can have them, glad to have you take 'em away. I'm thinking of putting a pool and a deck out here, and I'm allergic to bee venom.'

Bowditch cautioned that R.J. didn't want to try to move the hives for another five or six weeks, until they had a serious cold snap that would put the bees into dormancy. 'Actually . . .' He consulted an inventory list. 'David owns eight more hives that he's rented out to Dover's Apple Orchards. You want those too?'

'I suppose I do.'

'Buying the house the way I'm doing raises some problems,' Kenneth Dettinger said. 'There are clothes in closets, bureaux

211

to be cleaned out. I don't have a wife to help me get the house shipshape. Only just divorced, you see.'

'I'm sorry.'

'Oh.' He grimaced and shrugged, and then he grinned ruefully. 'I'll have to hire somebody to clean everything out of the house and get rid of it.'

Sarah's clothes.

'Do you know anyone I could hire to do a job like that?'

'Let me do it. No money. I'm . . . a friend of the family.'

'Why, that would be fine. I would appreciate it.' He was studying her with interest. He had chiseled features. She didn't trust the strength she saw in his face; perhaps it meant he was accustomed to getting his way.

'I have my own furniture. I'll keep the refrigerator, it's only a year old. Anything you want, just take it. What's left . . . give it away or ask someone with a truck to haul it to the dump, and mail me a bill.'

'When will you need the house emptied of things?'

'If it can be done by Christmas, I'll be grateful.'

'All right, then.'

That fall in the hills was especially beautiful. The leaves turned wanton in October, and the rains didn't come to buffet them off the trees. Everywhere R.J. drove, to the office, to the hospital, to make a house call, she was struck by color viewed through a prism of cold, crystal air.

She tried to go back to living her life normally, concentrating on her patients, but it seemed to her that she was always one step behind. She began to worry that her medical judgement might be affected.

A couple who were near neighbors of hers, Pru and Albano Trigo, had a sick kid, Lucien, ten years old. They called him Luke. He was off his food, without energy, had explosive diarrhea. It persisted, on and on. R.J. did a sigmoidoscopy, sent him for upper GI X-rays, an MRI.

Nothing.

The boy continued to fail. R.J. referred him to a gastro-enterologist in Springfield for a consult, but the Springfield physician couldn't find anything wrong either.

Late one afternoon she crunched over dry leaves on the trail. Just as she reached the beaver pond she saw a body flash away underwater like a sleek, small seal.

There were beaver colonies up and down the Catamount River. The river ran through the Trigo property, just down-stream from R.J.'s.

She hurried to her car and drove to the Trigos' house. Lucien was lying on the couch in the living room, watching television.

'Luke, did you go swimming this summer? In the river?'

He nodded.

'Did you swim in the ponds made by the beaver dams?'

'Sure.'

'Did you ever drink the water?'

Prudence Trigo was paying very close attention.

'Oh yeah, sometimes,' Lucien said. 'It's real clean and cold.'

'It does look clean, Luke. I swim in it myself. But I just happened to think that the beaver and other wild creatures defecate and urinate in it.'

'Defecate and . . .'

'Shit and piss,' Pru said to her son. 'Doctor means they shit and piss in the water, and then you drink it.' She turned to R.J. 'You think that's it?'

'I think it might be. Animals infect water with parasites. If somebody drinks the water, the parasites reproduce and form a lining in the gut, so the intestine is no longer capable of absorbing nourishment. We won't be sure until I send a stool sample off to the government lab. In the meantime, I'll start him on a strong antibiotic.'

When the test came back, the report said that Lucien's diges-tive tract was laden with *Giardia lamblia* protozoa and showed

213

traces of several other parasites as well. Within two weeks he was eating again, and his diarrhea had disappeared. Several weeks after that, another test revealed that his duodenum and jejunum were free of parasites, and his pent-up energy had found such release that he was getting on his mother's nerves.

He and R.J. agreed that next summer they would swim in Big Pond instead of in the river, and that they wouldn't drink the lake water either.

The cold came down from Canada, the kiss of death for all the flowers except the hardiest chrysanthemums. The hayed fields, close-cut as the heads of convicts, turned brown under the lemonish sun. R.J. paid Will Riley to bring the bee hives to her place in his truck and stand them in her back yard in a row, between the house and the woods. Once they were moved, she completely ignored them, being occupied with treating humans. She had received advisories from the Centers for Disease Control, warning that one of this year's influenza strains, A/Beijing 32/92 (H3N2), was particularly virulent and debilitating, and for weeks Toby had been summoning aging patients to the office for flu shots. The vaccine didn't make an appreciable dent in the epidemic when it came, however, and suddenly R.J.'s days were too short. The telephone ring became hateful. She prescribed antibiotics to some whose infections appeared to be bacterial, but mostly all R.J. could do was tell them to take aspirin, drink lots of fluids, stay warm, get plenty of bed rest. Toby caught the flu, but R.J. and Peg Weiler managed to stay healthy despite the work load. 'We're too ornery to get sick, you and I,' Peggy said.

It was the second day of November before R.J. could make time to bring cardboard cartons to the log house.

It was as if she were closing out not only Sarah's life, but David's as well.

While she folded and packed Sarah's clothing, she tried to

shut off her mind. If she could have closed her eyes too while she packed, she would have done it. When a carton became full, she took it to the town dump and placed it in the bin for Salvation Army collection.

She stood for a long time over Sarah's collection of heartrocks, trying to decide what to do with them. She couldn't give them away or discard them; finally, she packed them all carefully and carried them out to the car as if they were jewels. Her guest room became a rock room, trays of heartrocks everywhere.

She threw away the things in David's medicine chest, ruthlessly dumping Sarah's Clearasil and David's antihistamines. Inside her there was a growing coldness at him for making it necessary for her to do these hurtful things. She saved the letters she found on his desk without reading them, placing them in a brown paper bag. In the lower left-hand drawer of the desk, she opened a typing-paper box and found his book manuscript, which she took home and placed on the high shelf in her closet next to old scarves, mittens that didn't fit any more, and a Red Sox cap she had had since college.

She spent Thanksgiving Day working, but the epidemic had already started its downward curve. The following week she managed to take two days in Boston for an important occasion. Her father was ten months beyond the university's mandatory retirement age of sixty-five. Now he had to leave the chair at the medical school that he had occupied for so many years, and his department colleagues had invited R.J. to join them at a dinner in his honor at the Union Club. It was a mellow evening, full of praise, affection, and reminiscences. R.J. was very proud.

The next morning her father took her to breakfast at the Ritz. 'Are you all right?' he said gently. They had already discussed Sarah's death at length.

'I'm absolutely fine.'

215

'What do you suppose has happened to him?'

Her father asked timidly, afraid to cause her more hurt, but she had already faced the question squarely, and she realized she might never see him again.

'I'm certain he's lost in a bottle somewhere.'

She told her father she had paid off one-third of the bank loan for which he had cosigned, and both of them were relieved to change the subject.

What lay ahead for Professor Cole was a chance to write a textbook he had been planning for years and the teaching of several courses as a guest professor at the University of Miami.

'I have good friends in Florida, and I thirst for warmth and sunshine,' he said, holding up hands that arthritis had made gnarled as apple tree branches. He told R.J. he wanted her to have the viola da gamba that had been his grandfather's.

'Whatever would I do with it?'

'Perhaps learn to play it. I don't play it at all nowadays, and I want to travel light.'

'Are you giving me Rob J.'s scalpel, as well?' She had always secretly been very impressed by the antique family scalpel.

He smiled. 'Rob J.'s scalpel doesn't take up much room. I'll hold on to it. You'll be getting it soon enough.'

'Not for a very long time, I hope,' she said and leaned over the table to kiss him.

He was going to place the apartment's furnishings in storage, and he asked her to take whatever she might want.

'The carpet in your study,' she said at once.

He was surprised. It was an undistinguished Belgian rug, beige and almost threadbare, not worth anything. 'Take the Hamadan that's in the living room. It's a much better carpet than the one in my study.'

But she already had a fine Persian rug, and what she wanted was something that was a part of her father. So the two of them went to the apartment and rolled up the rug and tied it. Even with both of them carrying an end it was a chore to get it

216

downstairs and into the rear cargo space of the Explorer. The viola da gamba took up the entire rear seat as she drove back to Woodfield.

She was glad to have the instrument and the carpet, but she wasn't pleased with the fact that she kept inheriting the belongings of people who mattered to her.

34

Winter Nights

One Saturday morning Kenneth Dettinger arrived at the log house to find R.J. going through the last of the Markus possessions. He helped her sort through the tools and the kitchen utensils.

'Hey, I'd like to keep the screwdrivers and some of the saws.'

'Okay. You've paid for them.'

Doubtless she sounded as depressed as she felt. He gave her a searching look. 'What's going to happen to the rest of this stuff?'

'You're giving it to the church ladies for their tag sale.'

'Perfect!'

They worked together for a time without speaking. 'You married?' he asked finally.

'No. Divorced, same as you.'

He nodded. She saw an ache fly across his features, fleeting as a bird, coming and going in an instant. 'It's a hell of a big club, isn't it?'

R.J. nodded. 'Members all over the world,' she said.

*   *   *

She spent a lot of time with Eva, talking about the old days of Woodfield, discussing events that happened when Eva was a little girl or a young woman. Always, she watched the old woman closely, made uneasy by what was clearly a winding down of vitality, a gradual fading that had begun in Eva shortly after her niece's death.

R.J. asked her again and again about the Crawford children, still held captive by the mystery of the infant skeleton. Linda Rae Crawford had died in her sixth year, and Tyrone had died when he was nine, both before they had reached child-producing age. So it was on the other two siblings, Barbara Crawford and Harry Hamilton Crawford Jr, that R.J. focused her attention.

'Young Harry was a sweet-natured boy, but not cut out for a farm,' Eva remembered. 'Always had his head buried in a book. He studied at the state college in Amherst for a while, but then he got thrown out, something to do with gambling. He just went away somewheres. I think California, or Oregon. Some place out there.' The other daughter, Barbara, was a steadier kind of person, Eva said.

'Was Barbara pretty? Did she have men who . . . you know, came around and courted her?'

'She was pretty enough, and a very nice girl. I can't remember her having any particular feller, but she went away to the normal school in Springfield and married one of her teachers.'

Eva became impatient with R.J.'s questions and cranky about her presence. 'You don't have young ones, do you? Or a man at home?'

'I do not.'

'Well, you're making a mistake. I could have gotten me a good man, I know I might have, if only I'd been free.'

'Free? Why, Eva, you talk as though you were a slave back then. You've always been free.'

'Not really. I couldn't break away. My brother always needed me to stay on the farm,' she said stiffly. Sometimes while they talked she grew visibly agitated, the fingertips of her right hand plucking at the table top or the bedspread or the flesh of her other hand.

She had had a hard life, and R.J. saw that it disturbed her to be reminded of it.

There were numerous and growing problems involving her present life. The church volunteers who cleaned her house and cooked her meals had reacted splendidly to a crisis, but they weren't able to do it on a long-term basis. Marjorie Lassiter was empowered to hire someone to clean the apartment once a week, but Eva needed extended care, and the social worker confided to R.J. that she had begun to look for a nursing home that would take her. Eva was querulous and raised her voice a lot, and R.J. suspected that most nursing homes would try to keep her sedated. She saw problems ahead.

In mid-December, suddenly there was snow to match the cold. Sometimes R.J. dressed in layers and ventured out onto the trail on her skis. The winter woods were still as a deserted church, but there were signs of occupancy. She saw the fresh pugmarks of a wildcat and tracks of deer of varying sizes, and a bloodied and fur-strewn patch of broken snow. Now she didn't need David to tell her that a predator had taken a rabbit; it was coyotes, their dog tracks were in the snow all about the kill.

The beaver ponds were frozen and snow-covered, and the winter river gurgled and rushed over, under, and through an atmosphere of ice. R.J. wanted to ski along the riverbank, but that was where the cleared trail ended, and she had to turn around and go back the way she had come.

Winter was beautiful in the woods and the fields, but it would have been better shared. She ached for David. Perversely, she was tempted to telephone Tom and talk out her troubles, but she knew he was no longer available to her. She was lonely, frightened about the future. When she ventured forth into the cold whiteness, she felt like a tiny mite lost in the enormous deep freeze.

Twice she hung beef suet in net onion bags for the birds, and each time it was stolen by a red fox. She saw his tracks and caught glimpses of him skulking, a wary thief. Finally she carried a ladder out to a young ash tree at the edge of the woods and, teetering but climbing high, hung another chunk of suet too far up for the fox to leap. She refilled her two bird feeders daily, and from the warmth of her house she watched chickadees, several kinds of nuthatches and grosbeaks, tufted titmice, a huge hairy woodpecker, a pair of cardinals. The male cardinal pissed her off; he always sent the female to the feeder first, in case there was danger there, and the female always went, a perpetual potential sacrifice.

When will we ever learn? R.J. asked herself.

When Kenneth Dettinger telephoned, he caught her by surprise. He was back in the hills for the weekend, and he wondered if she would care to join him for dinner.

She opened her mouth to refuse the invitation and began arguing with herself. She should go, she thought, as the moment lengthened and he waited for her reply until the pause was embarrassing.

'I would like that,' she said.

She groomed carefully and chose a good dress she hadn't worn in a while. When he picked her up he was wearing a tweed jacket, wool slacks, lightweight black hiking boots, and a heavy down jacket, the hill country dress-up outfit. They went to an inn on the Mohawk Trail and took their time over wine before ordering. She had become unaccustomed to alcohol; the wine relaxed her, and she discovered he was an interesting man, a good conversationalist. For several years he had spent three weeks annually working in Guatemala with children who had been traumatized by the murders of one or

221

both of their parents. He asked insightful questions about her practise in the hills.

She liked the meal, the talk about medicine and books and movies, enjoying herself enough so that when he took her home it felt natural to invite him in for coffee. She asked him to light the fire while she started the coffee.

When he kissed her, that somehow felt natural too, and she enjoyed the experience. He was a good kisser, and she kissed him back.

But her lips became like wood, and very soon he stopped.

'I'm sorry, Ken. The timing is very wrong, I guess.'

If she had hurt his ego, it didn't show. 'Do you give rain checks?'

She hesitated too long, and he smiled. 'I'm going to be in this town a lot in the future.' He held up his coffee mug to her. 'Here's to better timing. After a while if you would like to see me, let me know.'

He kissed her on the cheek when he left.

A week later he came up from New York for three days over the Christmas holiday, with another man and two very attractive women, both young.

When R.J. passed them on the road in the Explorer, Ken honked his horn at her and waved.

R.J. spent Christmas Day with Eva. She had made a small turkey at home, and she brought it over with the side dishes and a chocolate cake, but Eva derived little enjoyment from the meal. She had been told that in two weeks she would be transferred to a nursing home in Northampton. R.J. had gone there to check it out. She had told Eva it was a good place, and the old woman had listened quietly and had nodded her head without comment.

Eva began to cough while R.J. was cleaning up after their meal. By the time the dishes were put away, her face was hot and flushed.

R.J. had had sufficient experience with influenza to make it an easily recognizable enemy. It had to be a flu strain not included in the vaccine Eva had received.

R.J. toyed with the idea of sleeping in Eva's apartment or of getting one of the local women to stay the night.

But Eva was so frail. In the end, R.J. called the ambulance and rode in it to Greenfield, where she signed the papers admitting Eva to the hospital.

The next day, she was glad she had done so, because the infection had impaired Eva's respiratory system. R.J. ordered antibiotics in the hope that the pneumonia was bacterial, but it was a viral pneumonia, and Eva sank rapidly.

R.J. waited in the hospital room. 'Eva,' she said. 'Eva, I'm here with you.' She drove back and forth between Woodfield and Greenfield and sat by the bedside holding Eva's hands, feeling the old woman's life wind down and saying goodbye to her without any more words.

R.J. ordered oxygen to ease her labored breathing, and toward the end, morphine. Eva died two days before the new year.

The ground in the Woodfield cemetery was hard as flint, and a grave couldn't be dug. Eva's casket was placed in a holding vault. Her burial had to await the spring thaw. There was a memorial service at the Congregational Church, sparsely attended because in ninety-two years not many people in town had known Eva Goodhue very well.

The weather was beastly, a series of what Toby called 'three-dog days.' R.J. had not even one dog to cuddle with against the cold, and she saw the spiritual danger of unremitting grey skies. She took responsibility for herself. In Northampton she found a teacher of viola da gamba, Olga Melnikoff, a woman in her seventies who had spent twenty-six years with the Boston Symphony. She began to have weekly lessons, and now in the still, cold house at night she sat and clamped the great viol between her knees as if it were a lover. The first strokes of the bow gave off sonorous bass vibrations that thrust their way deep into her body, and soon she was lost in the exquisite business of making sound. Mrs Melnikoff started her on the basics, grimly correcting the way she wanted to hold the bow, ordering her to repeat the musical scale again and again. But R.J. already was a musician of piano and guitar, and soon she was doing exercises and then a few simple songs. She loved it. Sitting alone and playing, she felt that she was accompanied by the generations of Coles who had made melody with this instrument.

It was a time to spend wood on the fire and stay in bed nights. She knew the wild creatures must be suffering. She wanted to leave hay in the woods for the deer, but Jan Smith dissuaded her. 'Deliver them from our kindness. They're best off when we leave them completely alone,' he said, and she tried not to think of the animals and birds during weather when tree trunks cracked open from the cold like pistol shots.

The hospital announced that any doctor with a modem could access a patient's chart in a few seconds and could give the nurses instructions over the telephone instead of making the long, slippery drive to Greenfield. There were nights when she still had to go to the hospital in person, but she invested in the equipment and was thankful to embrace some of the technology she had left behind in Boston.

The great blazes she built nightly in the fireplace kept her warm despite the winds that shook the house on the verge. She sat by the fire and went through journal after journal, never quite catching up but making great inroads on her medical reading.

One night she went to the closet and took down David's manuscript. Seated by the fire, she began to read.

Hours later, suddenly conscious that the room was cold, she stopped to rebuild the fire, to use the bathroom, to make fresh coffee. Then she sat and read again. Sometimes she chuckled; several times, she wept.

The sky outside was bright when she was through. But she wanted to read the rest of the story. It was about farmers who had to change their lives because the world had changed, but who didn't know how. The characters were alive but the manuscript was unfinished. It left her deeply moved but wishing to scream. She couldn't imagine David would abandon such a book if he were able to complete it, and she knew he was either gravely ill or dead.

35
Hidden Meanings

January 20.

Sitting at home, warming the air with music, R.J. struggled with the feeling that tonight was special; a birthday? some kind of anniversary? And then she had it, a message from Keats that she had had to memorize for Sophomore English Lit.

> St Agnes' Eve – Ah, bitter chill it was!
> The owl, for all his feathers, was a-cold;
> The hare limp'd trembling through the frozen grass,
> And silent was the flock in woolly fold.

R.J. had no idea how the flocks were doing, but she knew that the creatures who couldn't be in a barn must be doing miserably. On several mornings a pair of large wild turkeys, females, had moved slowly over the snow-covered fields. Each successive snowfall had frozen with an icy crust, forming a series of impermeable layers. The turkeys and the deer couldn't dig through them in order to reach the grass and plants they needed for survival. The turkeys made their way across the meadow like a pair of arthritic dowagers.

R.J. wondered if the Gift worked with animals. But she didn't have to touch them to know the turkeys were close to death. In the orchard they gathered themselves and made weak and unsuccessful efforts to flutter up into the apple trees to get at the frozen buds.

She could stand it no longer. At the farm store in Amherst she bought a large sack of cracked corn and threw handfuls of the feed over the snow in several places where she had seen the turkeys.

Jan Smith was disgusted with her. 'Nature managed nicely without human beings for millennia. So long as man doesn't destroy the animals they do fine without our help. The fittest will survive,' he said. He was even scornful of bird feeders. 'All they do is allow a lot of people to see their favorite songbirds up close. If the feeders weren't there, the birds would have to move their asses a little in order to live, and it would do them good to work harder.'

She didn't care. She watched with satisfaction as the turkeys and other birds ate her largesse. Doves and pheasants came, and crows and jays, and smaller birds she couldn't identify from a distance. Whenever they had eaten all the cracked corn, or when it snowed and covered what she had last thrown, she went outside and threw some more.

Cold January became frigid February. People ventured outside wrapped in a variety of protective layers, knit sweaters, down-filled coats, old fleece-lined bomber jackets. R.J. wore heavy long underwear and a woolen stocking cap that she kept pulled over her ears.

The lousy weather brought out the pioneering spirit that had drawn people into the mountains in the first place. One morning during a blizzard R.J. staggered through drifts to make her way into the office, where she stood, covered with white. 'What a day,' she gasped.

'I know!' Toby said, her face glowing. 'Isn't it *marvelous*?'

It was a month for warm and hearty meals shared with friends and neighbors, because winter stayed forever in the hills and cabin fever was ubiquitous. Over bowls of chili at Toby and Jan's house, R.J. talked about American artifacts with Lucy Gotelli, a curator in the museum at Williams College. Lucy said her lab had the ability to date objects with comfortable accuracy, and R.J. found herself describing the plate found with the baby's bones in her pasture.

'I'd like to see it,' Lucy said. 'There was a Woodfield Pottery here in the 1800s that turned out serviceable, unglazed dishware. Perhaps they made your piece.'

A few weeks later, R.J. brought the plate to Lucy's house.

Lucy examined it with a magnifying glass. 'Hey, looks to me like a Woodfield Pottery product, all right. Of course, we can't be certain. They had a distinctive marking, a merged T and R in black paint on the bottom of every piece. If this plate ever had the marking, it's been worn away.' She looked curiously at the seven surviving rusty letters on the face of the plate – *ah* and *od*, and *o* and again, *od*, and picked with a fingernail at the *h*. 'Funny color. Is that ink, do you think?'

'I don't know. It looks like blood,' R.J. ventured, and Lucy grinned.

'Nah. I guarantee it ain't blood. Look, why not let me take this to work with me, and see what I can come up with?'

'Sure.' So R.J. left it with Lucy, though she was curiously reluctant to give up the plate even for a short time.

Despite the cold and the deep snow, there was a scratching at the door early one evening. And another scratching. To R.J.'s relief when she opened the door, instead of a wolf or a bear the cat walked in and ambled from room to room.

'I'm sorry, Agunah. They're not here,' R.J. told her.

Agunah stayed less than an hour, and then she stood before the door until R.J. opened it and let her out.

Twice more that week she came and scratched on the door,

searched the house disbelievingly, and then departed without deigning to look at R.J.

It was ten days before Lucy Gotelli telephoned, apologizing for the delay. 'I've done your plate. Nothing to it, really, but we've had one minor crisis after another at the museum, and I wasn't able to deal with it until day before yesterday.'

'And?'

'It *is* made by Woodfield Pottery, I detected the latent mark very plainly. And I analyzed a bit of the substance that formed the letters on the top surface. It's casein paint.'

'All I remember about casein is that it's a milk component,' R.J. said.

'Right. Casein is the chief protein in milk, the part that curdles when the milk sours. Most of the dairy farmers around here made their own paint in the early days. They had plenty of skimmed milk, and they let the curds dry and ground them between stones. They used the casein as a binder, mixing it with pigment and milk and egg white and a little water. In this case, the pigment used was red lead. The letters are printed in red barn paint. A very bright red, actually. Turned into rust by time and the chemical action of the soil.'

All she'd had to do was place the plate under ultraviolet radiation, Lucy said. The porous clay had absorbed paint, which fluoresced under the ultraviolet, absorbing energy and remitting it right back.

'So, were you able to detect the other letters?'

'Yes, certainly. Got a pencil handy? I'll read them back to you.'

She spelled them out slowly, and R.J. wrote them on her prescription pad, and when Lucy had finished talking she sat and looked without blinking, almost without breathing, at what she had written:

ISAIAH NORMAN GOODHUE
GO IN INNOCENCE TO GOD
Nov 12, 1915

So Harry Crawford's family had had nothing to do with the skeletal discovery. R.J. had been barking up the wrong family tree.

She checked the town history to make certain Isaiah Norman Goodhue was indeed the brother Norm with whom Eva had lived alone for most of her life. When she saw that he was, instead of solutions she was left with questions and assumptions, each more disturbing than the last.

Eva would have been a fourteen-year-old girl in 1915, of childbearing age but in important ways still a child. She and her older brother had lived alone in the remote farmhouse on Laurel Hill Road.

If the child had been Eva's, had Eva been impregnated by some unknown male, or by her brother?

The answer seemed to be implicit in the crude name marker.

Isaiah Norman Goodhue had been thirteen years older than the girl. He never married; he spent his life in isolation, working the farm alone. He would have depended on his sister to cook, to tend the house, to help with the animals and the fields.

. . . And his other needs?

If the brother and sister had been the parents, had Eva been forced? Or had there been an incestuous love affair?

The terror and bewilderment the girl must have felt over the pregnancy!

And afterward. R.J. could imagine Eva – frightened, guilt-ridden because her infant was buried in unconsecrated earth, pained by the birthing and what must have been crude or nonexistent aftercare.

Clearly, their neighbor's marshy pasture would have been chosen as burial site because it was wet and worthless and never would be turned over by a plow. Had the brother and sister done the burying together? The clay plate had been buried shallower than the baby. R.J. thought it likely that Eva had marked it to record her dead son's name and birth date – the only memorial available to her – and then had stolen down to bury it above her infant.

Eva had spent most of her life looking down the hill at that marsh; what must she have felt, seeing Harry Crawford's cows wading there, adding their piss and manure to the muck?

Dear God, had the child been born alive?

Only Eva would have been able to answer the dark questions, so R.J. would never really know, which was just as well. She no longer wished to display the plate. It spoke to her too loudly of tragedy, too plainly of the unhappiness of a rural girl caught in deep despair, and she wrapped it in brown paper and placed it away in the bottom drawer of her breakfront.

36
On the Trail

Thoughts of the youthful Eva cast a ghostly shadow over R.J. that not even purposeful music-making could dispel. Now each day she left her house for the office eagerly, needing the contact with human beings that her practise provided, but even the office was a difficult place, because Toby's inability to conceive was affecting her ability to deal with the daily tensions. Toby was snappish and short-tempered, and what was worse, R.J. saw that she was aware of her own unsteadiness.

R.J. knew that eventually they would have to discuss it, but Toby had become more than an employee and a patient. They had grown to be close and caring friends, and R.J. was putting off confrontation as long as possible. Despite the added stress she spent long hours at the office, returning only reluctantly to the quiet house, the lonely silence.

She took consolation from the fact that winter was dying. The mounds of snow at the sides of the road shrank. The warming earth drank the melt, and the maple syrup folks began their yearly labor of tapping the trees to collect sap. Back in December, Frank Sotheby had stuffed a pair of old tennis shoes and some moth-eaten ski pants with rags.

Outside his general store, he had stuck what looked like a human lower torso into a snow pile waist-first, along with one ski and a ski pole, as though a skier had taken a header. Now his sight-gag melted with the snow. When he removed the sodden garments, R.J. told him it was the surest sign that spring had come.

One evening she opened the door to a now-familiar scratching, and the cat entered the house and made her usual ambling inspection.

'Oh, Agunah, stay with me this time,' she said, reduced to begging for an animal's company, but Agunah soon returned to the front door and demanded her freedom, and slipped out and left R.J. alone.

She began to welcome and respond to evening ambulance calls, although the rule was that the crews would call on her only if they had a situation they couldn't handle. The last night in March also offered up the last snowstorm of the season. On the highway leading out of Main Street, a drunken driver skidded across to the wrong side of the road in his Buick and met a small Toyota head-on. The man who was driving the Toyota slammed into the steering wheel, fracturing his ribs and making an island of his sternum, a condition known as flail chest. Whenever he breathed he experienced great pain. Worse, the loose chest wall segment didn't move in and out with the rest of his chest when he respirated; in effect, the bellows was broken.

All the EMTs could do for the injured man in the field was to tape a small, flat sandbag over the loose sternum, and then give him oxygen and get him into the medical center. The ambulance people were already doing that when R.J. reached the scene. For a change, too many EMTs had responded, among them Toby. The two of them watched the ambulance people preparing the man for transport, and then R.J. motioned Toby away from the volunteer firemen who were cleaning glass and pieces of metal from the road.

They walked down the highway to a place where they could look back at the accident.

'I've been thinking a lot about you,' R.J. said.

The night air was chill, and Toby was shivering slightly in her red ambulance jacket. The urgent yellow ambulance light, turning like a beacon viewed from out at sea, illuminated her features every few seconds. She wrapped her arms about her body and looked at R.J.

'Yeah?'

'Yeah. There's a procedure I'd like you to have.'

'What kind of procedure?'

'Exploratory. I want somebody to take a good look at what's happening inside your pelvis.'

'Surgery? Forget it. Look, R.J., I'm not going to be opened up. Some women . . . it just isn't in the cards for them to be mothers.'

R.J. grinned mirthlessly. 'Tell me about it.' She shook her head. 'They don't have to open you up any more. Nowadays they make three tiny little incisions in your abdomen: one through your navel and the other two below, roughly over each ovary. They use a very narrow fiber optics instrument with an incredibly sensitive lens that lets them see everything in sharp detail. If necessary, other special instruments allow them to do corrective procedures, right through those three tiny incisions.'

'Would they have to put me out?'

'Yes. You'd have general anesthesia.'

'. . . Would you do the . . . what do you call it?'

'Laparoscopy. No. I don't do that. I'd send you to Danny Noyes. He's very good.'

'No way.'

R.J. allowed herself to lose patience. 'But why? You so desperately want to have a child.'

'Look, R.J. You're so fucking pious when you preach about women needing to have the right to choose what happens to their own bodies. Well, this is my body. And I choose not to

234

have surgery unless my life or health is threatened, which it doesn't seem to be. So leave me the hell alone, understand? And thank you for your concern.'

R.J. nodded. 'You're welcome,' she said sadly.

In March she tried to enter the woods behind the house without skis or snowshoes, and she failed, going thigh-deep into snow that had refused to melt on the shaded trail. When she tried again in April, some snow remained but she was able to walk, if somewhat clumsily. Winter had made the wild place wilder, leaving the trail the worse for wear, with downed branches that had to be cleared. She seemed to feel the djinn of the forest, staring down at her. In a patch of snow she saw what looked like the tracks of a barefoot man with fat feet and ten sharp claws. But the big toes were the outer ones, and R.J. knew the marks had been left by a large bear. She puckered up and whistled as loud as she could blow, for some reason choosing as her bear-frightening song 'My Old Kentucky Home', although she thought it might put the bear to sleep instead of sending it galloping away.

In three places, trees had fallen across the path. R.J. went back to the barn and got a Swedish bow saw and tried to use it on the blown-down trees, but the saw was inadequate and the work too slow.

There were some things for which she needed a man, she told herself with bitter resignation.

For a few days she pondered whom she might hire to clear the path of debris and perhaps extend the trail along the river. But a few afternoons later, she found herself in her favorite farm supply store, attempting to learn all about chainsaws.

They looked lethal, and she knew they could be as deadly as they looked. 'They scare the bejeezus out of me,' she admitted to the salesman.

'Well, they should. They'll cut off your limb as easily as they'll cut off a tree's,' he said cheerfully. 'But so long as you stay scared, they're perfectly safe. The people who get hurt are the ones who get comfortable enough to handle them carelessly.'

The saws came in several brands and a number of different weights and lengths. The salesman showed her the smallest, lightest model. 'A lot of women favor this one.' But when she told him she wanted to clear a trail through woods, he shook his head and offered her another saw. 'This one is medium-heavy. Your arms will tire quicker, and you'll have to rest more frequently than with the small saw, but you'll get a lot more accomplished.'

She made him show her half a dozen times how to start it, how to stop it, how the automatic brake should be set so the whirling chain wouldn't cut her head open if the saw caught on something and kicked back.

By the time she brought it home, along with a supply of oil and a filled gasoline can, she had second thoughts. After supper she read the instruction manual carefully and knew the purchase had been a folly. The saw was too complicated, too wickedly capable of destruction, and she would never have the courage to go into the woods alone and use the dangerous tool. She set everything in a corner of the barn and did her best to forget all about it.

Two afternoons later, she came home from work and, as usual, she took the mail out of the mailbox by the road and carried it down the long driveway to the house. Seated at the kitchen table, she separated it into several piles: things to be dealt with later, consisting of bills, catalogs she wanted to read, and magazines; letters; and junk mail to be thrown away.

The envelope was square, medium-sized, light blue. The moment she saw the handwriting the air in the room became heavy and warm and harder to breathe.

She didn't rush to tear it open. Instead, she treated it as if it were a letter-bomb, examining it carefully on both sides.

236

There was no return address. It was postmarked three days before, and it had been mailed from Chicago.

She picked up her letter-opener and slit the envelope neatly across the top.

It was a greeting card: Wishing You a Happy Easter.

Inside, there was David's cramped, slanted handwriting.

My Dear R.J.,

    I scarcely know what to say, how to start.

    I suppose I must begin by saying that I am mortally sorry if I have caused you unnecessary anxiety.

    I want you to know I'm alive and healthy. I've been sober for some time, and I'm working hard to stay that way.

    I'm in a safe place, surrounded by good people. I am coming to terms with life.

    I hope you may find it in your heart to think kindly of me, as I think of you.

        Yours sincerely,
        David

Think kindly of me?

Wishing You a Happy Easter?

She threw the card and the envelope onto the mantel. Gripped by an icy, disgusted fury, she wandered through the house and finally went outside and into the barn. She picked up the new chainsaw and strode down the wood road until she came to the first fallen tree.

She did as she had been instructed by the salesman and the manual: knelt; placed her right foot on the bottom of the rear handle, pinning the saw to the ground; set the handguard; fixed the choke and turned on the ignition switch; held the front handlebar down firmly with her left hand and pulled the starter handle with her right hand. Nothing happened after several pulls, and she was preparing to give up when she pulled again, and the saw started with a cough and a sputter.

She pulled the trigger, and gave it gas, and it roared. She turned to the fallen tree, pulled the trigger again, and placed the blade against the trunk. The chain whipped around, its teeth biting into the wood, and went down through the trunk easily, quickly. The noise was music.

The power! she thought. The power!

In a very short time, the tree was in pieces small enough for her to move them off the trail. She stood with the roaring saw in her hand as dusk fell, reluctant to shut it off, drunk with success, ready to cut away all of her problems. She no longer was trembling. She didn't fear the bear. She knew the bear would flee from the sound of her vibrating, ripping teeth.

She could do this, she thought exultantly. The spirits of the woods were witnesses to the fact that a woman could do *anything*.

37

One More Bridge to Cross

Two afternoons in a row, she took her chainsaw into the forest and vanquished the other pair of fallen trees. Then on Thursday, her day off, she entered the woods early, while the silent, druid-like trees were still wet and cold, and commenced to extend the trail. There was only a short distance to go before the lane reached the Catamount, and she attained the river just before breaking for lunch. It was a thrill to turn the corner and begin to work downstream, along the bank.

The saw was heavy. She had to stop from time to time, and she used the intervals to gather the branches and small trees she had severed and drag them off the path, piling them so they would be nesting places for rabbits and other small creatures. There was snow here and there along the banks but the water ran like liquid crystal, fast and full. Just beyond where skunk cabbages pushed through the snow, she saw a blue cordiform stone in the shallow current. When she pushed up the sleeve of her sweater and plunged her hand into the water, her arm seemed to crystallize too, the shock of the cold telegraphing all the way to her toes. The stone was well shaped, and she wiped it dry tenderly with her handkerchief and dropped it into her pocket. All afternoon as she pushed the trail forward, she felt the magic of the heartrock giving her strength and power.

At night she was serenaded by the soprano yipping of coyotes and the baritone roar of the swollen river. Mornings, eating breakfast in the kitchen, making the bed, straightening up the living room, she saw from her windows a porcupine, hawks, an owl, buzzards, the great northern ravens that had taken over her land as if on a long-term lease. There were lots of rabbits and several deer, but there was no sign of the two turkeys she had fed in the winter, and she feared for them.

Now every day she rushed home from the office, changed her clothes, and took the chainsaw from the barn. She worked hard, with satisfaction that was almost a quiet glee, pushing the great circuit of trail back in the direction of her house.

There was a new softness in the air. Each day darkness fell later, and suddenly the back roads had become goo. She had learned about her environment and knew now when to park the Explorer and slog in on foot to make a house call, and she didn't use the come-along or need to have her car towed out of the mud.

The muscles of her arms and back and thighs tightened from the work in the woods and were so sore that she grunted when she walked, and then her body hardened and adjusted to the steady labor. Pushing the saw into branches to get the blade close to the treetrunks, she sustained numerous scratches and shallow gouges in her hands and arms. She tried wearing long sleeves, and gloves, but the sleeves snagged and the gloves didn't allow her to grip the saw tightly enough, so she disinfected the wounds carefully each night after her bath and wore the scabs like service stripes.

Sometimes an emergency kept her from working on the trail, a house call or the need to drive to the hospital to see a patient. She became miserly about her spare time, spending every moment in the woods. It was a long hike to the end of the trail, growing longer every time she found a few hours to work. She learned to leave her cans of gasoline and oil in the woods, in well-secured plastic bags. Sometimes she saw signs in the woods that disturbed her. In a place where she had worked only the previous afternoon, she found the scattered long feathers and soft inner down of a turkey that had been taken by something during the night, and she hoped foolishly that it hadn't been one of 'her' birds. And one morning when she walked out, she found an enormous pile of bear droppings like a special delivery letter. She knew that the black bears slept off and on all winter without eating or defecating; in the spring they gorged until they had an enormous bowel movement that expelled a hard, thick fecal plug. She had read of the plug and now examined it, and she noted the wide caliber of the droppings, indicating a very large animal, probably the bear whose paw marks she had seen in the snow. It was as if the bear had shat on her trail to serve notice that it was his territory and not hers, and she grew anxious again about working in the woods.

All through April she pushed the trail home, attaining now a few difficult feet, now an easier advance. Eventually she came to the last major challenge, a brook to be bridged. Over a very long time the brook had eaten deeply into the forest floor, draining the wet pasture into the river. David had made three wooden bridges where they had been needed in other places; she didn't know if she could make the fourth – perhaps it would take more strength and construction experience than she possessed.

One day after she came home from work she studied the high banks and then visited the bridges David had made, analyzing what she would need to do. She could see that the job would require at least a full day, so it would have to wait for her day off, and she turned away and declared a holiday with whatever light remained of the afternoon. The river was swollen and fast, still too high for fishing, but she went home and got her spinning rod and dug half a dozen

241

worms next to the compost pile. She cast out into the largest of the beaver ponds and alternately watched the little bobber and admired the work of the beavers, which had built up the dam and thinned an impressive number of trees. Before the bobber moved at all, a kingfisher came and mocked her with its cry, and it dove into the pond and flew away bearing a fish. R.J. felt inferior to the bird, but eventually she caught two beautiful small brook trout, which she had for supper with a mess of steamed fiddleheads, tasting the season in the wild greens.

After supper, bringing out her garbage, she came upon a small black heartrock where she had dug the worms, and she pounced on it as if it could scuttle away. She brought it inside and washed it and rubbed it to bring out its sheen, and placed it on top of the television set.

Once the earth was bared of snow, it was as if R.J. somehow had been singled out to inherit Sarah Markus's serendipitous ability to discover heart-shaped stones. Everywhere she went, her eyes fell upon them as if directed by Sarah's spirit. They came in all shapes – stones with the heart's upper cheeks curvy as a pear and deeply indented as a perfect fundament, stones with angular but balanced cheeks, stones with lower points that were sharp as fate or shaped like the shallow arc of a kindergarten swing.

She discovered a stone that was as tiny as a smooth, brown birthmark, in a plastic bag of purchased plant soil. She found one the size of a fist at the base of the crumbling stone wall on the western boundary of her property. She came upon them while working in the woods, while walking on Laurel Hill Road, while doing errands on Main Street.

Very quickly, people in Woodfield observed the doctor's preoccupation with cardioid stones and began finding them for her, dropping them off with pleased smiles at her home and her office, helping her with her hobby. She became accustomed, on coming home, to emptying her pockets of stones, or taking stones from her purse or from paper bags. She washed and dried them and spent anxious moments wondering where to put them. The collection quickly outgrew the guest room. Soon the heartrocks were displayed all over the living room as well, on the wall mantels and above the fireplace. And on end tables and the coffee table. And on the kitchen counter, and in the bathroom upstairs, and on her bedroom bureaux, and on the toilet tank in the lavatory on the ground floor.

The stones spoke to her, a sad, wordless message reminding her of Sarah and David. She didn't want to hear it, but still she collected them compulsively. She bought a geology manual and began to identify the stones, taking pleasure in the knowledge that this one was basalt from the lower Jurassic era, when monster creatures had roamed the valley; that that one was solidified magma that had poured, liquid and boiling, up from the molten core a million years ago when the earth had hiccupped fiery vomit; that this stone of fused sand and gravel came from a time when ocean depths covered these now-inland hills; that that piece of glittering gneiss most likely had been a drab rock before colliding continents had transformed it in the pressure cooker of metamorphism.

One afternoon in Northampton, R.J. walked past the site of a sewer line replacement on King Street. The excavation was a trench perhaps five feet deep, cordoned off from the public by wooden saw-horses, metal barriers, and yellow plastic rope. In the corner of the hole was something that made her eyes widen, a reddish, well-shaped stone about fifteen inches long and eighteen inches wide.

The petrified heart of a vanished giant.

The worksite was abandoned. The laborers had finished work for the day and were gone, or she would have asked someone to get it for her. Too bad, R.J. thought and passed it by. But she hadn't taken five steps before she turned and went back. She sat in the dirt on the lip of the trench with her feet dangling, never mind her new slacks, and ducked her head inside the rope; then she pushed off with her hands and dropped into the hole.

The rock was fully as good as it had looked from above. But it was heavy, very difficult for her to lift, and she had to raise it the height of her neck in order to push it out of the trench. She accomplished the feat on the second try, as an act of desperation.

'Lady, what the hell?'

He was a police officer, glaring down at her in disbelief from the side of the trench that faced the road.

'Do you mind giving me a pull up?' she asked, holding up her hands. He was not a large police officer. But in a moment he had hauled her out, exhibiting as much strain as she had shown when she lifted the stone.

Breathing hard, he stared at her, seeing the dirt smudge on her right cheek, the black slacks streaked with gray clay, and the mud on her shoes. 'What were you doing down there?'

All she could do was give him a beatific smile and thank him for his help. 'I'm a collector,' she said.

Three Thursdays came and went before she had an opportunity to spend the day building her bridge. She knew what she had to do. She had walked the trail to the brook half a dozen times to study the site, and again and again she had gone over in her mind how it might be done.

She had to cut two matching trees whose trunks would provide the main bridge supports. The trimmed logs had to be heavy enough to hold weight and endure, yet light enough for her to be able to move them into position.

She had already chosen the trees and went right to them, the growl and whine of the saw a comfort, and she felt expert now as she cut the boles and trimmed them. The logs were deceptively slender. They were very heavy, but she discovered she was able to move each one a few feet at a time by lifting and heaving first one end and then the other. The thud each time a log dropped seemed to shake the earth and made her feel she was an Amazon, except that she was tiring very quickly.

With a pick and a shovel she dug four shallow sockets, two on each bank, into which the log ends needed to nest to give them stability.

Slowly but surely, she moved the logs into place, ultimately getting into the brook and lifting the logs on her shoulder to maneuver each end into its prepared slot. When she was finally done, it was lunchtime, and the blackflies and mosquitoes had begun feeding on her, so she beat a retreat.

She was too excited to spend time preparing much of a meal, eating peanut butter smeared hastily on sliced bread, and a cup of tea. She longed to soak in a hot bath, but she knew she wouldn't finish the bridge if she did, and she could smell victory. So, freshly sprayed with repellent, she went back outside.

She had bought a truckload of black locust slabs from Hank Krantz – they were piled in the back yard – and she measured and cut four-foot lengths of slab, trying to select pieces that were more or less uniformly thick. Then she carried them, three or four at a time, to the bridge site. By this time she was really tired, and she stopped for more tea. But she knew that what remained to be done was clearly within her range of capabilities, and the knowledge drove her as she placed the slabs one by one and drove in the long nails, the sound of her hammer blows daring any wild critter to challenge her in her territory.

Finally, as the late afternoon shadows darkened the woods, she finished. The bridge was strong. It lacked only elegant white birch rails that she would install another day. It was springier than it would have been if she had been able to handle thicker logs, she admitted to herself. But it was a good job, and it would serve her well.

She stood in the middle of it and danced a triumphant little tarantella.

And on the east side of the brook, the right-hand corner of the bridge moved slightly.

When she went closer and jumped up and down, the corner sank. She jumped several times, cursing, and the corner went down quite a bit more. Her tape measure told her the bridge ended up fourteen inches lower on that side than on the other.

R.J. had set the stage for the problem by neglecting to firm the soil under the log on that side, and the weight of the bridge had done the rest. She saw that it would have been wise to have placed a flat rock under each log end, as well.

She went back into the brook and tried to lift the bridge on the low end, but it was impossible for her to move it, and she surveyed the slanting structure bitterly. It would be possible to cross it gingerly, if it didn't drop any more. But it would be folly to try to get across it while carrying a heavy load, or while pushing a laden wheelbarrow.

She collected her tools and made her slow way home, bone weary and terribly disappointed. It would no longer be easy or pleasurable to boast to herself that she could do anything, if she had to add a qualifier:

'. . . Almost.'

38

The Reunion

George Palmer came to R.J.'s office one day when every seat was taken in the waiting room, and Nordahl Petersen was sitting outside on the front steps. Still, when she had finished talking with George Palmer about his bursitis, explaining why she wasn't going to give him any more cortisone, he nodded and thanked her but showed no sign of leaving.

'My youngest child is Harold. My baby,' he said sardonically. 'Now forty-two years old. Harold Wellington Palmer.'

R.J. smiled and nodded.

'Accountant. Lives in Boston. That is, he *has* been living there, past twelve years. Now he's going to be living with me again. He's coming back to Woodfield.'

'Oh? That should be nice for you, George,' she said cautiously, having no way to know whether or not it would be nice until he came to the point.

It turned out that it might not be at all nice for George.

'Harold is what they call HIV positive. He's coming here with his friend Eugene. They've been living together for nine years . . .' He seemed to lose his train of thought and then found it again with a start. 'Well, he's going to need a doctor's care.'

R.J. put her hand on George's. 'I'll look forward to meeting him and being his doctor,' she said, and squeezed his hand. George Palmer smiled at her and thanked her and left her office.

There wasn't a great deal of forest between the end of the trail and her house, but the sadly sagged bridge had dampened her enthusiasm for trail building, and she turned to her vegetable garden with relief. It was too early for tender vegetables. The gardening books said she should have planted peas several weeks earlier instead of working in the woods, but the cool mountain climate gave her leeway, and she spread peat moss, compost, and two bags of purchased greensand on the raised beds that she and David had made, and dug everything in. She planted edible pod peas, of which she was especially fond, and spinach, knowing that neither would be bothered by the heavy frosts that still fell at night with regularity.

She watered carefully – not too much, to avoid damping off, not too little, to avoid aridness – and was rewarded by a row of seedlings that lasted scarcely a week. At the end of that time they had vanished, and the clue to where they had gone was a single perfect print in the velvet earth.

A small deer.

That night she went for coffee and dessert to the Smiths' house and told them what had happened. 'What do I do now? Replant?'

'You can,' Toby said. 'You might still have time to get a crop.'

'But there are a whole lot of deer out in the woods,' Jan said. 'You'd better take steps to keep the wild animals away from your garden.'

'You're the fish and game expert,' R.J. said. 'So how do I do that?'

'Well, some folks collect human hair from barber shops and

spread it around. I've tried that myself. Sometimes it works, sometimes it doesn't.'

'How do you protect your own garden?'

'We pee all around it,' Toby said calmly. 'Well, *I* don't.' She jerked her thumb at her husband. '*He* does.'

Jan nodded. 'Best thing. One whiff of human piss, the critters find an excuse to make a business trip elsewhere. That's what you should use.'

'Easy for you to say. There is a certain physiological dissimilarity that makes my situation more difficult than your own when it comes to spraying. Would you consider coming over to my place, and . . .?'

'Nope,' Toby said firmly. 'His supply is limited, and spoken for.'

Jan grinned and offered a final word of advice. 'Use a paper cup.'

That was what she did, after replanting her peas. The problem was, she had a very limited supply too, even when she forced herself to drink more fluids than her thirst demanded. But she anointed the area next to the portion of the raised bed where she had replanted her peas, and this time when the seedlings came up, they weren't eaten.

One day R.J. heard a sound like multiple motors in her back yard, and when she left the house, she saw that a buzzing host was lifting from one of the hives. Thousands of bees rose in twisting, dancing ropes that coalesced and merged at roof height into a thick column that looked almost solid at times, so closely packed and multitudinous were the small bodies. The column became a cloud that contracted and expanded, shifted and grew, and eventually it lifted and moved darkly over the trees and into the woods.

Two days later, another hive swarmed. David had worked hard on his bees, and R.J. had ignored them, but their loss gave her no feelings of guilt. She was busy with her own work and interests, and she had decided that she had her own life to live.

The afternoon of the second swarm she received a telephone call at the office. Gwen Gabler was coming from Idaho to visit her. 'I need to be in western Massachusetts for a couple of weeks. I'll explain when I see you,' Gwen said.

Marital problems? But no, it didn't sound like that at all: 'Phil and the boys send their love,' Gwen said.

'Give my love to them. And hurry from there to here. Hurry,' R.J. told her.

R.J. wanted to pick her up, but Gwen knew what a doctor's schedule was like, and she arrived by cab from the Hartford airport, the same wise-ass, warm, wonderful Gwen!

She came in the afternoon accompanied by a spring rainstorm, and they hugged damply and kissed and stared at one another and hooted and laughed. R.J. showed her the guest room.

'Never mind that. Where's the toilet? I've held it in since Springfield.'

'First door on the left,' R.J. said. 'Ooh, wait.' She ran into her own room, grabbed four paper cups from the bureau top, and hurried after Gwen. 'Here. Would you use these, please? I'd appreciate it greatly.'

Gwen stared. 'You want a specimen?'

'As much as you can give. It's for the garden.'

'Oh, for the garden.' Gwen turned away, but her shoulders were already shaking, and in a moment she was roaring, leaning against the wall helplessly. 'You haven't changed, not one marvelous cell. God, how I have missed you, R.J. Cole,' she said, wiping her eyes. 'For the garden?'

'Well, let me explain.'

'Don't you dare. I don't ever want to hear it. Don't spoil a thing,' Gwen said, and clutching the four cups, ran into the bathroom.

*   *   *

That night they were more serious. They stayed up and talked late, late, while outside the rain drummed against the windowpanes. Gwen listened as R.J. spoke about David and told her about Sarah. She asked a question or two and held R.J.'s hand.

'And what of you? How is life in the HMO?'

'Well, Idaho's beautiful and the people are really nice. But the Highland Family Health Center is a health maintenance organization from hell.'

'Ah, Gwen, damn. Your hopes were so high.'

Gwen shrugged. She said that in the beginning it had appeared ideal. She believed in the HMO system, and she had received a bonus for signing her contract. She was guaranteed four weeks of paid vacation time and three weeks to attend professional meetings. There were a couple of doctors who seemed to her to be less than geniuses, but she saw at once that four of the staff physicians were first-rate, three men and a woman.

But almost immediately, one of the good male doctors, an internist, had left the Highland Center and had gone to work at a nearby Veterans Administration hospital. Then another man – the HMO's only other ob-gyn – had moved to Chicago. By the time the woman doc, a pediatrician, had bailed out, Gwen had a good idea what the exodus was about.

The management was very bad. The company owned nine HMOs throughout the western states and advertised that its driving goal was quality care, but the bottom line clearly was profit. Its regional manager, a former internist named Ralph Buchanan, now did time-and-motion studies instead of practicing medicine. Buchanan reviewed all the case reports to determine where money was 'wasted' by the employee-physicians. It didn't matter whether a doctor sensed something in a patient that made him or her want to investigate further. Unless there were citable 'book reasons' for ordering a test, the physician was brought to account. The company had something they called the Algorithmic

Decision Tree. 'If A occurs, go to B. If B happens, go to C. It's truly medical practise by number. The science is standardized and spelled out for you, with no allowance for individual variations and needs. Management insists that the non-clinical details of a patient's life – the background that sometimes points us to the real causes of trouble – must be ignored as a waste of time. There's absolutely no room for a doctor to practice the art of medicine.'

It wasn't the HMO system that failed, Gwen insisted. 'I still believe managed health care can work. I think medical science has progressed sufficiently so we can work under time and test restrictions established for each ailment, so long as the physicians have the right and ability to depart from "the book" without having to spend time and energy defending themselves from management. But this particular HMO is owned and run by bozos.' Gwen smiled. 'Wait. It gets worse.'

To fill in for the loss of the three good practitioners, she said, Buchanan hired what was available – an unboarded internist whose hospital privileges had been revoked for shoddy practise in Boise, a sixty-seven-year-old man who never had practiced but had spent his professional life doing research, and a young rent-a-doc general practitioner from a medical temp agency, who would work until the company was able to find another physician.

'The one remaining good physician, besides yours truly, was a bushy-tailed New Age doc in his thirties. Marty Murrow. He wore blue jeans to the office, had long hair. Actually went to medical conventions to learn new things. Tried to read everything in sight. He was a terrific young internist in love with medicine. Remember?

'Anyway, the two of us got into immediate trouble.'

It began for her, she said, when the company assigned 'the klutz from Boise' to cover for her on her days off. Many calls ensued from her to Buchanan, at first polite and friendly, rapidly becoming acerbic. She told him that she was a boarded obstetrician-gynecologist and she wasn't going to allow an unqualified person to share responsibility for her patients. That she had inherited a lot of cases from the departed ob-gyn. That she was far beyond the caseload limit specified in her contract, the limit at which she could continue to function as a physician at a quality level, and that they damn well better find another ob-gyn to share the burden.

'Buchanan reminded me that this was a team operation, that I had to be a team player. I told him he could stuff that up his flexura sacralis recti unless he hired another qualified obstetrician. So I became an honored name on his shit list.

'Meanwhile, Marty Murrow was getting into far worse trouble. His contract called for him to treat 1,600 patients, and he was handling more than 2,200 people. The lousy new doctors were each "caring for" from 400 to 600 patients. The researcher just didn't know very much about internal medicine. Whenever he was in the ICU, he had to ask the nurses to write his orders for him. He lasted less than two months.

'The patients soon caught on that there were some lousy doctors at the Highland Family Health Center. When Highland got the contract to provide health care for a small factory with fifty workers, forty-eight requested Marty Murrow as their doctor. He and I began to freak out. We didn't recognize a lot of the names on the charts. Often we were asked to sign prescription forms for other doctors' patients, to order drugs for people we didn't know and whose illnesses we weren't familiar with. And because doctors were just employees, we had no control over the general lack of quality in the place.'

One of the nurses, Gwen told R.J., was particularly bad. Marty Murrow caught her in repeated mistakes when she brought prescription refills for his signature – 'ordering the patient to take Zantax instead of Xanax, things like that. We had to watch her.' It bothered Gwen that the receptionist was rude and sarcastic in the office and over the telephone and often neglected to deliver patients' messages and questions to the doctors.

'Marty Murrow and I screamed and called them names,' Gwen said. 'We both telephoned Buchanan regularly to complain, which he liked because it gave him an opportunity to put us in our places by ignoring us. So Marty Murrow sat down and wrote to the president of the company, a retired urologist who lives in Los Angeles. Marty complained about the nurse, the receptionist, and Buchanan, and he asked the president to replace all three of them.

'Buchanan got a telephone call from the president and sent letters to the nurse and the receptionist informing them of Dr Murrow's charges. When he met them subsequently, they both told him the same story: Dr Martin B. Murrow had harassed them sexually.

'One can imagine Buchanan's pleasure. He sent Dr Martin B. Murrow a registered letter telling him of the sexual harassment charges and informing him that he was suspended for two weeks while an investigation would be held. Marty has a very attractive wife he talks about all the time and two small daughters who take every moment he can spare from medicine. He told his wife what was happening. It was the beginning of a terrible experience for both of them. Buchanan confided to several people that he had suspended Marty, and why. Almost at once, some of the Murrows' friends began to hear the rumors.

'Marty telephoned his big brother, Daniel J. Murrow, a partner in the Wall Street law firm of Golding, Griffey, and Moore. And Daniel J. Murrow telephoned Buchanan and told him that indeed there should be an investigation as announced, and that his client, Dr Martin Boyden Murrow, insisted that every single person in the office should be interviewed.'

R.J. sat up a little straighter. Although she had turned her back on the law, part of her would always respond to the right kind of case. 'Are you certain Marty Murrow didn't . . .'

Gwen smiled and nodded. 'The nurse in question is in her

late fifties and quite heavy. As somebody who is getting older and fatter all the time, I don't denigrate the aging or the obese, but I don't imagine they're more sexually alluring than young women who have never had to deal with cellulite. As for the receptionist, she is nineteen, but she's scrawny and nasty. There are eleven females who work with Marty regularly, and three or four of them are knockouts. Every one of them said Dr Murrow never had harassed her. One nurse did recall a Monday morning when she told Marty she had a test for him. 'If you're such a hot diagnostician, look into Josie's and Francine's eyes, and tell us which one got laid this weekend.' He said it must have been Francine, because she was the one with the smile on her face.'

'Not very incriminating,' R.J. said drily.

'That was the worst thing they were able to get on him. Neither of the two complainants could come up with specifics, and it was obvious they had colluded to bring the charge after he had complained about them. Others in the office had the same complaints about their work performance, and following the investigation the nurse and the receptionist were terminated.'

'And Buchanan?'

'Dr Buchanan still has his job. The offices he supervises turn in a very healthy profit. He sent Marty a letter informing him that the investigation had not resulted in conclusive evidence to substantiate the charges that had been made against him, therefore he was reinstated to practice medicine for the Highland Family Health Center.

'Marty replied at once that he planned to sue Buchanan and the two discharged employees for defamation of character and the HMO for breach of contract.

'The president of the company flew in from California. He met with Marty and asked him about his future plans. When Marty said he intended to go into private practise, the president said the company wanted to help him do that, to avert the negative publicity of litigation. He offered to pay for the unexpired portion of Marty's contract, fifty-two thousand in cash. In addition, Marty could take all the furnishings in his office and in his two examining rooms, as well as an EKG machine and sigmoidoscopy equipment that none of the other doctors had bothered to learn how to use. Marty agreed at once.'

At that point, Gwen said, she knew she didn't want to stay at the HMO either. 'But I was in a quandary. My husband had discovered that he loved to teach, and I hesitated to interfere with his career. Then, at a national meeting of business school educators in New Orleans, Phil met the dean of the business school at the University of Massachusetts, and they both agreed he would be just right to fill an opening on the UMass business faculty.

'So I promptly threatened Buchanan with a suit of my own, for breach of contract, and after a little horse-trading, he agreed to pay our expenses when we move east. We're coming back here in September, and Phil will be teaching in Amherst.'

Gwen stopped and grinned at the sight of her friend, capering like an excited and very happy child.

39
A Naming

'So? What will you do when you get here?' R.J. asked.

Gwen shrugged. 'I still believe managed care is America's only chance to get health coverage for everybody. I'll look for another HMO to hire me, I guess. And make certain it's a good one this time.'

In the morning she went to the village with R.J. They walked the length of Main Street, and she watched wistfully as people called out a greeting to the doctor or gave R.J. a smile. In the office she went from room to room, observing everything, stopping now and again to ask a question.

While R.J. saw patients, Gwen sat in the waiting room and read gynecology journals. They ordered sandwiches at the general store for lunch.

'How many ob-gyns are there in the hilltowns?'

'None. The women have to travel to Greenfield or Amherst or Northampton. There are a couple of midwives based in Greenfield, who come up into the hills. All the hilltowns are growing, Gwen, and there are enough women here now to provide a gynecologist with patients.' It would be too much for her to hope that Gwen would practice in the hills, and she wasn't surprised when Gwen merely nodded and went on to talk of something else.

That evening Toby and Jan had them to dinner. During the meal the phone rang and someone reported to the fish and game officer that a hunter had wounded a bald eagle in Colrain, so as soon as he had eaten, Jan asked their forgiveness and went to see what that was all about. It was just as well. Left to their own devices, the three women settled down in the living room and talked comfortably.

R.J. had sometimes found it dangerous to meet the close friend of a close friend. The experience could go either way – jealousy and rivalry could sour the meeting, or the two newly introduced people could see in each other what their mutual friend saw in each of them. Happily, Toby and Gwen responded to one another warmly. Toby learned all about Gwen's family, and she was frank in describing her yearning for a child and the weariness she and Jan had come to feel as a result of their unsuccessful efforts.

'This woman is the best ob-gyn I have ever met,' R.J. told Toby. 'I'd feel so much better if she were to examine you at the office in the morning.'

Toby hesitated, and then she nodded. 'If it's not too great an imposition?'

'Nonsense. It's not an imposition at all,' Gwen said.

Next morning, the three of them met in the inner office after the examination. 'You have random abdominal pain?' Gwen said.

Toby nodded. 'Sometimes.'

'I wasn't able to find any overt problems,' Gwen told her slowly. 'But I think you should have a laparoscopy, an exploratory procedure that would tell us exactly what is going on internally.'

Toby made a face. 'That's what R.J. has been trying to get me to do.'

Gwen nodded. 'That's because R.J. is a good doctor.'

'Do you do laparoscopies?'

'I do pelviscopies all the time.'

'. . . Would you do mine?'

'I wish I could, Toby. I'm still licensed in Massachusetts, but I'm not on a hospital staff. If it could be arranged before I have to go back to Idaho, I'd be happy to scrub up and participate as an observer, and consult with the surgeon of record.'

And that's how the arrangements were made. Dan Noyes's secretary was able to book the operating room for three days before Gwen was scheduled to go home. When R.J. talked with Dr Noyes, he was amiably willing to have Gwen stand at his elbow as an observer.

'Why don't you come, too,' he said to R.J. 'I have two elbows.'

Gwen spent the next five days visiting HMOs and physicians in a number of communities located within commuting distance of Amherst. On the evening of the fifth day, she and R.J. sat and watched a televised debate about national health care in America.

It was a frustrating experience. Everyone acknowledged that the health care system in the United States was inefficient, exclusive, and too expensive. The simplest and most cost-effective plan was the 'single-payer' system used by other leading nations, in which the government collected taxes and paid for the health care of all its citizens. But while American capitalism provides the best aspects of democracy, it also provides the worst, as represented by paid lobbyists applying enormous pressures on Congress to protect the rich profits of the health care industry. The enormous army of lobbyists represented private insurance companies, nursing homes, hospitals, the pharmaceutical industry, doctors' groups, labor unions, business associations, pro-choice groups who wanted abortion paid for, anti-abortion groups who wanted abortion excluded, welfare groups, the aged . . .

The fight for dollars was mean and dirty, not pretty to watch. Some Republicans admitted they wanted the health care bill killed because if it were passed, it would help the President's chances for re-election. Other Republicans declared themselves for universal health care but said they would fight to the death against either a raise in taxes or funding of health insurance by employers. Some Democrats who faced re-election campaigns and were dependent on the lobbyists for funds talked exactly like the Republicans.

The business suits on the television screens were agreeing that any plan must be phased in gently, over many years, and that they should be satisfied to cover 90 percent of the United States population eventually. Gwen got up suddenly and switched off the television in anger.

'Idiots. They talk as if 90 percent coverage would be a wonderful achievement. Don't they realize that would leave more than twenty-five million people without care? They'll end up creating a new caste of untouchables in America, millions of people who are poor enough to be allowed to sicken and die.'

'What's going to happen, Gwen?'

'Oh, they'll blunder through to a workable system, after years and years of wasted time, wasted health, wasted lives. But just the fact that Bill Clinton had the courage to make them face the problem is making a difference. Superfluous hospitals are closing, others are merging. Doctors aren't ordering unnecessary procedures . . .'

She looked at R.J. moodily. 'Doctors may have to change things without much help from the politicians, try to treat some people without charge.'

'I already do.'

Gwen nodded. 'Hell, you and I are good physicians, R.J. Suppose we started our own medical group? We could begin by practicing together.'

The thought swept R.J. into momentary excitement, but

very quickly reason took over. 'You're my best friend and I love you, Gwen. But my office is too small for two doctors, and I don't want to move. This has become my town, the people are my people. What I've made for myself here . . . it suits me. How do I explain? I can't risk ruining it.'

Gwen nodded and placed her fingers on R.J.'s lips. 'I wouldn't want to do anything to spoil things for you.'

'Suppose you set up an office of your own, nearby? We could still incorporate, and maybe form a cooperative network of good independent physicians. We could buy our supplies together, cover for one another, contract together for lab work, refer patients to one another, share someone to do our billing, and try to figure out how to provide treatment for uninsured people. What do you think?'

'I think I like it!'

The following afternoon they began searching for office space for Gwen in nearby towns. Three days later they found the space she wanted, in a two-story redbrick building in Shelburne Falls that already housed two lawyers, a psychotherapist, and a studio that taught ballroom dancing.

On a Tuesday morning they got up in the dark, had time only for coffee, and drove to the hospital through the pre-dawn chill. They went through the scrubbing process with Dr Noyes, achieving antisepsis in the prescribed routine that was at the same time necessary practise and a rite of their profession. At 6:45 they were in an operating theater when Toby was wheeled in.

'Hey there, kiddo,' R.J. said behind the mask, and winked.

Toby smiled blearily. She had already been started on an intravenous solution of lactated Ringer's solution to which a relaxant had been added – Midazolam, R.J. knew from her conversation with Dom Perrone, the anesthesiologist who was overseeing the attachment of EKG, BP, and pulse oximeter. R.J. and Gwen stood with folded arms safely outside the sterile field, watching while Dr Perrone gave Toby 120mg of Propofol.

Ta-ta, my friend. Sleep well, Tobe, R.J. thought tenderly.

The anesthesiologist administered a muscle relaxant, inserted the endotrachial tube and began the flow of oxygen, adding nitrous oxide and Isoflurane. Finally he grunted in satisfaction. 'She's all set for you, Dr Noyes.'

In a few minutes, Dan Noyes had accomplished the three tiny incisions and inserted the fiber optics eye, and presently they were watching a screen that revealed the interior of Toby's pelvis.

'Endometrial growths on the pelvic wall,' Dr Noyes observed. 'That would explain the occasional random pain noted on her chart.' In a moment they were zeroed in on something else, and he and his visitors exchanged nods; the screen showed five small cysts between the ovaries and the fallopian tubes, two on one side, three on the other.

'That might explain why there's been no pregnancy,' Gwen murmured.

'Probably it does,' Dan Noyes said cheerfully and went to work.

In an hour both the endometrial growths and the cysts had been removed, Toby was resting comfortably, and Gwen and R.J. were driving back down the Mohawk Trail so R.J. could keep office hours.

'Dr Noyes did a neat job,' Gwen said.

'He's very good. Retiring this year. He has a lot of women from the hills in his practise.'

Gwen nodded. 'Hmmm. Then remind me to drop him a letter and admire him a whole lot,' she said and shot R.J. her warm grin.

She was leaving on Friday, so they wanted to make Thursday count. 'Let's see,' Gwen said, 'I've contributed mightily and generously to the welfare of your sugar pod peas, I've altered

262

my entire life in order to become your associate and neighbor, and I've collaborated to try and help Toby. Is there anything else I can do before I leave?'

'As a matter fact. Come with me,' R.J. said.

In the barn she found the three-pound maul and the enormous old crowbar, long and thick, that had been left there perhaps by Harry Crawford. She gave Gwen work gloves and the maul, and she carried the crowbar as she led Gwen down the trail and around by the river, all the way to the final bridge. The three flat rocks were still just where she had abandoned them.

They got down into the brook. She positioned the crowbar and let Gwen hold it while she drove it firmly beneath the framework log on the far bank.

'Now,' she said. 'We try and lift it together.

'On the count of three. One . . . Two . . .' R.J. had been in junior high school when she learned about Archimedes' claim that, given a long enough lever, he could move the planet. Now she had faith. 'Three.'

Sure enough, as she and Gwen grunted together and lifted their arms, the end of the timber rose.

'Little more,' R.J. said judiciously. 'Now,' she said, 'you're going to have to hold it alone.'

Gwen's face went blank.

'Okay?'

Gwen nodded. R.J. let go, and dove for the flat rocks.

'R.J.' The lever wobbled as R.J. lifted one of the rocks and slid it into place. She bent for another rock, as Gwen gasped.

'R.J.! For . . .'

The second rock was in place.

'. . . crying . . . out . . . LOUD!'

'Hold it. Hold it, Gwen.'

The last rock thumped into place just as Gwen let go and sank to her haunches in the bed of the brook.

It took all of R.J.'s remaining strength to pull the crowbar from beneath the log. It grated on the top rock, but the three rocks stayed in position. R.J. climbed out of the brook and walked onto the bridge.

It was reasonably level. When she stamped on it, it appeared to be strong, a bridge for generations.

She did her tarantella. The bridge quivered a bit because it was flexible, but it didn't move. It felt firm and permanent. She threw back her head and stared into the leafy greenness of the trees, stamping her feet as she danced.

'I christen thee the Gwendolyn T. for Terrific Gabler Bridge.' Below her, Gwen was trying to whoop but was achieving only strangled laughter.

'I can do anything. *Anything*,' R.J. told the spirits of the forest, 'with a little help from my friends.'

40

What Agunah Feared

May was soft and good. The warmed earth could now be gardened, and graves could be dug in it again. On the fifth day of the month, two days before the annual Town Meeting, the body of Eva Goodhue was taken from the keeping vault at the Woodfield Cemetery and buried. John Richardson conducted a simple, moving graveside service. Only a handful of townfolk were there, mostly old people who remembered that Eva had come from a family that went far back in the town's history.

When R.J. came back from the funeral, she planted one of her two raised beds. She set the seeds in broad rows a foot wide, so there would be little room for weeds. She planted two kinds of carrots, three varieties of lettuce, red and white radishes, shallots, beets, basil, parsley, dill, and fava beans. It was somehow meaningful to her that Eva was now part of the earth that could bestow such beneficence.

It was late afternoon by the time she finished and put the gardening tools away. She was washing up in the kitchen when the telephone rang.

'Hello. This is Dr Cole.'

'Dr Cole, my name is Barbara Eustis. I'm director of the Family Planning clinic in Springfield.'

'Oh?'

Speaking slowly and quietly, Barbara Eustis conveyed her desperation. Her doctors had been intimidated by the violence of the anti-abortion zealots, the threats, the murder of Dr Gunn in Florida.

'Well, they gave that murderer a life sentence. Surely that will be a deterrent.'

'Oh, I hope so. But the thing is . . . a lot of doctors aren't willing to place themselves and their families at risk. I don't blame them, but I'm afraid that unless I get some physicians to help, the clinic will have to close. And that would be tragic, because women really need us. I was talking with Gwen Gabler, and she suggested I give you a call.'

She didn't! Damn you, Gwen, how could you? R.J. tasted brass.

Barbara Eustis was saying she had a couple of gutsy people who were willing to work. Gwen had promised she would work one day a week after she moved east. The voice on the phone begged R.J. to give the clinic one day a week also, to do first-trimester abortions.

'I'm sorry. I can't. My malpractise insurance premiums come to thirty-five hundred dollars a year. If I work for you, they'll go up to more than ten thousand dollars.'

'We'll pay your insurance.'

'I'm as lacking in courage as anyone. I'm just plain scared.'

'Of course you are, and with reason. Let me tell you that we spend real money on security. We have armed guards. We have volunteer bodyguards and escorts who meet our doctors and accompany them to and from the clinic.'

R.J. didn't want to have to contend with that. Or with the controversy and the crowds and the hatred. She wanted to spend her day off working in the woods, taking a walk, practicing the viola da gamba.

She never wanted to see an abortion clinic again. She knew

she would be forever haunted by what had happened to Sarah. But neither could she escape awareness of what had happened to the young Eva Goodhue and all those other women. She sighed.

'Suppose I give you Thursdays,' she said.

There was a fairly short stretch of woods between the Gwendolyn T. for Terrific Gabler Bridge and the back yard of her house, but it was mostly tough brush and close-set trees. She had only one Thursday left before starting work at the Springfield clinic, and she determined that she would attempt to finish the trail that day.

She arose early and got breakfast out of the way, eager to get outside and go to work. As she was putting away the breakfast things, there was a scratching at the door, and she let Agunah in.

As usual, Agunah ignored R.J., made her inspection of the house, and waited by the front door to be let out again. R.J. had abandoned offering pleasantries to the aloof visitor. She opened the door and waited for the cat to leave, but Agunah hung back, her spine becoming round, her tail rising. She looked like a cartoon caricature of a frightened cat, and she turned and ran into R.J.'s room.

'What is it, Agunah? What are you afraid of?'

She closed the door, compulsively turning the key in the lock, and began to peer out the windows.

There was a very large black shape moving at an unhurried pace across the meadow and toward her house.

The bear waded through the tall grass. R.J. had never imagined that a bear in the Massachusetts hills could become so large. The great male was doubtless the one whose signs she had been seeing in the woods for weeks. She stood transfixed, unable to leave the window long enough to run and search for her camera.

When he neared the house, he stopped at the crabapple

tree and stood on his hind legs to sniff at a couple of wrinkled apples left over from last year. Then he dropped back onto all fours and shambled out of her vision to the side of the house.

R.J. raced up the stairs to the bedroom window and looked directly down at him. He was staring at his reflection in the glass of the first-floor window; she was certain he thought he was looking at another bear, and she hoped he wouldn't attack and break the glass. The shaggy black hair on his neck and shoulders appeared to bristle. His great, wide head was slightly bent, and his eyes, too small for the large head, glittered with hostility.

After a moment he turned from the mirrored image. From where she watched, the power of the massive shoulders and the surprisingly thick, long legs was overwhelming. For the first time in her life R.J. actually felt the hair on the back of her neck lifting. Agunah and I, she thought.

She watched until the bear entered the woods, then she returned to the kitchen and sat in a chair without moving.

The cat went to the front door again, somewhat furtively. When R.J. opened it, Agunah hesitated only a moment and then slipped out and ran in the opposite direction from the one in which the bear had disappeared.

R.J. continued to sit. She told herself that she couldn't go into the woods now.

Yet she knew if she didn't finish the trail that day, she might not have a free day for a long time.

When half an hour had passed, she went into the barn and filled the chainsaw with fuel and oil, then she carried it onto the wood path. Jan Smith had told her that bears lived in fear of human beings and avoided them, but the moment she entered the dark, shaded trail she was terrified, aware she had left her own territory and entered the bear's. Jan had assured her that when bears were warned of human presence they would depart, and she picked up a stick and tapped it against the handle of the saw. He had also told her that it didn't warn a bear if you whistled, because they were accustomed to the sound of the birds. So she began to sing at the top of her voice, songs she had sung as a teenager in Harvard Square, 'This Land is Your Land', and then 'Where Have All the Flowers Gone?' She was well into 'When the Saints Go Marching In' when she came to the last bridge and clumped across.

It wasn't until the motor of the chainsaw had roared to life that she felt secure, and she moved quickly to overcome her fear with the hardest labor she could perform.

41
Kindred Spirits

The Family Planning clinic in Springfield was in a handsome old brownstone house on State Street, now a bit shabby but in good repair. R.J. had told Barbara Eustis that, at least for the moment, she preferred to come and leave unaccompanied, not believing that an escort offered any real protection. But now, as she parked a block away and walked to the clinic, she wondered about the wisdom of that decision. A dozen protesters were already there with signs, and as soon as R.J. started to mount the steps, the hooting began and the signs were jabbed in her direction.

One of the demonstrators held a signs saying 'JESUS WEPT'. She was a woman who looked to be in her thirties, with long honey-colored hair, a narrow nose with sculptured nostrils, regretful brown eyes. She didn't scream or wave her sign, she just stood there. Her gaze clicked onto R.J.'s, who knew they had never met but somehow felt that they knew one another, so that she nodded, and the other woman nodded back. And then she was up the stairs and inside the building, and the tumult was left behind.

*   *   *

First-trimester abortions were simple to resume, but the increased tension was back as a part of her life.

The horror was there every Thursday, the terrorizing took place all through the week. They identified her car almost at once. The telephone calls to her home began only two weeks after she started work at the clinic, and they came with regularity – the name-calling, the accusations, the threats.

Murderer, you'll die. Die, die, in pain. Your house will burn, but it won't be smoking ruins for you to find when you get home, because you'll be in the ashes. We know the house well, on Laurel Hill Road in Woodfield. Your apple trees need pruning, your roof soon will need some work, but don't bother to have it done. Your house will burn. You'll be in it.

She made no attempt to get an unlisted number; the townsfolk had to be able to reach their doctor.

She stopped at the police station in the basement of the town hall one morning and had a chat with Mack McCourtney. The Woodfield police chief listened hard when she told of the threats.

'You have to take them seriously,' he said. 'You must. I'll tell you something. My father was the first Catholic to move into this town. Nineteen thirty-one, it was. The Ku Klux Klan came at night.'

'I thought that happened only in the South.'

'Oh, no, oh, no . . . They came at night in their Yankee bedsheets and burned a big cross in our pasture. The fathers and uncles of a whole lot of the people you and I know, folks we serve every day, burned a big wooden cross near my father's house because he was a Chicopee Catholic who had dared to come here to live.

'You're a wonderful woman, doc. I know, because I've seen you in action and I've watched you closely when you didn't even know I was looking. Now I'll watch you even closer. You and your house.'

* * *

R.J. had had three HIV positive patients; a child who had contracted the AIDS virus from transfused blood, and a man who had given it to his wife.

George Palmer's son, Harold, came to the office one morning, accompanied by his friend. Eugene Dewalski read a magazine in the waiting room while she examined Harold, and then at her patient's request she called Mr Dewalski into the office while she discussed her findings.

She was certain that the things she discussed with them came as no surprise; they had known for more than three years that Harold Palmer was HIV positive. Just before coming to Woodfield he had been diagnosed with his first Coxsackie tumors, the onset of the full-blown disease. During the intake interview in her office, the two men sat and answered her questions with dry, expressionless voices. When they finished discussing his symptoms, Harold Palmer told her brightly that it was wonderful for him to be back in Woodfield. 'You can't ever take the country out of a country boy.'

'How do you like the town, Mr Dewalski?'

'Oh, I love it.' He smiled. 'I was warned about coming to live with a lot of cold Yankees, but so far the Yankees I've met have been warm. Anyway, they seem to be outnumbered by Polish farmers hereabouts, and we've already had two invitations to come over and sample homemade kielbasa and golumpki and galuska. We accepted them eagerly, too.'

'*You* accepted them eagerly,' Harold Palmer said, smiling, and the two men left amid badinage about Polish cooking.

The following week Harold returned alone for a shot. Within minutes he had collapsed into R.J.'s arms, weeping wildly. She cradled his head against her shoulder, stroked his hair, hugged him, spoke to him a long time – practiced the art of medicine. They established the relationship they would need as he entered the long, downward spiral.

It wasn't an easy time for many of her patients. The newscasters on network television reported that the stock-market index was rising again, but in the hilltowns the economy was bad. Toby became furious because a woman had made an appointment to have only her little girl examined, then had brought all three of her children for the doctor to look at. But Toby's fury died when she realized there was no insurance and almost assuredly no money to pay for three examinations. That evening, on the television news R.J. heard a United States senator reiterate smugly that there was no medical care crisis in America.

Sometimes on Thursday mornings she found a large group demonstrating in front of the clinic, at other times there were only a few people. R.J. noticed that they would show up to demonstrate during a single day of lousy weather, but they tended to dwindle away after several consecutive days of rain, except for the woman with the quiet eyes. She was there every Thursday morning no matter what the weather, never shouting, never waving her sign.

Every week she and R.J. nodded to one another, offering arcane, almost grudging concession of one another's humanity. On a morning of heavy, lashing rain R.J. came early to see the woman standing alone in the street, wearing a yellow slicker. They nodded as usual, and R.J. started up the stairs but then came back. Water was dripping from the woman's rainhat.

'Listen, let me buy you a cup of coffee. In the coffee shop at the corner.'

They looked at one another silently. The woman made up her mind and nodded. On the way to the coffee shop she stopped to stash her sign in the back of a Volvo station wagon.

The coffee shop was warm and dry, full of the clatter of dishes and the ragging voices of men talking about sports. They took off their rain clothes and sat facing one another in a booth.

The woman smiled faintly. 'Is this a five-minute truce?'

R.J. looked at her watch. 'Make it ten minutes. Then I have to go in. I'm Roberta Cole, by the way.'

'Abbie Oliver.' After a moment's hesitation she held out her hand, and R.J. shook it.

'Doctor, aren't you?'

'Yes. You?'

'Teacher.'

'Of?'

'Freshman English.'

They each ordered decaffeinated coffee.

There was a moment or two of anxiety as they awaited the first unpleasantry, but none was forthcoming. Every fiber of R.J.'s being wanted to confront this woman with facts – to tell her, for example, about Brazil, where as many illegal abortions are done annually as are done legally in the United States. The difference is that in the United States ten thousand women go to the hospital every year for complications of abortion, while in Brazil four hundred thousand women are hospitalized for the same reason.

But R.J. knew the woman opposite her no doubt was aching to present arguments of her own, perhaps to tell her that each blob of tissue she suctioned contained a soul screaming to be born . . .

'This is like a lull in the Civil War,' Abbie Oliver said, 'when soldiers climbed out of the trenches and exchanged food and tobacco.'

'It is, isn't it. Except, I don't smoke tobacco.'

'I don't either.'

They talked about music. It turned out each of them had a passion for Mozart and admired Ozawa and mourned the loss of John Williams as conductor of the Boston Pops.

Abbie played the oboe. R.J. told her about the viola da gamba.

Eventually, though, the coffee was finished.

R.J. smiled, pushed back her chair, and Abbie Oliver nodded and said thank you. She went back out into the rain while R.J. paid. By the time R.J. came out, the woman had retrieved her sign and was walking in front of the clinic, and they avoided one another's eyes as R.J. climbed the front stairs.

42

The Ex-Major

She had planted her garden during stolen half-hours late in the afternoons, after returning home from her office. Several times she had worked through the dusk and into the darkness, and she had been forced to put her small tomato and green pepper plants into the earth during a misty rain, not good gardening practise for several reasons, but the only time she had available. It was catch-as-catch-can gardening, but something within her responded to the process, enjoying the gritty promise she felt whenever there was dirt on her hands.

Still, the garden thrived. She was harvesting greens from it late on a Wednesday, bent over the raised beds, when a car with Connecticut license plates hesitated at the entrance of her driveway and turned in.

She stopped picking and watched as the driver left the car and walked toward her with a limp. Slim, but with a thick waist. Middle-aged, high hairline, iron-grey hair and brushy mustache.

'Dr Cole?'

'Yes.'

'I'm Joe Fallon.'

For a moment the name meant nothing, and then she remembered David telling her of the rocket attack that had wounded him, killing a chaplain whose name she didn't remember, and hitting the third chaplain in the troop carrier.

Involuntarily she looked at his legs.

He was perceptive. 'Yeah.' He lifted his right knee and rapped his knuckles against his lower leg, a solid thunking. '*That* Joe Fallon,' he said and grinned.

'Were you the lieutenant or the major?'

'The major. The lieutenant was Bernie Towers, may he rest. But I haven't been a major for a long time. Haven't been a priest for a long time, for that matter.'

He apologized for dropping in on her without notice. 'I'm on my way to a retreat with the Trappists at the monastery in Spencer. Due there tomorrow, and I saw on the map that I could come by here with only a little detour. I'd like to talk with you about David.'

'How did you find this place?'

'I stopped at the firehouse and asked how to get to where you lived.' He had a nice smile, an Irish charmer's smile.

'Come into the house.'

He sat in the kitchen and watched while she washed the greens.

'Have you eaten?'

'No. If you're free, I'd like to take you to dinner.'

'Very few restaurants in the hills, and a long way to drive. I was about to make a very simple supper, eggs and salad. Would you care for some?'

'It would be very nice.'

So she tore lettuce and arugula, cut up a store-bought tomato, scrambled eggs, toasted frozen bread, set the food on the kitchen table. 'Why did you stop being a priest?'

'I wanted to get married,' he said, so easily that she knew he'd answered the question many times before. He bent his head. 'For what we are about to receive, we thank you.'

'Amen.' Ill at ease, she stifled a desire to eat too fast. 'What do you do now?'

'College professor. Loyola University, Chicago.'

'You've seen him, haven't you?'

'Yes, I have.' Fallon broke toast, dropped it into his salad and pushed it around with his fork to soak up the dressing.

'Recently?'

'Fairly recently.'

'He got in touch with you, did he? Told you where he was?'

'Yes.'

She tried to blink back the tears of fury that sprang into her eyes.

'It's complicated. I'm his friend – maybe his best friend – but I'm just good-buddy Joe. So he could let me see him in . . . an emotionally frail condition. You are terribly important to him in a very different way, and he couldn't risk it.'

'Couldn't risk letting me know he was alive, all those months? I know what Sarah meant to him. What her loss must have done to him. But I'm a human being too, and he showed no regard. Certainly no love.'

Fallon sighed. 'There's a lot you can't be expected to understand.

'Try me.'

'It began for us in Vietnam. There were these two priests and a rabbi, like the beginning of a bigot's joke. David and Bernie Towers and me. All day long the three chaplains would try to offer comfort to the maimed and the dying in the hospitals. In the evening we'd write letters to the families of the dead, and then the three of us would go out on the town, tear up the pea patch. We lapped up a whole lot of alcohol.

'Bernie drank as much as David and me but he was a special priest, like a rock where his vocation was concerned. I was already having trouble keeping my vows and it was to the Jew I turned for talk and understanding, instead of to my fellow priest. David and I became very close over there.' He shook his head.

'It's strange, really. I've always felt I should have been the one to be killed instead of that wonderful priest Bernie, but . . .' He shrugged. 'A mysterious way. His wonders to perform.

'When we got back to the States, I knew I had to leave the priesthood, and I couldn't face it. I became a real lush. David spent a lot of time with me, got me started in AA, straightened me out. And then when his wife died, it was my turn to help him, and now it's my turn again. He's worth it, believe me. But he's a man who is not without problems,' he said, and she grunted in agreement. When she started to take the things away from the table, he stood and helped. She put coffee on, and they went into the living room.

'What do you teach?'

'History of religion.'

'Loyola. Catholic school,' she observed.

'Well, I'm still very much a Catholic. Did everything by the book, like an old soldier. Asked the Pope's permission to renounce my priestly vows, and the request was granted. Dorothy – my wife now – did the same. She was a nun.'

'You and David . . . you've stayed in close touch ever since the army?'

'In close touch most of the time. Yes, we're members of a small but growing movement. Part of the larger group of theological pacifists. After Vietnam we each knew we never wanted to see war again. We gravitated to certain kinds of seminars and workshops, and it became obvious that there were a number of us, clergymen and theologians of every religious stripe, who all felt pretty much the same.' He broke off as she went to pour the coffee and bring it back. When she gave him the cup he took a sip, nodded and resumed.

'See. All over the world, and ever since humanity was born, people have believed in the existence of a greater power, and they have yearned desperately to break through to the

279

deity. Novenas are said, *b'rokhot* are sung, candles are lit, donations are made, prayer wheels are spun. Holy men rise, kneel, prostrate themselves. They call on Allah, Buddha, Siva, Jehovah, Jesus, and a wide variety of weak and powerful saints. We each have our unique vision of God. We each believe our candidate is the genuine article and all the others are fakes. To prove it, we've spent century after century killing the followers of the false religions, telling ourselves we're doing the holy work of the one true God. Catholics and Protestants still kill one another, Jews and Moslems, Moslems and Hindus, Sunnites and Shiites. And on and on.

'So. After Vietnam we began to recognize kindred souls, men and women in religion who believed we could each look for God in our own way without waving our bloody swords. We were attracted to one another, and we've formed a very loose group – we call it the Peaceful Godhead. We're working to raise money from religious orders and foundations. I know of a piece of land and a building that's available in Colorado, and we'd like to buy it and set up a study center where people of every religion can meet and talk about the search for true salvation, the best religion, which is permanent world peace.'

'And David is a member of . . . the Peaceful Godhead.'

'Indeed he is.'

'But he's an agnostic!'

'Oh. Forgive my impertinence, but it's obvious that in some ways you don't know him at all. Please don't take offense.'

'That's true, I'm aware I don't know him,' she said sullenly.

'He talks a great agnosticism. But deep where he lives – and I know whereof I speak – he believes that something, a greater being than he, is directing his existence and the world's. It's just that David can't identify the power in terms precise enough to satisfy him, and so he drives himself nuts. He's perhaps the most religious man I've ever met.' He paused. 'I'm certain, after talking to him, that he

280

plans to try and explain his actions to you in person, some day soon.'

She felt sad, frustrated. She had felt that Sarah and David had offered her a warm and quiet life after a stormy and unhappy one. But Sarah was dead. And David was . . . away, chased by demons she couldn't even imagine, and not caring enough for R.J. even to contact her. She wanted to talk about it with this man, but found that she couldn't.

They carried their own cup and saucer to the sink. When he moved to wash the dishes, she stopped him. 'Don't bother to do that. I'll do them after you've gone.'

He was embarrassed. 'Well, there's something I'll ask you. I'm on the road all the time, telling the different religious orders about the Peaceful Godhead, talking to foundations. Trying to raise money to establish the center. The Jesuits pay for some of my travel, but they're not notorious for lavish expense accounts. I've a sleeping bag . . . I wonder if you'll let me camp in your barn?'

She gave him a wary, searching look, and he chuckled.

'Rest easy, I'm safe as safe. My wife is the best woman in the world. And when you've already abrogated one important set of vows, you become very careful about the other vows in your life.'

She showed him the guest room. 'Heartrocks everywhere in your house,' he said. 'Well, she was a fine young person, Sarah.'

'Yes.'

She washed the dishes, he wiped. She gave him a bath towel and a washcloth. 'I'm going to be in and out of the shower quickly, and to bed. You take as long as you wish. About breakfast . . .'

'Oh, I'll be long gone by the time you wake.'

'We'll see. Good night, Mr Fallon.'

'Sleep well, Dr Cole.'

After her shower she lay in the dark and thought of a lot of things. From the guest room she heard the soft drone, the rise

281

and fall of his evening prayer. She couldn't make out words until the end, when his satisfied voice rose a bit in relief: 'In the name of the Father and the Son and the Holy Spirit, Amen.' Just before she slept, she remembered what he had said about having already abrogated one important set of vows, and it crossed her mind to wonder if Joe Fallon and his nun Dorothy had made love before receiving the Pope's dispensation.

In the morning she was awakened by the sound of the motor of his rental car. It was still dark, and she fell back into sleep for another hour, until the alarm went off.

The guest room was as before, except that the bed was made tighter than she usually accomplished, and with military corners. She unmade it, folded the blankets, put the sheets and the pillow cases in the hamper.

She and Toby had begun to meet early Thursday mornings for an hour of paperwork before she drove to Springfield. That morning they went through the forms that required her signature, and then Toby gave her a different little smile.

'R.J. I think maybe . . . I think the laparoscopy worked.'

'Oh, Toby! Are you certain?'

'Well, I'll let you tell me for sure. But I believe I already know. I want you to do the delivery when the time comes.'

'No. Gwen will be here long before then, and there's no better obstetrician. You're so lucky.'

'Grateful is what I am.' Toby began to cry.

'You stop that, you damn fool,' R.J. said, and they hugged each other until it hurt.

43

The Red Pickup

On the afternoon of the second Thursday in July, driving away from the Family Planning clinic, R.J. saw in the Explorer's rear mirror that a battered red pickup truck also had pulled away from the curb. It stayed behind her in traffic as she crossed the city of Springfield, heading for Route 91.

She pulled over onto the grass at the edge of the highway and stopped her car. When the red pickup sailed past, she drew a deep breath and sat there for a minute or two until her pulse slowed, and then she drove the Explorer back onto the road.

Half a mile down the highway the red pickup waited by the roadside. When she passed, it moved onto Route 91 behind her.

Now she was trembling. When she came to the turnoff to Route 292 that would bring her onto the winding back road up Woodfield Mountain, she didn't take it, instead staying on I-91.

They already knew where she lived, but she didn't want to lead them onto lonely, untrafficked roads. Instead she stayed on Route 91 all the way to Greenfield and then took Route 2 west, following the Mohawk Trail up into the mountains. She drove slowly, watching the truck, trying to commit things to memory.

She stopped the Explorer in front of the Shelburne Falls barracks of the Massachusetts state police, and the red pickup truck stopped across the road. The three men in the truck sat and looked at her. She wanted to walk up to them, tell them to go to hell. But people were shooting doctors, and she got out of the Explorer and ran into the building where it was dark and cool in contrast to the bright early summer sun outside.

The man behind the desk was young and tanned, with short black hair. His uniform was starched, the shirt ironed with three vertical creases, sharper than a Marine's.

'Yes, ma'am? I'm Trooper Buckman.'

'Three men in a pickup truck have been following me all the way from Springfield. They're parked outside.'

He got up, walked out the front door while she followed. The place where the truck had been parked was empty. Another pickup truck came down the highway at a good clip and slowed when the driver saw the trooper. It was yellow. A Ford.

R.J. shook her head. 'No, it was a red Chevvy. It's gone.'

The trooper nodded. 'Come on back inside.'

He sat down behind his desk and filled out a form, her name and address, the nature of the complaint. 'You're certain they were following you? You know, sometimes a vehicle just happens to be going the same place you are, and you think it's a tail. It's happened to me.'

'No. There were three men. Following me.'

'Well now, most likely a couple good ol' boys had a schnapps or two under their belt, doctor, you know? They see a pretty woman, follow her for a while. Not a nice thing to do, but no real damage.'

'It's not like that.'

She told him about her work at the clinic, about the protests. When she finished she saw he was looking at her through a great coldness. 'Yes, I imagine there are people don't like you all that much. So what do you want me to do?'

'Can't you notify your patrol cars to watch for their truck?'

'We have a limited number of cars and they're on the main roads. There are country roads in every direction, into Vermont, down to Greenfield, south all the way to Connecticut, west all the way into New York State. A majority of the people in the country drive pickup trucks, and lots of them are red Fords or Chevrolets.'

'It was a red Chevrolet with running boards. Not new. There were three men in the cab. The driver wore rimless eyeglasses. He and the man near the passenger door were thin, or at least average. The man in the middle looked fat and had a good-sized beard.'

'Their ages? Color of hair, color of eyes?'

'I couldn't tell.' She reached into her pocket and pulled out the prescription pad she had scribbled on. 'The truck had Vermont license plates. The number is TZK-4922.'

'Oh.' He wrote it down. 'Okay, we'll check it out, get back to you.'

'Can't you do it now? While I stay here?'

'It's liable to take some time.'

Now she returned his dislike. 'I'll wait.'

'Up to you.'

She sat on a bench near the desk. He made certain he didn't do anything about her for at least five minutes, then he picked up the telephone and called a number. She heard him repeating the Vermont license plate number and then thanking somebody and hanging up.

'What did they say?'

'Have to give them time. I'll call back.'

He busied himself with paperwork and ignored her. Twice the telephone rang, and he had brief conversations that had nothing to do with her. Twice she got up restlessly and went outside to look at the highway, seeing only the traffic, heightened by people driving home from work.

When she returned the second time, he was talking on the telephone about the pickup's license plate.

'Stolen plate,' he told her. 'It was removed from a Honda sedan this morning at the Hadley Mall.'

'So . . . that's it?'

'That's it. We'll put out a bulletin, but by now they have some other number plate on the truck, you can be sure.'

She nodded. 'Thank you.' She started to leave and was struck by a thought. 'They know where I live. Will you kindly telephone the Woodfield police department and ask Chief McCourtney to meet me at my house?'

He sighed. 'Yes, ma'am,' he said.

Mack McCourtney went through her house with her, room by room. Cellar and attic. Then the two of them walked the wood path together.

She told him about the harassing calls. 'Isn't there equipment the phone company offers now that gives you the telephone number for every call?'

'Yeah, Caller ID. The service costs a few dollars a month, and you have to buy a piece of equipment that costs about the same as an answering machine. But you're left with a bunch of phone numbers, and New England Telephone won't reveal who they belong to.

'If I tell them it's a police matter, they'll set up an annoyance call trap. That service is free, but they'll charge you three dollars and twenty-five cents for every number they trace and identify.' Mack sighed. 'The trouble is, R.J., these creeps who are calling are organized. They know all about this equipment, and all you're going to get is a lot of numbers that belong to pay phones, a different pay phone for every call.'

'So you don't think it's worth trying to trace them?'

He shook his head.

They saw nothing on the wood trail. 'I'd bet a year's pay they're long gone,' he said. 'But here's the thing, these woods are deep. Lots of places to hide a pickup truck off the road. So I'd like you to lock your doors and windows tonight. I'm off at nine o'clock, and Bill Peters is the night man. We'll keep driving by your house, and we'll keep our eyes peeled. Okay?'

'Okay.'

It was a long, hot night, and it passed slowly. Several times headlights coming down the road sent light dancing into her bedroom. The car always slowed when it passed her house; she assumed it was Bill Peters in the squad car.

Toward dawn the heat was stifling. Keeping the windows closed on the second floor was silly, she decided, since she would certainly hear it if anyone set a ladder against the house. She lay in bed and enjoyed the coolness from the window, and a little after five o'clock the coyotes started to howl behind the house. That was a good sign, she thought; if humans were in the woods, probably the coyotes wouldn't howl.

She had read somewhere that much of the time the howling was sexual invitation, used to arrange mating, and she smiled as she listened: Aa-ooo-ooo-ooo-ooo-yip-yip-yip. Here I am, I'm ready, come and take me.

It had been a long time of abstinence for her. Humans after all were animals too, as ready for sex as the coyotes, and she lay back and opened her mouth and let the sound come out. 'Aa-ooo-ooo-ooo-yip-yip-yip.' She and the pack howled back and forth as the night turned pearly grey, and she smiled to realize she could be so scared and so horny, all at the same time.

44

Early Concert

It was a rich summer of joys and sadnesses for R.J., practicing among people she had come to admire for their many strengths and for the humanness of their frailties. Janet Cantwell's mother, Elena Allen, had been suffering with diabetes mellitus for eighteen years, and finally circulatory problems had developed into gangrene that forced the amputation of her right leg. With trepidation, R.J. was treating atherosclerotic lesions on her left leg as well. Elena was eighty years old, with a mind perky as a sparrow. On crutches she showed R.J. her prize-winning late lilies and huge tomatoes, already beginning to ripen. Elena tried to foist some of her surplus zucchini onto the doctor.

'I have my own squash,' R.J. protested, laughing. 'Would you like to accept some of mine?'

'Glory, no!'

Every gardener in Woodfield grew zucchini. Gregory Hinton said that anyone who parked a car on Main Street had better lock it, because if he didn't, when he came back to it he would find that somebody had put zucchini in the back seat.

Greg Hinton, R.J.'s early critic, had become her loyal

supporter and friend, and it wounded her when he developed small-cell lung cancer. By the time he came to her, coughing and wheezing, he was in trouble. He was seventy. He had been a two-pack-a-day cigarette smoker from the time he was fifteen, and he thought there were other causes of the disease as well. 'Everybody says how healthy it is to be a farmer, to work out of doors and all that. They don't think of the poor fella inhaling hay chaff in closed barns, and breathing in chemical fertilizers and weedkillers all the time. It's an unhealthy job in lots of ways.'

R.J. sent him to an oncologist in Greenfield. After an MRI showed a small, ring-shaped shadow in his brain, R.J. comforted him after radiation treatments and administered chemotherapy and suffered with him.

But there were also positive moments and weeks. There hadn't been a mortality all summer, and R.J.'s environment was fecund. Toby's abdomen had begun to expand like a popcorn bag in a microwave oven. She was racked with morning sickness that extended into the afternoon and evening. She found that intensely cold sparkling water containing slices of lemon helped to quell the nausea, so between vomitings she sat behind her desk in R.J.'s office holding a tall glass whose ice tinkled as she took small, dignified swallows. R.J. had scheduled her for amniocentesis in the seventeenth week of pregnancy.

Other births had already caused ripples in the placid surface of the town. On a moist day of dreadful humidity R.J. had delivered Jessica Garland of triplets, two girls and a boy. They had known for a long time that three babies were coming, but after the uneventful birth the whole community celebrated. It was R.J.'s first delivery of triplets, and probably her last, for she had decided to refer all maternity cases to Gwen after the Gablers moved into the hills. The babies were named Clara, Julia, and John. R.J. had once thought that country doctors had babies named for them, but she supposed that no longer happened.

One morning when Gregory Hinton came to the office for his chemotherapy, he lingered.

'They tell me, Dr Cole, that you perform abortions in Springfield.'

The formal address put her on guard; for some time he had been calling her R.J. But the question didn't take her by surprise; she had been careful not to be secretive about what she was doing. 'Yes, I do, Greg. I go to the clinic there every Thursday.'

He nodded. 'We're Catholics. Did you know that?'

'No, I didn't.'

'Oh, yes. I was born here and raised Congregational. Stacia was raised a Catholic. She was Stacia Kwiatkowski, her father was a chicken farmer in Sunderland. One Saturday night she and a couple of girlfriends came to a dance at the Woodfield town hall, and that's where I met her. After we were married, it seemed simpler to go to one church, and I started to attend hers. No Catholic church here in town, of course, but we go to Holy Name of Jesus, in South Deerfield. Eventually, I converted.

'We have a niece lives in Colrain, Rita Hinton, my brother Arthur's daughter. They're Congregational. Rita was going to Syracuse University, got herself pregnant, and the boy took off. Rita quit school, had the child, a little girl. My sister-in-law Helen takes care of the baby, Rita does housecleaning to support her. We're very proud of our niece.'

'You certainly should be proud of her. If that's what she chose to do, you should support her and be happy for her.'

'The point is,' he said quietly, 'we can't abide abortion.'

'I don't like abortion much myself, Greg.'

'Then why do you do it?'

'Because the people who come to that clinic are in desperate need of help. A lot of women would die if they didn't have a safe, clean abortion option. It doesn't matter to one of those women what any other pregnant woman did or didn't do, or what you think, or what I think, or what this group or that group thinks. The only thing that matters to her is what's happening in her own body and soul, and she must personally decide what she has to do in order to survive.' She looked into his eyes. 'Can you understand that?'

After a moment, he nodded. 'I believe I can,' he said grudgingly.

'I'm glad,' she said.

Still, she didn't want to go on dreading the approach of Thursdays. When she had agreed to help out she had told Barbara Eustis her participation would be temporary, only until Eustis had an opportunity to recruit other doctors. On the final Thursday in August, R.J. went to Springfield intending to give Eustis notice that she was through.

A demonstration was in progress when she drove past the clinic. As usual, she parked several blocks away and walked back. One effect of the Clinton administration's influence was that now police officers had to keep the demonstrators across the street, where they could no longer physically impede the progress of anyone entering the clinic building. Still, as a car turned into the clinic driveway, the signs and placards were shaken and raised into the air, and the shouting began.

Through a bullhorn: 'MOMMY, DON'T KILL ME! MOMMY, DON'T KILL ME!'

'Mother, don't kill your baby!'

'Turn back. Save a life.'

Someone must have identified R.J. when she was half a dozen steps from the door.

'MURDERER . . . MURDERER . . . MURDERER . . . MURDERER . . .'

Just before she went inside, she saw that the window of the administration office had been broken. The inside door of the office was open, and Barbara Eustis was on her hands and knees, picking up shards of glass.

'Hi,' she said calmly.

'Good morning. I wanted to talk to you for a moment, but obviously . . .'

'No, come in, R.J. Always have time for you.'

'I'm a little early. Let me help you pick up the glass. Whatever happened?'

'Not what, who. A boy maybe thirteen years old came walking past all by himself, carrying a paper bag. Right under my window, he took *that* out of the bag and threw it.'

A rock the size of a baseball was sitting on Barbara's desk. R.J. could see that it had hit a corner of the desk and splintered it. 'It's good it didn't land on your head. Were you cut by the glass?'

Eustis shook her head. 'I was in the ladies' room at the time. Very lucky, a providential urge.'

'Did the kid belong to one of the demonstrators?'

'We don't know. He ran up the street and down an alley that goes to Forbes Avenue. Police searched but they never found him. Probably he was picked up by a waiting car.'

'Lord. They're using children. Barbara, what's going to happen? Where are we heading with this thing?'

'Into tomorrow, doctor. The United States Supreme Court has upheld the legality of abortion in this country. And now the government has okayed the testing of the abortion pill.'

'You think it will make a real difference?'

'I think it will make every difference.' Eustis dumped pieces of glass into her waste basket, swore, sucked a fingertip. 'RU-486 should test fine in the United States, because it's already been in use for years in France, Britain, and Sweden.

'Once physicians are able to administer the pills and give follow-up treatment in the privacy of their offices, the war will have been won, more or less. Lots of people still will have very strong moral objections to abortion, of course, and they'll still hold demonstrations from time to time. But when women can terminate a pregnancy just by dropping in on their family doctor, the abortion struggle will pretty much be over. It's impossible for them to protest everywhere.'

'When will it happen?'

'It will take about two more years, I think. In the meantime, our job is just to hold on somehow. There are fewer and fewer doctors working in the clinics every day. In the entire state of Mississippi, there's only one man who performs abortions. In North Dakota, only one woman does them. Doctors your age won't do this work. A lot of the clinics are open only because elderly, retired physicians staff them.' She smiled. 'Old doctors have brass balls, R.J., a lot more courage than the younger physicians. Why is that?'

'Maybe they have less to lose than younger doctors. The younger ones still have families to raise and careers to build and worry about.'

'Yeah. Well, thank God for the old ones. You're a real exception, R.J. I'd give anything to find another doc like you. So tell me – what is it you want to talk about?'

R.J. dropped pieces of glass into the basket and shook her head. 'It's growing late, I'd better get to work. It wasn't important, Barbara. I'll catch you some other time.'

On Friday evening she was making vegetable stir-fry for supper and listening to the radio, Mozart's Violin Concerto, when Toby telephoned.

'Are you watching television?'

'No.'

'Oh, God, R.J. Turn it on.'

In Florida, a sixty-seven-year-old physician named John Bayard Britton had been shot and killed outside the abortion clinic where he worked. The weapon, a shotgun, had been fired by a fundamentalist Protestant minister named Paul Hill. The murder had taken place in the city of Pensacola, in the same city in which, in the previous year, Michael Griffin had killed Dr David Gunn. R.J. sat and listened to detail after detail, scarcely moving. When the stink of burning cabbage brought her from her trance she leaped to turn off her supper and dump the smouldering mess into the kitchen sink, then she came back and watched some more.

The assassin Hill had approached the doctor's car just as it had pulled up to the door and had fired the shotgun into the front seat of the car at point-blank range.

The car door and window were riddled, and the doctor had died at once. In the car with him were two volunteer escorts, a man in his seventies seated with Dr Britton in the front, who was also killed, and the man's wife seated in the rear, who was hospitalized.

The newscaster said Dr Britton hadn't liked abortion but had worked at the clinic in order that women might have a choice.

There were film clips of the Reverend Paul Hill being interviewed at earlier demonstrations, during which he had praised Michael Griffin for eliminating Dr Gunn.

There were interviews with anti-abortion religious leaders who decried violence and murder. There was a soundbite of the leader of a national anti-abortion organization, who declared that his group found the murder regrettable; but the network then showed the same man exhorting his followers to pray that calamity would come to any doctor who performed abortions.

A news analyst recounted the recent setbacks that had occurred to the anti-abortion movement in the United States. 'In the light of these new laws and attitudes, more acts of violence are expected from the most radical individuals and groups within the movement,' he said.

R.J. sat on her couch, hugging herself very tightly, as if she couldn't get warm. Even after the news broadcast was replaced by a game show, she remained transfixed by the flickering screen.

All weekend she steeled herself for trouble. She remained

294

inside the house behind locked doors and shuttered windows, wearing little clothing in the heat, trying to read and to sleep.

Early Sunday morning she left the house to make an emergency house call. When she returned, she locked the door again.

On Monday when she went to work, she parked off Main Street and approached the office on foot. Three houses away, she turned into a driveway. The back yards were unfenced, and she walked to her office and entered through the rear door.

All day at work she was distracted. That night she lay sleepless, a bundle of nerves because the harassing telephone calls had stopped. She flinched at every sound, each time the old house creaked or the refrigerator motor shuddered into life.

Finally at 3 a.m. she got out of bed and opened all the windows and unlocked the doors.

Barefoot, she carried a folding chair outside and set it by the raised beds of her vegetable garden. Then she went back to the house and brought the viola da gamba outside and sat under the stars, digging her toes into the grass and drawing out of the instrument a chaconne by Marais, a piece she had been working on. It sounded wonderful in the black morning air, and as she played, she pictured the animals in the woods listening to the strange and mystical sounds. She made mistakes but didn't care; it was music to serenade lettuce by.

The music was a transfusion of courage, and after that she was able to behave calmly. She drove to the office next day and parked in her usual place. She functioned normally with her patients. Every morning she found time to walk the trail before work, and when she returned in the afternoon she weeded the garden. She replanted bush beans and arugula that had gone to seed.

On Wednesday Barbara Eustis telephoned and told her the

clinic had arranged for volunteers to pick her up and drive her to the clinic.

'No. No volunteers.'

'Why not?'

'Nothing's going to happen, I feel it. Besides, volunteers didn't help that doctor in Florida very much.'

'. . . All right. But you drive right into the parking lot. There will be someone there, holding the parking space next to the door. And there are more police cars here than we've ever seen before, so we're very secure.'

'Fine,' R.J. said.

On Thursday, panic returned.

She was grateful when a police cruiser picked her up at the Springfield line and followed her discreetly, a couple of cars behind, all the way across the city.

There were no demonstrators. One of the clinic secretaries was holding the parking space, as promised.

Her day turned out to be uneventful and easy, and by the time the last case was finished, even Barbara was visibly relaxed. The police, and nobody else, followed her all the way back to the city line, and suddenly she was again just one of the many drivers going north on I-91.

When she reached home, she was happy to see that a small bag had been left on the front porch, containing tender new potatoes the size of golf balls and a note from George Palmer telling her to enjoy them boiled, with butter and a little fresh dill. They cried out to be accompanied by trout, so she dug a few worms and collected her fishing rod.

It was seasonally warm. As the trail entered the woods the coolness was like a welcome. The sun through the tree canopy cast a rich dappled pattern.

When the man moved out of the deepest shade, it was like her fantasies of an attack by the bear. She had time to see that he was large and bearded, long-haired as Christ, then her arm rose and fell, the fishing rod whipped across the upper part of his body, and she was striking at him. The fishing rod snapped but she kept striking at him because suddenly she knew who he was.

The strong arms wrapped themselves around her, his chin on her head hurt her.

'Careful, the hook's come loose, it will dig into your hand.'

He spoke into her hair.

'You finished the trail,' he said.

IV
THE COUNTRY
DOCTOR

45

The Breakfast Tale

Minutes after David had terrified her on the wood trail, they sat in R.J.'s kitchen and regarded one another, still a bit fearfully. They had a very difficult time beginning to talk. When last they had been together, they had stared at each other over the body of his dead child.

Each wasn't what the other had remembered. It was as though he were in disguise, she thought, missing the ponytail and intimidated by the beard. 'Do you want to talk about Sarah?'

'No,' he said quickly. 'That is, not now. I want to talk about us.'

She clasped her hands in her lap very tightly, trying to keep from trembling, fluctuating between hope and despair, beset by strange combinations of emotions – joy, a fluttering exhilaration, enormous relief. Yet there was also ruinous anger. 'Why have you bothered to come back?'

'I couldn't stop thinking about you.'

He looked so healthy, so *normal*, as if nothing had happened. He was too calm, too matter of fact. She wanted to say tender things to him, but what came out of her mouth was different. 'I'm gratified . . . Just like that. Not a word for a year, and then, "Hello, good old R.J. I'm back." How do I know that the first time we have an argument you won't get in your car and disappear into thin air for another year? Or five years, or eight years?'

'Because I tell you so. Will you at least think about it?'

'Oh, I'll think about it,' she heard a shrewish voice say with such bitterness that he turned away.

'Can I stay here tonight?'

It was on her lips to refuse him, but she found she couldn't. 'Why not,' she said, and laughed.

'I'll need a lift to my car. I left it on the village road and walked in over Krantz's land to pick up the wood trail at the river.'

'Well, you just walk yourself back to it while I make supper,' she said cruelly and a bit wildly, and he nodded without replying and left the house.

When he returned, she was under control. She told him to put his suitcase in the guest room, speaking to him politely now, as she would to any guest, to keep him from hearing her gladness, her eternal availability. She gave him a meal that wasn't a prodigal's feast – warmed-over veal burgers, yesterday's baked potato, applesauce from a jar.

They sat to eat, but before she had taken a bite, she left the table and went quickly to her room, closing the door. David heard the television being turned on and then canned laughter, a rerun of Seinfeld.

He also heard R.J. Somehow he knew it wasn't for them that she was sobbing, and he went to the door and knocked softly.

She was lying on the bed, and he knelt beside her.

'I loved her too,' she whispered.

'I know.'

They wept together as they should have done a year before, and she skooched over and made room for him. The first kisses were soft and tasted of tears.

302

'I thought about you all the time. Every day, every moment.'
'I hate the beard,' she said.

In the morning R.J. felt strangely that she had spent the night with someone she had just met. It wasn't only the facial hair and the missing ponytail, she thought as she stood in her kitchen and mixed juice.

By the time she had made toast and scrambled the eggs, he joined her.

'This is pretty good. What is this stuff?'

'I mix orange juice with cranberry juice.'

'You never used to drink it this way.'

'Well, I drink it this way now. Things change, David . . . Did it occur to you that I may have met someone else?'

'Have you?'

'You don't have a right to know any more.' Her anger broke through. 'Why did you contact Joe Fallon but not me? Why did you never telephone? Why did you wait so very long to write to me? Why didn't you let me know you were all right?'

'I wasn't all right,' he said.

The eggs on their plates were untouched and growing cold, but he began to talk, to tell her.

The color of the air had seemed to me strangely tinged after Sarah died, as if everything had been washed in a very pale yellow. Part of me was functional. I telephoned the funeral director in Roslyn, Long Island, scheduled the funeral for the next day, directed my car to New York behind the hearse, driving carefully. Carefully.

I stayed at a motel. In the morning, the service was simple. The rabbi at our former temple was new; he hadn't known Sarah, and I instructed him to make things very brief. Employees of the funeral home served as pallbearers. The funeral director had placed a notice in the morning paper, but only a few people saw it in time to attend the funeral. At the Beth Moses Cemetery in West Babylon, two girls who had been Sarah's friends in grammar school held hands and wept, and five adults who had known our family when it had been young in Roslyn stood distressed as I sent away the gravediggers and filled in the hole myself, the stones in the first shovelfuls thumping onto the coffin, the rest just dirt on dirt until it was level with the rest of the ground and then mounded.

A heavy woman I hardly recognized, who had been Natalie's best friend in a slimmer, younger version, sobbed and clasped me to her, and her husband begged me to come home with them. I was scarcely aware of what I said to them.

I left at once, after the hearse. I drove a mile or two and turned into the empty parking lot of a church, where I waited more than an hour. When I returned to the cemetery, the people who had attended the funeral were gone.

The two plots were close together. I sat between them, with one hand on the edge of Sarah's grave and one hand on Natalie's. No one bothered me.

I knew only my grief and an incredible aloneness. Late in the afternoon I got into my car and drove away.

I had no destination. It was as though the car were driving me, down Wellwood Avenue, over turnpikes, across bridges.

Into New Jersey.

In Newark I stopped at Old Glory, a workingman's bar just off the Jersey Pike. I had three quick drinks there but became aware of the staring, the silences. If I had had on overalls or jeans, it wouldn't have mattered, but I wore a ruined and earth-stained single-breasted navy blue Hart Schaffner & Marx suit, and I was a ponytailed man, no longer young. So I paid and left the bar, walking to a package store and buying three fifths of Beefeaters that I took to the nearest motel.

I've heard hundreds of drunks talk about the taste of liquor. Some describe it as 'liquid stars', 'sipping nectar', 'stuff of the gods'. I've always hated the taste of grain alcohols and stick to vodka or gin. In the motel room I sought oblivion, drinking until I fell asleep. Whenever I awoke, I would lie there puzzled for a few moments, fumbling with my mind, and then terrible pain, calamitous memory

304

would flood in, and I would drink again.

It was an old, familiar pattern, which I had perfected long ago, drinking in locked rooms where I was safe. The three bottles kept me drunk for four days. I was wretchedly ill for a day and a night, and then I had the blandest breakfast I could find and checked out of the motel and let the car take me somewhere.

It was a routine I had lived before, familiar and easily re-adapted. I never drove when drunk, understanding that I was kept from disaster only by my car, my wallet with its plastic cards, and my checkbook.

I drove slowly and automatically, my mind numb, trying to leave reality behind. But there always came a moment, sooner or later, when reality entered the car and rode with me, and whenever the pain grew beyond bearing I stopped, bought a couple of bottles, and checked into a room.

I got drunk in Harrisburg, Pennsylvania. I got drunk outside of Cincinnati, Ohio, and in places I never identified. I was drunk on and off through the change of seasons.

One warm, early autumn morning – very early morning – badly hung over, I found myself driving down a country road. It was a nice rolling landscape, although the hills were lower than in Woodfield, and there were more worked fields than forest. I pulled the car around a horse-drawn black buggy driven by a bearded man wearing a straw hat, white shirt, and black pants with suspenders.

Amish.

I passed a farmhouse and saw a woman in a long dress and a little prayer cap, helping two boys unload winter squash from the back of a flat wagon. Across a cornfield, another man drove a five-horse rig, harvesting oats.

I was nauseated and my head hurt.

I drove slowly through the farm country, houses all white or unpainted, wonderful barns, water towers with windmills, well-tended fields. I thought perhaps I was back in Pennsylvania, maybe near Lancaster, but pretty soon I came to the town line and learned I was driving out of Apple Creek, Ohio, and into the township of Kidron. I had a powerful thirst. Had I known it, I was

305

less than a mile and a half from stores, a motel, cold Coca-Cola, food. But I didn't know it.

I could easily have driven by the house, but I came upon an empty buggy with the shafts resting on the macadam of the road, the broken leather traces telling a mute story of how the horse got away.

I passed a man running after a mare that seemed to know what she was doing, keeping just ahead.

Without a second thought, when I drove past the horse, I turned my car to block the road, then I got out and stood in front of the car and waved my arms at the approaching animal. There was a fence on one side of the road and high corn on the other; when the mare slowed I went forward, talking soothingly, and grabbed the bridle.

The man came puffing up, glowering. 'Danke. Sehr danke. You know how to handle these creatures, yes?'

'We used to own a horse.'

The man's face started to swim, and I leaned back against the car.

'You are krank? Help you need?'

'No, I'm fine. Just fine.' The dizziness was passing. What I needed was to get out of the sun's bright hammer. I had Tylenol in the car. 'Perhaps you know where I can get some water?'

The man nodded and pointed at the nearby house. 'Those people, they will give you water. Knock on their door.'

The farmhouse was surrounded by cornfield but it wasn't owned by Amish – I could see into the back yard where a number of automobiles were parked. I had already knocked on the door when I noted the small sign: Yeshiva Yisroel. *The Study-House of Israel.* Through the open windows came chanted Hebrew, unmistakably from one of the psalms, Bayt Yisroel barachu et-Adonai, bayt Aharon barachu et-Adonai. *O house of Israel, bless the Lord, O house of Aaron, bless the Lord.*

The door was opened by a bearded man who looked Amish down to the dark trousers and the white shirt, but there was a skullcap on his head, his left shirtsleeve was rolled up, and phylacteries were *wound about his forehead and his arm. Beyond him, men were seated at a table.*

He peered at me. 'Come in, come in. Bist ah Yid?'

'Yes.'

'We've been waiting for you,' he said in Yiddish.

There were no introductions. Introductions came later. 'You're the tenth man,' a greybeard offered. I understood that I made the minyan, enabling them to stop chanting the psalms and begin morning prayers. A couple of the men smiled, another grouchily muttered that Gottenyu, it was about time. Inwardly, I groaned. Under the best of circumstances I wouldn't wish to be captive to an Orthodox service.

Yet under these circumstances, what could I do? There were water and glasses on the table, and first they let me drink. Somebody handed me phylacteries.

'No, thank you.'

'What? Don't be a nahr, you must put on the tefillin, they don't bite,' the man growled.

It had been too many years, they had to help me wrap the thin leather strap down my forearm, correctly across my palm, around the middle finger. And fix the box containing the Scripture between my eyes. In the meantime two other men came in and put on tefillin and said the brocha, but nobody hurried me. I learned later they were accustomed to irreligious Jews stumbling in on them; it was a mitzvah, it counted as a blessing to be able to give instruction. When the prayers started I found my neglected Hebrew rusty but very serviceable; at the seminary, in ancient days, I had been praised for my beautiful Hebrew. Near the end of the service three of the men stood for Kaddish, the prayers for the recently dead, and I stood with them.

After we prayed, we breakfasted on oranges, hardboiled eggs, kichlach, and strong tea. I was wondering how to escape when they cleared the table of breakfast things and brought out oversized Hebrew books, the pages yellowed and tattered, the corners of the

307

leather covers bent and worn.

In a moment they were studying as they sat on their unmatched kitchen chairs, but not just studying – contradicting, arguing, listening with the keenness of full attention. The topic was the extent to which humankind is composed of yetzer hatov, good inclinations, as opposed to yetzer harah, inclinations toward doing evil. I was amazed at the infrequency with which they consulted the texts before them; they plucked from their memories entire passages of the oral law redacted by Rabbi Judah eighteen hundred years ago. Their minds sped through both the Babylonian and Jerusalem Talmuds, easily and with style, like kids doing tricks on rollerblades. They engaged in pilpulistic debate over points in The Guide to the Perplexed, the Zohar, a dozen commentaries. I realized I was witnessing daily scholarship as it had been practiced for almost six thousand years and in many places, in the great Talmudic academy of Nahardea, in the beth midresh of Rashi, in the study of Maimonides, in the yeshivas of eastern Europe.

The discussion was sometimes waged in quicksilver bursts of Yiddish, Hebrew, Aramaic, colloquial English. Much of it I couldn't understand, but often it slowed as they considered a citation. My head still pounded, but I was fascinated by what I was able to comprehend.

I could identify the head man, an elderly Jew with a full white beard and mane, a fat little belly under his prayer shawl, stains on his tie, round steel spectacles magnifying intense, agate-blue eyes. The Rebbe sat and answered the questions that were put to him from time to time.

Somehow, the morning sped. I felt that I was a captive in a dream. When they broke for lunch at midday, the scholars went to get their brown-bag lunches, and I shook myself out of my reverie and prepared to leave, but the Rebbe beckoned.

'You will come with me, please. We will eat something.'

I followed him out of the study hall, through two small classrooms with rows of worn desks and children's Hebrew homework pinned to the walls next to the blackboards, and up a flight of stairs.

It was a small, neat apartment. The painted floors shone, there were lace doilies on the parlor furniture. Everything was in its place; clearly, it wasn't the home of small children.

'Here I live with my wife Dvora. She is at her job in the next town, women's klayder she sells. I am Rabbi Moscowitz.'

'David Markus.'

We shook hands.

The saleswoman had left tuna salad and vegetables in the fridge, and the Rebbe deftly plucked slices of challah from the freezer section and popped them into the toaster.

'Nu,' he said when he had blessed the food and we were eating. 'So what do you do? Salesman?'

I hesitated. To say I sold real estate would provoke awkward curiosity about what might be up for sale locally. 'I'm a writer.'

'Truly? About what do you write?'

It was what happened when one wove a tangled web, I lectured myself. 'Agriculture.'

'There's lots of farming here,' the Rebbe said, and I nodded.

We ate in companionable silence. When we were through, I helped clear the table.

'Do you like apples?'

'Yes.'

The Rebbe took some early macintosh from the refrigerator. 'Do you have a room to stay tonight?'

'Not yet.'

'So be by us, we rent our extra room, it isn't dear. And in the morning you will help make the minyan. Why not?'

The apple I bit into was tart and crisp. On the wall I saw a picture calendar from a manufacturer of matzos, showing the Wailing Wall. I was very tired of being in my car, and when I had used the bathroom, it had been spotless. Why not, indeed? I thought dizzily.

Rabbi Moscowitz got up several times during the night to go to the bathroom, shuffling on bunioned feet in carpet slippers; I figured he had an enlarged prostate.

Dvora, the Rebbe's wife, was a small, grey woman with a pink face and lively eyes. She reminded me of a kindly squirrel, and each morning she sang Yiddish love songs and lullabies in a sweet, quavering voice as she prepared breakfast.

I didn't unpack my clothing into the bureau drawers but lived out of my suitcase, aware I would be leaving soon. Every morning I made my own bed and put my things away. Dvora Moscowitz told me everybody should have such a boarder.

On Friday for dinner there was the same fare my mother had served me when I was a boy, gefilte fish, chicken soup with mandlen, roast chicken with potato kugel, fruit compote, and tea. Friday afternoon, Dvora made a cholent for the following day, when it was forbidden to cook. She placed potatoes, onions, garlic, white pearl barley and navy beans into an earthenware pot and covered them with water. She added salt, pepper, and paprika, and set it to boiling. A couple of hours before the onset of the Sabbath, she added a large flanken and placed the pot into the oven, where it baked in low heat all through the Shabbos, until the following evening.

There was a wonderful baked crust over everything when the cholent pot was opened, and the rich blend of aromas made me swallow.

Rabbi Moscowitz took a bottle of Seagram's Seven Crown whiskey from a cupboard and filled two shot glasses.

'Not for me.'

The Rebbe spread his hands. 'No shnappsel?'

I knew if I took the drink the bottle of vodka would come out of my car, and this house wasn't the place to get sodden drunk.

'I'm an alcoholic.'

'Ah. So . . .' The Rebbe nodded and pursed his lips.

It was as if I had been able to step into a story I had heard my parents relating about the Orthodox Jewish world into which they had been born. But sometimes at night I awoke and recent memory flooded in, bringing pain that made me want to reach for the bottle. Once I left my bed and walked downstairs and out into the dew-wet yard in my bare feet. I opened the trunk of the car and found the vodka and drank two great life-saving swallows, but I didn't bring the bottle back in with me when I reentered the house. If either the Rebbe or Dvora had heard me, neither of them said anything to me in the morning.

Every day I sat with the scholars, feeling like one of the cheder children who came to the classrooms in the afternoons. These men had sharpened their intellects throughout their lifetimes, so that the least of them was light years beyond my own feeble scholarship of the Bible and halakha, Jewish law. I made no mention to them that I had been graduated from the Jewish Theological Seminary of America and ordained as a rabbi. I knew that to them a Conservative or Reform rabbi wasn't a rabbi. And certainly not a rebbe.

So I listened in silence as they debated about human beings and their capacity for good and evil, about marriage and divorce, about treyf and kashruth, about crime and punishment, about birth and death.

I found myself especially interested in one exchange. Reb Levi Dressner, a trembling old man with a husky voice, pointed out three different sages who said a good old age could be a reward for righteousness, but even the righteous could meet death early in life, a great misfortune.

Reb Reuven Mendel, stout and fortyish, with a red face, cited work after work that allowed those who survived to be comforted with the thought that in death young people often were reunited with a mother or a father.

Reb Yehuda Nahman, a pale boy with sleepy eyes and a silky brown beard, cited several authorities who were certain the dead carried on a connection with the living and had an interest in the affairs of their lives.

46

Kidron

'So, did you spend the entire year with the Orthodox Jews?'
R.J. asked.

'No, I ran away from them, too.'

'What happened?' R.J. said. She picked up a triangle of cold
toast and took a bite.

*Dvora Moscowitz was quiet and respectful in the presence of her
husband and the other scholars, but as if aware that I was different,
when she was alone with me, she became chatty.*

*She was working hard to make the apartment and the study-house
spotless in time for the High Holidays, and in between washings and
polishings and scrubbings she filled me in on the history and legends
of the family Moscowitz.*

*'Twenty-seven years I have been selling dresses at the Bon Ton
shop. I am really looking forward to next July.'*

'And what will happen then?'

'I'll be sixty-two years old, and I'll retire on Social Security.' *She
relished weekends because she didn't work Fridays and Saturdays,
her Shabbos, and the shop was closed on Sundays, the owner's
sabbath. She had given the Rebbe four children before she was*

unable to bear more, God's will. They had three sons, two of them in Israel. Label ben Shlomo was a scholar in a study house in Mea-Shearim, Pincus ben Shlomo was rabbi of a congregation in Petah-Tikva. Her youngest, Irving Moscowitz, sold life insurance in Bloomington, Indiana. 'My black sheep.'

'And your fourth child?'

'She was a daughter, Leah, died when she was two years old. Diphtheria.' There was a silence. 'And you? You have children?'

I found myself telling her, not only forced to face it, to think about it, but to put it into words.

'So. It's a daughter you're saying Kaddish for.' She took my hand. Our eyes became moist, I was desperate to escape. Presently she made tea and plied me with mandel bread and carrot candy.

In the morning I got up very early, while they still slept. I made my bed, left money and a brief note of thanks, and stole away with my suitcase to the car while darkness still hid the stubbled fields.

I stayed drunk throughout the Days of Awe – in a flophouse in the town of Windham, in a rickety tourist cabin in Revenna. In Cuyahoga Falls, the manager of the motel let himself into my locked room after I had been drinking for three days and told me to leave. I sobered sufficiently to drive that night to Akron, where I found the shabby old Majestic Hotel, a victim of the motel age. The corner room on the third floor needed paint and was full of dust. Through one window I saw smoke from a rubber factory and through another glimpsed the brown flowing of the Muskingum River. I stayed holed up there for eight days. A bellman named Roman brought liquor whenever I ran dry. The hotel had no room service. Roman went someplace – it must have been a distance because it always took him so long – to fetch bad coffee and greasy hamburgers. I tipped generously so Roman wouldn't roll me while I was drunk.

I never learned whether that was the bellman's first or last name.

One night I awoke and knew someone was in the room.

'Roman?'

I turned on the light, but no one was there.

I even searched the shower and the closet. When I switched off the light, I felt the presence again.

'Sarah?' I said at last.

'Natalie? Is it you, Nat?'

Nobody answered.

I might as well call out to Napoleon or Moses, I thought bitterly. But I couldn't rid myself of the certainty that I wasn't alone.

It wasn't a threatening presence. I kept the room unlit and lay in the dark, remembering the discussion in the study-house when Reb Yehuda Nahman had quoted sages who had written that the beloved dead never are far away, and that they take an interest in the lives of the living.

I reached for the bottle and was struck by the thought of my wife and daughter watching me, seeing me weak and self-destructive in this foul room stinking of vomit. There was enough alcohol already in me to bring a sodden sleep, finally.

When I awoke I felt that I was alone again, but I lay on the bed and remembered.

Later that day I found a Turkish bath and stretched out on a bench in the steam and sweated booze for a long time. Then I took my filthy clothes to a laundromat. While they were drying I found a barber and received a very bad haircut, saying goodbye to the ponytail; time to grow up, try to change.

The next morning I got into the car and left Akron. I wasn't surprised when the car drove me back to Kidron in time for the minyan; I felt safe there.

The scholars greeted me warmly. The Rebbe smiled and nodded as if I were just returning from an errand. He said the room was vacant, and after breakfast I carried my things upstairs. This time I emptied the suitcase, hanging some things in the closet and placing the rest into the bureau drawers.

*   *   *

314

Autumn became winter, which in Ohio was very much like winter in Woodfield except that the snow scenes were more open, field upon field. I dressed as I had in Woodfield, long underwear, jeans, woolen shirt and socks. When I went outside, I wore a heavy sweater, a stocking cap, an ancient red muffler Dvora gave me, and a Navy pea coat I had bought secondhand in Pittsfield my first year in the Berkshires. I walked a lot, my skin roughening in the cold.

Mornings I participated in the minyan, more as a social obligation than because prayer made full contact with my soul. I was still interested in listening to the scholarly discussions that followed each service and found that I was understanding more of what I heard. Afternoons, the cheder children came noisily into their classrooms adjoining the study room, and some of the scholars taught them. I was tempted to volunteer to help in the classrooms, but I understood that the teachers received payment, and I didn't want to break anyone's rice bowl. I read a lot from the old Hebrew books, and occasionally I asked the Rebbe a question and we talked.

Each of the scholars knew it was God who made it possible for him to study, and they took their work seriously. When I watched them, it wasn't quite like Margaret Mead studying the Samoans – after all, my grandparents had belonged to this culture – but I was only a visitor, a stranger. I listened hard and like the others often dove into the tractates on the table in an attempt to buttress an argument. Once in a while I forgot my reticence and blurted a question of my own. This happened during a discussion of the world to come.

'How do we know there is an afterlife? How do we know there's a connection with our loved ones who have died?'

The faces around the table turned to me with concern.

'Because it is written,' Reb Gershom Miller murmured.

'Many things that are written are untrue.'

Reb Gershom Miller was irate, but the Rebbe looked at me and smiled. 'Come, Dovidel,' he said. 'Would you ask the Almighty, Blessed Be He, to sign a contract?' and reluctantly I joined in the general laughter.

*   *   *

315

One evening at supper we discussed the Secret Saints, the Lamed Vav. *'Our tradition says that in every generation there are thirty-six righteous men, ordinary humans going about their daily work, on whose goodness the continued existence of the world depends,' the Rebbe said.*

'Thirty-six men. Couldn't a woman be a Lamed Vovnikit*?' I asked.*

The Rebbe's hand crept into his beard, scrabbled about as it did whenever he pondered. Through the open door to the pantry, I saw that Dvora had stopped what she had been doing. Her back was turned to my vision, but she was a statue, listening.

'I believe she can.'

Dvora resumed her work with great energy. She looked pleased as she carried in the salmon salad.

'Could a Christian woman be a Lamed Vovnikit*?'*

I asked it quietly, but I sensed that they felt the weight of the question in my voice and knew it stemmed from something intensely personal. I saw that Dvora's eyes searched my face as she set the plate on the table.

The Rebbe's blue eyes were inscrutable. 'What do you think is the answer?' he said.

'Of course she can.'

The Rebbe nodded without surprise and gave me a little smile. 'Perhaps you are a Lamed Vovnik*,' he said.*

I took to waking up in the middle of the night with a perfume in my nostrils. I remembered breathing it in when my face was buried in your throat.

R.J. looked at David, and then she looked away. He waited a few moments before he began to speak again.

I dreamed of you sexually and my sperm leaped from my body. More often I saw your face, watched you laugh. Sometimes the dreams didn't make sense. I dreamed of you sitting at the kitchen table with the Moscowitzes and some Amish. I dreamed of you driving a team of eight horses. I dreamed of you dressed in the long shapeless Amish garb, the Halsduch *over your breast, the apron around your waist, a demure white* Kapp *on your dark hair . . .*

In the yeshiva I was offered good will to a point, but little respect. The scholarship of the men of the study-house was deeper than my own, and their faith was different.

And everyone at the yeshiva knew I was a drunk.

On a Sunday afternoon the Rebbe officiated at the marriage of the daughter of Reb Yossel Stein. Basha Stein was united with Reb Yehuda Nahman, the youngest of the scholars, a seventeen-year-old who throughout his life had been an ilui, a prodigy. The wedding was held in the barn, and everyone in the yeshiva community came. When the couple was beneath the canopy, they sang lustily:

> He who is strong above all else,
> He who is blessed above all else,
> He who is great above all else,
> May he bless the bridegroom and bride.

Afterwards, no one turned to me to offer a glass when the schnapps was poured, as no one ever offered me a glass of wine at the Oneg Shabbat that marked the end of each Sabbath service. They treated me with gentle condescension, performing their mitzvot, their good deeds, like bearded boy scouts being nice to the maimed in order to earn their merit badges toward the ultimate reward.

I felt the onset of spring weather like new pain. I was certain my life was going to change, but I didn't know how. I stopped shaving, deciding to try a beard like all the other men around me. I toyed very briefly with the idea that I might make a life for myself in the yeshiva, but I recognized that I was almost as different from these Jews as I was from the Amish.

I watched the farmers become busy in their warming fields. The *heavy, honeyed stink of manure was everywhere.*

One day, I sought out Simon Yoder on his farm. Yoder was the farmer who rented and worked the yeshiva's land; it was his runaway horse I had stopped the day I had come to Kidron.

'I'd like to work for you,' I said.

'Doing what?'

'Whatever you need.'

'You can drive?'

'Behind horses? No.'

Yoder looked dubiously at me, studying this strange English. 'We don't pay minimum wages here, you know. Much less.'

I shrugged.

So Yoder tested me, put me to work on the manure pile, and I shoveled horseshit into the spreader all day. I was in heaven. When I returned to the Moscowitz apartment that evening, muscles in protest again and clothing reeking, Dvora and the Rebbe assumed that either I had gone back to drinking or I had lost my mind.

It was an abnormally warm spring, slightly dry but with enough moisture for decent crops. After the manure was spread, Simon plowed and disked with five horses, and his brother Hans plowed behind a row of eight great beasts. 'A horse produces fertilizer and other horses,' Simon told me. 'A tractor produces nothing but bills.'

He taught me how to drive. 'You already do a good job of handling one horse. That's really the most important part. Into the traces one at a time you back them. One at a time you take off the harness. They are used to working as a team.' I found myself working behind two horses, plowing the corners of all the fields. By myself, I planted the cornfield surrounding the yeshiva. As I walked behind the horses, holding the reins, I was conscious that each window was filled with scholarly, bearded faces watching my every move as if I were a man from Mars.

Soon after planting was done, it was time for first hay to be cut. Each day I worked in the fields, breathing in a work perfume, a mixture of horse musk, my own sweat, and a heady olfactory slap, the scent of large areas of cut grass. I grew dark from the sun, and my body

318

gradually strengthened and hardened. I let my hair grow long, and the beard sprang from my face. I was beginning to feel like Samson.

'Rebbe,' I asked one night at the supper table, 'do you believe God is really all-powerful?'

The long white fingers scrabbled in the long white beard. 'In every thing except one,' the Rebbe said finally. 'God is in each of us. But we must give Him permission to come out.'

All through the summer, I found genuine joy in work. I thought of you as I labored, allowing myself to do this because I believed I was becoming my own master. I had begun to dare to hope, but I was a realist and knew I was a drunk because I lacked a certain kind of courage. All my life I had been running away. I had run from the horror I had witnessed in Vietnam, into booze. I had run from the rabbinate, into real estate. I had run away from personal loss, into degradation. I had few illusions about myself.

A pressure was building in me. As summer waned, I tried to divert it, sometimes almost frantically, but finally it couldn't be denied. On the hottest day of August, I helped Simon Yoder store the last of the second cutting of hay in the barn, and then I drove to Akron.

The package store was just where I remembered it. I bought a liter of Seagram's Seven Crown whiskey; in a kosher bakery I found kichlach, and in the Jewish market I bought half a dozen jars of pickled herring. One of the jar lids must have been loose. Before I had driven far, my car was filled with the sharp, greasy odor of fish.

I went to a jeweler and made one more purchase, a single pearl on a delicate gold chain. I gave the little pendant to Dvora Moscowitz that evening, and a rent check in lieu of notice to vacate. She kissed me on both cheeks.

Next morning after the service, I broke out the food and whiskey for the minyan. I shook hands with everyone. The Rebbe followed me out to the car and gave me a bag Dvora had left for me, tuna sandwiches and streusel squares. I expected something more portentous from Rabbi Moscowitz, and the old man didn't disappoint.

319

'May the Lord bless you and keep you. May He shine His countenance on you and bring you peace.'

I thanked him and started the motor. 'Shalom, Rebbe.' I was aware that for once I was departing a place properly. This time I told the car where to go, driving it straight toward Massachusetts.

When finally he reached the end of the narrative, R.J. looked at him.

'So . . . shall I stay?' he asked her.

'I think you should, at least for a time.'

'For a time?'

'I'm not certain about you now. But stay for a little while. If we decide we shouldn't be together, at least . . .'

'At least we can bring it to a decent end? Closure?'

'Something like that.'

'I don't have to consider. But you take your time. R.J., I hope . . .'

She touched the smooth, familiar but unfamiliar face. 'I hope so, too. I need you, David. Or somebody like you,' she said to her own astonishment.

47
Settling In

That evening, R.J. came home from the office to the rich smell of roasting leg of lamb. There was no need to announce that David had returned, she realized. If he had gone to the general store to buy the lamb, by now most of the people in town knew he was back.

He had made a wonderful meal, baby carrots and new potatoes browned in the gravy, corn on the cob, blueberry pie. She let him do the dishes while she went to her room and took the box from the bottom drawer of her bureau.

When she held it out to him, he wiped his soapy hands and carried it to the kitchen table. She could tell he was afraid to open the box, but finally he removed the cover and lifted out the fat manuscript.

'It's all there,' she said.

He sat and held it, examining it. He riffled through it, hefted it.

'It's so *good*, David.'

'You read it?'

'Yes. How could you just abandon it like that?' The question was so absurd, even she had to laugh, and he put it into perspective.

'I walked away from you, didn't I?'

People in the town had various reactions to the news that he had come back and was living with her. At the office, Peggy told R.J. she was happy for her. Toby said reassuring things but was unable to hide her apprehension. She had grown up with a father who drank, and R.J. knew her friend was afraid of what the future held for someone who loved an addict.

Toby quickly changed the subject. 'We're about reaching saturation point in the waiting room every day, and you never get to go home at a reasonable hour any more.'

'How many patients do we have now, Toby?'

'Fourteen hundred and forty-two.'

'I guess we'd better not take any more new patients once we reach fifteen hundred.'

Toby nodded. 'Fifteen hundred is exactly what I figured would be right. The trouble is, R.J., some days you get several new patients. And are you really going to be able to send people away untreated, once you reach fifteen hundred?'

R.J. sighed. They both knew the answer. 'Where are the new patients coming from, mostly?' she asked.

Together, they huddled over the computer screen and pored over a map of the county. It was easy to see that she was drawing patients from the far outskirts of her territory, mostly in towns to the west of Woodfield, where people had an extremely long trip to get to a doctor in Greenfield or Pittsfield.

'We need a doctor right here,' Toby said, placing her finger on the map at the town of Bridgeton. 'There would be lots of patients for her – or him,' she said with a quick smile. 'And it would make life a lot easier for you, not having to go that far for house calls.'

R.J. nodded. That night she telephoned Gwen, who was

involved with the task of moving her household three-quarters of the way across the continent. They discussed the patient population at length, and over the next couple of days, R.J. wrote letters to the chiefs of medicine of several hospitals with good residency programs, including details of the needs and possibilities of the hilltowns.

David had gone to Greenfield and brought home a computer, a printer, and a folding worktable, which he set up in the guest room. He was writing again. And he had made a difficult telephone call to his publisher, fearing that maybe Elaine Cataldo, his editor, no longer was working there, or perhaps had lost interest in the novel. But Elaine came on the line and spoke to him, very carefully at first. She voiced frank concerns about his dependability, but after they talked at length, she told him she had suffered terrible personal losses too, and that the only thing to do was to go on with life. She encouraged him to finish the book and said she would work out a new publication schedule.

Twelve days after David's return, there was a scratching at the front door. When he opened it, Agunah came in. She walked around and around him, pressing her furry body against his legs, reclaiming him with her scent. When he picked her up, her tongue lapped at his face.

He petted her for a long time. When finally he set her down on the floor, she walked through every room before she lay down on the rug in front of the fireplace and went to sleep.

This time she didn't run away.

Suddenly, R.J. found herself sharing her household. At David's suggestion, he bought and prepared their food, provided the firewood, did the household chores, and paid the electric bill.

All of R.J.'s needs were tended to, and she no longer came home to an empty house when her work was done. It was a perfect arrangement.

48
The Fossil

Gwen and her family arrived the Saturday after Labor Day, exhausted and cranky after three days of driving. The house she and Phil had bought overlooking the Deerfield River in Charlemont had been cleaned and was ready, but the moving van with all their furniture had broken down in Illinois and would be two days late. R.J. insisted that they move into her guest room for two nights, and she went to a rental store on Route 2 for a pair of folding cots for the children, Annie, eight, and Julian, six, whom they called Julie.

David labored mightily to make their meals a pleasure, and he got on very well with Phil, with whom he shared a love for team sports in all the seasons. Annie and Julie were attractive and loveable but they were children, full of pent-up, noisy energy, and they made the house seem small. The first morning they were at R.J.'s, the kids got into a loud and physical fight, Julie wailing because his sister insisted he had a girl's name.

Phil and David finally took them down to the river to fish, leaving the two women alone for the first time.

'Annie's right, you know,' R.J. said. 'He does have a girl's name.'

'Hey,' Gwen said sharply. 'It's what we've always called him.'

'So? You can change. Call him Julian. It's a perfectly good name, and it will make him feel like a grownup.'

R.J. was certain Gwen was going to tell her to mind her own business, but after a moment her friend grinned at her. 'Good old R.J. You still have all the answers. I like David, by the way. What's going to happen between you two?'

R.J. shook her head. 'I don't have *any* of the answers, Gwen.'

David started writing early each morning, before she left for her office, sometimes even before she was out of bed. He told her that by remembering the Amish he was able to flesh out his descriptions of people who had lived in the Massachusetts hills a hundred years ago, and describe their evenings by lamplight and their days filled with work.

The writing filled him with tension that could only be released through physical labor of his own. Late each afternoon he worked about the place, picking fruit in the small orchard, harvesting the late garden vegetables and pulling up exhausted plants and adding them to the compost pile.

He was grateful that R.J. had saved his bee hives, and he set out to rehabilitate them. They offered him all the busy-work he could ask for.

'They're a mess,' he told R.J. cheerfully.

Only two of the hives still contained healthy swarms of bees. David started to be watchful, and whenever he saw bees going into the woods he followed, hoping to recapture one of the swarms that had gotten away. In some of the hives that remained, the bees were weakened by disease and parasites. He built himself a worktable of unpainted lumber in the barn and set up a honey house. He dug right in, cleaning and sterilizing hives, dosing bees with antibiotics, and turning nests of mice out of two of the hives.

He wondered aloud what had happened to his honey separator, and to all the empty honey jars and printed labels.

'Those things are in a corner of the barn on your old place. I put them there myself,' R.J. told him.

That weekend, he telephoned Kenneth Dettinger. Dettinger looked in the barn and reported all the things were still there, and David drove over and collected them.

When he returned, he told R.J. that he had offered to buy back the separator and the jars, but Dettinger had insisted that he take them, along with his old honey sign and his entire inventory of filled jars, almost four dozen of them. 'Dettinger said he didn't want to be in the bee business. He said he'd settle for an occasional jar of honey. He's a nice guy.'

'He is,' R.J. said.

'Would you mind if I sold honey again, from here?'

She smiled. 'No, that would be good.'

'I'll have to put out the sign.'

'I like the sign.'

He drilled two holes on the underside of her sign that hung out front, then he screwed in eyebolts and hung his sign under hers.

Now somebody passing the house received a barrage of messages.

The House
On the Verge
R.J. Cole MD
I'm-In-Love-With-You
HONEY

She began to be hopeful about the future. David started going to Alcoholics Anonymous meetings again. She went with him one evening, sitting in the low-ceilinged meeting room of a graceful stone Episcopal church with perhaps forty other people. When David's turn came, he rose and faced the group.

'I'm David Markus, and I'm an alcoholic. I live in Woodfield, and I'm a writer,' he said.

They never quarreled. They got along sunnily, and she wouldn't have been troubled save for one fact she could not sweep away into a cranny where it didn't have to be examined.

He never talked to her about Sarah.

One afternoon when David had been digging up, splitting, and transplanting the tough, woody rhubarb roots that had been old when R.J. had bought the place, he came inside the house and washed something at the kitchen sink.

'Look here,' he said as he wiped it dry.

'Oh, David. It's amazing!'

It was a heartrock. The piece of reddish shale was an irregular heart, but what made it wonderful was the clear imprint of an ancient, armored fossil that was imbedded in its surface, slightly off center.

'What is it?'

'I don't know. It looks like some sort of a crab, doesn't it?'

'It's like no crab I've ever seen,' R.J. said. The fossil imprint was less than three inches long. It recorded a wide head, with prominent eye sockets, empty as Orphan Annie's. Its body shell was made up of many linear segments in a row, in three distinct longitudinal lobes.

They looked under 'fossils' in the encyclopedia.

'I think it's this one,' she said, pointing to what the book said was a trilobite, a shelled animal that lived more than 225 million years ago, when a warm, shallow sea had covered much of the United States. The little shelled animal had died in the mud. Long before the mud hardened into rock, the flesh had rotted and carbonized, leaving a hard chemical film over the imprint that was left to be discovered under a rhubarb plant.

'What a find, David! How could there be a better heartrock? Where shall we put it?'

'I don't want to display it in the house. I want to show it to a couple of people.'

'Good idea,' she said. The subject of heartrocks reminded her of something. That morning when she had brought in the mail, there had been an envelope for him from the Beth Moses Cemetery in West Babylon, Long Island. She had read in the newspaper that before the Jewish High Holidays was a traditional time for visiting cemeteries.

'Why don't the two of us go to visit Sarah's grave?'

'No,' he said shortly. 'I can't face that just now. I'm sure you understand,' he said, and he put the shale stone in his pocket and went out to the barn.

49
Invitations

'Hello?'

'R.J.? This is Samantha.'

'Sam! How are you?'

'I'm especially fine, that's why I'm calling. I want to get together with you and Gwen and share a little surprise, a little good news.'

'Sam. You're getting married.'

'Now, R.J., don't you start making all sorts of outrageous guesses, or you're going to make my little surprise seem shabby by comparison. I want you two to come to Worcester. I've already talked to Gwen, welcoming her back to Massachusetts. She said she knows you have a free day next Saturday, and she'll come if you will. Say you'll do it too.'

R.J. checked her book and saw that Saturday was still clear, except that she had dozens of chores. 'Okay.'

'Wonderful. The three of us together again. I can't wait.'

'It's a promotion then, isn't it? Full professor? Associate chair of pathology?'

'R.J., you're still an eminent pain in the ass. Goodbye. I love you.'

'I love you too,' R.J. said, and hung up, laughing.

* * *

Two afternoons later, as she drove home from her office, she came upon David, walking in the road. He had come out to intercept her, down Laurel Hill Road and up Franklin Road, knowing it was the route she took.

He was two miles from home when she spotted him, and she grinned when she saw him sticking out his thumb like a hitchhiker, and opened the car door.

He climbed in, beaming. 'I couldn't wait to tell you. I've been on the phone with Joe Fallon all afternoon. The Peaceful Godhead has been given a grant by the Thomas Blankenship Foundation. Big money, enough to establish and support the center in Colorado.'

'David, how wonderful for Joe. Blankenship. That English publisher?'

'New Zealander. All those newspapers and magazines. How wonderful for all of us who want peace. Joe asked us to come out there with him, in a couple of months.'

'What do you mean?'

'What I said. A small group of people will live and work at the center, and participate in its interfaith peace conferences as a permanent staff. Joe's inviting you and me to be among them.'

'Why would he invite me? I'm not a theologian.'

'Joe feels you'd be valuable. You could contribute a medical viewpoint, scientific and legal analysis. He's interested in having a doctor there to take care of the rest of the members. You would have your work.'

As she turned the car onto Laurel Hill Road, she shook her head. She didn't have to put it into words for him.

'I know. You already have your work, and this is where you want to be.' He reached over and touched her face. 'It's an interesting offer. I'd think about accepting it if it weren't for you. If this is where you want to be, this is where I want to be.'

*   *   *

But in the morning when she awoke, he was gone. There was a scrawled sheet of paper on the kitchen table.

Dear R.J.,
  I have to go away. There are some things I must do.
  I should be back in a couple of days.
    Love.
    David

At least this time he left a note, she told herself.

50

The Three of Them

Samantha came down to the lobby of the medical center as soon as the receptionist called and told her R.J. and Gwen had arrived. Success had given her quiet assurance. Her black hair, worn short against her beautifully shaped head, had a thick white streak over her right ear; once Gwen and R.J. had accused her of helping nature along with chemicals for dramatic effect, but they knew it wasn't so. It was Samantha's way to accept what nature had given her, and to make the very best of it.

She hugged each of them twice in turn, exuberantly.

Her announced schedule called for lunch in the hospital, followed by a guided tour of the medical center, dinner in a wonderful restaurant, and late talk in her apartment. Gwen and R.J. would stay overnight and go back to the western hills first thing in the morning.

They had scarcely started to eat their lunch before R.J. gave Samantha her lawyer's stare. 'All right, woman – give us the news we've driven two hours to hear.'

'News,' Samantha said sedately. 'Well, this is news. I've been offered the job of chief pathologist at this place.'

Gwen sighed. 'Oh, boy.'

They beamed and offered their congratulations. 'I knew it,' R.J. said.

'It's not going to happen for another eighteen months, until Carroll Hemingway, the present chief, leaves for the University of California. However, they've offered the job early, and I've accepted, because it's what I've always wanted.'

She smiled. 'But . . . that is not the news.'

She turned around the plain gold ring she wore on the third finger of her left hand, to reveal the stone. The blue diamond in the setting wasn't large but it was beautifully cut, and R.J. and Gwen were out of their seats and hugging her again.

Samantha had had a number of men in her life, but she had stayed unmarried. While she had made an enviable life for herself as a single woman, they were happy she had found someone to share it.

'Let me guess,' Gwen said. 'I'll bet he's in medicine, a full professor of something-or-other.'

R.J. shook her head. 'I won't guess. I have no idea. Tell us about him, Sam.'

Samantha shook her head. 'He'll tell you himself. He's meeting us for dessert.'

Dana Carter proved to be tall and white-haired, a compulsive forty-mile-per-week runner who was slender almost to the point of underweight, with coffee-colored skin and young eyes.

'I am nervous as a cat,' he told them. 'Sam told me meeting her family in Arkansas was going to be easy, but that satisfying you two would be the true test.' He was the human resources manager of a life insurance company, a widower with a grown daughter who was a freshman at Brandeis University, and he was funny as well as warm. He won them at once; it was obvious he was sufficiently in love to satisfy even Samantha's closest friends.

By the time he left them, it was mid-afternoon, and they spent another hour learning details of his history – he had been born in the Bahamas but raised in Cleveland – and telling Samantha how fortunate she was, and how 'damned all-out lucky' Dana was.

Sam looked very happy as she took them through the medical center, showing off her department, and then the trauma center and the heliport that serviced it, the up-to-date library, and the labs and lecture rooms of the medical school.

R.J. found herself wondering if she envied Samantha her success and her authority. It was easy to observe that the promise everyone had predicted for her when they were students had been fulfilled. R.J. saw the deference with which people at the medical center addressed her, the way they listened when she spoke and moved to carry out her suggestions.

'I think you guys should come to work here. This place is the only large medical center in the state to have a department of family medicine,' Sam said to R.J. 'Wouldn't it be nice,' she said wistfully, 'if the three of us could work in the same building, see each other all the time? I know both of you could find good slots here.'

'I already have a good slot,' R.J. said, a trifle crisply, sensitive that perhaps she was being patronized, annoyed that well-meaning people kept trying to change her life.

'Listen,' Samantha said, 'what do you have up there in the hills that you couldn't have here? And don't give me that bull about fresh air and a sense of community. We breathe very well here, and I'm as active in my community as you are in yours. You two are superb physicians, and you ought to be participating in tomorrow's medicine. We're working on the absolute forward edge of medical science in this hospital. What can you do in a rural backwater, *as a doctor*, that you couldn't do here?'

They smiled at her, waiting for her to run down. R.J. wasn't inclined to argue. 'I love practicing where I am,' she said calmly.

'I can already tell I'm going to feel the same way about the hilltowns,' Gwen said.

'I'll tell you what, you take all the time you need to answer that question,' Samantha said loftily. 'If you can think of any answer at all, you drop me a line, okay, Dr Cole?'

R.J. smiled at her. 'I'll be glad to accommodate you, Professor Potter,' she said.

The first thing R.J. saw when she turned into her own driveway the next morning was a Massachusetts state police prowl car, parked by her garage.

'Are you Dr Cole?'

'Yes?'

'Good morning, ma'am. I'm Trooper Burrows. Nothing to be alarmed about. There was a little trouble here last night. Chief McCourtney asked us to keep an eye out for your return and give him a holler on the radio.'

He leaned into his own car and did just that, telling Mack McCourtney that Dr Cole had arrived home.

'What kind of trouble?'

Shortly after 6 p.m. Mack McCourtney, driving by the deserted house, had noticed an unfamiliar blue van, an old Dodge, on the lawn between the house and the barn. When he investigated, he had found three men behind her house, the trooper said.

'Had they broken in?'

'No, ma'am. They hadn't had a chance to do anything. It looks like Chief McCourtney drove up at just the right moment. But the van contained a dozen cans full of kerosene, and materials that would have allowed them to construct a delayed-action fuse.'

'Dear God.'

She had nothing but questions, and the state trooper had few answers. 'McCourtney knows a lot more about this than I do. He'll be here in another minute or two, and then I'm leaving.'

In fact, Mack arrived before R.J. had taken her overnight

bag from the car. They sat in the kitchen, and he told her he had arrested the men and kept them overnight in the cramped, dungeon-like old cell in the basement of the town hall.

'Are they there now?'

'No, they're not, doc. I couldn't charge them with arson. The incendiary materials hadn't been removed from their van, and the men claimed they were on their way to burn brush and had stopped at your house to seek directions to the Shelburne Falls Road.'

'Might that have been true?'

McCourtney sighed. 'I'm afraid not. Why would they pull the van up onto the lawn, off the driveway, just to ask for directions? And they had a burning permit, to provide cover for a possible alibi, but it was a permit to burn grass in Dalton, all the way over in Berkshire County, and they were a long way from that town.

'Besides, their names turned out to be on the attorney general's list of known anti-abortion activists.'

'Oh.'

He nodded. 'Yeah. The van's plates were stolen, and the owner was arraigned on that charge in Greenfield. Somebody showed up right away with bail money.'

Mack had their identities and addresses, and he showed R.J. Polaroid pictures he had taken of them in his office. 'These guys look familiar to you?'

Perhaps one of them, overweight and bearded, was one of the men who had followed her from Springfield.

Perhaps not.

'I can't be certain.'

McCourtney, ordinarily a gentle officer completely protective of the civil rights of citizens, had allowed himself to step beyond his position, he admitted, 'in a manner that could cost me my job if you discuss it with anyone else.' While he had had the men in his jail he had told them, calmly and clearly, that if they or any of their friends bothered Dr Roberta

336

Cole again, he personally guaranteed them broken bones and permanent disabilities.

'At least we kept them in the lockup overnight. That cell is really miserable,' he said with satisfaction. McCourtney stood and patted her shoulder clumsily, then he left.

David came back the following day. They were constrained as they greeted one another, but when she told him what had happened, he came and put his arms around her.

He wanted to speak to McCourtney, so they went together to meet Mack at his little basement office.

'What shall we do to protect ourselves?' David asked him.

'You own a gun?'

'No.'

'You might buy one. I'd help you get it licensed. You were in Vietnam, right?'

'I was a chaplain.'

'Right.' McCourtney sighed. 'I'll try to keep a close watch on your place, R.J.'

'Thank you, Mack.'

'But I'm responsible for a lot of territory when I cruise,' he said.

The following day an electrician placed spotlights on all sides of the house, with heat sensors that turned on the lights as soon as a person or a car got within forty feet. R.J. called a company that installed security systems, and a crew worked all day installing alarms that would go off whenever an exterior door was opened by an intruder, and heat and motion sensors that would trigger the alarm if anyone should succeed in gaining entry. The system was designed to summon police or firefighters within seconds.

Little more than a week after the installation of all the electronics, Barbara Eustis hired two full-time doctors at the clinic in Springfield, and R.J. wasn't needed there any longer.

She was able to regain her Thursdays.

Within a few days, she and David largely ignored the security system. She knew the protesters wouldn't be interested in her any more; they would learn about the two new doctors and concentrate on them. But even though she was free again, there were times she didn't believe it. She had a recurring nightmare in which David hadn't come back, or perhaps he was gone again, and the three men had come for her. Whenever she was pulled from sleep by the dream or by the old house creaking in the wind or groaning the way arthritic houses do, she reached to the panel by the bed and pressed the button that filled the electronic moat and sent the dragons out on patrol. And then she moved her hand stealthily under the covers to see if it really hadn't been a dream.

To see if David was still there.

51
A Question Is Answered

When R.J. had written to hospital medical chiefs, informing them of the opportunity for a new practice in the Berkshire hills, she had emphasized the beautiful countryside and the opportunities for fishing and hunting. She hadn't anticipated a deluge of replies, but neither had she expected that her letter would go unanswered.

So she was pleased when finally she received a telephone call from Peter Gerome, who said he had completed a residency in medicine at the New England Medical Center and had followed it with a post-residency fellowship in family medicine at the University of Massachusetts Medical Center. 'Right now, I'm working in an emergency room while I look around for a country practice. I wonder if my wife and I could visit you?'

'Come as soon as you can,' R.J. told him.

Together they worked out a date for the visit, and that afternoon she sent Dr Gerome directions to her office, transmitting them on her latest concession to technology, a fax machine that would allow her to receive messages and records from the hospitals and other doctors.

She was bemused by the upcoming visit. 'It's too much to

expect that the one respondent we've had will be any good at all,' she told Gwen, anxious to make the visit an attractive one. 'At least the scenery will be at its very best for him. The leaves have already begun to turn.'

But as sometimes happens in the autumn, a drenching rain began to fall on New England the day before Peter Gerome and his wife were to arrive. The downpour drummed on the roof of the house all through the night, and in the drizzly morning R.J. wasn't surprised to see that most of the colorful foliage had been stripped from the trees.

The Geromes were a likable couple. Peter Gerome was a large teddy bear of a young man, with a round face, gentle brown eyes behind thick glasses, and almost ashen hair that he kept brushing away as it fell over his right eye. His wife, Estelle, whom he introduced as Estie, was an attractive brunette, slightly overweight, who was a registered nurse-anesthetist. She was very much like her husband in temperament, with a calm, pleasant demeanor that R.J. warmed to at once.

The Geromes came on a Thursday. She took them to meet Gwen, and then she drove them throughout the western county and into Greenfield and Northampton to visit the hospitals.

'How did it go?' Gwen asked her that night on the phone.

'I couldn't tell. They weren't exactly bubbling over with enthusiasm.'

'I don't think they're the kind to bubble over. They're thinkers,' Gwen said.

They had liked what they saw well enough to come back, this time for a four-day visit. R.J. would have wanted them to stay with her, but the guest room had been turned into David's office. Portions of his manuscript were all over the room, and he was working feverishly to end his book. Gwen wasn't sufficiently established yet to have houseguests, but the Geromes found a room at a bed and breakfast on Main Street, two blocks from R.J.'s office, and she and Gwen settled for having them to dinner every evening.

R.J. found herself hoping they would move to the area. Each of them had had exemplary training and experience, and they asked sensible, practical questions when she discussed with them the loose, HMO-like medical group she and Gwen wanted to establish in the hills.

The Geromes spent the four days driving around the county, stopping to talk with people in town halls and general stores and firehouses. The afternoon of the fourth day was chill and overcast, but R.J. took them walking on the wood trail, and Peter was appreciative of the Catamount. 'It looks like a good little trout river.'

R.J. smiled. 'It is, very good.'

'Well, may we fish it when we come out here to live?'

R.J. was very pleased. 'Of course you will.'

'I suppose that settles it, then,' Estie Gerome said.

Change – more than the change of seasons – was in the chill, leaden air. Toby was less than two-thirds through her pregnancy but she was leaving R.J.'s office. She planned to spend a month preparing for the baby and helping Peter Gerome to find and set up an office. After that, she would serve as business manager of the Hilltowns Medical Cooperative, splitting her time among R.J.'s office and Peter's and Gwen's, doing all the billing and purchasing and keeping the three sets of books.

Toby recommended her own successor as R.J.'s receptionist, and R.J. hired her, knowing that Toby's instincts about people were very good. Mary Wilson had been a member of the town planning board when R.J. had appeared before that group to get permits for her office renovations. Mary would probably be a fine receptionist, but R.J. knew she would miss seeing Toby every day. To celebrate Toby's new job, R.J. and Gwen took her to dinner at the inn in Deerfield.

They met at the restaurant after work. Toby couldn't drink because of her pregnancy, but the three of them were quickly in good humor without wine, and they toasted the new baby and the new job with cranberry juice. R.J. felt deep affection for both of her friends, and she had a very good time.

It began to rain during the drive home, when she and Toby were halfway up Woodfield Mountain. By the time she dropped Toby off it was pelting, and R.J. drove slowly, peering through the windshield wipers.

Intent on her driving, she was almost past Gregory Hinton's farmhouse when she became aware that the light was on in the barn, and she glimpsed, through the open barn door, a figure seated inside.

The road was slick, and she didn't try to brake, but she slowed the car, and when she came to the rough lane leading into the Hintons' pasture, she turned the car around and went back. Gregory was in the midst of a combined course of radiation and chemotherapy, and he had lost his hair and was suffering from the side effects of the treatment. It wouldn't hurt to say hello to him, she thought.

She drove right up to the barn door, and he turned as she slammed the car door and ran in through the rain. He was seated in a folding chair by one of the stalls, wearing overalls and a barn coat, his new baldness covered by a cap that advertised a fertilizer company.

'Whew, what a night. Hi, Greg, how are you doing?'

'R.J. . . . well, you know.' He shook his head. 'Nausea, diarrhea. Weakness like a baby.'

'This is the worst part of the treatment. You'll feel much better when it's done. The thing is, we've got no choice. We have to stop that brain tumor from growing. Shrink it if we can.'

'Damn disease.' He motioned to another metal folding chair deeper in the barn. 'Set a while?'

'I will.' She went to get the chair. She had never been in his barn; it stretched before her into the animal-warmed gloom like an airplane hangar, cows in the stalls on both sides. Far above her under the vast roof something fluttered and dove and fluttered again, and Greg Hinton saw the direction of her glance.

'Just a bat. They stay high.'

'Some barn,' she said.

He nodded. 'Made from two old barns, really. This part was original. The rear half was another barn, moved here by oxen about a hundred years ago. Always figured I'd put in one of those fancy milking parlors, but I never did. Stacia and I milk 'em old-fashioned, with their necks in stanchions so they can't move on us.'

He closed his eyes, and she reached over and put her hand over his.

'You think they'll ever find a cure for this rotten thing, R.J.?'

'I think they will, Greg. They're working on genetic cures for lots of diseases, including different kinds of cancer. The next few years are going to make an enormous difference. It's going to be a new world.'

His eyes opened and found hers. 'How many years?'

The big black-and-white cow in the stall in front of them lowed suddenly, a loud, complaining bawling that startled her. How many years, indeed. She steeled herself. 'Oh, Greg. I don't know. Maybe five? Just a guess.'

He gave her a bitter trace of a smile. 'Well, however many years. I won't be around to see that new world, will I?'

'I don't know. Lots of people with your disease live a number of years. I think it's important that you believe – *really believe* – that you'll be one of them. I know you're religious, and it won't hurt if you pray a lot right now.'

'Will you do me a favor?'

'What's that?'

'Will you pray for me too, R.J.?'

Oh, glory, wrong number. But she smiled at him. 'Well, that can't do any harm either, can it?' she said, and promised him she would. The creature in front of them suddenly let out a great call that was answered first by a cow at the other end of the barn and then by others.

'What are you doing sitting out here by yourself, anyway?'

'Well, this one is trying to drop a calf, and she's in trouble,' he said, motioning with his chin at the cow in the stall. 'She's a heifer cow. You know, never had a calf before?'

R.J. nodded. A primigravida.

'Well, she's tight, and the calf is hung up on her insides. I've called the only two veterinarians around who handle big animals any more. Hal Dominic is down bad with the flu, and Lincoln Foster is all the way over to the south county with two or three jobs still to do. He said he'd try to be here by eleven o'clock.'

The cow sounded again and clambered to her feet. 'Easy, there, Zsa Zsa.'

'How many cows do you have?'

'Seventy-seven, at the moment. Forty-one of them milkers.'

'And you know their names?'

'Just the cows that are registered. See, you have to put names on the registration papers. The ones that aren't registered have numbers painted on their sides instead of names, but this cow is named Zsa Zsa.'

The Holstein sank down again as they watched, dropping onto her right side with her legs sticking straight out.

'Shit. *Shit!* Beg your pardon,' Hinton said. 'They only go to their side like that when they're almost gone. She'll never last until eleven o'clock. She's been trying to give birth for five hours.

'I've got money sunk into her,' he said bitterly. 'A registered cow like this, I can expect eighty to a hundred pounds of milk per day. And the calf would have been worthwhile. I paid a hundred dollars just for the semen from a specially good bull.'

The cow moaned and shuddered.

'Isn't there something we can do for her?' R.J. asked.

'No, I'm too sick to handle this, and Stacia's absolutely worn out from doing most of the milking. Stacia's no longer young either. She tried to deal with this for a couple of hours and just couldn't, had to go into the house and lie down.'

The cow bellowed in pain, climbed to its feet, sank back onto its belly.

'Let me have a look,' R.J. said. She took off her Italian leather jacket and placed it on a bale of hay. 'Will she kick me?'

'Not likely, lying down like that,' Hinton said drily, and R.J. approached the cow and squatted in the sawdust behind her. It was a strange sight, a manurial anus like a great, round eye above the enormous bovine vulva in which she could see one pathetic hoof and a flaccid red object dangling to the side.

'What's that?'

'Calf's tongue. The head's just below there, out of sight. For some reason, calves often are born sticking their tongues out at you.'

'What's holding it back?'

'Normal birth, the calf would be born with the two front hooves first, then the head – the way a diver goes into the water holding his hands out in front of him. This one has the left hoof in the proper position, but the right leg is doubled back somewhere in there. What the veterinarian has to do is push the head back into the vagina and reach his hand in to see what's wrong.'

'Why don't I give it a try?'

He shook his head. 'Takes some little bit of strength.'

She watched the cow shudder. 'Well, it can't hurt to try. I've never lost a cow yet,' she said, but it was wasted, he didn't even smile. 'Do you use a lubricant?'

He eyed her doubtfully, then shook his head. 'No, you wash your whole arm and just leave plenty of soap on it,' he said, leading her to the sink.

She rolled up both sleeves of her shirt until they were all the way to the shoulders, and then she scrubbed in the cold water, using the thick, stained block of laundry soap that was there.

Then she went back behind the cow. 'Now, Zsa Zsa,' she said, and then felt silly to be speaking to a rear end. As R.J.'s fingers and then her hand entered the warm moistness of inner space, the cow extended her tail, straight and rigid as a poker.

The calf's head was indeed just below the surface, but it felt immovable. When she looked at Greg, she saw that despite his concern his eyes held a clear I-told-you-so, and R.J. took a breath and leaned into it, as if trying to push a swimmer's head down into almost-solid water. Slowly, the head began to recede. When there was room, she pushed her hand into the cow's vagina, wrist deep, then halfway to her elbow, and her fingers found something else.

'I can feel . . . I think it's the calf's knee.'

'Yeah, probably is. See if you can reach below it, pull the hoof up,' Hinton said, and R.J. tried.

She worked her hand and arm deeper but suddenly felt a kind of cosmic ripple as undeniable as a small earthquake, then a rolling force that pushed a tsunami of muscle and tissue against her hand and forearm and simply moved them up and out like a seed spat out so forcefully that her entire body fell back.

'What the hell,' she whispered, but she didn't need Greg to tell her it was a variety of vaginal contraction she had never met before.

She took the time to resoap her arm. Back at the cow, she spent several minutes of experimentation before she realized what she was up against. The contractions came once a minute and lasted about forty-five seconds, leaving her only a fifteen-second window in which to work. She pushed her arm deep into the straining butt in front of her as soon as she felt a contraction slacken – past the knee, along the foreleg.

'I can feel a bone, the pelvic bone,' she told Greg.

And then, 'I've got the hoof, but it's caught under the pelvic bone.'

The rigid tail switched, perhaps in pain, and smacked R.J.

in the mouth. Sputtering, she grabbed the tail with her left hand and held it. She was warned by new ripples and had just enough time to grasp the hoof and hold on while a vaginal vise clamped her arm from fingertips to shoulder. After a moment there was no danger her arm would be expelled, because the pressure around it had become too tight. The pressure pushed the front of her wrist against the cow's pelvic bone. The pain made her gasp, but her arm quickly became numb, and R.J. closed her eyes and dug her forehead into Zsa Zsa. Her arm was captive all the way to the shoulder; she had become a prisoner, joined to this cow. She felt faint and experienced a sudden fantasy, a terrible certainty that Zsa Zsa was going to die, and they would have to cut up the cow's carcass in order to free her.

She didn't hear Stacia Hinton come into the barn, but she caught the woman's cranky challenge: 'What's that girl think she's doing in there?' and an inaudible mumble as Greg Hinton replied. R.J. smelled manure, and the internal odor of the cow, and the animal stink of her own sweat and terror. Then the contraction was over.

She had delivered enough human babies to know now what had to be done, and she withdrew her numbed hand as far as the calf's knee and pushed it back. Then she was able to reach past it, in and down. When her hand found the hoof again, she had to fight against a panic that made her want to rush things, because she didn't want to be in the vagina when the next contraction came.

But she worked carefully, grasping the hoof, working it up the vagina, and finally out and next to the other hoof, where it belonged.

'Heyyyy!' Greg Hinton breathed in delight.

'Good girl!' Stacia called.

At the next contraction, the calf's head appeared.

Hello, there, R.J. told it silently, enchanted. But they were unable to pull more than the forelegs and head from the cow. The calf was stuck like a cork in a bottle.

'If only we had a calf puller,' Stacia Hinton said.

'What's that?'

'It's kind of a winch,' Greg said.

'Tie the hooves together,' R.J. said. She went to the Explorer and released the hook of the come-along, and pulled the cable into the barn.

The calf was drawn out so easily – such an argument for technology, R.J. thought.

'Bull calf,' Greg said.

R.J. sat on the floor and watched Stacia wipe mucus, the remains of the water bag, from the little bull's nostrils. They brought the calf around to the front of the cow, but Zsa Zsa was exhausted and barely moved. Greg began rubbing the newborn's chest with clumps of dry hay. 'This gets the lungs working, that's why the cow always gives the calf a rough licking with her tongue. But this little fella's momma is too tired to lick a stamp.'

'Will she be all right?' R.J. asked.

'Sure she will,' Stacia said. 'I'll get her a nice bucket of warm water in a while. That'll help her pass the placenta.'

R.J. raised herself from the floor and went to the sink. She washed her hands and arm, but it would be impossible to get herself clean there, she saw at once.

'Got some – ah, manure in your hair,' Greg said delicately.

'Don't touch it, it'll just smear, dear,' Stacia said.

R.J. stowed the come-along cable and, carrying the leather jacket well in front of her, placed it in the back seat of the car, as far from her as possible.

'Good night.'

She scarcely heard their expressions of gratitude. She drove home trying to make as little contact as possible with the car upholstery.

When she was in her kitchen she took off her shirt. The sleeves had rolled down and the front was smeared as well; she identified blood, mucus, soap, manure, and a variety of

348

birth fluids, and she shuddered and rolled it up and dropped it into the trash bin.

She stayed under the hot shower a long time, massaging her arm and using a great deal of soap and shampoo.

When she got out, she brushed her teeth and then put on her pajamas in the dark.

'What?' David called.

'Nothing,' she said, and he went back to sleep.

She had intended to go to sleep too, but instead she went back down to the kitchen and put water on the stove for coffee. Her arm was bruised and aching, but she flexed her fingers and her wrist and her elbow and saw that nothing was broken. She took paper and a pen from her desk and sat at the table to make certain she could write.

She decided to send a letter to Samantha Potter.

Dear Sam,

You told me to write if I thought of something a doctor can do in the country that she can't do in a medical center.

Tonight, I thought of something:

You can put your arm into a cow.

Yours truly,

R.J.

52

The Calling Card

One morning R.J. realized to her discomfort that the date was approaching when she would be required to renew her license to practice medicine in the Commonwealth of Massachusetts, and she wasn't prepared to apply. The state license had to be renewed every two years, and to safeguard the public, the law required that every physician who applied for relicensing must submit evidence that he or she had taken a hundred hours of continuing medical education.

The system was designed to update medical knowledge and continually sharpen skills, and to prevent doctors from falling below the standards of their profession. R.J. thoroughly approved of the concept of continuing education, but she realized that over a period of almost two years she had accrued only eighty-one CME points. Busy establishing her new practice and working at the Springfield clinic, she had neglected her educational program.

The local hospitals frequently offered lectures or seminars worth a few points, but she didn't have enough time left to fulfil her obligation that way.

'You need to attend a large professional meeting,' Gwen said. 'I'm in the same position myself.'

So R.J. began to study the meeting announcements as she read her medical journals, and she noted that a three-day cancer symposium for primary care physicians would be held in New York City, at the Plaza Hotel. Sponsored jointly by the American Cancer Society and the American Board of Internal Medicine, it offered twenty-eight continuing medical education points.

Peter Gerome agreed that he and Estie would come and stay at her house while she was gone, so Peter could cover for her. He had applied for hospital privileges but they hadn't come through yet, and R.J. arranged for a Greenfield internist to admit any patients who might have to be hospitalized.

David was laboring on his next-to-last chapter, and they agreed he couldn't interrupt his work. So she drove to New York alone, through the pale-lemony sunshine of early November.

She found that although she had been happy to flee the city pressures when she had left Boston, now she was ready to embrace them. After the solitude and quiet of the country, New York seemed like a colossal human anthill, and the interaction of all those people was a powerful stimulant. Driving through Manhattan was no pleasure, and she was content to surrender her car to the doorman at the hotel, but she was glad she had come.

Her room was on the ninth floor, small but comfortable. She took a short nap and then had just enough time to shower and dress. Registration was combined with a cocktail party, and she had a beer and helped herself hungrily to the lavish buffet.

She saw no one she knew. There were many couples. At the buffet a doctor whose nametag said he was Robert Starbuck from Detroit, Michigan, struck up a conversation.

'And where in Massachusetts is Woodfield?' he said, peering at her nametag.

'Just off the Mohawk Trail.'

'Ah. Old mountains, worn down to loveliness. Do you drive around all the time, looking at the scenery?'

She smiled. 'No. I just observe it when I go out on house calls.'

Now he peered at her face. 'You make house calls?'

His plate was empty, and he deserted her for the buffet table, but soon he was back. He was a moderately attractive man, but he was so openly and so hungrily seeking something other than conversation that she found it easy to leave him along with the dirty dishes when she had finished eating.

She took the elevator to the lobby and walked outside, into New York City. Central Park wasn't the place to go at night and didn't tempt her; she had trees and grass at home. She moved slowly down Fifth Avenue, stopping at almost every window and spending a long time at some, studying the lavishness of apparel, luggage, shoes, jewelry, books.

She walked down half a dozen blocks, crossed the street, and walked uptown again until she returned to the hotel. Then she went upstairs and went to bed early, as she had always done before classes during the long years of scholarship. She could hear Charlie Harris telling her, 'Gotta take care of business, R.J.'

It was a good conference, designed to be intensive and meaty, with a continental breakfast served during the first session of every morning, and lectures during lunch and dinner. R.J. treated it very seriously. She didn't skip a session, she took careful notes, and she arranged to purchase the tape recordings that were made of several of the lectures that particularly interested her. Evenings were reserved for entertainment, with several good choices. The first evening she saw a revival of *Show Boat* and enjoyed it a lot, and on the second evening she watched the Dance Theater of Harlem, with great pleasure.

By the third morning she had accumulated enough points

to guarantee her relicensing. Only the earliest of the third-day presentations interested her, and she thought that perhaps she would break away from the conference and do a little shopping before leaving New York.

On the way back to her room to pack, she suddenly had a better idea.

The concierge was a determinedly cheerful woman of late middle age. 'But of course,' she said when R.J. asked her if she had a road map of greater New York.

'Can you tell me how to drive to West Babylon, Long Island?'

'If madam will give me but a moment.' The woman consulted the map and then she drew in the route with confident sweeps of her ink marker.

R.J. stopped at the first filling station she saw once she had left the freeway, and asked the way to the Beth Moses Cemetery.

When she came to it, she followed its perimeter until she came to the cemetery entrance. There was an administration building just inside the gate, and she parked the car and went inside. A man about her own age, wearing a blue suit and a white skullcap on his head of sparse blond hair, sat behind a desk signing papers. 'Good morning,' he said without looking up.

'Good morning. I would like some help in finding a grave.'

He nodded. 'Name of deceased?'

'Markus. Sarah Markus.'

He swiveled his chair around to the computer behind him and typed in the name.

'Yes, we have six by that name. Middle initial?'

'None. Markus with a K, not a C.'

'Ah. But there are two. Was she sixty-seven years old, or seventeen?'

'Seventeen,' R.J. said thinly, and the man nodded. 'There are so many,' he said apologetically.

'You have such a large cemetery.'

'Sixty acres.' He took a paper bearing a diagram of the cemetery and drew directions with his pen. 'Twelve sections down from this building, you turn right. Eight sections beyond that, take a left. The grave you seek is midway in the second row. If you get lost come back, I'll take you there myself . . . Yes,' he said, glancing at the monitor to confirm the location.

'We have everything on computer,' he said with pride, 'everything. I see there was a dedication there last month.'

'A dedication?'

'Yes, when the memorial stone was unveiled.'

'Oh.' She thanked him and left, clutching her paper.

So R.J. walked slowly down the narrow roadway of gritty rock dust. Beyond the cemetery wall cars zoomed, a motorcycle burred past, brakes squealed, the sound of a horn intruded.

Counting the sections.

R.J.'s mother was buried in a cemetery in Cambridge, with grassy spaces between headstones. These graves were terribly close to one another, she thought. They were so many, indeed, people moving out of one city and into another.

. . . Eleven . . . twelve.

She turned right and marched down eight sections.

It should be here.

In the section beyond, people sat in chairs next to a hole in the ground. A man in a skullcap finished talking, and mourners lined up to place a shovelful of dirt in the grave.

R.J. went to the second row in her section, trying to move unobtrusively. Now she was looking at individual stones, not sections. Emanuel Rubin. Lester Rogovin.

Many of the gravestones had small stones on top of them, calling cards left to mark a visit by the living. Some graves had been planted with flowers or shrubs. One was obscured by an overgrown yew; R.J. pushed aside the branches and read the name, Leah Schwartz. There were no stones on Leah Schwartz's memorial.

She went through the Gutkind family plot, many Gutkinds,

and then saw a double stone with two handsome, weather-proofed portraits, of a young man and a young woman. Dmitri Levnikov, 1970–1992, and Basya Levnikov, 1973–1992. Husband and wife? Brother and sister? Did they die together? In a car accident, in a fire? It must be a Russian custom, the photographs on the headstone, she thought. It marked them as refugees; how sad, to come all that distance, through the sound barrier of cultures, to this.

Kirschner. Rosten. Eidelberg.

Markus.

Markus, Natalie J., 1952–1985. *Adored Wife. Beloved Mother.*

It was a double stone, one half engraved, the other half blank.

Next to it: Markus, Sarah, 1977–1994. *Our Cherished Daughter.* On a simple stone of square granite like Natalie's, but this one unweathered, unmistakably new.

On each headstone, one small 'calling-card' stone. It was the small stone on Sarah's monument that caused R.J. to stand transfixed: a piece of reddish shale shaped like an irregular heart, imprinted clearly with the crablike head and lobed body of a trilobite that had lived many millions of years ago.

She didn't speak to Natalie or Sarah, she didn't think they would have heard. She recalled that somewhere, in a college course probably, she had read that one of the Christian philosophers – Thomas Aquinas? – had expressed doubts that the dead had knowledge of the affairs of the living. Still, how could Aquinas have known? What did anyone know, Aquinas or David Markus or any other presuming human creature? It occurred to R.J. that Sarah had loved her. Perhaps in some way there was magic in this heartrock, a magnetism that had drawn her here and made her realize what it was necessary for her to do.

R.J. picked up two pebbles nearby and placed one on Natalie's marker and one on Sarah's.

The neighboring funeral was over, the mourners were dispersing, and many of them were coming her way, passing nearby.

They averted their heads from the disturbing but commonplace sight of a broken woman by a grave. They couldn't know that she wept as much for the living as for the dead.

As a doctor she had always found it terrible to talk about death with those involved, and the next morning, seated in her kitchen, she struggled as she forced herself to talk with David about the death of their relationship. But she managed to tell him it was time to put an end to it.

She asked him to recognize that it would never work.

'You told me you had gone away to research the book. But you went to dedicate your daughter's headstone. Yet when I've asked you to take me there, you've refused.'

'. . . I need time, R.J.'

'I don't think time will make a difference, David,' she said gently. 'Even people who have been married for a long time often divorce after the death of a child. I might be able to deal with your alcoholism and the fear that some day you might drift off. But deep inside, you blame me for Sarah's death. I believe you'll always blame me, and I can't deal with that.'

His face was pale. He made no denials. 'We were so good with one another. If only it hadn't happened . . .'

Her vision of him blurred. He was right. In many ways, they had been good for one another. 'It did happen.'

He accepted the truth in what she said but was slower to accept its inevitable consequence. 'I thought you loved me.'

'I did love you. I do love you, I'll always love you and wish you happiness.' But she had made a discovery. She loved herself, too.

That evening she was late at her office, and when she came home, he told her he had decided to go to Colorado to join Joe Fallon's group.

'I'm going to take the honey separator and a couple of the

356

best hives with me, and set the bees up on the mountain. I thought I might empty the other hives and store them in your barn.'

'No. It would be better if you sold them.'

He understood what she was saying, the finality of it. They looked at one another, and he nodded.

'I won't be able to leave for ten days or so. I want to finish the script and get it off to my publisher.'

'That's reasonable.'

Agunah walked by and gave R.J. a cold stare.

'David, I would like you to do me a favor.'

'What's that?'

'This time when you go, take the cat.'

Now the hours passed very slowly, and they worked at avoiding one another. Only two days had gone by before she received a telephone call from her father, but it had seemed like a much longer time.

When her father asked about David, she was able to tell him that she and David were parting.

'Ah. Are you all right, R.J.?'

'Yes, I am,' she said, fighting tears.

'. . . I love you.'

'I love you, too.'

'What I'm calling about is this. How about coming down here for Thanksgiving?'

Suddenly she wanted to see him, talk with him, absorb his comfort. 'Suppose I come down early. Like right away?'

'Can you arrange it?'

'I don't know. Let me try.'

When she asked Peter Gerome if he could come back and fill in for her for another two weeks he was bemused, but he was obviously happy to agree. 'I really like working up there,' he said, and she telephoned the airline and then called her father and told him she was coming to Florida the next day.

357

53

Sunshine and Shadows

Her heart lifted when she glimpsed her father, but his appearance troubled her; he seemed to have shrunk into himself somehow, and she was aware that between their last meeting and this, he had grown old. But his spirits were fine, and he seemed giddy with pleasure at seeing her. They began to argue almost at once, but without heat; she wanted a porter for her two pieces of luggage, knowing he would want to carry one.

'Now, R.J., that's foolish. I'll take the suitcase and you can carry the garment bag.'

Laughing in despair, she let him have his way. The moment they left the airport building, she blinked in the sunny dazzle and wilted under the moist slap of the tropical air.

'What's the temperature, Dad?'

'High eighties,' he said proudly, as if the warmth were a personal reward for his good teaching. He drove out of the airport and into the city as if he knew where he was going. He had always been a confident driver. She glimpsed sailboats on the painted ocean and missed the familiar cold breath of her woods.

He lived in a white tower owned by the university, in

an impersonal two-bedroom apartment that he had barely attempted to make his own. Two oil paintings of Boston hung in the living room. One was of Harvard Square in the winter. The other depicted a moment in the Charles River regatta, with the grimacing BU oarsmen frozen in an explosive effort to skim their racing shell off the canvas, while the buildings of MIT were a vague suggestion on the far shore. Other than the pictures and a few books, the place was militarily neat but pleasureless, like the expanded cell of a modern scholar-monk. On the desk in the guest room, which doubled as her father's office, was the glass case containing Rob J.'s scalpel.

In his bedroom was a photograph of R.J., near a sepia picture of her mother, a smiling young woman in an old-fashioned one-piece bathing suit, squinting against the sun on a Cape Cod beach. On the other dresser was a photograph of a woman R.J. didn't recognize.

'Who's this, Dad?'

'Friend of mine. I've asked her to join us for dinner, if you feel up to it?'

'Oh, I certainly will, once I've had a long shower.'

'I think you'll like her,' he said. Evidently, she realized, her father was not a monk after all.

He had made reservations at a seafood restaurant where they could watch the marine traffic move up and down a canal as they dined. The face in the photograph belonged to a well-dressed woman named Susan Dolby. She was chunky but not overweight, and somehow athletic. Her hair was cut in a tight grey helmet, and her nails were short and glowed with colorless polish. Her face was tanned, with laugh lines in the corner of eyes that were almost almond-shaped. Were they green? Brown? R.J. was willing to bet she was a golfer or a tennis player.

She was also a physician, an internist with a private practice in Fort Lauderdale.

The three of them sat and talked medical politics. While the restaurant's speakers spouted 'Adeste Fideles' – too early in the season, they agreed – sun glare bounced off the water, and sailboats moved by like expensive swans.

'Tell me about your practise,' Susan said.

R.J. told them about the town, and the people. They talked about influenza in Massachusetts and in Florida and compared their problem cases – shop talk, doctor talk. Susan said she had been in Lauderdale ever since finishing her internship at Michael Riis Medical Center in Chicago. She had gone to medical school at the University of Michigan. R.J. was drawn to her open manner and easy friendliness.

Just as their shrimp dinners were being served, Susan's pager beeped. 'Uh-oh,' she said, and excused herself and went off to find a telephone.

'Well?' R.J.'s father said a few moments later, and she realized this woman was important to him.

'You were right. I really like her.'

'I'm glad.'

He had known Susan for three years, he said. They had met when she came to Boston to attend a conference at the medical school.

'After that, we saw each other occasionally, sometimes in Miami, sometimes in Boston. But we couldn't meet often enough, because both of us have crowded schedules. So before I retired in Boston, I contacted colleagues at the university here and was happy to get an offer.'

'Then this is a serious relationship.'

He smiled at her. 'Yes, we're becoming serious about one another.'

'Dad, I'm so happy for you,' R.J. said, taking his hands in hers.

For a moment she was conscious only that his fingers had become more gnarled with arthritis. Then she was aware of a descending, a gradual loss of energy even as she leaned toward him, smiling.

Susan was returning to the table. 'I took care of it by phone,' she said.

'Dad, are you feeling all right?'

Her father was pale, but his eyes were alert as he looked at her. 'Yes. Shouldn't I be?'

'Something is going on,' R.J. said.

Susan Dolby regarded her. 'What do you mean?'

'I think he's having a heart attack.'

'Robert,' Susan said steadily, 'are you experiencing chest pains? Shortness of breath?'

'No.'

'You don't seem to be sweating. Do you have muscular pain?'

'No.'

'Listen. Is this some kind of family joke?'

R.J. felt a sinking, the falling of an internal barometer. 'Where's the nearest hospital?'

Her father was watching her with interest. 'I think we'd better listen to R.J., Susan,' he said.

Puzzled, Susan made up her mind, nodded. 'Cedars Medical Center is only minutes away. The restaurant has a wheelchair. We can call the emergency room on my car phone. It will take less time to drive him than to wait for an ambulance to get here.'

Her father began to gasp with his first pains just as they turned into the medical center drive. Nurses and a resident were waiting in front of the door with a gurney and oxygen. They gave him a shot of streptokinase, hustled him into an examining room, and wheeled up the portable EKG.

R.J. stood to one side. She was listening hard, watching ferociously, but these people were good, and it was best to leave them alone so they could do their jobs. Susan Dolby was at her father's side, holding his hand. R.J. was a bystander.

*   *   *

361

It was late evening. Her father was resting comfortably in an oxygen tent in the intensive care unit, hooked up to beeping monitors. The hospital cafeteria was closed, so R.J. and Susan went to a small restaurant nearby and ate black bean soup and Cuban bread.

Then they returned to the hospital and sat alone in a small waiting room.

'He's doing very well, I think,' Susan said. 'They got the anticoagulants into him so quickly, 1.5 million units of streptokinase, aspirin, five thousand units of heparin. We're lucky.'

'Thank God.'

'Now. How did you know?'

As sparely and factually as possible, R.J. told her.

Susan Dolby shook her head. 'I would say it's your imagination, a fairy tale. Except that I saw it happen.'

'My father calls it the Gift . . . There have been times when I've thought it was a burden. But I'm learning to live with it, learning to use it. Tonight, I'm so grateful for it,' R.J. said. She hesitated. 'I don't talk about this to other physicians, as you can understand. I would appreciate it if you wouldn't . . .'

'No. Who would believe me? But why did you tell me the truth? Weren't you tempted to make up a story?'

R.J. leaned over and kissed the tanned cheek. 'I knew we would keep it in the family,' she said.

Her father was in pain, and sublingual nitroglycerine didn't do much good, so they gave him morphine. It made him sleep a lot. After the second day she could go away from the hospital for an hour or two at a time. She drove his car. Susan had patients to see but she pointed out the best beach, and R.J. swam. She slopped on sunscreen like a good doctor, but it felt good to have sea salt dry on her skin again, and for a few minutes she lay on her back with an orange glow above her closed eyes, and nursed hurtful regrets about

362

David. She prayed for her father and then for Greg Hinton, as promised.

That evening she asked for a conference with her father's cardiologist, Dr Sumner Kellicker, and was glad when Susan wanted to join them. Kellicker was a red-faced, fussy man who wore gorgeous suits and obviously didn't relish patients with physicians in the family.

'I'm apprehensive about the morphine, Dr Kellicker.'

'Why is that, Dr Cole?'

'It has a vagotonic effect. It can cause bradycardia or advanced degrees of heart block, no?'

'Well, yes, that happens. But everything we do has risks, a down side. You know that.'

'How about giving him a beta-blocker instead of morphine?'

'Beta-blockers don't always work. Then he's back with the pain.'

'But it would be worth a try, wouldn't it?'

Dr Kellicker glanced at Susan Dolby, who had been listening intently, watching R.J. 'I agree,' she said.

'If that's what the two of you want, I have no objection,' Dr Kellicker said sourly. He nodded and walked away.

Susan stepped close to R.J. She looked into R.J.'s eyes and put her arms around her. They stood there, swaying, and R.J. hugged her back.

She made several telephone calls. 'On your first day there, he had the attack?' Peter Gerome said. 'What a way to begin your vacation!' Everything was in complete control, he assured her. People told him they missed her. People sent love. He didn't mention David.

Toby was terribly concerned, first for R.J.'s father and then for R.J. When R.J. asked her how *she* was, Toby said dolefully that her back hurt constantly and she felt she had been pregnant all her life.

Gwen made her go over every detail of her father's case history, and said R.J. had been wise to request the beta-blocker instead of continued use of morphine.

She was right. The beta-blocker was successful in keeping away the pain, and after two days R.J.'s father was allowed to leave the bed and sit in a chair, twice a day for half an hour. Like many physicians, he was a terrible patient. He asked a lot of questions about his own condition and demanded the results of his angiography, as well as a complete report from Kellicker.

His mood vacillated wildly, from euphoria to severe pessimism, and back again. 'I'd like you to take Rob J.'s scalpel with you when you leave,' he told his daughter during a depressed moment.

'Why?'

He shrugged. 'It will be yours some day. Why not have it now?'

Her eyes locked his. 'Because it's going to continue to be yours for many years,' she said, and firmly closed the subject.

He made progress. On the third day he began standing next to his bed for short intervals, and the day after that he began to walk in the corridor. R.J. knew that the first six days after an attack were the most dangerous, and when a week had passed without mishap, she began to breathe easier.

On R.J.'s eighth morning in Miami, she met Susan at a hotel for breakfast. They sat on the terrace overlooking the beach and the sea, and R.J. breathed in the soft salt air. 'I could become accustomed to this.'

'Could you, R.J.? Do you like Florida?'

Her remark had been a joke, an appreciation of unaccustomed luxury. 'Florida's very nice . . . I don't really enjoy extreme heat.'

'One becomes acclimated, though we Floridians do love our air-conditioners.

'R.J., I'm planning to retire next year. My practise is

established, and the income from it is very good. I wonder if you would be interested in taking it over?'

Oh.

'. . . I'm so flattered, Susan. And I thank you. But I've sunk roots in Woodfield. It's important to me that I practice medicine there.'

'Are you certain you don't want to think it over? I could give you lots of details to consider. I could work alongside you for a year . . .'

R.J. smiled, shook her head.

Susan made a quick chagrined face at her and smiled back. 'Your father has become so important to me. I liked you at once. You're smart and caring, and obviously you're a very good doctor – the kind of doctor I admire, the kind my patients deserve. So I thought, here is a perfect way in which to serve everyone – my patients, R.J., Robert . . . and myself – all in one neat package. I don't have family. You will forgive someone who should know better, but I allowed myself to fantasize about being a family. I should have realized that there never are perfect solutions that answer everyone's needs.'

R.J. admired Susan's frankness. She didn't know whether to laugh or cry; a little more than a year before, she had spun the same fantasy for herself.

'I like you too, Susan, and I hope you and my father do end up together. If you do, we'll get together regularly and often,' R.J. said.

That noon when she came into her father's room, he put aside his crossword puzzle. 'Hi.'

'Hi.'

'What's new?'

'New? Nothing much.'

'Did you meet Susan this morning and have a talk?'

Ah. They had discussed it before Susan had talked with

her. 'Yes, I did. I told her she's a dear, but I have a practise of my own.'

'For Pete's sake, R.J. It's a terrific opportunity,' he said crankily.

It occurred to R.J. that perhaps there was something about her personal chemistry that made people suggest how and where she should live. 'You have to learn to let me say no, Dad,' she said quietly. 'I'm forty-four years old, and capable of making personal decisions.'

He turned away. But in a little while, he turned back to her. 'You know something?'

'What, Dad?'

'You're absolutely right.'

They played gin rummy, and he won two dollars and forty-five cents from her and then took a nap.

When he woke, she told him about her practise. He was pleased that it had grown so quickly and approved that she had closed the practice at 1,500 patients. But it worried him when she told him she was getting ready to pay the remaining debt on the bank note he had co-signed.

'You don't have to wipe away the debt in two years, you know. You shouldn't do without things you may need.'

'I don't do without anything,' she said and held his hand.

Calmly and deliberately, he placed his other hand in hers.

It was a frightening moment for her, but the message she received from his hands placed a smile on her face as she bent to kiss him, and his relief could be seen in his own quick smile.

On Thanksgiving Day, she and Susan arranged to have hospital trays with him in his room.

'I ran into Sumner Kellicker this morning when I made rounds,' Susan said. 'He's very pleased with your condition and said he hopes to release you in another two or three days.'

R.J. knew she had to return to her patients. 'We'll have to get somebody to stay at the apartment with you for a while.'

'Nonsense. He's coming to stay at my house. Aren't you, Robert?'

'I don't know, Susan. A patient is not the way I want you to think of me.'

'I think it's time we thought of each other in every possible way,' she said. In the end, he agreed to go to her house.

'I have a good cook who comes weekdays to prepare dinner. We'll watch Robert's diet and see that he gets just the right amount of exercise. You're not to worry about this man,' she said, and R.J. promised that she wouldn't.

She took the 6:20 p.m. plane for Hartford the next day. As they circled Bradley Airport, the pilot announced: 'The temperature on the ground is twenty-two degrees. Welcome to the real world.'

The night air was sharp and rough to breathe, New England air in late autumn. She drove home slowly, into Massachusetts and up into the hills.

When she turned into her driveway, she sensed that something was different. She braked the car for a moment and studied the dark house that hugged the verge, but nothing seemed changed. It wasn't until the next morning that she glanced through the window at her shingle hung by the road at the end of the driveway, and saw that the hooks below it were empty.

54

The Sowing

It was chill in the darkness before sunrise when the wind blew down from the mountain slopes and swept across her meadow to buffet the house. In half-sleep, R.J. liked the wind sounds as long as she was snug; she was awakened by burgeoning daylight and huddled under her warm double quilt and thought long thoughts until she forced herself up and out, to turn up the thermostat and jump into the shower.

Her period was several weeks late, she realized as she toweled, and she frowned at a possibility that pushed its way into her consciousness: premenopausal amenorrhea. It forced her to confront the fact that now, or soon, her body would be slowing and changing as obsolescent organs began to shut down, presaging the permanent disappearance of menses; and then she pushed the thought from her mind.

It was Thursday, her free day. As soon as the sun rose fully, it warmed the house, and she turned down the thermostat and built a fire in the stove. It was nice to build wood fires again, but they dried the air and caused an efflorescence of thin grey ash to settle on every surface, and the heartrocks that were everywhere made dusting her house an Augean task.

She found herself standing and staring at a rounded grey

river stone. Eventually she set down her dustcloth and went to the closet where she stored her knapsack. She put the grey stone into the knapsack and began to walk about the house, collecting the heartrocks.

When the knapsack was almost full, she lugged it out the back door to the big construction wheelbarrow and let the contents clatter and thump into it. Then she went back into the house and collected more. She kept only the three heartrocks Sarah had given her, and the two stones she had given Sarah, the crystal and the tiny black basalt.

It took her five trips with the knapsack to clear the house of the stones. She dressed for winter – down jacket, stocking cap, work gloves – and went out and grabbed the wheelbarrow handles. The big barrow was more than a third full, and the aggregate of the stones weighed a lot more than she could move in comfort. It took effort to bull it across twenty-five feet of lawn, but once she entered the wood trail, the ground began to dip toward the river, and the barrow seemed to move of its own accord.

The little sunlight that came through the canopy of branches beautifully dappled the rich, deep shade. It was cold in the woods, but the trees broke up the occasional wind gusts, and the wheelbarrow's balloon tire hissed over the damp packed pine needles and then thumped over the spaced boards of the Gwendolyn Gabler Bridge.

She stopped pushing as soon as she reached the river, which was brisk and burbling from the autumn rains. She hadn't emptied the last knapsack load into the barrow, and now she took the knapsack and began walking along the trail. The river-bank was lined with trees and brush, but there was access between the treetrunks, and every now and then she would pause and take a heartrock from the knapsack and throw it into the water.

She was a woman of practical method, and she quickly realized a pattern of dispersal: the small rocks were carefully thrown into the shallows at the edge, while the larger specimens went into the depths, mostly in the occasional pools. When she had emptied the knapsack she went back to the barrow and pushed it along the trail, upstream. Then she filled the knapsack and continued to throw away heartrocks.

The heaviest rock in the barrow was the large one she had rescued from the construction ditch in Northampton. Back straining, shoulders hunched, she carried it to the deepest pool, just downstream of a tall and wide beaver dam. It was too heavy to throw; she had to try to carry it out along the brushy dam, to the middle of the pool. At the outset her foot slipped, and she got a boot full of icy water, but slowly and gradually she made her way to a place that satisfied her and dropped the stone heart like a bomb, watching it sink to the bottom and settle in the sand.

R.J. liked to see the rock there, where soon it would be covered with ice and snow at the winter's coldest. In the spring mayflies might lay their eggs on it, and trout could suck up the larvae and then shelter from the current behind the heart. She imagined that in the secret silence of summer nights, beavers might hang suspended over the rock and join in the clear moonlit waters like birds coupling in midair.

She made her way off the beaver dam, and in similar fashion she emptied the remaining contents of the barrow into the river that flowed through her land, like the funerary scattering of ashes. She had turned half a mile of beautiful mountain river into her memorial to Sarah Markus.

It had become a river where you could find a heartrock when you needed one.

She pushed the empty wheelbarrow home and put it away.

She took off her outer garments in the mudroom, and her shoes and sodden socks. Barefoot, she walked to get dry woolen socks and put them on. Then in her stockinged feet she started in the kitchen and dusted every room in her house.

When she was through, she went into the living room. The

house was empty and polished, silent but for the sound of her own breathing. There was no man, there was no cat, there was no ghost. It was solely her own house again, and she sat in the living room in the silence and the gathering darkness, waiting for what was going to happen to her next.

55

Coming of Snow

November became December under a sky of greasy clouds. In the woods the deciduous trees were bare of leaves, their branches like upraised arms, the twigs like reaching fingers. R.J. had walked the trail unafraid all summer long, yet now that most of the bears had gone into hibernation, she was perversely afflicted with fear that she would meet the big bear face-to-face on the narrow path. Next time she went to Greenfield, she stopped at a sporting goods store and bought a boat horn, a small can with a button that gave a great blast of sound when pressed. She wore the noisemaker in a belly pack when she went into the woods, but the only animal she saw was a large buck that moved through the woods not far from where she stood without scenting her; if she had been a hunter, it would have died.

For the first time, she was fully aware of her aloneness.

All the trees along the trail had dead lower branches, and one day she carried an extension pruning saw into the woods in mittened hands and sawed, freeing tree after tree of dried, barkless limbs. She liked the appearance of the pruned trunks, rising cleanly like natural pillars, and she determined to prune the trees all along the trail, a long-term project.

Snow came on the third day of December, a heavy, dumping storm with no early flurries or warning. It snowed for a day and most of a night, and she wanted to ski the trail but had to contend with the nameless, irrational fear that had plagued her for days. She went to the phone and called Freda Krantz. 'It's R.J., Freda. I'm going skiing on my wood path. If I don't call you again in about an hour and a half, will you ask Hank to come in and get me? I don't expect any difficulty, but . . .'

'Smart girl,' Freda said firmly. 'Sure. You enjoy yourself out there, R.J.'

The sun was high, in a blue sky. The new snow dazzled her, but once she was in the woods, it wasn't so bright. Her skis hissed along; it was too soon after the storm to see many tracks, but she saw a rabbit's, a fox's, and some mice prints.

There was only one bad, precipitous drop in the whole loop of trail, and on the way down her balance vanished and she fell heavily, but into snow that was new and deep. She lay in the soft cold with her eyes closed, vulnerable to whatever might spring onto her from the nearby wooded cover – a bear, a thug, a bearded David Markus.

But nothing came, and in a little while she got up and skied home and telephoned Freda.

There seemed to be no lasting effects of the fall, no breaks or sprains or even bruises, except that her breasts ached and were sensitive.

That night when she went to bed, for the first time in a long time she turned on the security alarm.

She decided to get a dog. She began by taking books from the library and reading about the different breeds. Everyone she talked with had a different preference, but she spent several weekends visiting pet shops and kennels, and she kept narrowing the list until finally she decided she wanted a giant

373

schnauzer, a breed developed several centuries ago to provide huge, tough dogs that could herd cattle and protect cows from predators. The breeders had matched the handsome, intelligent standard schnauzer with sheepdogs and Great Danes; one of the books said the result was 'a wonderful watchdog, large, loyal, and strong'.

She found a kennel in Springfield that specialized in giant schnauzers. 'It's best to get a puppy that will imprint on you while it's young,' the owner cautioned. 'I've got just the little fella.'

R.J. was seduced by the puppy at once. He was small and clumsy, with enormous paws, a wiry black-and-grey coat, a blunt, square jaw, and stubby whiskers. 'He's gonna stand over two feet tall and weigh eighty pounds,' the kennel man said. 'Be warned that he'll eat a whole lot.'

The dog had a hoarse, excited bark that reminded R.J. of Andy Devine, the wheezy-voiced actor in the old movies she sometimes saw on television late at night. She called him Andy for the first time on the way home, when she reprimanded him for wetting the car seat.

Toby was having terrible backaches. She managed to go to church on Christmas morning, but R.J. roasted a turkey and made Christmas dinner at the Smiths' cabin. She had purposely bought a turkey that was too large, so leftovers would provide the Smiths with meals for the next few days. Several of Toby's friends had been cooking and delivering meals; it was something that was done in Woodfield when it was needed, a small-town custom R.J. particularly admired.

After dinner, R.J. played carols on their old piano, and the three of them sang, and afterwards she sat sleepily in front of the fire, surprised by her own exhaustion. Sometimes there were long, comfortable silences, and Toby commented on them. 'We don't have to talk. We can just sit here and wait for my kid to be born.'

'I can wait at home,' R.J. said crankily, and kissed them and wished them a Merry Christmas and a good night.

After she got home, she received her best present, a phone call from Florida. Her father sounded good to her, strong and happy. 'Susan is kicking me back to work next week,' he said. 'Wait a moment. We have something to tell you.'

Susan came on the phone extension, and they told her they had decided to get married in the spring. 'The last week of May, we think.'

'Oh. Dad . . . Susan. I'm so happy for you.'

Her father cleared his throat. 'R.J., we were wondering. Could we be married up there, at your house?'

'Dad, that would be perfect.'

'If the weather is nice, we'd like to be married outside, in the meadow, with those hills of yours looking down. We'd like to invite a few people from Miami. Some of my friends from Boston, and a couple of Susan's closest relatives. About thirty guests in all, I think. We'll pay for the reception, of course, but R.J., could you make the arrangements? You know, find a good caterer, a minister, that sort of thing?'

She promised she would. When they said goodbye and hung up, she sat before her own fire and tried to play the viola, but her mind wasn't on the music. She got pen and paper and began to make lists of what would be needed. Music, perhaps four pieces; fortunately, there were wonderful musicians in the town. The food would take careful thought, and consultation. Flowers . . . lilacs would be everywhere in late May, and perhaps early roses. The first haying of the meadow would have to be done early. She would rent a tent, a small one with open sides . . .

Planning Dad's wedding!

It had taken several weeks of grim determination for R.J. to housebreak Andy, and even after that was accomplished, the puppy sometimes lost control of his kidneys when excited.

She decided he would be a cellar dog, and fixed him a soft bed next to the furnace. She gave in only on New Year's Eve. Dateless and home alone, she spent the evening trying not to indulge in self-pity. Finally, she went down to the cellar and fetched Andy, who was pleased to lie next to her chair in front of the fire. R.J. toasted him with cocoa. 'Here's to us, Andy. The old lady and her dog,' she told him, but he had fallen asleep.

The annual epidemic of colds and flu was well under way, and that week the waiting room at her office was crowded with hackers and sneezers. R.J. had avoided catching cold, but she felt rundown and irritable; her breasts still hurt, and her muscles ached.

During her lunch hour on Monday, stopping at the small stone library to return a book, she found herself staring hard at Shirley Benson, the library clerk.

'How long have you had that black mark on the side of your nose?'

Shirley grimaced. 'Couple of months. Isn't it ugly? I've soaked it and tried to squeeze it, but nothing seems to work.'

'Let me have Mary Wilson make an immediate appointment for you to see a dermatologist.'

'No, I don't want to, Dr Cole.' She hesitated, coloring. 'I can't afford to spend money on something like that. I'm only part-time here, so I don't have medical insurance from the town. My kid is a senior in high school this year, and we're really worried about paying for college.'

'I suspect that mark may be a melanoma, Shirley. Maybe I'm wrong, and you'll waste some money. But if I'm right, it could metastasize fast. I'm certain you want to be around to see your son go to college.'

'All right.' Moisture glinted in Shirley's eyes. R.J. didn't know whether the tears were caused by fear or by anger at her despotism.

Wednesday morning the office was busy. She did several annual physical exams and changed Betty Patterson's medication regimen to deal with her tendency toward insulin infection. She sat and discussed with Sally Howland what the echocardiogram had indicated about her tachycardia. Polly Strickland came in because she had had such a heavy monthly flow that it had frightened her. She was forty-five years old.

'It could be the start of menopause,' R.J. said.

'I thought that's when periods stopped.'

'Sometimes at the very beginning they get heavy, then irregular. There are many patterns. With a smaller percentage of women, menstruation just turns off, like a faucet.'

'Lucky.'

'Yes . . .'

Before leaving to buy her lunch, R.J. read through several pathology reports. Included was one informing her that the neoplasm removed from Shirley Benson's nose had been a melanoma.

After the office closed R.J. felt that she needed nourishment, and she drove to the restaurant in Shelburne Falls and ordered a spinach salad, changing her mind in the same breath and telling the waitress to bring her a large sirloin, medium rare.

She ate the steak with mashed potatoes, squash, a Greek salad and rolls, and apple pie and coffee.

Driving back to Woodfield, it occurred to her to consider what she would do if a patient came to her with the symptoms she had been displaying for several weeks: irritability and mood swings, muscular pains, a ferocious appetite, aching and sensitive breasts, and a missed menstrual period.

377

It was an absurd thought. She had spent years trying to conceive a child without the slightest success.

Still.

She knew what she would do if someone else were the patient, and instead of going home, she drove to her office and parked near the door.

The office was locked and dark, but she used her key and switched on the lights. She took off her coat and went around pulling down the window shades, as nervous as if she were an addict about to shoot up.

She found a sterile butterfly needle she knew was easy to use and attached a tube to it and then tied a tourniquet around her left arm. She scrubbed the inside of her elbow with an alcohol patch and made a fist. It was clumsy taking her own blood, but she found the medial cubital vein with the needle and drew the dark, brown-red fluid.

She had to use her teeth to remove the tourniquet. And then she detached and capped the tube and placed it in a manila envelope, put her coat back on, turned off the lights and locked the door, and carried the blood to the car.

She drove straight back down the Mohawk Trail, this time all the way to Greenfield.

The blood lab in the hospital basement was open twenty-four hours a day. There was a single phlebotomist on duty, holding down the evening shift alone.

'I'm Dr Cole. I'd like to leave a sample with you.'

'Sure, doctor. Is the case urgent? This time of night, the only stat work we do is for emergencies.'

'It's not an emergency. It's for a pregnancy test.'

'Well, I can accept it, and they'll do the testing tomorrow. Have you filled out the form?'

'No.'

The tech nodded and got one from a drawer. For a long moment R.J. intended to write a false name after *patient*, and to sign it legitimately as the attending doctor; and then she felt great fury at herself and scribbled her own name twice, both as the patient and as the physician.

She gave it to the phlebotomist and saw careful blankness on the young woman's face as she took in the two signatures.

'I'd like you to telephone the results to my home phone instead of to my office.'

'We'll be glad to, Dr Cole.'

'Thank you.' She went to her car and drove home slowly, as if she had just run a long way.

'Gwen?' she said into the phone.

'Yeah. R.J.?'

'Yes. I know it's a little late to call . . .'

'No, we're still up.'

'Are you free for dinner tomorrow? I need to talk.'

'Well, no, I'm in the midst of packing a bag. I still need fourteen CME points for my license renewal, and I'm taking your solution. I'm leaving in the morning, going to a conference on caesarean delivery, in Albany.'

'Oh . . . Good idea.'

'Yeah. I don't have a patient due for the next couple of weeks, and Stanley Zinck is covering for me. Look, do you have a problem? Do you want to talk now? Or I can cancel. I don't have to go to this conference.'

'No, of course not. It's nothing, really.'

'I get home Sunday night. How about we talk about it over early dinner on Monday, after work?'

'You're on, that sounds good. You drive carefully, now.'

'Okay, luv. Good night, R.J.'

'Good night.'

56

Discoveries

A restless night. She was out of bed early on Thursday, sleep-starved and cranky. Her breakfast cereal tasted like bits of cardboard. She wouldn't hear from the lab for hours. It might have been easier if it hadn't been her day off; perhaps work would have occupied her mind. She determined to substitute household chores and began by washing the floor in the mudroom. It took energetic scrubbing to remove the accumulated grit and stain, but eventually the old linoleum shone.

When she looked at the clock, only three-quarters of an hour had passed.

The two woodboxes were almost empty, and she lugged in logs from the woodshed, three or four at a time, and dropped them into the big pine box near the fireplace and the cherry woodbox next to the stove. Then she swept up the wood chips and sawdust.

Shortly after 10:30 she got the silver polish and set the silver service on the kitchen table. She put a Mozart CD on to play, *Adagio for Violin and Orchestra*. Ordinarily Itzhak Perlman's violin could carry her through anything, but this morning the concerto sounded intrusive and jangling, and she got up after a while and washed the polish from her hands and went to the CD player.

As soon as the music stopped, the telephone rang, and she took a deep breath and said hello.

But it was Jan. 'R.J., Toby's in real pain. Her backache is worse than ever, and now she has cramps.'

'Let me talk to her, Jan.'

'She's too upset to talk, she's crying.'

Toby wasn't due to deliver for another three and a half weeks.

'I guess I'd better drop over there.'

'Thanks, R.J.'

She found Toby agitated, wearing a flannel nightgown with tiny roses printed on it, and pacing shoeless, in argyle socks that R.J. knew Peggy Weiler had given her for Christmas.

'R.J. I'm so scared.'

'Listen, sit down. Let's see what's going on here.'

'Sitting down makes my back worse.'

'Well, lie down. I want to take your vital signs,' R.J. said easily but briskly, inviting no argument.

Toby was breathing a little fast. Her blood pressure was 140 over 86, and her heart rate was 92, not bad at all, considering that she was excited. R.J. didn't bother to take her temperature. When she put her palm on the convex abdomen, the contraction was unmistakable, and she took Toby's hand and placed it so she would understand.

R.J. turned to Jan. 'Will you call the ambulance and tell them your wife is in labor, please? Then call the hospital. Tell them we're coming in, and ask them to notify Dr Stanley Zinck.'

Toby started to cry. 'Is he any good?'

'Of course he's good, Gwen wouldn't allow just anybody to cover for her.' R.J. pushed into sterile gloves. Toby's eyes were large. R.J. had to ask her several times to raise her knees, the last time sharply. The digital exam was

381

unremarkable; she had scarcely dilated, perhaps three centimeters.

'I'm so afraid, R.J.'

R.J. hugged her. 'You're going to be just fine. I promise.'
She sent her into the bathroom to empty her bladder before
the ambulance got there.

Jan came back. 'She'll need to take a few things,' R.J.
told him.

'She's had a bag packed for five weeks.'

Steve Ripley and Dennis Stanley came with the ambulance,
especially eager because Toby was one of theirs. When they
arrived, R.J. had just taken a second set of vitals and recorded
them, and she handed the paper to Steve.

Jan and Dennis went out to get the gurney.

'I'm coming with her,' R.J. said. 'She's frightened. It would
be good if her husband rode in back with us, too,' she said,
and Steve nodded.

The ambulance was crowded. Steve stood beyond Toby's
head, closest to the driver and the radiotelephone; Jan stood
by his wife's feet, and R.J. was in the middle, the three of
them swaying together and fighting for balance, especially
after the ambulance left the secondary roads and was on the
curving highway. It was warm inside the ambulance because
the heaters were powerful. They had removed the blankets
from Toby at the beginning of the run, and R.J. had raised
her nightgown well above her swollen belly. At first R.J. had
covered Toby with a light sheet for modesty's sake, but Toby's
thrashing legs had kicked it down.

Toby had started the trip white-faced and silent, but soon
her face was reddened by the exertion of fighting the pains,
and she was making a succession of grunts and moans, with
an occasional sharp cry.

'Shall I give her some oxygen?' Steve asked.

'It can't hurt,' R.J. said.

But after a few breaths, Toby was having none of it and ripped the mask from her face. 'R.J.,' she called frantically, and moved back from the great gush that came from inside her and leaped out onto R.J.'s hands and jeans.

'It's all right, Tobe, it's just your waters breaking,' R.J. said and reached for a towel. Toby opened her mouth wide and stuck out her tongue as if trying to give a great scream, but no sound came out. R.J. had been watching closely and had seen a little additional dilation, perhaps to four centimeters, but now she looked down and saw that Toby's vulva was a full circle crowning the top of a small, hairy skull.

'Dennis,' she called, 'pull over and park.'

He turned the ambulance smartly to the side of the road and set the brake. R.J. thought they might be there a long while, but something about the sound of Toby's grunt made her realize otherwise. She brought her hands down between Toby's legs, and a small, rose-colored baby slid out and filled them.

The first thing R.J. noticed was that, premature or not, the baby had a matted head of hair, as light and fine as its mother's.

'You've got a boy, Toby. Jan, you have a son.'

'Will you look at that,' Jan said. He never stopped rubbing his wife's feet.

The baby was wailing, a sharp, indignant little sound. They wrapped him in a towel and laid him down close to his mother. 'Take us in, Dennis,' Steve called. The ambulance was just past the Greenfield town line when Toby began to pant again. 'Oh, God. JAN, I'M HAVING ANOTHER ONE.'

She thrashed, and R.J. lifted the infant out of her way and gave it to Steve for safekeeping. 'Better stop again,' she called.

This time Dennis turned the ambulance into a supermarket parking lot. All around them, people were getting in and out of cars.

Toby's eyes bulged. She held her breath, grunted, and bore down. And held her breath, grunted, and bore down, again and again, lying partially on her left side and staring hopelessly at the ambulance wall.

'She needs some help. Lift her right leg high, Jan,' R.J. said, and Jan held her knee in his right hand and leaned on her thigh with his left hand to keep her leg flexed.

Now Toby screamed.

'No, hold her!' R.J. said, and delivered the placenta. In the process, Toby had a small bowel movement; R.J. saw, and covered it with a towel, marveling that this was how the world was made, all those millions of people for millions of years, each produced in just this kind of slime, blood, and agony.

As Dennis drove again, through the center of town, she found a plastic bag and put the placenta into it.

They laid the baby next to Toby again, and the placenta next to the baby. 'Shall we cut the cord?' Steve asked.

'With what?'

He opened the ambulance's useless little obstetrics kit, and held up a single-edged razorblade. R.J. thought of using it in the moving vehicle and suppressed a shudder. 'We'll wait and let somebody use a sterile scissors,' she said, but she took the two laces from the kit and tied off the cord, first an inch above the baby's abdomen and again near the opening of the plastic bag. Toby was inert, her eyes closed. R.J. massaged her abdomen, and just as the ambulance turned in to the hospital, through the thin, smooth skin of the slack belly she felt the uterus respond and contract, starting to become firm and ready in case some day there might be another birth.

In the staff toilet, R.J. stood at the sink and scrubbed her hands and arms, washing away the amniotic fluid and diluted blood. Her clothes were saturated and gave off an earthy, pungent smell, and she stripped off her jeans and sweater and rolled them into a tight ball. There was a pile of freshly laundered grey scrubsuits on a shelf, and R.J. helped herself to a bottom and a top and put them on. When she left the toilet she carried her clothes in a paper bag.

Toby lay in a hospital bed. 'Where is he? I want him.' Her voice was hoarse.

'They're cleaning him up. His daddy is watching him. He weighs five pounds, ten ounces.'

'That's not much, is it?'

'He's healthy. Just small because he was born a little early. That's why you had such an easy time.'

'I had an easy time?'

'Well . . . fast.' That reminded her, just as one of the nurses came into the room. 'She has some small tears in the perineum. If you give me some sutures, I can sew her.'

'Oh . . . Dr Zinck is on his way. He's officially the obstetrician. Don't you want to wait, and let him do it?' the nurse suggested delicately, and R.J. got the message and nodded.

'You plan to name him after the good old doctor, the one who answered your call?' R.J. said.

'Nix.' Toby shook her head. 'Jan Paul Smith, same as his father. But you'll have a piece of him. You can talk to him about hygiene, and how to treat all those girls. Stuff like that.'

Her eyes closed, and R.J. brushed back her damp hair.

It was 2:10 when the ambulance dropped R.J. at her car. She drove home slowly, down the town's familiar roads. The sky had turned gray over the snow-covered fields. Between meadows, stretches of forest offered shelter, but in the open the wind leapt across the long spaces like a weather wolf, chasing frozen snow pellets to rattle against her car.

When she reached the house, she went directly to the telephone answering machine, but no one had called.

She brought food and fresh water to Andy in the cellar, gave him a good scratching behind the ears, and then climbed the stairs and got into a long, hot shower, a blessing. When she left it, she toweled luxuriously and then dressed in her most comfortable clothes, sweatpants and a ragged sweatshirt.

She had put one shoe on when the telephone sounded, and she dropped the other shoe and hobbled to pick up the receiver.

'Hello? . . .

'Yes, this is she . . .

'Yes, what did it show? . . .

'I see. What are the numbers? . . .

'Well, will you please send a copy of the report to my home? . . .

'Thank you very much.'

She wasn't conscious of putting on the other shoe. She wandered about the house. Eventually, she made herself a peanut butter and jelly sandwich and drank a glass of milk.

A long-term dream come true, winning the globe's best lottery.

But . . . the responsibility!

The world seemed to be growing bleaker and meaner as technology shrank it. Everywhere, people were killing people.

Maybe, this year, a child will be born who . . .

So unfair, even to think of placing on unborn shoulders the burden of being a secret saint, or even of becoming a Rob J., next in the line of the Cole physicians. It will be enough, she thought incredulously, to produce a human being, a good human being.

It was such an easy choice.

This child would come home to a warm house and would be familiar with good smells of cooking and baking. R.J. thought of what she would have to try to teach her/him – gentleness, how to love, how to be strong and deal with fear, how to exist with the live things in the woods, how to read a river for trout. How to make a trail, choose a path. About the legacy of heartrocks.

She felt as though her mind would burst. She wanted to walk for hours, but the wind was still outside, and it had begun to snow heavily.

She turned on the CD player and sat in a kitchen chair. Now the Mozart concerto made sense and spoke to her sweetly of joy and anticipation. R.J. calmed as she sat and listened, her palms on her stomach. The music swelled. She could feel it being carried from her ears down nerve pathways through tissue and bone. It was powerful enough to travel to her soul and to the very core of her being, down to the little pool where the tiny fish swam.

About the Author

CHOICES is the third book of Noah Gordon's trilogy about the Cole family of physicians down through the centuries. The first two novels in the series, THE PHYSICIAN and SHAMAN, have been international best-sellers. The author has received the James Fenimore Cooper Prize in the United States, the Golden Pen Award in Germany and twice has received the Silver Basque Prize in Spain. In addition, SHAMAN was a *Premio Selezione* in the Bancarella book competition in Italy.

Noah Gordon lives with his wife, Lorraine, in the Berkshire hills of western Massachusetts. They have three grown children, Lise Gordon, Jamie Beth Gordon, and Michael Seay Gordon.